c

PAPER ROSES

(Inspired by a True Story)

DEBBY SHOW

FIELDMERE PRESS

Published by The Fieldmere Press

2242 Overlook Drive Walnut Creek, CA 94597

Painting: *Marrakech* used with permission from the artist Gerald Heinen.

Fieldmere Press First edition 2025

Paper Roses Trade Paperback ISBN::979-8-9996027-7-0

The Library of Congress has catalogued Fieldmere Press paperback edition as follows

ISBN :979-8-9996027-7-0

San Jose, CA USA—Fiction 2. Morocco—Fiction 3. World War II Era North Africa—Fiction 4. Betrayal—Fiction, Crime—Fiction 5. Multi-generational trauma—Fiction, 6. North African Sephardic Jews—Fiction, 7. North 7. Muslim-Jewish Relationships—Fiction, Con artists—Fiction.

To Wes

ACKNOWLEDGEMENTS

To my writing coach and developmental editor, Gila Green. Without your patience and support, this book would never have been completed. To my editors—Janet Gay (who salvaged Abi) and Paige Lawson—a million thank-you's. I also want to acknowledge my parents, Bruce and Nelly Show. If they knew better, they would've done better. And to my kid sister—Know I am grateful that, either by accident of DNA or birth order, I am not in your shoes. Although I have chosen not to continue my relationship with you on earth, I am confident we will meet again in the afterlife, where unity and love flow freely.

I am forever grateful to my former husband, Dan, who taught me humility and opened my heart to more empathy and care than I thought possible. And to our son Wes—along with his wife Jazmine and the little one on the way—you give us hope for the future. All I can say, Dan, is that; we did it. The cycle ends with us.

Gratitude goes to my fifth-grade teacher, Mrs. Mills, and to my first therapist, Dr. Sharon Diane Walker. Mrs. Mills, you were at Steindorf Elementary for just one year, but what a year it was. (Your last name was my security password for longer than was probably wise.) And Dr. Walker—what can I say? Your kindness and support saved me.

To my childhood friends Pam, Sarah, Sheila, and Gerald, you are still my chosen family, and I love you all. Thanks go to Cyndi, an anchor-friend I wish I'd met decades earlier, and Halleh, the friend who gave me insights on Iran and its culture.

Lastly, I want to express my appreciation to my new friend Loriann, who truly has the voice of an angel for narrating the book with such passion. Thanks also goes to her and to Zak at ZG3 Productions for the amazing job you did recording and editing and to Erick Gutierrez from the pristine Neighborhood Wache Studios Los Angeles for providing such a great space.

CHAPTER 1

Behind the Eight Ball

Abigail – 1973

Mimouna is the biggest Jewish Moroccan food festival-slash-moveable party of the year. Celebrated on the evening after Passover, it's a tradition for us to go from house to house picking up treats—like Halloween, but better. Because Antonia Symonds, San Jose's Moroccan housewife extraordinaire, is organizing a gathering afterward. This Mimouna is going to blow all others out of the water. Dinner, dancing, music—you name it. Antonia is letting me help, which makes me feel not thirteen.

Stacked on my dresser, in front of the free-with-a-fill-up Dolls of the World set Dad brought me, are four dozen tissue paper roses and a bunch of miniature sheaves of wheat I tied by hand. I made those.

What I don't plan on is being behind the eight ball from Minute One. As soon as I open my eyes, too much light is pouring through the window. It's disorienting—a total trip—so it takes me a minute to realize I've already missed half the morning. With Good Friday and Easter coming up, and our grades already out, we're mostly playing trivia and Scrabble in school now. Still, school is my happy place.

Dad can't handle noise, especially not in the morning. No alarm, no clock radio, no blow dryer—unless we want to start World War III. It's been like this since seventh grade started. Usually, I wake on my own, but Mom makes sure. Except today. Not only is Dad's Rambler not in the driveway, but Mom's nowhere to be found. The story that comes out later is he's taken extra shifts at the gas station, but I wasn't born yesterday.

Mom's Starfire sloppily parked a few houses down doesn't make sense either. Mom might be taking a break from school, but she doesn't like it here any more than I do. Most mornings, she'll pop a convenience-store pancake in the toaster, throw the half-frozen disc in a napkin, and hand it to Nikki. Often, they drive past me on my walk to school. Nikki waves and flashes a toothy grin like she's in a toddler beauty pageant. Crazy.

Mom's been all gung-ho about the gym ever since they started offering free babysitting. If she works out long enough, she gets to add guilt-free carbs to her diet—meaning she won't be living on Tab and carrot sticks, which is exhausting. After that, it's on to one of Mom's Moroccan friends. While they socialize, Nikki will play with the woman's son, who's the same age as her but light years behind in terms of sophistication. When the Tehranpours are traveling, which is often, it's off to Valley Fair to get Nikki a pretzel from Hot Sam's. These days, they don't get home until 9, when Dad's party winds down and only a few stragglers are left. I imagine someone teasing Nikki about the salt crystals on her lips and chin, making some awful comparison. Luckily, I haven't been around for any of this. Let's just say I have my ways.

I better get to school. It won't look good if I skip the day and then show up at people's houses for goodies. I wander past Nikki's room— empty and unmade—to Mom and Dad's. I knock. No answer. I try my fist. Still no response, but when I turn the knob, it's unlocked. And there's Mom, still in her negligee, face-planted on the bed. A few of the pink foam rollers from last night are still in her hair; the others spread out across her pillow.

Seeing her like this doesn't even register on the Richter scale. Nothing fazes me anymore. You'd think the open Librium bottle and the water carafe with lipstick on the rim would stress me out, but I'm numb these days. Mom told me the diet pills make her jangly, and she needed something to take the edge off. Her walrus snore tells me it worked.

In the living room, the Starburst clock above the fireplace says 12:05. Nikki is planted in front of the TV, hand deep in a bag of Cocoa Puffs, cereal stuck to her nightshirt and spilled across the floor. Mom's been out of it—but leaving cereal out during Passover? Really?

I was hoping to make it to school by lunch, then fifth period.

There's no flippin' way.

Next to my sister is my old See and Say toy, which is *kaput* from having its string pulled one too many times. I figure Nikki hasn't been up long because, the minute she gets bored, she goes off the rails. A few times, she's stripped naked and bolted when no one was watching. The ground outside is wet, so maybe that's probably why she hasn't. So far, so cool. She's stuffing Cocoa Puffs in her mouth, singing along with Bert and Ernie in a flat, robotic voice.

Nikki's range of emotions goes from A to B, but I'm not concerned. Unlike me, who's shut down, this kid's sharp. She's crazy smart. She's never been to preschool, but she already knows the alphabet. I feel bad for her. My parents might've gone through the motions with me, but at least there was some semblance of normal. Dad was affectionate, once. He said kind things that softened Mom's rough edges.

My parents have never been easy. I never knew when Mom was going to push me into a room or Dad was going to slap me upside the face. I had to maneuver around landmines, but I never had to duck to avoid hand grenades. Not like Nikki.

Dad's party must've gone longer than usual. Someone emptied the ashtrays and threw the beer cans in the trash, but powdery ash is all over the coffee table. Mom's tried to make this house into a showplace, but Dad's torpedoed that. Last summer, she spent all day pasting floral wallpaper, and now it's peeling like the posters on my wall turning yellow. The gold-and-mushroom drapes she and Grandma made are grimy and stink of smoke.

Moody shades of brown and green dominate, which I guess is "in," but even Nikki's room feels like a dungeon. She once got her head stuck in the crib rails trying to climb out. At her first birthday, she crashed face-first into the cake, chocolate all over her frilly pink dress. Oblivious, she sucked the Betty Crocker Devil's Food frosting off her fingers. It would've been cute if it had stopped there. Since then, she's slammed into plate-glass windows, stolen candy from the grocery store even though God says it's wrong and we make her put it back. Mom can't contain her. Not that I can help. These days, I spend more time than is advisable in a fantasy world.

I might be a space cadet half the time, but I know I'm going to be great someday. The poem I'm writing is light years ahead of the Nancy

Drew rip-off I wrote for Highlights. But let's be real—I'm deluded. It's not the masterpiece I think it is.

To lure Nikki away from the TV—which isn't healthy—I try Pick Up Stix. Not exactly thrilling, but come on. Nothing she's allowed to do besides TV holds her attention.

"Let's play Barbie," I say, handing her a box with two dolls (hair totally jacked) and a pile of tiny dresses and shoes. Within 30 seconds, Nikki drives her knee into one of the Barbies.

"She's dead," she says.

It gives me the heebie-jeebies. Her blank eyes flash black. I want to give her the Hamsa Mrs. Tehranpour gave me for my birthday. Nikki needs it more than I do.

"Nikki," I say, in my best kindergarten-teacher voice. "That's not how you play. How would you feel if someone stomped on you?"

"Lemme go outside," she says.

"It's sprinkling, Nikki. I've got school."

"Outside."

I pick up another Barbie and hand it to her. "Let's try this one. This time, Barbie's going out with Ken. Here. You pick her shoes."

"That's stupid!" she says.

"How 'bout changing the channel? Look. Electric Company's on."

I stand in front of the TV like it's a prize. Keeping her mesmerized is the only thing left in our toolkit when it comes to Nikki. I heard about shrinks who help kids play in the sand. Maybe. For once, Mom and Dad wouldn't have trouble paying. Dad still pumps gas, but there's money.

Cash for Mom's on-again, off-again real estate classes. For the Starfire. For Vegas. Dad buys Mom pearls, diamonds, emeralds—wrapped in Tiffany boxes. Peace offerings, all of them. Mom's awash in jewels. There's even a Doughboy in the backyard. Every room but Nikki's has a waterbed, sloshing around and smelling like mildew, while my clothes—and Nikki's— aren't a priority. My socks are so old the elastic's blown. The hems on my dresses unravel constantly. There's always a string hanging, like if someone pulled it, everything would come undone.

On TV, two puppets from Channel 2 are talking about the March of Dimes carnival contest. I entered last year. And what do you think second place got me? Nada. I didn't need that bike, but I deserved to win. Me and the Heinzzman twins climbed a chain-link fence and dove into a dumpster behind Gemco looking for prizes. We found clackers, black lights, and posters. Scavengers. We made booths out of discarded boxes. Unfair.

While I'm stewing, Nikki gets up and switches the channel to KQED 9. She's immediately hooked by something on PBS—thank goodness. Little Houdini's staying put, giving me a chance to pick up where I left off in my book. This week it's *The Wizard of Oz*. By the light of the TV, I squint, hold the page close to my face, and use a bookmark to track the words.

Why I can stay calm in my real life while freaking out over fictional characters, I'll never know. But when the Wicked Witch sends the winged monkeys, I skip ahead. I can't relax until the Queen of the Field Mice gives Dorothy the golden whistle. L. Frank Baum knows something I don't—about evil-doers and their enablers.

It's a while before I look up. When I do, Mr. Rogers is on the screen, singing about good feelings.

It takes a minute to register: Nikki's gone, but it's way too wet outside for me to worry. What would she be doing anyway? She's here, playing Hide and Seek. I go from room to room.

"Ready or not, here I come!"

Then it dawns on me. How could I expect reruns to keep her entertained? That and my busted old toys didn't stand a chance. The evidence is right there: the captain's chair didn't move itself from the kitchen to the front door. She must've pushed it slowly, pausing now and then to make sure I was still reading, making sure the legs didn't catch in the carpet.

Like I'd believe furniture moves on its own. Like I wouldn't notice the smidge of golden-brown curls poking above the top of the chair.

But it's the sound of her laugh, heard up close and later further in the distance, that alerts me. I open the door and call her name.

What I don't know yet is this won't be the last time Nikki runs. Right now, it's easy—evading one half of Tweedle Dee and Tweedle Dum. Just a practice run. If you'd told me the cops would be the ones chasing her someday, I would've said you were crazy-loco.

There she is: in her birthday suit, barreling down Fawn Drive on a borrowed Big Wheel.

It's no mystery how she pulled it off. She made it to the foyer, positioned the chair in front of the door, climbed up, and unlatched the chunky gold chain. Once outside, she rolled her clothes into a ball and tossed them into the hydrangeas by the porch.

What Nikki didn't plan for was the drizzle falling from a trio of dark clouds. I imagine her feeling the moisture on her skin, not noticing the dull gray sky above her.

Undeterred, she walked across the lawn and snagged the Big Wheel from the neighbor boy—he always leaves it out. She climbed on, gripped the wet plastic handles, and shook the water from her hair. Water drips from her forehead to the tip of her chin. She's finding it difficult to wipe her eyes, and her naked brown bottom sticks to the wet plastic of the tricycle. Once her grass-stained feet find the pedals, she'll need to pump furiously, but the tiny pedals are not up to the job.

As it turns out, she's as impervious to the rain as she is about everything else. As her feet move the pedals, she lets out a tinkling laugh. It floats through the air and settles nowhere.

I've never heard her sound more human.

She's a genius, but what good is that if you've got zero common sense? All it adds up to is an emergency.

I race to Mom's room. "Nikki's escaped!" I yell, voice sharp and loud.

"What, what?" Mom mumbles, dazed. Like this is new.

I yank open the curtain. "She's circling the block."

"Give me a second, Abi."

But from the way Mom's talking in slo-mo, I'm pretty sure it's going to be longer. I knew Librium relaxed a person, but her words are dragging like she's acquired a southern drawl. When her head starts to bobble, I become alarmed.

"Mom. Get up. Nikki's gone."

"I'm already up," she slurs.

That's debatable.

Her eyes are glassy. When she stands, she's wobbly. I think about warning her it's raining, but I don't have time to hunt for an umbrella. Mom's never prepared. In her head, she's always in Morocco—where it's hot or hotter.

She grabs a sleeveless dress from the closet and puts it on backward. An easy mistake—it looks the same both ways.

"My good clothes are at the cleaners," she offers, like I care.

Mom doesn't do sneakers. She calls them déclassé. She shoves her feet into kitten-heeled slippers—plastic, with feathers.

Walking her to the living room, I shove everything she might trip over out of the way. Meanwhile, I'm filled with dread. By now, Nikki and her Big Wheel are going at maximum speed. She's buzzed by the monotony of manicured lawns and perfectly trimmed hedges at the end of the street, the rain bringing them into sharp relief.

The only thing Mom has in her favor is Nikki wants attention. Also, she might get bored. I mean, her game can't be as much fun as it was a week ago when it was sunny, when she was the talk of the neighborhood. Her, riding around in circles, Mom chasing after her as if catch-me-if-you-can was a sport in the 1972 Olympics.

When Nikki spies Mom in the distance, it's her cue to venture further. From there, the chase is on, the tires of the Big Wheel skidding and sliding across the sidewalk, Mom tripping over her heels. When Nikki manages to turn onto Leigh Avenue, even I stop breathing.

Leigh Avenue's the worst. It's like when a street has a stop sign and a yellow line through the middle—all bets are off. Chain-smoking drivers throw still-lit cigarettes out the window. There's broken glass. People there get their beer by the case, people there park their cars on lawns instead of driveways, leaving them to rust in various stages of disassembly until so much motor oil has absorbed into the grass it reeks, until the adjoining concrete walkways are stained black.

My stomach lurches when I see Clyde Smith peeking out from under his car in time to give Nikki his signature slimy smile. I recognize him from the Al's Liquors where Dad has me get cigarettes. Geezer makes me want to hurl. He's always offering to buy me a bottle, like I'll owe him something.

He's shirtless today. Saggy chest. Belly over his belt. Can't even zip his pants.

I want to scream. But some otherworldly force must be watching over Nikki. She passes him.

Then her wheels bump over broken glass. When she slides over a trio of banana slugs, they squish under her wheel and cause the tricycle to skid. She's still good enough on three wheels to regain control.

Mom spots her as she's circling back onto the safety of Fawn Drive. At this point, though, all I want to give her credit for is reproducing. Mom's doing her best, but no matter how hard she tries, Nikki's still out of reach. The cat-and-mouse game has Nikki checking over her shoulder to make sure she's still chasing her—grinning like crazy.

"What did I say about running away?" Mom calls, zero authority in her voice.

Nikki twists her neck in a sassy no-no. The distance between them is large now. The sound of Nikki's laugh floating further away.

That's when Bramford, a built-like-a-tree-trunk firefighter, springs into action. If there's anyone who knows how to solve problems, it's him. A regular Mr. Fix-it, his garage is floor-to-ceiling with tools, all organized like a hardware store.

He steps from behind his Ford pickup and gives Nikki one of his don't-mess-with-me looks. Would've turned me to stone. It doesn't faze Nikki. He steps in front of her trike, and with one giant fist, he grabs a hold of the console of the Big Wheel.

Although Nikki looks like she wants to peel out, what Bramford's done has given Mom time to catch up. But when Mom tries to swoop in, one of her heels slips off. She does manage to grab Nikki, tucking her under an arm like a loaf of French bread. When Nikki tries squirming, Mom tightens her hold.

Bramford's eyes dart between my rail-thin mom and my squirming sister. Mom's mortified. She talks in a high, nervous pitch.

"This was Abi's fault," she says. "She was supposed to watch her. It won't happen again. I promise."

It takes everything in me not to yell. She can't be serious. She's too busy cramming her feet into slippers to notice her kid's gone rogue.

Bramford pats my head. He knows. I should've been at school. It's Mom's responsibility.

"You need a better lock," he says. "Tell Hugh Orchard Supply will fix him up."

Then, like it's just another Tuesday: "You'd better get going; that child of yours is going to catch cold."

He gives Nikki one more hard look like it would serve her right— would've made me pee my pants.

The walk home is a blur.

The second we're inside, I let out a warbled sigh. I'm soaked. I'm tired. School's a lost cause. But somehow, Nikki saved Mimouna. She got Mom out of bed—dynamite-style.

Mom smiles at Nikki like she's proud of her derring-do.

"Let's get my Lil' Pumpkin cleaned up," she says before turning to me and asking me to draw Nikki a bath.

I don't decline. Five minutes and half a box of Mr. Bubbles later, Nikki's in the tub, in pigtails with a froth of foam hanging from her chin, complaining the whole time.

"Mama, Abi made the bath too hot!" she bellows.

"Not true. I tested the water myself," I say.

"Ow, ow, ow," she cries. But those are crocodile tears. She's acting.

"You were filthy. Look—the water's brown."

Mud's still caked on her neck. I think about leaving it, but Mom's flipped over less.

After scrubbing, I toss her a towel. "You can get out yourself. Any kid big enough to run away … Also, if I were Mom, I'd make you apologize. Stealing's wrong."

From the hallway, Mom calls, "Abigail Jane, don't be so hard on your sister. You may have the face, but she's got legs for miles. A future showgirl."

I swallow a sigh and touch the Hamsa tied to my bracelet.

If Mom's right about Nikki, what does it mean for me? Mom put me in a Little Duckie's dance class when I was eight with a bunch of four-year-olds. I still couldn't keep up. It makes me mad. I want to be measured by my own yardstick. And who the heck wants this for their kid? It scares me imagining Mom and adult Nikki. Mom isn't exactly a silverware-stealing, murdering Stage Mom like Gypsy Rose Lee's mother. She'd be swallowed up. When I imagine Nikki in her element, in nothing but a feather boa and fan, surrounded by a band of admirers, flying monkeys all, my mind drifts to the Little Duckie's dance class. Me, surrounded by toddlers twirling circles around me.

That feeling—like I'll never measure up—

I hate it.

CHAPTER 2

Cast Away

Yasmina – Fint Oasis, Morocco – 1941

The sun is barely over the ridge, and a faint streak of orange lights the sky. My Hand of Fatima amulet presses against my chest as I stand in the doorway, a bag beside me. Mma—my word for mother in my native Tamazight—fastened it around my neck just before I became a wife two years ago. I thought it would protect me.

Inside our mud hut, my mother-in-law, Adrina Mouloudji—who wants this done before the neighbors can see—is still gathering my things and placing them into bags. The one beside me holds a special occasion dress, sandals, scarves, miswak for my teeth, and a two-sided comb carved from olive wood. The other will contain a tunic and head covering for modesty, lambswool socks, and horse-hide slippers. Everything is expertly packed—but then again, my mother-in-law never does anything halfway.

After setting the last bag on the dirt floor, she pulls me into a hug.

"Allah have mercy," she says.

That I flinch surprises even me. I abhor false affection. For two years, this woman acted like the picture of kindness and piety, and I believed her. Every word. Every smile. Now, I want to pull away—to say something, anything—but I don't.

She's hoping I will. She wants me to break, so she can pretend she's the one who's been wronged. But I've been taught better. Obedience isn't a choice; it's all I've ever known. My mother-in-law may have turned out to be a chameleon, but Mma told me, "Always remain quiet." Where I come from, a girl who shows anger is a girl without dignity.

That doesn't stop my hands from going numb, or keep me from feeling like I've stepped outside my body. I watch her every move—the way she raises her chin, the way she rolls her shoulders back.

"You better take her before she makes a scene," she says to my brother-in-law.

Oh really? I want to say but don't. All my life I've been restrained, passive.

Idir, just in from the stable, with straw on his djellaba, looks confused. "I got the ticket like you said. Second class," he says.

"Get her to Marrakech," my mother-in-law replies. "After that, I don't care."

Although my face is puffy from crying all night, I won't give her the satisfaction. I want to press my fingers to my temples—it's too much to process. Last night, at the creek, beneath the date palm, was when I learned the truth. The sun hung low in the sky. Someone appeared on the horizon. I thought it was my husband.

But it was Idir.

"Brahim is divorcing you," he said, eyes dark and soulless in a way I hadn't seen before. "He adores you, Yasmina, but he's found someone else—someone who can give him a child. He hopes you'll understand."

"It's only been two years," I said.

Understand? What was there to understand?

Without the date palm behind me, I might have fallen. His words were such an earthquake to my soul, the ground didn't feel solid. Maybe he was testing me, seeing if I'd cry or beg. I didn't. I couldn't. I must be good. If they cast me off—where would I go? Back to Tacheddirt with nothing? Girls like me don't return home. They get passed around. They end up in unspeakable places.

I remember Idir crossing his arms, sneering. Then, as if reading my thoughts, he continued: "We're not throwing you away. Friends of ours found you a job in Morocco's capital—as a maid. You should be grateful. These positions aren't easy to find."

I pressed my fingers into my forehead. "What about Brahim?"

"You'll be happy there," Idir said, locking eyes with me. "We traded a few things with Monsieur Moab, your future employer. He's good and honest. The mellah—the Jewish section where you'll live—is safe. Clean."

I'd never felt more paralyzed. I might have argued my case—I am capable of it—if I weren't being lied to, if I didn't have too much pride. I couldn't go back to Tacheddirt. There was no dowry, no place for me. I'd be soiled.

A wife must keep her husband happy. If she fails and he chooses divorce, it is the woman who has betrayed the man—not the other way around. It is she who must hang her head.

It never even crossed my mind that Brahim, who was fifteen when we married, might be too fickle and immature for such an endeavor. But he wanted what he wanted. If only he hadn't had that magical way of weaving words—of turning dreams into reality, of persuading even the most die-hard skeptics—I wouldn't be here now.

That this confident boy was able to convince my parents to let me travel 150 miles away to live with a family they'd never met is beyond comprehension.

It's true—I was smitten. But had my parents forbidden the marriage, I would have obeyed. Brahim's charm and good manners won him many admirers, including my parents. It didn't hurt that he was handsome, though I'm used to it now. His hair, eyes, and skin were the color of cinnamon. His teeth: even and white. His body: lean and tall. And the way he'd sweep his cloud-like hair off his brow—we swooned.

Idir climbs onto the camel and waves a hand in front of my face. "Time to go, stupid," he says.

"Not yet, Idir," my mother-in-law interrupts. "Fatima needs to say goodbye."

I crane my neck for one last look at the place I've called home. This modest red-earth dwelling once seemed like a palace. Everything had meaning. The loom had to face backward. The kitchen—always rich with the scent of oil and fried dough—was set at the periphery. This layout, I was told, protected the virtue of the unmarried daughter: ten-year-old Fatima. I heard it often: "Only men can live in the light. It is unsafe for a woman to do the same."

But to me, that kitchen had gone. I'd never seen anything more beautiful. The giant wood pile, the earthenware jugs on one side of the counter so we didn't have to go for water every day. And there were small clay jugs and grass baskets that stored too many delicacies to count. At any time, we'd have couscous, millet, yams, beans, rice, dates, and dried meat.

And now I'm thinking, *are the Mouloudjis not grateful?* I was thirteen when I arrived, but I'd brought so much. In Tacheddirt, I learned how to treat sick animals with a poultice of turmeric, onion, and oregano oil, sealed with thick bandages. I'd helped cows give birth. I knew how to forage. In Fint Oasis, I did all this and more. When food was scarce, I tracked wild herds, followed bees to hives, and hacked through thickets for wild thyme and dandelion. We gathered so many seeds, fruits, herbs.

When the water ran out, it was me who traveled the winding path and crossed the bridge. Even though they believed only in Allah, it was me who thanked Gaia, goddess of the Earth and patron saint of Tacheddirt. And now this family has taken my trust, and with it, my innocence.

I've always swallowed my emotions, so when anger bubbles to the surface, it registers as irritation. I pull at the camel's mane. It grunts. Fatima wraps a donut in a napkin and hands it to Idir. She says goodbye to him, but not to me. It doesn't matter.

This commune of artisans and farmers has always been kind to me, but I sensed they'd had enough of the Mouloudjis. Not the parents. Not the sister. Especially not the father, who spends his days hoeing rocky soil and planting millet. It's the sons they mistrust.

It's whispered that while the Mouloudji boys lack skill with clay or paint, they make up for it in hustle. They're negotiators. Maybe even cheaters. But the villagers rely on them to sell. So they go back and forth—from Ouarzazate to Marrakech, sometimes farther, especially since the war began.

"Stop thinking so much," Idir says. "I need you to pay attention."

By now, we're at the creek. While Idir squats to fill the canteens, I absentmindedly pick fleas from the camel's mane.

Idir is right. But can you blame me?

Until last night, I believed every act—good or bad—was proof the gods were smiling down on me. This oasis was what connected me to them. It made life's slings and arrows bearable.

The realization that I'll never again dip my feet in this water, never wiggle my toes in the warm sand, makes me want to cry. But as I watch Idir—smelling of hashish and sweat—fasten the canteens to the camel's side, the tears won't come.

"Times are hard, Yasmina," he says. "Cigarettes, chocolate, nylons— that's what people are buying. For days, Brahim and I tried. Finally, we left the donkeys with a friend, took a few smaller items, and hitched a ride in a cargo truck. Next thing you know, we're in Spain."

I want to ask him something, but maybe it's better to stay quiet. Either he's lying, or he's confessing.

"They caught us—Germans. But you should've seen Brahim skip that chain-link fence. I can run marathon distances, but I can't jump and sprint like him. So what happened is, he got away."

"So now you're admitting it?"

"Brahim deserves a shot at prosperity."

"So he's throwing me away?"

Whatever Idir says next, I don't hear it. If he could lie last night, he can lie again. Even if some of what he says is true, how would I know?

I've heard of women being discarded. I never thought it would happen to me. I never thought my fate would depend more on the character of others than on my own.

The gods are fickle, and so is life. If I'm going to survive, I'll have to depend on myself.

This time, when I reach for my Hamsa, it isn't for comfort.

CHAPTER 3

Desert Winds

Yasmina

The rest of the morning passes almost without incident. Pink, cigar-shaped clouds float across the sky. Idir keeps insisting I not get lost in them, but he needn't worry. With each strike of the camel's foot, the closer we get to Marrakech, the sharper my awareness becomes. Soon, I'm no longer floating outside my body—I'm fully present.

Idir, however, is headed in the opposite direction. Every time he takes a drink, he grows more unsteady. It dawns on me: This is who I'm depending on? A foolish man without a shred of decency or honor?

You'd think my anger at him would be as fierce as a thousand white-hot suns, with silence the only way I can suppress it. But I'm still blaming myself.

As the afternoon drags on, the breeze grows stronger. I'd experienced the ferocity of the sirocco winds before, but only from the safety of our hut. As they gather force around us, I'm gripped by fear. I had almost looked forward to Rabat and the Moabs—for the freedom it might offer me. But with Idir as useless as he is, constantly glancing at his watch, it takes everything I have to stay brave.

Idir's traveled this road many times, but something inside me, maybe it's my anger, develops the beginnings of a plan. Before I can set it into motion, it's the overworked camel who stages a revolt at just the right moment, stopping so abruptly that the inebriated Idir topples face-first into the sand. He's not hurt, but the fall sobers him enough to take action. He begins setting up a barrier behind a sand dune.

While I tend to the camel, I watch as he removes a tent from his bag and tries to set it up. But the winds are growing fiercer. Idir needs to shield his face from the sand as the wind twists the tent flaps and bends the poles, which collapse before he can secure them. Even without my help, he would never accept it, a rough structure eventually begins to take shape.

With a date palm tree as refuge, with the wind drumming at my back, I try to care for the camel. I apply salve and wet bandages to its swollen legs. After the animal accepts a rotten persimmon and a drink, I pull an apple from my pocket and take a bite.

I'm never as angry with the gods when I need them.

After taking a swig from my canteen, I find comfort in my Hamsa and in prayer. My fingers, still sticky with salve, trace the engraving as I murmur a prayer to Shu, god of the winds—*Please, do not sweep us away.*

Once Idir gets the tent upright, another problem arises. The lamp, his kefir, and our fruit attract a swarm of mosquitoes. I want to scold him for not bringing netting, but I quickly realize I don't need to. The bugs are far more attracted to him.

He tries swatting them away, but it's useless. His hands and arms are covered in welts. He checks his watch again. I don't yet realize his suffering is about to become mine.

"No sense in sticking around here where sleeping's impossible," he mutters. "As soon as it's clear, we're out of here."

CHAPTER 4

In the Belly of the Beast

Yasmina

Idir takes a swig from his bottle and spits it out. Although it's morning, the siroccos are still howling. It occurs to me that Shu has abandoned me. The climate is as harsh and unforgiving as anything the wind god can conjure. Sand scratches my eyes and blurs my vision. Dust and flying insects cling to every pore. The wind twists my hair and knots the loose folds of my clothing. It whistles around our ears, as if to say: *I have you in my grip.*

I keep praying, but nothing improves. Now, with the wind hurling at me full force, I fear the next gust will be the one that levels me. I grab the fur at the camel's neck with one fist and latch onto Idir's shirtwaist with the other. Idir, usually brimming with misplaced confidence, clings to the camel. He pulls my hand around his stomach. A wave of disgust washes over me.

Then, out of nowhere, the wind calms just enough for us to see ahead. From there, we manage to reach the commune at Amerzgane, where we refill our canteens and gather provisions. I don't get a moment of relief— except when Idir is silent.

You'd think the last eight hours would've taught him something. But soon enough, he returns to his old self. There's a meanness in him I can't reconcile. When he wipes the sweat from his face, his eyes glisten with satisfaction. When I complain of a parched throat, he shares—but only reluctantly.

If I had begged, would he have taken me back to Tacheddirt? Even if it meant facing my parents' wrath?

Little do I know, once I'm settled in Rabat, my father-in-law will travel to Tacheddirt to inform Baba. The news—that I'm living with a middle-class family and earning a wage—will be welcomed. To everyone but me, this will feel like a triumph.

Under a grove of argan trees, I ask when we'll reach Marrakech.

Instead of answering, Idir picks at his teeth and tries to comb through his matted hair. "Soon enough," he says.

"I was told we'd see mountains and villages. All I've seen is desert."

"Listen. I'll get you there."

There's a sinister edge to his voice that makes me draw back. Sometimes I get premonitions. Something's about to happen—something even my evil eye charm can't protect me from.

It turns out I'm right.

Just as we finish our canteens, a vehicle appears on the horizon. As it slows, Idir comes alive in a way I've never seen. He signals the driver to stop—and then, the worst happens.

In one swift motion, Idir picks me up and hurls me into the back of the vehicle. Before I can make sense of anything, I hear the latch slam shut. I'm out of my mind with fear. On the other side of the door, Idir is screaming like a banshee—like he's the one imprisoned and I'm the one free.

"Go, go, go!" he yells.

Idir didn't expect me to fight. But I do. I claw and kick at the door. His reaction is chilling—he goes into a frenzy. And then it hits me: he's as frightened as I am.

"Shut up," he bellows, his voice as gritty and cruel as the sandstorm we just survived.

"What have you done? Where am I going?" I wail.

"Stupid woman. If we'd continued by camel, it would've taken seven more days—and the rest of the trip would've been even more dangerous. This way, you'll be in Marrakech by morning."

I'm furious. He's abandoning me with strangers—one or both of whom could harm me worse than I've already been soiled before, and the only bag he's given me is the one with the burqa and my canteen. He might as well left me with nothing. I try slamming my body against the door. I yell as loud as my voice will carry. I claw at the windows. When my behavior gets the attention of the men in the cab, it's clear Idir doesn't want a commotion. The men argue. I can't hear the words, but when Idir returns to the back of the van, he's subdued.

"Remain quiet and you won't get hurt," he says. "Otherwise … I can't promise."

"Idir—please," I whimper. "How could you? Haven't I been like a sister to you?"

"Okay. Okay," he mutters, slipping a piece of paper through a small opening at the bottom of the door.

"The driver, Old Fahood, is an associate of ours. He's older than the desert itself. The passenger won't hurt you. He prefers boys."

"This is your ticket," he adds. "You'll need it for the train."

He says it like he's handed me a brick of gold. As far as I'm concerned, if I didn't need it, I'd throw it out.

As long as Idir is there, I feel I still have some control. I don't expect him to walk away. When he does, I scream until my voice is hoarse.

I need to calm my breathing. To ground myself, I think of Madame Rubin—the bravest woman I've ever known. How lucky I was to have her as my teacher. What a terrible situation she'd been in.

She must have been so afraid—running from the Germans—but she never showed it. She was only supposed to be in Morocco for a few weeks while her husband gave Torah lessons to the boys in the encampment below. That's how she ended up with us. Hiding with other Jews in the Rhirhaia Valley was safe—but not safe enough.

If she could survive being ripped from everything she knew, then so can I.

"Don't turn from the shadows," she once told me. "It's there you will find your power."

Now, as the engine rumbles and the van's wheels kick up sand, her words echo in my ears. She hadn't wanted to upset my parents; she'd been hesitant to tell me the Jonah story. But since he was in her Bible and in the Quran, she decided to go ahead.

"God allowed Jonah to be swallowed by a large whale. Jonah was faithful and obedient, and in the end, he was rewarded for it."

I'm so vain as to believe my situation can compare to being inside a whale, but there are similarities. Having never been in a motorized vehicle before, it does feel like I'm in the belly of a whale. The diesel fumes make me sputter and cough.

If God tested Jonah, maybe He's testing me too.

I begin to believe that my prayers are what's moving the truck—what's taking me out of this place. A strange peace overtakes me. Maybe half my things are gone, but I'm still here. Maybe I'm not full of gratitude—but my faith endures.

For a moment, as the wind hits the van full force and sends it swerving, I believe I'm going to die.

A rage like I've never known floods me. Furious, I tear at my arms. I bang my head against the floor. I slam my fists against the walls of the van until I collapse in exhaustion.

Then, the wind shakes open a compartment.

Inside is a multi-colored blanket, made from fine, hand-dyed wool. With water from my canteen, I soak a corner and begin to clean myself. Through the night, I wipe specks of sand and insects from my skin, picking them from my hair. When I'm clean enough, I wrap the blanket around myself, leaving only my arms free.

The next several hours are spent in continuous prayer. While not completely restored, I'm no longer adrift. My dress will have to be good enough for the train. Wearing my burqa would be a shock, especially one as restrictive as this. Old Fahood said I would need it, but didn't Madame Rubin tell me Marrakech and the coastal cities to the north were quite tolerant? In the end, I follow Allah's lead. Any changes I make will be in his time.

The next time the van careens around a corner, I'm at peace. When I hear panicked voices from the cab, I pay them no mind. Their day of reckoning will come. Nothing—not even a vehicle with the power of ten horses—is impervious to the wrath of Allah.

CHAPTER 5

The Iron Path

Yasmina

At the first whisper of dawn, the usually buzzing city of Marrakech is wrapped in quiet stillness. It feels so unreal I press my nails into my palm to make sure I'm not dreaming. The ticket in my pocket feels heavier than it should, as if the future itself is a burden. It reads 22 May 1941. In less than three hours, I will be on a train bound for Rabat, where I'll join the household of Monsieur Moab.

I am hopeful, having had many positive interactions with those of the Jewish faith. There's Madame Rubin, of course, but in Tacheddirt, we worshipped and celebrated alongside a tribe of nomadic Jews who were very much like us. They attended our weddings, and we went to theirs.

Leaving Tacheddirt hadn't been hard—I wasn't alone then. But leaving Fint Oasis feels like walking blindfolded. I've never had to stand alone before. Will I be rejected where I'm going? To be discarded again … I couldn't bear it.

Except for the mews of an abandoned kitten, the silence is suffocating. A stillness presses against my throat. I feel the weight of every step. And here I am, depending on Old Fahood, a man so frail and bent that he could barely unlatch the back of the van to help me to my feet.

Maybe it's a blessing that Marrakech, at this hour, is not as Madame Rubin described it. By God's grace, I am seeing the city at its most desolate. We are in front of Souk Marche, a few blocks from the train station on Avenue de France. Can you imagine? Had I witnessed the full, overwhelming buzz of the market—the colors, sounds, and smells—I might've fainted. Too much for a country girl to take in.

As it is, the only living creatures are cats. With scratched-out eyes and battle scars, they fight, play, and drink from bowls left out for them. In a few hours, throngs of people will flood the streets. Musicians, snake charmers, merchants, shoppers, beggars, and children will push past one another, their voices and instruments forming a single wall of sound.

But by then, I'll be long gone.

Old Fahood tells his companion to stay in the van while he escorts me to the station. At first, he tries leading me like I'm his daughter, but when he sees his touch angers me, he backs off. I can't help it. God wants me to forgive—but I can't. Had I believed in the dark arts, I might've cast a spell. And yet, there's enough newness here to provoke a teenager's curiosity. The people may be gone, but the remnants of yesterday's commerce remain.

We step around a pile of feathers, shards of pottery, and wet newspaper. The putrid stench of rotting animals is unbearable. I cover my nose. Old Fahood does not.

"Above you," he says, pointing to the sky.

It feels like an insult—his kindness. I don't want to look up. But when I do, I'm mesmerized. Overhead are lattices covered in palm leaves and desert flowers, all in bloom.

"They're for shelter," he says.

He starts telling a story, but a dog's bark interrupts him. In a nearby alley, two skin-and-bones dogs huddle together. My heart aches. Old Fahood notices and looks at me with confusion. My sympathy surprises him—dogs in Morocco are seen as unclean. Unlike cats, they don't tidy themselves or fetch water. That they must steal from the cats just to survive seems deeply unfair.

Old Fahood motions for me to turn. A man in a heavy hooded djellaba and white turban stirs a large black kettle over a fire made from argan branches. Whatever he's preparing, it isn't food—it smells medicinal and foul.

"When people live too close together," Old Fahood says, "there's a lot of disease." He points ahead. "There, on your right, is the station."

I don't know how much Idir paid him, but he leads me in. He opens the heavy door and motions for me to go ahead. As I do, it's like I've been struck by a lightning bolt. I've heard stories of villagers buckling under the weight of seeing a modern city for the first time. Their feet give out, and sometimes they need smelling salts or are carted off to the hospital. At first, it feels like I'm disconnected from my body, like someone else is experiencing this. Much of it, I've blocked out. It's too much to absorb. More people than I've ever seen. The number of languages spoken is mind-boggling. The memories I do have return to me in fragments. A pale man in a fedora and trench coat stamps out a cigarette. A man in a swastika armband barks commands in a guttural language I can't understand. His face is menacing, hard. At his waist is a shotgun.

"I'll stay with you until it's time to board," Old Fahood says.

I'm so dazed I can barely nod.

"Can I help you to your seat? Get you a book? A gâteau? Tea?"

I raise a hand to refuse. He's proven not to be a jackal, but I'd still rather starve than accept his help.

Undeterred, he offers cookies, a thermos of mint tea. He swipes a newspaper and a dog-eared Vogue from a nearby seat and hands them to me. When I toss them aside, he grabs me gently by the shoulders.

"When someone offers you what you need, take it," he says. "Here's another piece of advice: Pretend you're a married woman traveling between towns to visit your sister. Pretend your husband is in another train car conducting business. And whatever you do—cover yourself."

If that had been his only counsel, I might've found it in my heart to forgive him.

But what he says next is a violation.

He slams his keys onto the bench and juts out his chin.

"You're not stupid like the rest," he says. "Still, I've never met a Shilha who doesn't worship a mishmash of nothing—Allah, Egyptian gods and goddesses, even bits of the Jew religion. Believe me, the city will beat that out of you. You'll be too busy working to dance around like a wood nymph."

His judgment rattles me. Is this what I can expect from city people?

Who says we must abandon our other gods? It is our openness—our embrace of many paths—that we are proud of. Yes, we revere the god of Abraham. When Mma had complications after childbirth, Baba made a pilgrimage to Ouirgane to pray at the shrine of Rabbi Abraham Ben Hammou.

Old Fahood sets the thermos, food, and reading materials on the seat beside me and walks away.

I don't know why, but I feel empty and alone. However, I cannot indulge these feelings. There is the blare of a beacon to contend with, not to mention the rattle of the platform vibrating under my feet, and the pillows of smoke billowing everywhere. The smell of diesel, introduced to me in the truck hours before, is strong here. The fumes and smoke from the engine saturate my nostrils.

I eat four ginger nibbles and discard the rest. I sip from the thermos. I might be stubborn—how dare he?—but it's not like he's watching. Besides, I've been too overcome by grief to eat. The nibbles settle my stomach, and the newspaper steadies my jangly hands.

Berbers, Europeans, East Africans, and other Arabs scurry around like ants—which feels strange, because aside from the soldiers, isn't everyone already where they need to be? Yet instead of being frightened by the massive locomotive, I find it strangely grounding. Only a powerful god could've created something so impressive. Just looking at it makes me feel invincible. For the first time in days, I feel myself settling back into my body.

The locomotive releases a tremendous cloud of steam. For a long while, all I can see is a faint dot of light. When it finally clears, a caravan of connected cars and carriages comes into view. They seem to stretch on forever.

One train car after another is loaded and unloaded with supplies, food, livestock, and other goods. The armored cars on flatbeds—carrying munitions and barbed wire—I thought I'd erased from memory. But I still have the newspaper article. A ship bound from Spain, carrying 1,700 souls—Jewish refugees from France—was forced to turn back. Other dispatches from the war are too technical for me to fully understand. Madame Rubin once told me the Germans were among the vilest of the Europeans—even though she was one herself. Everything I've read confirms it. Hitler, the leader of Germany and the Nazi Party, wants to take over the world. Morocco is under Vichy control, sympathetic to the Nazis. But not our king. He says the Jews are his subjects. He refuses to hand them over.

I'd hoped the newspaper would serve as cover. But the sight of a Berber girl engrossed in print draws attention. People are staring. Brahim didn't mind me being literate—he used to bring me newspapers from vendors and train stations. But when he brought home an underground pamphlet, more on the forced imprisonment of Jews, he snatched it away before I could finish reading. Madame Rubin always said knowledge was power. Now I wonder if it was too much—if maybe that pamphlet dimmed the light between Brahim and me. I had stumbled on his secret.

The chair feels hard against my tailbone. I shift in my seat. Across from me are two soldiers in steel helmets. They carry rifles. On the front of their coats is a swastika.

I take a long swig of tea. Thank God Madame Rubin isn't here.

The next few hours blur. Many European women look like they've stepped out of the Vogue magazine I'm holding. Tall and slim, they're considered beautiful by someone's standards, though not mine. They have powdered faces and thin lips, which they paint in shades of coral or scarlet. Strings of pearls adorn their necks, and oversized butterfly-shaped brooches are pinned to their lapels. Their derby hats, made from wool and decorated with feathers, fruit, or flowers, are sometimes so tiny they no longer serve their purpose. As for the men, I could say they are dashing, matched-set counterparts to the women, but I would be lying. There are as many distinct shapes and sizes of the white men as there are stars in the sky.

When we start to line up, I go with the other Berbers, who are all traveling third class. What I don't realize is that the passenger cars are not separated by nationality but by ticket price. Within minutes, I'm lost in the crowd. The chef de train checks my ticket, frowns, and points to another line, but I'm pushed aside by other passengers. Irritated, he grabs my elbow and leads me to a quieter car, guiding me up the stairs and to the first empty seat he sees.

"Asseyez-vous," he says sternly.

I obey without question.

When I look up, the Nazi soldiers from the station are standing across from me. I take a deep, steadying breath. I try to settle into my seat, but it's made of a hard material that feels stiff against my back. When I crane my neck and see dim amber lamps suspended from the ceiling, it makes me curious. This is the electricity Madame Rubin taught me about.

What puzzles me is that, as more people enter the train and take up the available seats, I realize I'm not only the youngest person on this train—I'm the only Berber. No turbans, no djellabas, no shift dresses, burqas, or caftans. Around me are cinched-waist dresses, trench coats, woolen trousers, and shoes so polished I can see my reflection. And unlike Madame Rubin, most of these Europeans are tall. Some of the men have to duck to avoid bumping the lamps.

As the train lurches forward, I brace myself against the seat in front of me. The lamps swing wildly. I close my eyes and whisper a prayer, asking the gods for strength.

I try to bury myself in the magazine, but when thoughts of Brahim creep in, it becomes impossible to concentrate. Part of me wants to cry. I could. No one would notice. But another voice inside says: *Have you no pride? Stop dreaming. Brahim's not coming to Rabat—or anywhere else.*

The train whistles, and as it picks up speed, there's a rush of air. The familiar yet unfamiliar *clickity-clack* sound of wheel meeting rail fills the air. A European woman with brown eyes and chestnut hair, captured in a net, sashays past me. As she walks by, a stringed hatbox and a bag graze my knee. She smells of roses, jasmine, and vanilla. She doesn't want to be anywhere near the soldiers either. I'd go too, but all the seats are taken. One of the Nazis clears his throat and spits. The wad lands within an inch of my foot.

Suddenly, it all feels too real—the cruelty of others, the relentlessness of life. No one cares. For three days, my fate has been in other people's hands. Every time I think I've found solid ground, it shifts beneath me. I imagine a soldier's boot on my neck, a pistol at my head. Panic tightens in my chest. I want to reach for my amulet—for comfort—but I refuse. I don't want them to know I'm afraid.

By the time the train bumps over a bridge, making a hollow rattle, I've convinced myself I'm too small to bother with. I occupy myself with the scene outside. The outline of a city is taking shape over the horizon. A figure, possibly a maid, rushes home. Under her arm is a parcel wrapped in newspaper. That she's covered from head to toe in a burqa makes me recoil. It's not that my own dress is scanty by comparison. Old Fahood is right. My heart hurts thinking about the excessive modesty. Until now, if I wore a scarf, it barely skimmed my hair. I'd spent summer days at the river with my friends, splashing in the sun. By the time we were done, our dresses clung to us so tightly there was little left to the imagination.

I trace an opening in the fogged window. There she is again—the maid—greeting another woman. They clasp hands and kiss each other's cheeks. Comfort. Friendship. Just like back home. Maybe this is part of God's plan for me. Maybe I will learn something with this new family.

I begin to lose myself in the thought, imagining all the ways I can be useful, when a voice crackles over the loudspeaker:

"Next stop, El Jadida Station."

My heart leaps. Casablanca's next. Then Rabat. The closer we get, the more I convince myself: Stop resisting. Madame Rubin always said, "When in Rome …"

It's time.

I grab my bag, push through to the next carriage, and find the lavatory. Once inside, I see it—a spot of red on my underwear. Tears spring to my eyes. I knew I wasn't infertile. I knew it was a lie.

I roll toilet paper into a wad and place it in my underwear. My dress is stained. I have no choice—I have to change. Putting on the burqa is difficult. It's heavy, cumbersome, and now, thanks to the van, it smells like dust and sand.

When I open the door and reenter the corridor, I imagine everyone is watching me. I'm almost to my seat when the train begins to rock.

"El Jadida," a voice says over a loudspeaker.

The words make my heart leap. Hopefully, I can get a look at the vast ocean Madame Rubin told me about. But it turns out El Jadida is a city of large stone walls. Out the window, men load and unload the cars. There are more bundles of barbed wire, more men in djellabas and skull caps. There are women in long robes and face coverings who, like me, only have their eyes showing. This causes a flush of heat to rise through my body. Self-conscious, I smooth the burqa and wrap my scarf tighter around my neck. How do women tolerate this? It's stifling. With no air from the window, I fan myself with the cardboard insert from the magazine.

The train stops. The door opens. The Nazis are the first to exit. I exhale.

As we roll forward, snaking over another bridge, a coyote howls in the distance. This time, I reach for my amulet, unafraid. I'm thankful for every sound—joyful or not—that God allows me to hear.

Just as the sun slips behind a hill, the train begins to slow.

"Another unscheduled stop," someone says. "The war."

I want to read, but the light is too dim. Until the train speeds past a grove of fig trees, past the familiar papyrus of my youth with their long, reedy stalks and spicy aroma, there hasn't been much to see except for a lone yew tree. Not a minute later, two young men who could be brothers are pulling a cart full of straw bales. I'm thinking of them and of the journey ahead when the train comes to a sudden halt, another unplanned stop.

Outside, the sun has moved behind a distant mountain, taking with it smears of pink, gold, and orange. In this light, the village in front of me resembles Fint Oasis so closely I have to shut my eyes to be sure I'm not imagining it. Everyone is gathered around a man playing a flute. A cobra dances at his feet. People are singing, laughing, dancing.

My heart sinks into my stomach.

My eyes, heavy with exhaustion, begin to close.

CHAPTER 6

A Gift of Plums

Yasmina

I wake to the trill of a desert lark—a sound so familiar, I almost forget. But there's no lark. I'm on a train, hurtling toward Rabat. Not home in bed, where there are no whistles or horns, no grinding brakes. No voices crackling over loudspeakers. No electric lights swaying above. At home, even my emotions were still. Now, they swirl.

It wasn't just Brahim's family—my own parents discarded me. I'd been the much-anticipated, much-loved eldest daughter. Baba planted a tree for me. He used to say I was so fine, so lovely, that even the sky god and his rainbow wife took notice.

As for Mma, she believed too much in the basic goodness of humanity. Why else would she send me into the world with nothing but an evil eye amulet to protect me? Madame Rubin wasn't exactly against the marriage, but she wanted me to take my time.

"Do not trust too early or too easily," she told me. "He who lords over the underworld is as clever as he is devious. His minions walk among us. Watch for them. They are capable of such a deft impersonation of humanity, even God can be fooled."

Mma told me to trust fellow travelers. She believed the world was harsh and that we had to depend on one another to survive. "It is a sin against Allah to assume the worst without proof," she'd say.

But now I ask myself: should we never trust our instincts? Much of the evil in this world is done in the dark. I am the only witness to what the Mouloudjis did, and if I hadn't seen it for myself, I wouldn't have believed them capable of it. Yet they were. My mother-in-law acted like getting rid of me was no worse than taking an animal to slaughter. I'm thinking all this when the train spits out a cloud of smoke and slows to a stop.

I squeeze my eyes shut. When I open them again, there's a Berber girl sitting across from me. Judging by the sun's position, I've only slept half an hour. How did she get on board? Did I sleep through another stop?

For a moment, I think she's a vision.

She's no more than 10 or 11, very pretty, and has a kind, open-flower face framed by a multi-colored scarf grazing her chin and flowing over her shoulders. She's wearing an embroidered cyan-blue dress, and she has a dozen gold bangles around her wrists. My first thought: *Where are her parents?* I could go on—why she's dressed like this—but honestly, who cares?

She reaches behind her back and retrieves a gift wrapped in silver-leaf paper and balances it on her lap. "For my wedding," she says. "I've no idea what's in it."

I fix my gaze on the window, trying to be polite. "Nice."

That she's a child becomes even more obvious by what she does next. Only a kid laughs off things that should be frightening. When the train rocks before clattering to a stop, she sings. Her voice is better than average, but it's annoying—the way she watches me when she finishes, like she thinks we're the only two people on board.

"Hope you don't mind. I watched over you while you slept."

Her friendliness would be disarming, her convivial blend of warmth and concern, but my mother-in-law was the same way, and she turned out to be fake. Besides, why would I want to waste my time with some pesky juvenile I'm never going to see again?

"I don't mean to be rude, but do you mind?" I ask. "I've never seen the ocean."

"Seen it a hundred times, and I can tell you, it's nothing special." She shrugs, then jiggles the box. "Wouldn't you rather see what's inside?"

When she opens it, I'm surprised. I expected a necklace, maybe a scarf. But inside are a dozen of the most beautiful dark purple plums I've ever seen.

I've been too upset to think about food. Now it takes everything in me not to drool. My stomach growls.

"Think I should save or share?" she grins.

"Sharing's better," I say, trying not to sound greedy.

She waves a plum in the air. "All right. First, you have to tell me your name. You look like an eldest daughter. And from what you're wearing, I'm guessing … Fatima?"

"There were plenty of Fatimas in my village," I say. "But my parents were rebels. I'm Yasmina."

She drops a plum into my hand. "Nice to meet you," she says, overly dramatic in a way only kids can be.

Biting a plum while veiled is not easy. I try to eat fast so no one notices—and also make it look like I'm not starving. Though it does nothing for my hunger, it's almost a relief when it's gone.

For a while, there's silence, which is how I want it to be. The only other thing on my mind, besides her volunteering to give me another piece of fruit, is getting a view of the ocean. But when I look out the window, it's one heavily fortified city after another. Each has a medina with a courtyard, in the middle of which forms its hub. At every center is a fountain where children frolic, women gossip, and men discuss commerce.

Just as I'm getting bored, outside Bir Jedid Saint-Hubert, I see a gazelle resting on the tracks. Panic grips me. With only seconds to spare, the train blares its horn. The gazelle bolts—but not before the train clips its leg.

I clutch my amulet and mouth, "Praise be to God." The girl, unfazed, wraps silver thread around her finger and flashes a gold-toothed smile.

"I have one just like that at home," she says, pointing to my amulet. "I'm not superstitious, but I wear it sometimes."

"You didn't see the gazelle?" I ask.

"I knew he'd be okay."

"How?"

She shrugs. "Didn't, really. Want another plum?"

"I could give you a gift too," I say. "A comb? Socks?"

"Don't be ridiculous. They'll spoil in the heat. Accept half as my apology for being such a bother."

"Stop," I laugh. "You remind me of my sister."

She nods at my dress. "Must be difficult."

"There's always a first time," I smile. "It'll take getting used to."

"Don't tell me you married one of those husbands."

"I—I don't have one. Not anymore."

The words spill out before I can stop them. I regret them instantly. My eyes sting.

"I didn't mean to—Are you okay?" the girl asks. "I'll be quiet."

And she is—for a while. But curiosity gets the better of her. She doesn't ask directly if I'm divorced, but her questions become more cautious.

"Why veil your face?" she asks.

"I might change my mind later," I say. "But we're with strangers. It's not safe."

The chef de train enters the compartment.

"Next stop: Bus to Berrechid."

The girl offers to switch seats so I can get a better view. Even so, the landscape isn't what I imagined. Maybe it's the train, but these coastal cities aren't like how Madame Rubin described them.

"I've been to the best perfumeries in Paris," Madame Rubin said. "The sea-salt air blended with the scent of jasmine and gardenia. Nothing beats it."

We pass through the souk's butcher quarter, and the only thing in my nostrils is the stench of sun-dried carcasses—thick, metallic, unmistakable. The train rattles on. Someone must have cranked a window open. But who? Through the glare, men with machetes cut pieces of lamb, beef, and goat into thin slices. Next to them are the glutinous brown globs used for making soap. It feels like a cruel joke. I'd wanted the ocean, and I get this.

A voice crackles over a loudspeaker.

"Watch for it, everyone—on your left. A fabulous view of the coast."

I crane my neck. So does the girl. Despite myself, my heart warms. She may be just a child, but since she came, I haven't felt quite so alone. And there it is: gray, bleak, majestic. The ocean. I fall silent. It feels like the life Madame Rubin had could be mine.

For a while, I sit in stillness. Then someone taps my shoulder. It's the girl.

"A ginger snap?" she asks, offering a tin. "I'm Amira." She settles in beside me. "An hour ago, I was in third class with my parents. But they insisted I come here."

I nod.

"Mma wants me to stay clean and tidy," she says, then lowers her voice. "But the truth is—my future in-laws are meeting us on the platform. I can't be seen getting off a cattle car."

I study her. She's so young. I fear for her wedding night. What happens when her in-laws discover the deception?

"I'll stay close," I say softly.

"Will you be living in Rabat?" she asks. "I'll be a maid in a Jewish household. My husband will take care of the gardens."

With that in common, we lose ourselves in conversation. We share what little we know, of the Moabs, of Amira's young man ... It's possible the people waiting for us on the other side of the platform will be impossible to please. How will we handle it? The next two hours are spent encouraging each other.

"Change into your usual clothes," she says when there are only two minutes left.

I'd consider taking her advice, but my dress is stained with blood. When the door slides open, Amira is one of the first to leave.

"I'll be in touch," she calls with a wave.

Passengers spill out. I hesitate. Not quite fear—just the weight of being so thoroughly covered. My world feels narrowed. I scan the platform for Amira. She's gone.

I nibble a knuckle. The last thing I want is to cry when meeting Madame Moab.

I look around. I was told to look for a light-skinned woman with short, light-brown hair wearing a bright blue dress, accompanied by her brother. A respectable man.

Idir left out one detail: Elise Moab is visibly pregnant. Her dress is tight over a watermelon-sized belly. She's carrying low and in front, which means she's either going to have a boy or she's about to deliver any minute. Standing next to her is a man in his early twenties, wearing European-style clothes. A package of cigarettes juts out from his shirt pocket.

It is she who recognizes me first. There aren't many travelers in second class fitting my description. My first reaction is to freeze. I would hug her, but the baby.

I blurt out how very delightful it is to meet her.

"I look forward to a long, fruitful employment."

She doesn't mean to be cold. She doesn't mean to treat me like an employee and nothing more. It still stings.

What I don't know is that her demeanor has nothing to do with me—and everything to do with what's happening in Europe.

As we near the Moab home, the truth clicks into place. The train, the soldiers, the barbed wire, the warnings—all of it. The Jews of Morocco are in more danger than I imagined.

Swastikas cover the walls of the mellah. In red paint: **We are coming for you.**

When one Moab boy flings himself onto my lap and another grabs my knee, reality rushes back in. I'd been holding my breath this entire time. But now I'm here, in this real place, and soon these memories will be softened by daily life.

Still, at night, when I close my eyes, I see another girl—pale, soft-looking, with straight hair and strange clothes—mouthing words I can't understand.

CHAPTER 7

Paper Roses

Abigail – 1973

The Purple Panther, Ida Price Junior High's Only Student-Run Newspaper April 1, 1973

<u>Gabbie's Gossip.</u> Holy cow. 1973 is speeding along! So far, Junior High's a gas. I can't believe how many friends I've made. New couple alert. RV is going with CS, JR with CL, LR with BP, and BB with DS. By the way, Coach Callium told me to tell you she's still holding spots on the cheer team for ANY 7th grader who wants to try out. It's about school spirit, but she can't mean no talent is necessary. There are to be cuts but they won't happen till late fall, which won't give nearly enough time for the uncoordinated. Because someone can rhyme and sing, and I'm talking to you AJ. What do you want to do? Embarrass yourself royally? Anyways, see ya later, Panthers. PS, If you were hurt by anything I wrote, lighten up. It's April Fools!

I bolt upright. I don't have time to daydream, but my mind drifts anyway. I'm in the desert. A girl from long ago is watching over me, like she knows something I don't.

It's Mom's voice—high-pitched, a shriek, really—that brings me back.

"Abigail, you there?" she says.

"You off?" I answer, trying my best to be Miss Mellow Yellow—until I hear her jiggling the knob.

Even through the door, I can feel her temper spike.

"What did I say about locking your room?"

I hide the panic in my voice. "Still in a towel, Mom."

Thank God she didn't catch me in my Ida Price pom-pom girl uniform. I yank a T-shirt over my head and open the door.

She comes at me in a cloud of hairspray. Her hair's done up like Jackie O's, and she's doused in Prince Matchabelli. She's wearing a cream-colored pantsuit with a matching yellow belt and heels. Snazzy.

"You're not thinking of wasting your time with cheerleading, are you?" she says.

I stifle a sarcastic sigh. A month ago, she dragged me to practice and shelled out money for a secondhand uniform. I didn't even want to do it— but the second I started enjoying it, she insisted I quit. To heck with her.

"Wasn't cheerleading your idea in the first place?" I ask. Carefully, because I don't want to set her off.

Practice, which turns out to be the best thing that ever happened to me, starts in less than an hour and I figure the minute Mom gets in her Starfire and sets off toward real estate class, the party Dad's having in the living room is going to go from unbearable to mildly dangerous. No way I want to be around his creepy friends.

"I thought it would help you be less clumsy," she says. "But I can see it's a lost cause. Besides, you think I'm going to let you go with the mess you made? It looked like Bombay exploded."

"A bomb, Mom," I say, trying to keep my tone neutral. "But don't worry. After I clean up, I'll be working on my book report."

It's disrespectful, me being fake—but come on. If she can lie to the bill collector, what goes around comes around.

"Just making sure," she says.

I want to double over. I want to throw up.

I don't need to be in the living room to imagine it: the scale, the mountain of pot, the Reefer Madness rolling papers, the straight white powdery lines on the coffee table. Bald, bandana-wearing, tatted-up Tom Timmerson—six-foot-four and menacing, hates kids. Kermit McDougal—

taller, and likes kids way too much. And my four-year-old sister Nikki, center stage, pretend mic in hand, tunelessly warbling a Grace Slick song.

The idea of being trapped in my room with smoke from Dad's hash pipe seeping under the door is too much. Plus, the girls are counting on me. I'm such a klutz they toss me in the air. I'm the top of the pyramid. I have to practice.

"And since I won't be around," Mom says, "be hospitable. I know you'd rather be under the covers reading, but for once, try to hide your disgust. They're our guests."

"Sure thing, Mom," I say, all sugary-ass.

Seriously—the gall. Dad's friends are in there making straws out of twenty-dollar bills, and I have to be nice?

"What do you think of my outfit?" she says, thrusting a stockinged leg into the light. "Bob Thornton says I'm a gazelle."

I want to tell her she looks like a toothpick.

"You're going to be late for real estate class," I say.

"Oh, I quit that. I thought my English was good, but the teacher kept testing me with, 'How you say—tricky questions.'"

My stomach clenches.

"Isn't that going to delay things?" I ask, trying to sound casual, though I'm freaking out inside.

She's been hinting at not allowing me to go anymore. Seeing me on the edge of popularity for the first time in my life, having so much fun. She can't handle it. I'd already pressed my cheerleading uniform and laid it out under my sheets. The bag with my nylons and shoes, I'd hidden in the bush behind the trash cans. Since I can't walk past Dad and his gang of stoners, I'd planned on jumping. Besides, it makes me mad at how she quits everything she tries.

When I'm about ready to give up, when the situation feels too unpredictable, Mom pulls the top of her sleeve over her shoulder. The price tag is still there—just visible enough. I know the game. She'll wear the Halston a few times, then return it for a refund. Once Dad gets paid, she'll buy something else—maybe Mary Quaint or another big name—and parade around in it.

She'll get all the mileage she can from that Halston.

"I'll retake the class another semester," she says. "Teachers are supposed to help—but you know. Jealousy. I'll be sure to get a male professor next time. Anyway, I'm off to Dr. Eastman's. A chicken's warming in the oven. Rice is on the counter. Dad won't be hungry, but feed your sister."

"How long will you be gone?" I ask, trying to keep it breezy.

Her real estate class gave me a solid three-hour window. But her new schedule? Who knows.

"The doctor is lonely," she says, brushing a blue-black curl from her brow. "His wife took their girls to Paris. She married him for status. Now he's old, and she's never around."

The comment makes me flinch. She once told me he makes her feel how she did back in her modeling days.

Still, I'm proud of myself. No eye-rolls. No sighs. I look her dead in the eye and say the fakest thing I've ever said:

"Can't keep him waiting."

God, I should be arrested for fraud.

But it works.

"Oh my goodness, you're right," she says. "Can't have him getting bored of me. Toodle-doo!"

Through a lull in the music, I hear her stiletto heels clicking across the linoleum, then sinking into the brown looped carpet. I picture her saying goodbye to Nikki, Dad, and the guests in her chirpy voice. I watch her wobble past a row of cars and the lone Harley in our driveway, stepping over an oil stain. She's so bony her pants barely cling, even with the belt. Her clutch purse looks massive in her twiggy hands. She looks like a child.

Once she hits the curb, it should be smooth sailing.

Hurry up, Mom. Get in your Starfire. Rev the engine. Go.

As soon as her car rounds the corner, someone cranks up a record— some acid rock song about the devil's grandma. Nikki starts singing along. Even if my walls weren't paper thin, it would still feel like my entire room is pulsating.

But honestly, I'm grateful for the acid rock. If Dad plays a country song, he gets teary, then drags me out to sing *Paper Roses* in front of everyone. I don't mind doing it once in a while—but not today.

By now, Mom's Starfire has crossed Geneva Street, well past Leigh Avenue.

It's Go Time.

I pull on my blue-and-gold Ida Price Junior High cheerleading uniform and head to the window. It sticks, like everything else in this house. I throw my shoulder into it. A hairline crack splits across the glass—by tomorrow, it'll be a full spider. Dad won't care. Mom will.

Goosebumps rise on my arms. My hands, which smelled of florist's tape and Elmer's glue from a craft I'm working on, are ice.

But there's a good explanation for why I'm running away. My homeroom teacher is a guy named Mr. Lew Anderson. He says behavior has two functions, either to get something or to run away from it. For me, it's an escape. As the will-go-well-into-the-night party gathers steam in the living room, I think about how tired I am of pulling an electric blanket over my head, praying for slumber. I'm tired of being a caterpillar in a cocoon. I'm tired of all my possessions smelling like pot. I had to take my Bobby Sherman posters down because they started turning yellow. Even the blue first-prize rosette I won for writing Highlights Magazine's best children's poem of 1972 smells bad.

My BFF's sister Renee has promised to take me to practice after her San Jose State class is over. She still has to go to her shift at K-Mart, which means I have exactly ten minutes. Straddling one leg on each side of the windowsill, I try to gather the courage to jump. What I don't count on is the skirt of my limp piece of crap uniform catching on a tiny construction nail, or the one-inch run in the polyester.

Some not-so-nice cheerleader will definitely let me know.

But what's really stressing me out more is what's right in front of me, the half-story jump. I hesitate. We're not in leafy, hermetically sealed Los Gatos. We're in Cambrian Park, a still-to-be-established blue-collar San Jose neighborhood. It'd still be a prune orchard if IBM hadn't relocated here three decades ago, and if the Stanford Linear Accelerator Center wasn't up the peninsula.

I'm supposed to jump into a barely covered-over irrigation trench full of poison. I know what this has led to, a profusion of misshapen animals, frogs with missing or extra legs and eyes. I heard about one with two heads. A neighbor kid jumped a fence and landed on top of an industrial-size canister of VMR pesticide. Mom says, "No problem, that's why these houses were such a bargain."

What's on my mind, however, are the snakes. I imagine one hiding in a gopher hole, but then I think about what'll happen if I'm forced to quit. No more slumber parties with popular kids. More time spent under the covers with a booklight in my hand. How can I let down Sierra Blair, who taught me how to pluck and trim my bushy half-Moroccan eyebrows? And Paula Yocab, who had me swear off dairy and all my zits went away?

In the mirror is a symmetrical perfect-oval face and button nose, not the honker my mother and sister have. With my ears adorned with the diamond studs Lee and I got from the Piercing Station, I look like a damn cheerleader. A month ago, I'd wanted to punch their smug faces. Let them have a taste of the real world.

I mean seriously, what do I have to fear? We're the Joneses. It's like God gave us a pass on the laws of physics. Rules? Suggestions.

I'm about to jump when two freckled redheads stroll into my driveway, hands entwined. Gross.

Wait—it's Gina Cleary, freshly returned from what we've been told is a fat farm in Utah.

"She's packed on too many Christmas pounds," her parents said at the time.

Rumor is though she got pregnant with Geoff Garcia's baby and went away for a while. She's clearly regained her head-cheerleader figure. However, as far as I know, she still hasn't shown up at school. Her companion, who is not Geoff, looks like a real cretin with matted shoulder-length hair and a heavily pockmarked face. He stops to light a cigarette, and after taking a drag from it, tosses it on the ground. The grease oozes out of him.

That Gina and the slimeball are taking their time makes me angry. By the time they walk past and round the corner to Geneva Avenue, another minute will be lost. That's when I make my first mistake. Although there are as many of these specimens crawling around this neighborhood as there are misshapen frogs, I commit the cardinal sin of teenagerhood. *Don't stare.*

I can't help it. Ever since Gina returned from wherever she went, she has this dazed look like she's been hit with a brick. She still wears her trademark fire-engine red Pres-a-Ply nails, she still lays still while her sister steam irons her hair on the highest setting until it's as straight and flat as a measuring stick, but seriously.

I know staring's not polite. Besides, it's not like I want what they have. It's not them, but their orange-tagged Levis and desert boots I want. Even if I was dying to be in the in-group, Mom, who in this way is quintessentially Moroccan, doesn't waste money on kids' trends.

"I can make it for less," she says.

Out of nowhere, a rock hits the top of my window, making the spider even larger. Another one whizzes by. Seriously? Relief washes over me. The cretin did me a favor. And as long as the glass holds, I won't have to jump into a pile of shards.

"Up yours," I say.

"Creeper!" the guy yells.

"Takes one to know one!" I shoot back.

That's when Sugar—who knows a lowlife when she sees one, and who's been patrolling the fence line like a cop with a flashlight—springs into action. She barks, she snarls, she shows her teeth.

But when Gina locks eyes with her, Sugar just tucks her tail between her legs and whines.

"What's your Sugar gonna do? Pee on me?" Gina laughs. "Cocker Spaniel? Poor excuse for a dog. I bet you begged your mom for her. I heard you're one of Coach Callium's pity cases. Face it, kid. You're too much of a dork to make the squad."

I want to defend Sugar—she's the best dog ever—but there she is, belly-up on the ground. It's not what Gina said about Coach that bugs me. It's that word: dork.

I can handle bullying. I'm not a sniveling coward. I'm the queen of stiff upper lips. The problem is, my sense of humor is meaner than I am. I could say something about raising her future babies. I could remind her she's used goods. That continuation school doesn't even have a cheer squad.

Instead, I make a face and chuck one of my extra pom-poms out the window. It lands a foot away from the cretin's boot. He throws a fake punch in my direction.

Gina tells him to stop. Sugar barks. I look away. I've already wasted a minute with these jerks. The clock says 4 damned 57.

Then a miracle happens. When the far-outclassed Gina sees Renee's gray Oldsmobile turn onto Fawn drive, she gets this look of fear on her face. Not only does she scamper away, her slimy, butt-crack-showing boyfriend follows closely behind.

I'm more worried about how little time's left, honestly. The boy won't do anything. He's enough of a goon and about the right age to be one of Dad's revolving door of loser friends. It doesn't cross my mind that my super-nice, super-loving dad is helping ruin the entire neighborhood. If I have a sick feeling, I shove it down. I have one focus: jumping.

My legs, freshly shaved and smooth all the way up to my thighs, smell like Johnson's baby oil. Once I land in that pile of lawn clippings, it'll reek of Eau de Grass, and my uniform will be stained. But it's either that or go back inside and deal with Dad's "friends."

They're only going to get bolder. The smell of burning hemp will drift under my bedroom door again. I'd rather let Pepe Le Pew spray me with skunk oil. Seriously! While I'm waiting, someone puts another record on the player and turns the volume all the way up. Jefferson Airplane is blaring from the high-end Dolbys that inexplicably weren't a waste of money.

I'm seized by a pang of guilt thinking about Nikki the Brat being out there alone. I imagine her high on adrenaline and second-hand smoke, entertaining the guests, who are blotto. Her, belting it out like a miniature Gypsy Rose Lee. *Let me Entertain You* with a more modern twist. I don't understand. In what universe would any mom want us here?

Another Harley roars into the driveway. Panic. I want this more than ever.

The driver—bald, tattooed, with a kerchief—gets welcomed in. That's my cue. I can finally breathe.

I'm halfway out the window when I hear Nikki's thin voice cutting through the air.

"Don't you want somebody to love?" she croons.

I wasn't prepared for my heart to split in two.

The kid's high. She might be a brat, but … hell no. A girl has to do what she has to do.

In the end, it's a dog-eat-dog world. Nikki's going to have to figure it out.

Once I accept that, it's easy. I kiss the binding of the diary where I've hidden the amulet Mrs. Tehranpour gave me, toss it onto the bed, and jump.

The landing's nothing—just some dry grass clippings I brush off my skirt. But my duffel bag, stashed behind the trash can, smells like puke and piss.

I'm stepping around the shards of a broken beer bottle when I hear a voice.

"What ya doing?" Nikki says.

And there she is. Dilated eyes. Lopsided mouth. Not much shocks me—but a high four-year-old? Yeah, that does.

I'm sympathetic. But if there's one thing I know, Nikki is 100% snitch.

"I heard a noise," she says dreamily. "Dad says it's time for you to sing!"

What I do next—I don't feel bad about. She'll be too young, too zonked to remember.

"Can't. Going to Lee's house. Math homework."

I glance down at my outfit—dead giveaway—but press on.

"She wants to see one of my routines," I add.

"Mom said."

"I couldn't go to Ida Price."

"Dad says, sing. Abi, *pleeease*."

"You don't understand. Lee has a D. You know what that means?"

"Dad's friend says I have the funcking munchies."

Her voice is so casual. Like this is normal.

She might grow up to be a burnout.

But before I can worry too much, Renee's car coughs out a puff of exhaust across the street.

"Peace out, kid. There's food on the counter," I say.

What I don't expect is for her to bargain.

"Chick-O-Sticks," she says. "Bring some home and I won't tell. And I wanna wear your Hamsa. Just once. That's all I'm asking."

"Yes to the candy. As for the evil eye? Dad already gave you a rabbit's foot."

She won't let that slide. Nikki's a savant—like a 40-year-old used-car salesman in a 4-year-old body. When Mom and Dad brought her home, I wasn't expecting a Currier & Ives cherub. But this kid destroys everything she touches. And when she doesn't get her way? Total meltdown.

Luckily, I found a good hiding spot for my charm.

"Mom says you're supposed to feed me, and Dad says you're supposed to sing."

She slips into an imitation of Dad's voice. Only she's so disoriented the words come out all wonky.

"Listen to my Abigail. Radio-ready angel voice. Acapella."

It makes my eyes want to well up. She's trying to manipulate me back into the house, but she's too messed up to pull it off. At this stage, I can outsmart the little punk. I don't know that in a few years, she'll have honed her skills. She'll become a pro at playing victim.

Exhaust pours from the tailpipe of Renee's car.

"Give me a minute," I say. "I want to say hi to Lee's sister since she's always at school or at work. In the meantime, the sheet music for Paper Roses is on my desk. In my jewelry box, you'll find the charm."

Nikki nods her head, gives me a sly smile, and skips off.

As soon as she disappears inside, I bolt. Next thing I know, I'm in Renee's Oldsmobile, shimmying on suntan L'eggs, brushing out my hair, and swiping mascara across my lashes. By the time we turn onto New Jersey Avenue, I'm sitting up straight.

"Man, it's freezing. Can you turn the heater on?" I say.

"Sure. By the way, it's been forever since I babysat you. How are you doing?"

"Fine."

"Hope you don't mind me asking," she says, fiddling with the dial. "Why isn't your mom so gung-ho about cheerleading anymore? Wasn't she the one who signed you up? Told my mom it was for coordination."

"I dunno."

At a stop sign, she turns to look at me. Plum lipstick. Spun gold leaf earrings.

"If I didn't know better," she says, "I'd think your mom's competing with you. Like she doesn't want you to be happy. Exhibit A: that ghastly red checkered fake fur pantsuit she made you wear."

Here we go.

Yeah, Mom can be a bitch—a monster, even. But other people saying it? No way.

I look out the window.

"Hey, can we change the subject?" I say after a silence. "She likes to make things. She thinks she's helping."

"I'm sorry," she says. "Speaking of making things. You know those tissue roses you're making? Can you make some for me? I'm throwing a shower for my friend Rainy. They'll be perfect."

"Sure," I say. "But why fake when real is so much better? It's like the song Dad makes me sing about imitation love."

"Listen, kid. I'm rooting for you," Renee says. "Don't take things too seriously. Real flowers die. These we can keep forever. Anyway, keep making them. Keep writing your poetry. You never know."

There's wisdom in that. But I'm wary. I don't trust adults. Even cool 18-year-old ones.

The rest of the ride, I keep my hand on the door lever.

Renee pulls into the parking lot.

"Thanks for the ride," I say. "By the way—Mom and I are cool. Whatever she does, she doesn't mean it. She had a hard time growing up. A bunch of French girls at her lycée."

Renee nods. "You need a ride next Thursday?"

I shake my head. She doesn't know that from now on, I won't be going home after school. I don't care what I have to do—library, Jack in the Box, Winchell's—I'm never putting myself through that again.

I don't mean to, but when I step out of the car, I slam the door with a sharp click. The sound hangs in the air long after the engine fades down the road.

CHAPTER 8

Pom Poms and Pancakes

Abigail

How I found myself twirling a baton when I've always been the epitome of the anti-cheerleader has everything to do with Sierra Blair—aka Head Pom-Pom Girl at Ida Price Middle School. Teenage Sierra may resemble Hugh Hefner's latest girlfriend (minus the boob job), but don't be fooled; she couldn't care less about appearances.

Until just a year ago, she was homeschooled—not by choice, but because she lived in the Panama Canal Zone. She was five minutes from dense jungle, spent her days feeding mangoes to iguanas, and carried an 18-inch machete clipped to her waist to cut through sawgrass. She kept a snakebite kit with her at all times to handle the pit of fer-de-lance snakes lurking at the edge of her family's property.

And now, here she is, gracing us with her presence.

She told me the only reason she joined the squad was because it seemed like "the American thing to do." She didn't expect to be popular—but she is. Spectacularly. As far as I'm concerned, she could grow another head and every girl in school would follow suit.

The best thing about Sierra is she sees me as valuable—even when Mom and the other girls don't. I'm enough, just as I am.

"Mom's nickname for me is Pancake One," I tell a shocked Sierra. "You know, the first pancake that sticks to the bottom of the pan and has to be thrown out. My sister? She's Pancake Two—the perfect one."

When Sierra says, "There's no way!" my stomach clenches and does a somersault. I'm not used to such kindness. Besides, I thought all moms were like that. I'm used to Mom always saying exactly what she thinks. Her mom was the same way. I call them Nanette's gems. But those are only part of why I cling to friends like Velcro while trying to peel myself away from her.

Soon enough, it's Sierra this, Sierra that. She only gives me pointers when I ask, and she actually listens when I talk. Sierra knows more about the world than the rest of us—thanks to the education her mom gave her—but she still needs help with English. That's where I come in.

"If I'm going to take cosmetology in a couple years," she says, "I'll need practice now."

She's fourteen and already a wizard with a blow dryer, but her English needs work. I've had Mrs. Dubois for summer session. It'll be easy. I'll tutor her. Our friendship won't be one-sided.

But after Sierra goes too far with the Sun-In—making her hair golden blonde and mine burned orange—Mom, who seems to forget hair grows back, decides she's not a fan.

Because of Sierra, I have Cheryl Tiegs eyebrows. I'm channeling supermodel energy. Doesn't Mom realize?

Anyway, I haven't been in Sierra's "chair" for over a week thanks to Easter break and Passover. Mom's thrilled. I'm not. Already, dark hairs are sprouting above my eyes and over my nose—like black pen strokes on white paper. The beginning of a unibrow.

What happens next—just before Ben and his family pick us up for Mimouna—is Disaster City. Never have less-experienced hands held a pair of tweezers. Even if I had skill, I tend to mess things up when it counts. The first few plucks have me wincing in pain. After that, I go into a trance-like state, the feel of cold metal against warm skin, and the release. Before long, not much eyebrow is left on either side of my nose. What can I say? I like symmetry.

I jiggle Mom's vanity drawer, then rummage for an eyebrow pencil. All hers are jet black. Plan B: dry my bangs flat enough to reach my nose. It hides the eyebrows but creates a new problem. I tease the rest of my hair into oblivion, sealing it with so much Aqua Net that eventually, nothing comes out of the can but air.

It doesn't matter if I look weird. Soon, my baby-fine hair will be flatter than a tire with a nail in it.

Next: freckles. I find a jar of pressed powder. It's four shades too dark, so I mix in white eyeshadow. Not bad in the bathroom mirror, but when a bit of sun shines through the top of our frosted window, I'm sparkling in all the wrong places. The rest of me too. I could bump my hair to the high heavens and cake on a pound of makeup; I'd still look like a baby.

Even with the tomato-soup colored hair, you'd think my clear skin and once kind of good-enough eyebrows would've carried me. I mean, my face is good. But I'd overestimated the power of a teenager in a training bra to make a colossal mess out of myself. I was hoping looks and talent would carry the day. But now, looking at my tissue paper roses and hand-tied sheaves of wheat, I know they won't get me far. The older girls are bringing chocolate éclairs, croquembouche towers, cake-and-frosting masterpieces.

I do have a poem. But I'm only sharing it with one person.

When the phone rings, Mom—still wrapped in a towel—rushes to answer. Whoever it is must've complimented her, because when she hangs up, she's beaming.

She tells us to get moving. I pull a blue and silver caftan from the closet and slip it on, shoving my feet into sequined babouche slippers. I don't need makeup to sparkle.

Nikki, however, is not impressed.

"What'd you do? Smear sumpin' all over your face?"

"Henna tattoos hide a multitude of sins," Mom says, giving me an annoyed look. She dabs lotion onto a tissue and hands it to me. "Thirteen's a touchy age."

I wish I could come up with a snappy retort. Mom couldn't find a kid-sized caftan, so Nikki's dressed like a mini grown-up: bell-bottoms, a Handi-Wipe tube top, and a fringed, spangled vest. She looks like a disco munchkin.

Mom decides to give us henna tattoos. Nikki goes first. She's four—if she doesn't go first, she screams. She can't sit still, so she gets a blurry Hand of Fatima and a crooked four-leaf clover.

She squeals. Gives Mom a thumbs-up.

Mom and I get the same design—a delicate daisy chain of leaves and flowers. Mine goes above my eyebrows.

"She's not purty no more," Nikki says. "But I am."

"Be nice," Mom says, light but firm. She glances at me, brushes hair from my face, and stands. "Next time, Abi, don't pluck so far back. Our ride'll be here any minute."

CHAPTER 9

Boogie Baby

Abigail

The Lindner family van is spacious and air-conditioned—much better than Dad's Rambler and Mom's constantly breaking down Starfire. Mom is up front with her friend Lilianne and Lilianne's new husband, smiling and laughing like she's never had a care in the world. Us kids are in the two back rows.

Lilianne's daughters, Linda, 17, and Leesa, 16, are here. So is Leesa's twin, Ben. The girls' hands are covered in henna designs way more intricate than mine. Leesa, the cheery one, compliments Nikki on her blurry Hand of Fatima.

Linda's holding a sheet cake shaped like a lion—with candy corn teeth and a mane formed from curls of orange buttercream. When I take notice, she shrugs.

"I made a pattern and cut it out," she says. "It was easy. Not like your flowers."

I'm too self-conscious to take a compliment. My funky eyebrows, iridescent streaked makeup, and baby-fine Sun-In'd hair with bobby pins that keep slipping out. Ben, meanwhile, looks perfect. Even Mom, who never comments on how 16-year-old boys look, notices.

"Your face could launch a thousand ships," she says to Ben. "Such beauty, wasted on a boy. It's a Greek tragedy."

Mom doesn't read much—not in English, not in French—so her referencing Helen of Troy is impressive. But not only is she kind of insulting him, she's also missing the point. Yes, he's cute. But he's also funny, smart, kind—and totally tolerant of my obvious crush. My competition (ask any girl at the party) is probably just as enamored. I wonder how long they spent perfecting their hair, makeup, tiaras, and gold bangles.

We zip from house to house before arriving at the Symonds' home. Mom's jealous—Antonia has turned her backyard into a spring wonderland. There are paper lanterns, flags, and strands of blue and white lights. With no room left on the table, I assume my flowers will be shoved aside.

Nikki, with an almond cookie in one hand and a pain au chocolat in the other, looks greedy. If she could have it all, she would. Mom's plate? Just a couple dates, celery stalks, and a smear of cream cheese. If we weren't mortal enemies after the cheerleading debacle and her other general behaviors I'm really not fond of, I'd be worried. Next to the voluptuous Lilianne, she's a popsicle stick. I'm feeling sympathetic, but when she opens her big mouth to make a comment about me recently becoming a woman, all bets are off. Seriously, Mom?

Nikki, who hasn't been taught what menstruation is, laughs. Ben, however, looks secondhand embarrassed. His face goes beet red. Not long after, he pulls me aside.

"You okay?"

"Midol cures all ills," I say, instantly regretting it.

The worst. I'm the worst.

But just as I'm thinking I want to disappear, Antonia glides over. Instead of treating me like the almost-woman I am, she grabs my cheek and kisses it. Like I'm five.

"Such a talent you are, mignon," she says. "Such intricate flowers you've made."

Antonia's in the middle of her next sentence when she sees Mom and her face shifts from delight to concern. She grabs Mom by the sleeve and leads her inside, where a banquet is waiting.

"If this feast doesn't get you to eat, Nanette, nothing will."

And what a spread it is: Moroccan cigars stuffed with lamb, triangle-shaped pastries filled with potatoes, cold carrot and beet salads, couscous, and the pièce de résistance—a whole salmon topped with orange slices.

Mom does her best to comply. She nibbles a pastry, picks at a lamb cigar.

"The best I've ever tasted. Never better!" she says.

She could be faking it. If she downs Ex-Lax later, I won't be shocked. But I'm still encouraged when she dishes Nikki a big serving of couscous and fish, and a small portion for herself.

After we eat, Antonia pours boiling water from a decorative, gold-encrusted pot into tiny mint-filled glasses. When Grandma Moab hands Mom a bowl of sugar cubes, she drops in two.

Uncle Laurent, who's been waiting, finally asks about Dad.

"At an Atlantic Richfield convention," I say.

Truth is, this isn't a Jewish holiday serious enough for Dad to care. He's probably at a bar or playing pool with friends.

Uncle Laurent seems satisfied—he says nothing else.

We join a long row of picnic tables in the backyard, each one overflowing with sweets. What Antonia has assembled for dessert is cooler than cool. Forget Jolly Ranchers, mini Hershey's, and Life Savers—this is next-level: tray after tray of dried apricots, nuts and dates, honey gâteau, meskouta, and more Moroccan cigars—this time lemon-filled and rolled in powdered sugar. And there's Mom, munching on it all.

After dessert, Mom hands me the Polaroid camera.

"No problemo," I say.

What happens next is kind of sweet, kind of weird. I've only ever known Mom as high-strung—or vaguely sad. But as the photo develops, I'm stunned. Surrounded by her culture, her people, she looks … settled.

Years from now, I'll look back at the photo and be struck by how young she was. Thirty-one. Her melanin makes her look even younger. Nikki appears as a blur, a streak of lightning trying to wriggle out of her arms. Mom's barely-there grip on Nikki's knees is all that's keeping her from hitting Antonia's concrete patio.

I imagine Nikki hoisting herself out of the frame and into the middle of the action. Her caftan-free outfit makes escaping easy. She has no interest in joining the grandmas and aunties, who greet each newcomer with hugs and double cheek kisses.

Mom had Nikki in Little Duckie's dance studio practically before she could walk. So it's no surprise when she makes her way to the center of the dance floor. There, she dances with wild abandon but in the style of a 4-year-old, which makes her seem even wilder. She shimmies and shakes her way through the Boogaloo and the Jerk, adding in a few shuffle-ball changes as she goes along. The way she goes berserk is semi-adorable. The older girls pat her on the head and smile.

Someone puts on another record. This time, a flute is heard in the background. A male voice sings in an ancient language. None of us kids understand Arabic, but Grandpa Moab claps in rhythm, appreciating the lyrics and meaning. Others join in, snapping fingers, stomping feet. We're Rocking Moroccans, as the saying goes. The place pulses so hard I can feel it shift beneath me.

Nikki keeps perfect time with the drums, periodically stopping to check if Mom is watching. She isn't.

Why didn't any of the lovely older women step in? Mom clearly doesn't have a handle on things. But their energy is reserved for the true babies—those passed from great-grandmother to grandmother to great-aunt, feet never touching the ground.

"Je t'adore!" they exclaim. "Très mignon. Magnifique," they add, pinching each baby's chubby face. And as the evening winds to a close, each little one appears battle-worn, pink, and blemished from wear.

By the time *Hava Nagila* is on the record player, my mood has improved. Still, I'd rather watch from the sidelines. Nikki does the Bump, the Chicken Dance, and the Hustle, all the while stopping periodically to see who's watching. I would be nice to her, keep her occupied, but she's been a pill all day. However, all it takes is one look at Ben, who's spying at me from across the room, to make me change my stance. I don't want him to think I'm a bad sister.

During a lull in the music, I walk to the dance floor and tap her on the head.

"How ya doing, Squirt?"

"Jus' dancing."

"I didn't ask what, I asked how."

"I dunno. Fine, I guess."

"When you get tired, wanna come sit with me?"

"Has Mom seen me?"

"She's busy with her friends, Nikki."

"I don't care. Has she seen me?"

Before I can answer, the music starts again.

"My turn," Nikki says.

Then, as if on cue, Uncle Laurent's work friend tosses a string of Mardi Gras beads over Nikki's head. She giggles as they land around her neck and starts swaying like she's wearing a hula hoop.

"Play La Cucaracha!" she yells.

I would stay, but I'm not embarrassing myself. The only dance steps I know are from cheer. As I walk away, smiling like a fool, I nearly bump into Ben.

"You seem happy," he says. "Anyway, read any good books lately?"

Oh my God. He's such a dork. But he's Ben—sixteen, cute, and a literary genius. What am I supposed to say? That I've been reading Harlequin romances I checked out of the library? That I don't really understand Melville or Dickens or Homer?

"I haven't," I admit. "But I saw the movie The Picture of Dorian Gray. I even wrote a poem."

From his stricken expression, I can tell I've gone too far.

"Don't worry, Ben," I say. "Any relationship we have is purely intellectual."

His smile returns. I feel relief flood my chest.

"Dorian Gray was an evil dude," he says. "The way he treated people—especially women—was awful. Nothing happened to him, only to the painting. It's a cautionary tale. Be careful or you'll get it in the end."

My chest tightens. Not because I disagree—but because I live in a house where blame always finds me. I'll be fine. Nikki? I'm not so sure. But what about Mom and Dad? What'll happen to them when the reckoning comes?

"Here's the poem," I say. "I wrote it for you. But don't get a big head."

"I'm flattered, Abi. I'll keep it forever."

When the music stops, someone flips on the lights. People move about in sharp focus, putting things away, shutting things down. Piles of dirty dishes and trays are littered about. Stepped-on napkins are strewn across the floor.

And there's Nikki standing in the middle of the dance floor. Alone. Her Handi Wipe top is pulled up too high, and she's worked up such a sweat that the Hand of Fatima tattoo has melted off her face. Tonight, she made a full-throttled bid for love and affection, got it for a while, and now it's gone. The whole thing saddens me.

The next day at school, time will drag on. But as boring as my day will be, it can't be any worse than Nikki's. I imagine she'll be at home, watching TV, playing with my old, tired toys. Or at the gym daycare, crawling through one McDonald's-style plastic tunnel after another, supervised by some checked-out teen.

As I tuck my amulet under my caftan sleeve, I realize: I'll never know exactly what rolls around in that kid's head.

Little do I know, while I'll be learning about quadratic equations and Hernán Cortés, she'll be learning something else entirely.

I slide the amulet a little higher under my sleeve.

Pretty soon, we'll both be home. But at least I can count the days until I can leave.

It's hard pretending I wasn't meant for something else.

CHAPTER 10

Cowboy Games

Yasmina – Rabat, Morocco – December 1948

I've learned to be quiet. In silence, no one asks questions. In silence, you disappear just enough to survive. I've also come to learn it's the voices you can't see that teach you the most.

It's 1948, and Madame Moab is in her room listening to her favorite French soap opera, *La Famille Duraton*—one of those serials where nothing ever happens. I've heard her mimicking the accent of the lead actress, Blanchette Brunoy, again and again, trying to get the tone and phrasing just right. Though she can't see the actors, she knows from magazines that Mademoiselle Brunoy styles her hair in a confection of sun-kissed curls and waves. Her favorite photo of the actress is on page 49 of *Mon Film*, where Brunoy wears a white silk shirt with a notched collar, white gloves, and a hand-spotted mink draped over her shoulders.

Madame Moab is a wizard with needle and thread, able to recreate the latest fashions from whatever remnants she can scrounge. But now, well into her eighth pregnancy, she's put all that aside.

"Maternity clothes aren't exactly fashionable," she says. "It's better to concentrate on my face."

So, every day, she dusts her cheeks and nose with alabaster powder, and curls and pins her hair into perfect waves. She finishes with a dab of Chanel No. 5 on the back of her neck.

One glance in the mirror, and the transformation is complete. She is Blanchette Brunoy.

"N"Ne sois pas candidat à la mairie--

"Ne pas tu être candidat à la mairie!—Do not run for mayor," she says to a figment of actor Noël-Noël, Mademoiselle Brunoy's current paramour on the serial. That the real Noël-Noël wears a toupee, has a wife and two mistresses, and is five years older than Madame Moab's husband means nothing.

She lost all romantic interest in her husband the moment he was forced to put away his jeweler's loupe. I overheard her on the phone:

"I know it's political. Jews aren't making jewelry anymore," she told her sister. "Still, it takes everything I have to be with a man who smells of yeast. How would you like a man who's always picking dough out of his fingernails? Whose shirt sleeves and pant legs are perpetually dusted in flour?"

La Famille Duraton lasts 40 minutes; Madame Moab's fantasies stretch much longer. Meanwhile, one room over, six sons—lost boys all—wait for her to make an appearance. They play Cowboys and Indians shoot-up games with a velocity teetering on violence. This worries me. Their cap guns, which still smell faintly of gunpowder, go *pop-pop!* Their bow-and-arrow sets, though rubber-tipped, are dangerous enough at close range to put out an eye.

"I am Laurent, the last Lost Avenger," one of the twins shouts, loosening a length of rope from his waist. "Step aside, or me and my friend Lucky Luc will lasso you with our lariats!"

"The mighty Jews have won the shootout at the OK Corral. Surrender, Arabs, one and all!" yells the ten-year-old.

Their play fights always become Arab versus Jew, which is deeply unsettling. Even Aristide—barely older than baby Jean—has been indoctrinated. An almost 2,000-year cycle of battles, ceasefires, and détentes acted out by children.

"Quiet!" I say. "Your maman's going to have a fit. You don't want her to lose the baby, do you?"

They ignore me, as always. I'm a Berber, not an Arab, but try convincing them of that.

When the ten-year-old commands me to surrender, I leave them to their war games. Seven-year-old Nanette is in the kitchen, picking specks of dust off the floor. It makes me sad.

I'm about to scoop her up when Madame Moab's door creaks open. A moment later, she steps into the doorway.

"Oh, how your papa and I wish we had stopped at three," she says. "A bunch of unruly boys storming through the house at all hours—we can't get a moment's rest."

Not only is this incredibly hurtful to the boys, it takes everything I have not to roll my eyes. Lady, isn't it a little late to complain? Isn't this a speech you'll regret when someone has to take care of you one day?

It's a good thing I straighten my face just in time, because when Madame Moab turns to address me, her tone is civil and professional— with a thin veil of contempt I've never heard before.

"Since tomorrow is New Year's Eve, Hanukkah, and Shabbat all in one, can you, for once, get us a decent piece of fish?"

"I know just where to go," I say.

The boys, still bruised by their mother's words, fall silent. But the calm doesn't last. They return to their play with even more intensity. I admire their resilience—I wish I had it. But I can't afford to be reckless. It's not just the pregnancy making Madame Moab prickly. Since mid-May, when Jews began leaving Morocco for the new state of Israel, neither one of us knows how things stand. I've been their valued servant, renowned for my skill in the kitchen. Now it's clear I can be replaced.

Losing my job would be a threat to my very existence. Every maid in the mellah is on alert. Without a husband or a family to rely on, I'm particularly vulnerable. I strive to become indispensable, and with the Moabs, the only way is through their stomach. Monsieur and Madame don't share much in common, except that they both adore good cuisine. Refining my cooking becomes everything—even changing the way I engage with the children.

I don't notice when the boys get too wound up, or when two-year-old Olivier unstraps himself from his highchair and tumbles to the floor. Fortunately, twelve-year-old Henri, who's outgrown cowboy games, steps in. His comic book-inspired peace treaty is surprisingly mature.

"Even Arabs need to rest. And Jews. We can't always be fighting," he says.

Nanette isn't as tough. Or as easy to soothe. Maybe it's because she's not perfect that I've become so attached to her. I'd only been working here five days when she was born, and right away, it was clear: Nanette was several shades darker than her mother. Over time, her skin grew even more olive-toned. Her grandmother, aunties, and cousins whispered constantly about how ugly she was. They like to pretend they're European, but truthfully, every one of them has Berber blood in their veins.

As the only girl, Nanette is occasionally summoned by Madame Moab to model and twirl while her mother adjusts hems. The more attention she gets, the more the boys act out. Heaven forbid the new baby turns out to be the fair-skinned girl Madame Moab's always dreamed of. Nanette will be left behind.

I don't have time to ruminate on this. Olivier, the cherub, is tugging at my apron.

"Maman," he says.

"Non, non, petit mignon," I say. "Your maman is resting."

I admire Madame Moab, but she doesn't see what she has. If I had a husband—one of her babies! But Adrina Mouloudji's gossip ruined that possibility.

"Yasmina is unable to conceive," she told everyone. "Besides, she's bad luck."

So I can't marry. And going alone is unthinkable. Jews are leaving in droves. Where would I get another job? The Moab family is okay, but I know one wrong move, and I'm done for. Every day I feel myself crumbling more. I saw the postcard from Madame Moab's Aunt Fortuna telling her a life in Paris is possible.

When I eventually become a mother, my opinion of Madame Moab will change. After Adam's birth mother surrendered him and I picked him up from the airport, the first thing the toddler did was yank my earrings, stretch my earlobes into long slits, and draw blood. After days of refusing the bottle, me putting up with his ear-splitting scream for which nothing I do consoles him, in her shoes, maybe I would've had the same fantasies. And Adam is my only one. Madame Moab had eight, if you count the stillbirth.

I do wish she'd been able to bite her tongue. Her caustic words and criticisms, along with her habit of becoming self-absorbed, have torn through multiple generations. It needs to stop.

But it's not the Moab children I'm thinking about. I might be 22, but what if my boss decides to live out her Parisian dreams? Where will I end up?

One day, there's a postcard on the table lying face-up.

All you have to do is get Louis on board, it said. *Tell him, open a jewelry store. And the food here is amazing. Trout from the River Seine. Magnifique.*

Trout almondine becomes a mythical dish in my imagination—one so divine it could inspire a family to uproot and move. I see myself sleeping under cardboard, begging for francs. I'd have somewhere to go, but not for long. After Baba died, Mma and my brother moved to Fes. He has a wife, children, and Mma. I'd be a burden.

Maybe I don't know how to make trout almondine—yet. But I could learn. Amira's family loves her so much they say they'll never leave without her. I could master a cold salmon with couscous. It's a start. I know the rhythms of the Moab household after seven and a half years. I anticipate every need. But it's not enough. The fog in this house clouds the truth.

It's foolish to dream about bumping into Noël-Noël at a café in Paris or to pine for the Algerian mandolin player she once wanted to run away with—but that's Madame Moab. Monsieur Moab is more grounded. He knows he can't snap his fingers and open a jewelry shop on the Champs-Élysées. Still, with enough pressure, he might be convinced.

As for me? I can't shake the fantasy: that with one perfect bite, they'll forget everything happening around them. Monsieur Moab will put away his jeweler's loupe for good. He'll demand respect from his wife. He'll believe in his new vocation.

"As a jeweler, all I did was melt gold and silver into molds, chisel stones, and set them with prongs," he will say. "Baking is an art too, of the highest order. Making bread, for example. It takes talent to get the mixture to the correct consistency, knead the dough enough but not too much, watch it rise to the right height, shape it into perfect loaves, and bake it until it's crusty on the outside and soft on the inside, and perfectly brown."

CHAPTER 11

Fish and Fictions

Yasmina

When Madame Rubin told me the story of Jonah, she had no idea the effect it would have on me. That tale of faith and courage has stayed with me. So it's no big leap for me to believe a magical fish could change minds.

Loyalty to the Mouloudjis got me nowhere—but maybe it will be different with the Moabs.

All of this, of course, is a delusion. The Moabs no longer have the money they once did. If they leave Morocco, it will be with only the clothes on their backs. Still, the more I tell the story, the more believable it becomes. Farrah and Halleh—two of the other maids in the mellah—cling to the possibility. If it works for me, maybe it will work for them.

"For the best fish," Farrah said, "you must venture beyond the gates of the Bab Mellah to the sea. Walk along the river. You'll get there."

"You'll never find better," Halleh added. "As long as your arm and as wide as a fat man's belly. So plentiful, one cast of the net and you wouldn't believe. But you must leave early."

The last day of Hanukkah falls on New Year's Eve this year, so I figure it's the perfect day. Monsieur Moab will be home early, and everyone will be in good spirits. I've never left home before daybreak, and this morning in particular, there isn't a single star in the sky to light my way. Even the moon, a milky mélange of shadow and light, is covered in a thin morning mist. This discourages me at first. The first obstacle I have to get around are the mud and stone steps winding around the house. They reflect no light. Once I'm at the street, it becomes easier to see. Although some of the paving stones are dull, others glitter in the moonlight. I'm starting to get going, thinking, *so far, so good*, when I spot 12-year-old Henri standing on the balcony.

I motion for him to get back to bed, but instead of retreating, he crosses his hands over his chest.

"Listen, Henri," I say. "I should be back before anyone wakes up. If I'm not, don't say anything."

For whatever reason, he uncrosses his arms and heads back down the stairs. A few seconds later, he's gone.

Some alleyways are so dark I wish I mined silver—at least then I'd have a rope to hold or a rock to steady me. The farther I trudge, the more unsure I become that I'll return before the children wake. I consider turning back, but when I round a corner and find a path less dim, hope returns.

Eventually, I arrive at Monsieur Bohbot's vegetable market, where he's setting up for the day. I have no idea how much time has passed. I should keep walking—I can get vegetables later—but seeing him is a relief. I watch as he wraps asparagus in parchment and weighs the fennel and garbanzo beans I'll use for chickpea soup.

I'm not thinking about anything deep. But when I reach the gates of the Bab Mellah, I remember something Monsieur Moab once told me:

"After so many of us were expelled from Spain, Morocco welcomed us," he said. "Sheikh al-Watusi wanted to build a citadel to protect us but couldn't, so he walled us in. He figured if he placed us beside the medina, where the souks and shopkeepers were, anyone coming for us would have to go through them first."

The recollection makes me uneasy. Shortly after I'd arrived at the Moab home and was assured that burqas were only for the most observant women, I switched to a dress and a loose headscarf. Inside the walls of the mellah, no one looked twice. Out here, I'm not so sure.

The directions scribbled on my palm are detailed—I won't get lost or look confused, which would be worse. This is fortunate, because soon, a sliver of sunlight pierces the mist, and the streets begin to fill with pedestrians and cart-pushing vendors.

As the sun climbs higher, I grow more anxious about the time. I cross Boulevard Jaffe and the Triangle de Vues—names that mean nothing to me. It isn't until I reach the Lycée des Jeunes Filles, empty at this hour, that anything feels familiar. It's too early for school, but the silence feels eerie. What I don't realize—what will ruin everything—is that today is a holiday. I remember thinking how fortunate it was that the French-run schools started late. The children of diplomats and bureaucrats need their sleep.

In the mellah, the streets are so cramped I need to walk single-file. It's the same here, but in some places, the street opens up, allowing me to pick up speed. If I had the time, I'd stop to take in the grandness of it all. Intricate arches marking the beginning and end of each major street, the majestic palm trees lining each meridian, the endless communal spaces where people go to haggle over goats, milk … or fish.

When Rue Jaffe widens into a line of cafés, I know where I am. There, brightly dressed men and women sip tea from silver pots poured into tiny glasses. I'd love to be one of those early-bird couples—but that's a dream deferred. Keeping my job is the only priority.

Across the plaza, the street intersects with Rue de Bordeaux. I was told I'd see a government office there. A few more turns, and I'll reach the Bou Regreg River. From there, it's a straight shot to the sea.

I imagine Nanette wiping the cobwebs from her eyes, pulling her dress over her head, slipping her little feet into her slippers. I'd set the table for breakfast—but what a fool I was, thinking croissants and coffee would be enough to occupy her and six sleepy boys.

Nanette, always the first to wake, will come looking for me.

"Time for school," she'll say.

Then she and her older brothers will pile into the family sedan and leave.

As the sun brightens, panic threatens. But I reassure myself: Nanette will be fine. I picture her at her desk at the Institut Jeanne d'Arc—well-fed, alert, hands folded, the only Jewish girl in her Grade 1 class that she hates so much.

But what about the two too young for school? How long will they sleep?

I want to freeze right there—but I remind myself, I'll be fine.

We Shilha are resourceful. We've endured famine, war, disaster—and yet we survive.

Madame Moab will get her fish, and I'll keep my job. If not? She'll be the one left raising her brood alone.

It's for the children that I've dedicated myself. It's for them that I've mastered cookery. I remember Nanette as a toddler, delighting in the spicy, savory scent of sweet potato soup simmering on the stove. Her tongue licking salty sardine bits from her fingers. I see her now, standing on a stool, spoon in hand, pretending she's the chef.

Before I know it, I reach the place where the river meets the sea. The air feels lighter here, at the edge of the world. I inhale the scent of bougainvillea. Across the water, the Kasbah of the Oudaias glows orange in the sunlight. Beyond it: the sea.

Only a few fishing boats remain.

"Fifty feet ahead," the directions said. "Turn your back to the wall. You'll see it."

There are buildings painted blue, white, and yellow, with flowers in the windows—but no market. I follow a man with a cart down one alley and then another. The air turns sour—sweat, fish juice, animal dung. It overwhelms the ocean breeze.

Once I arrive, the scene is appalling—scampering rats, snakes, wild dogs, stray cats. And flies—hundreds of them.

The dress I'm wearing may be secondhand from Madame Moab's closet, but it's beautiful. I wore it for luck, thinking any woman who gifted me something so precious wouldn't abandon me. Hand-tailored, embroidered at the cuffs, she'd worn it only once—on a long-ago outing with the Algerian.

She looked wistful as I transformed it into a modern red-and-white poplin frock suitable for daytime.

Vendors are cocooned in stalls that display salmon, sole, hake, sunbeam, and mackerel, all swinging from metal hooks, staring at me as I walk by. I'm still used goods. The lies my mother-in-law spread have stuck to me like flypaper. But I don't care. Any man who allows bugs to cover so much of his catch is undeserving of me, whether I'm a barren troublemaker or not. The stray cats who lick at the newspaper shreds on the floor and salivate whenever a vendor takes out a knife to separate a fish from its hook do not bother me, but the flies, eating bits of fish skin and regurgitating it—sickening. A fishmonger, dressed in a chocolate-colored djellaba trimmed with camel hair, does his best to swat them with a rag. His movements are quick, his eyes lively—but his face and body are old.

"Hello, Beautiful Flower," he says.

His words rattle me. I've heard catcalls before, but coming from someone this old makes me want to recoil. Still, I've got my eye on a particular salmon. Large enough to feed nine Moabs—and definitely beyond budget. I'm embarrassed to ask the price.

He grins, almost toothless. I straighten my back and cough. The Moabs aren't getting mackerel. But I won't endure this.

"Well?" he says.

"That's my friend you're leering at," says a voice.

It can only be Amira. A tinkling laugh follows. She swings a burlap sack over her shoulder, and suddenly, she's beside me.

Our reunion, after so many months, is so sweet that even the vendor goes quiet.

"Ma chérie amie," she says, reaching for a hug. "How are you? Blessed, I hope."

We embrace. The customary one-on-each-cheek kiss. Amira's cheeks are soft and moist. She smells of lemon and kumquat oil.

"I'm good, my lovely," I say. "Thank Allah. And you?"

"Fine, fine," she says. "What brings you here? Not to see your friend Amira?"

Cupping my mouth with my hand, I whisper into her ear.

"Looking for a salmon that won't cost a fortune," I say. "But still—delighted to see you. How is Salim?"

"Wonderful as usual. I am blessed beyond measure."

Amira does seem content. Breezy and seemingly carefree, the girl of the tinkling laugh is dressed in a light caftan she didn't have to sew from scraps. It's midnight blue, adorned with purple medallions, and stitched with thread made from delicate gold leaf. When she touches her lips, her hands—stained with leftover henna from the many events she now attends as a married woman in a big city—move with casual grace. Her brown cheeks are full, and when she smiles wide, familiar dimples form at the corners of her mouth.

I hide my hands and reach into my pocket to rub my amulet. Amira proves Allah still answers some prayers—meaning there's still hope. I'd worried so much about her. The man she married was just a boy. Who knew how he would turn out? Her wedding had seemed more like a transaction than a celebration.

Afterward, it took her a while to locate me at the Moab household on Avenue 1 Botbut. She'd been apologetic.

"I thought you'd be easy to find," she'd said. "I should've introduced you. But I was afraid."

Later, she shared more.

"Imagine me—an eleven-year-old alone in a second-class train compartment. Can you picture it? Dressed the way I was? I was lucky. Salim's family was kind."

It doesn't matter now. The young woman in front of me is a marvel. Is it a testament to her marriage—or just to her? Since that day on the train, seeing her confirms it: people can get better with age. I think of Brahim. Somewhere in Spain, now, a fit husband for someone else.

When Amira raises her hand to her face, the sound of her gold bangles sliding to her elbow snaps me out of my thoughts. I'm embarrassed. Compared to hers, my hands are dry and chapped.

"All I do is work," I say. "But you should see the things I'm cooking."

"Lucky you. Since the Cohens' youngest left, they're a family of two," she replies. "So if you ever need help, me and the girls can lend a hand. Thank Allah they've kept me on. And forget about Israel—they'll never leave."

Amira must have been born under a lucky moon. Under different circumstances, she would've been doomed. Her parents never saw her as more than a doll they could dress and use for their gain. My parents allowed me to marry Brahim. Hers said it was ordained—God's will. In truth, they only saw opportunity in the match.

Maybe I'm not as fortunate, but things could've been worse. As a child, there were days I went hungry—and I may again. But look at the bounty in my basket. Full of delicacies.

Amira tucks a strand of hair behind her ear. "How's she treating you?" she asks.

"So-so. Madame's pregnant, which explains the moodiness. But she trusts me with her children. And she gave me this dress."

"Have you thought about me trying to play matchmaker again?" she asks. "A man like Salim—he appreciates everything I do. You've seen him. He's a good father. No guarantees I'll find someone just like him, but I can try."

For the first time, I consider it. Only because the alternative is the street.

"Okay," I say. "But—please. No more toothless ragmen. And no sixty-year-old widowers."

"Since you never seem to age, it's the youngsters I worry about."

"I don't know," I sigh. "What good is looking like a schoolgirl when my mother-in-law poisoned everything?"

Amira gives me a steady look.

"Yasmina," she says. "Remember when we went to the soothsayer, and she said you would travel far and wide? You can't do it alone."

"Have you stopped to think I've already fulfilled that prophecy?" I ask. "Rabat is a world away from where I came from."

"I guess you're right," Amira says, then grins. "Anyway, I assume you're here for a fish. Let's get you home before Miss Madame and her pregnancy hormones chop your head off. And don't worry about the price. Close to the ocean, fish is cheap. What they don't sell, they dry—or worse, throw out."

I laugh. I'd forgotten how dramatic Amira can be. And how easily she puts me in a good mood.

"She doesn't chop—she barks," I say.

Then, without warning, Amira's expression turns serious. It's unlike her.

"People may be leaving for Israel," she says. "But don't worry. The Moabs won't move. Not with eight children. We'll probably be the last maids left in Rabat."

"I hope you're right. But today, I need a fish," I say, pointing to a large salmon. "That one."

From there, it doesn't take long for Amira—daughter of grifters—to work her magic. She waves her hands, making a wild fuss. The fishmonger in the chocolate-colored djellaba doesn't stand a chance.

"That salmon my friend's pointing to? Smells like yesterday's catch," she declares. "Did you keep him overnight? If he gets any older, even the cats at your feet will turn up their whiskers."

The fishmonger protests, but it turns into a good-natured back-and-forth. The fish was caught this morning—they both know it.

When they settle on a price I still can't afford, Amira presses a five-franc coin into my hand.

"For the New Year," she says.

As the fishmonger wraps the salmon in yesterday's newspaper and ties it with twine, Amira says we must get together soon—for tea and biscuits.

She needs to return to her family now. But as she turns away, she pauses.

"I almost forgot to tell you," she says. "About that wicked ex-husband of yours—Brahim. From what I heard, finding a new match for you will be a lot easier."

She doesn't realize that mentioning his name is an affront. If it weren't Amira, I'd scream. He was never wicked. He was a seventeen-year-old boy.

But before I can form the words to say that kindly, I'm interrupted by a voice. For a split second, I wonder if it's him.

But Brahim would be in his mid-twenties now. This is a child's voice. I'm smoothing out my dress when its owner, none other than Henri Moab, comes into view. I'm relieved not to be face-to-face with my ex-husband. On the other hand, I want to explode.

"Why aren't you in school?" I say.

Henri, who bent down to tie his shoe, glances at Amira first, then at me.

"You forget it's a holiday," he says, still slightly breathless—like he ran all the way here.

The horror. Six children—alone with a fretful, past-her-prime, uncomfortably pregnant Madame Moab. And Henri, the only one besides me who can calm them, is miles away.

"The children?" I exclaim.

"Don't worry about that," he says. "This is an emergency!"

Amira, watching with wide eyes, shoots me a look. Her tale about Brahim can wait. She offers to help, but Henri waves her off.

"If you need me," she says softly, "you know where to find me."

She disappears down the alley. I press my knuckles to my lips and look at Henri.

"Nanette ran off," he says, with the urgency of a child—not a nearly thirteen-year-old young man. "It's my fault. I got tired of her hysterics. The way she manipulates Maman and Papa—always trying to be the center of everything. I want her to be real, but all she does is throw up smoke. Distract and deny. That's all she ever does."

I don't question what he says about Nanette. It's largely accurate, but being a child, she can be as easily changed as a ball of clay. It's the older Henri I worry about. His actions, whatever they were, were not in line with what's expected of a young man on the eve of his bar mitzvah. He needs to be realistic. He cannot let his anger take over.

"Listen, Henri. She's only seven and a half. She couldn't have traveled far."

As soon as the words leave my mouth, it occurs to me. If Nanette is hurt, it'll be my fault. I wouldn't blame the Moabs if they fired me on the spot.

"Anyone else know?" I ask.

Instead of telling me no, Henri goes into a speech. He's horrible, he disappointed the rabbi. He's worked for months to memorize hours and hours of the Torah. All for nothing.

"I told Nanette she came from the trash can," he says. "That Maman and Papa dug her out and brought her home. That's why she's as dark as an Arab."

I want to tell him not to feel so bad, but the way he says "Arab" makes my stomach lurch. Not one of the boys, including Henri, has the grace or discretion of their father.

I press my fingers to my forehead and shake my head.

"Did it need to come to this?" I ask.

"I didn't think she'd believe me," Henri says. "I forget how young she is. She doesn't act like it."

"Listen, as long as she's in the mellah, no one's going to lay a hand on her," I say. "Not Louis Moab's daughter. You know the story—when he was eighteen, he saved the ghetto."

Henri buries his face in his hands.

"Is that supposed to reassure me?" he says. "Papa has a gun, and he's not afraid to use it."

"A warning shot. To scare off a mob," I say. "He'd never hurt you. Not his first son. Anyway, I'd bet you all the fish here your sister's on her way to see your papa at the community oven."

Hope flashes in his eyes.

"If you're right, we'd better get there fast," he says. "She's only ever gone by car. She doesn't know the shortcuts."

I picture Nanette arriving at the ovens alone. Monsieur Moab—no access to a phone, no explanation—furious. In our world, problems stay in the family. The master baker, who's been at this longer than Monsieur Moab, who's burned his calloused hands countless times on hot brick, will scold him for not having control over his household. Nanette will be oblivious. She'll ask to stir in a handful of anise seeds. He'll say no. He'll set her on a stool. He'll cover ten perfectly shaped loaves with a cloth and leave them to rise. But by the time he slides them into the oven, he'll be ready to explode.

"Yel'an deen omak," he'll mutter in Arabic—curse words his children wouldn't understand.

The imagined scene makes me anxious. I pull my scarf tighter beneath my chin.

"Promise me," I say. "When we find Nanette—apologize."

"I will. On the graves of my ancestors."

It's hard to gauge his sincerity. His eyes plead, but his movements are quick. Before I can respond, Henri grabs my basket and bolts.

He runs so fast I can barely keep up.

The sun is almost at its peak, but for now, nothing matters except finding Nanette. Everything else—punishment, guilt, the future—can wait.

If I'm lucky, Madame Moab will be in her room pretending to be Blanchette Brunoy. But I also imagine five impatient boys pounding on the bedroom door. Eventually, even Madame Moab, unskilled in paying attention or managing her brood, won't be able to ignore the noise; it will get to be too much. For once, I'm grateful her mind drifts to fantasy. She's better at books and letter-writing, at embroidering and sewing, than she is with child-rearing. Whether she's changing a diaper or wiping a child's face, she's always preoccupied.

I puff out a breathless laugh.

"We'll find her, Henri," I say. "Nanette will accept your apology."

What I'm not sure of is whether the Moabs will accept mine. I shouldn't have left the children today. I shouldn't have gone so far. How did I not know the lycée was closed?

When we reach Avenue d'Egreach and step through the walled entrance of the mellah, I tighten my grip on Henri's hand. I imagine Nanette taking forever to get this far, weaving through doorways and shop stalls to avoid being seen, only to lose herself in some alley—or worse, the crumbling cemetery where two generations of her family are buried.

It might already be too late. The rabbi at the Slat Rabbi Chalom Zaou may have looked up from the Talmud and seen her. Or Monsieur Moreno, who runs the kosher butcher shop and has a phone, might've taken her home.

"The child's alone," he'll say into the receiver. "Where's the maid?"

Henri stops and lets go of my hand. "There she is!"

It takes a moment for me to register the tall-for-her-age figure standing outside the gate of the École L'Alliance Israélite Universelle. It's Nanette. Her hair is an untidy mess. And neither she nor her brothers attend this school.

Madame Moab, a former student, considers it a poor excuse for an educational institution. Her children are enrolled at the lycée.

But there Nanette is, poking her fingers through the chain-link fence. Two girls have stopped their hopscotch or jump rope games in favor of having a conversation with this mysterious girl.

Henri, who's more relieved than I've ever seen him, drops the basket, runs up to Nanette, grabbing her by the shoulders. Tears well up in my eyes.

"You belong to Maman and Papa," he declares. "Yasmina can say. She was there when you were born."

But Nanette isn't having it. She pulls away and runs into my arms.

I crouch to her level and hug her tight.

"Henri was mean to me, Yasmina," she says. "But now I know I belong. The girls here are dark. Like me. Like you. Even though you're an Arab and we're not."

"Berber," I correct gently. "And there's no shame in your skin. No matter what anyone says. Be proud of who you are. Now let's go home. You can help me make chickpea soup."

But Nanette isn't finished. She wants Henri to squirm.

"All these dark-skinned girls—none born in trash cans," she says. "You're lucky I stopped here. I was on my way to tell on you for lying. I still can."

Henri wrings his hands. "I won't do it again," he wails. "I swear. Please."

When Nanette only gives him a blank stare, he starts pulling at his hair like he's the most desperate person alive.

"Children," I say, "we can discuss this later. Right now, we need to get back to your maman. She must be worried sick. And Nanette—do you want your papa to get in trouble with his boss?"

That does it.

As we head home, I construct a fantasy in my head. Madame Moab's in her room, dusting her face with powder, attending to her hair. I imagine 11-year-old Laurent as a competent fill-in for his missing brother. I imagine him strapping Jean safely in his highchair, leaving the other children to play. I imagine them stopping their cowboy games, calling a truce.

CHAPTER 12

The Threads Unravel

Yasmina

Once I've prepared the salmon, I top it with preserved lemons and capers and place it in the icebox. The only thing I'm disappointed about is the chermoula—it hasn't had enough time to marinate. Otherwise, I'm satisfied. Half an hour later, the cold salad is nearly done, and the chickpea soup is simmering nicely. All it needs is a pinch of salt and a little more time.

Nanette stands beside me, looking every bit the mother's helper with her hair pinned back in a ponytail and a pinafore over her dress. I watch as she uses a pin to roll out dates and dried apricots to finish off the couscous. She's abnormally tall—seven years old and already almost at my eye level.

I wipe my brow with a towel and admire my work. As I hum a song Mma used to sing, I realize this is the first time I've felt at ease all day. I took a risk. Things nearly fell apart. And yet, Monsieur and Madame Moab are none the wiser.

Now, there's not much left to do but make the sauce. I use the fish bones, cream, garlic, and a splash of the Grand Marnier that Madame Moab's sister sent from Paris. Madame says liquor is fine—any alcohol will evaporate in the cooking. Just don't tell Monsieur. He wouldn't understand.

I've made a stew. The aroma from the tagine is so tantalizing that, one by one, the boys begin drifting in, asking for a bite.

The citrus aroma is so heavenly that when Madame Moab enters the kitchen, I half-expect her to swoon.

That's not what happens.

"You might want to come with me, Yasmina," she says, pointing to the door.

I don't know why, but I feel trapped. I can't catch my breath.

"Don't you like the—?" I begin, confused.

"Not now." She cuts me off. "We have a guest. He has a question for you."

At first, I interpret Monsieur Peres's presence in the living room as a welcome surprise. The kitchen is hot; I could use a break.

But it's Monsieur Peres. The neighborhood eavesdropper. He's the only one on the block with a phone—and he uses it. We know who's had an abortion and who hasn't. We know whose brand-new husband already has a mistress.

"Yasmina needs to hear it from the beginning," Madame says.

Her tone surprises me. She's moody around me, but always submissive around men.

"My friend Monsieur Moreno has a daughter, Berthe," Peres begins. "She's Nanette's age and attends L'Alliance. She's perfectly happy there, by the way."

He clears his throat.

"Today, she told a story about a strange girl throwing rocks from the other side of the fence. With all the unrest, my friend was concerned. Berthe never should've approached her—but she did. The girl told a tearful story about how her mother made her go to a French school where everyone was horrible. Then the bell rang. My friend knew immediately—it was Nanette."

I can't remember feeling this terrible, except maybe when Brahim left. It's like I have a rock on my chest. I resist the urge to look at the ground. I need to face Madame Moab, to take responsibility. She doesn't let me off easily. Her tone, the way she surveys me, tells me this all-in-one holiday (Hanukkah and New Year's Eve) and all the plans I had to go with it are over.

At dinner, Madame Moab has so much steam coming out of her ears, even the boys are silent. Making matters worse, the fish, while tastier than anything I could have bought in the mellah—was compromised. I shouldn't have experimented with the Grand Marnier. When I returned to the kitchen, I was so rushed and rattled that I forgot to strain all the bones from the sauce. The soup, hastily finished, never had time to develop flavor.

Despite Madame's anger, nothing more happens. Not right away. It is the most important night of Hanukkah, after all. After dinner, Monsieur and Henri light the candles and say the prayers. Seven subdued children open gifts and play dreidel.

Meanwhile, I'm filled with dread.

When it's time to bathe the children, it's Madame Moab—heavily pregnant—who does it.

It's the usually gentle Monsieur who delivers the blow.

"Please, don't fire me," I plead. "I was so preoccupied with the new year. This horror of a decade is one year closer to ending, and I just wanted to make it special."

If I was hoping for empathy, I don't get it. My words land on angry ears.

"Incroyable," he says. "How did you not know there wasn't school today? You know how dangerous it is. She could have been hurt."

"I thought you'd be taking her. New Year's isn't until tomorrow—"

"Not when it falls on a Saturday," he bellows. "And it was on the calendar. You can read."

"Monsieur Moab, I'm tired. All I do is work. You have seven children! How can you expect—?"

His eyebrows draw together. For a moment, his face softens. Surely he sees that they should've told me.

But then he speaks again. And I realize I'm out of a job.

"It pains me to say this, but we have to let you go. I know it will be difficult, especially with so many moving to Israel. But don't you have family in Fes?" He pauses. "I'll take you to the train tomorrow. My wife doesn't want me to pay for the ticket—but she needs to remember, I'm the one in charge."

Monsieur Moab was so angry, I never thought I'd see him again. So ten days later, when he knocks on the door of my brother's house at 4 Rue

Ahmed Hiba in Fes, I'm shocked—not just by his presence, but by how much he's changed.

Diminished, he's a far cry from the imposing, clean-shaven giant I remember. His brow is drenched with sweat. Thick black stubble covers his cheeks and chin, sharp as porcupine quills. He looks like he hasn't bathed or eaten since the new year. Without suspenders, his pants would fall to his knees. Even his overcoat hangs off him like a tent.

But I'm not about to be sympathetic.

"Forget something?" I ask.

I can't be faulted for the thoughts swirling in my head: *Maybe stop getting your wife pregnant. Maybe stop relying on a 22-year-old to raise your almost eight children.*

I could say at least some of these things. I have nothing left to lose. But it's not in my nature. Still, I can't deny it feels good when he starts to beg.

"You must come back," he says, removing his hat to reveal a mop of greasy hair. "No one else will help. The boys are wild. And Nanette—you don't want to know."

"Really?" I say. "With a thousand maids out of work?"

"Why didn't you tell the truth, Yasmina? You could've saved everyone a lot of grief. If I had known you were the hero …"

"What do you mean?" I ask.

"Henri admitted he was at fault. You took the blame to save him from the belt. Nanette confirmed it. Why, Yasmina? Why didn't you just say so?"

I can't help but be moved. The children didn't have to protect me— but they did.

"If it makes you feel better," he adds, "I'm sorry. And now we have a real emergency. Nanette says she won't eat until you come back."

"You know how she is. She's probably sneaking food under her pillow."

"You don't understand. She isn't well. You see how much weight I've lost? Double that for her. We're thinking about taking her to the hospital."

A tear slips down my cheek. "Is she taking any liquids?"

"Yes. But more than that … what I didn't mention—she's hysterical. She's been crying for seven days. Listen, I know you're worried we might move to Paris. If you're the only one who can save Nanette, we'll take you with us. You'll always have a home with us."

"To keep a maid around, she threatens starvation?"

My love for Nanette is stronger than my need for a job. I want to tell him not to give in to her—this will only make her more spoiled. I'm glad, but a part of me is aware: there will be complications. Harder times lie ahead.

"She says only you can save her."

"So now I'm the chosen one?" I say.

He doesn't respond. He doesn't have to. We both know this is Nanette and her games. I want to laugh, but there's nothing funny about what she's done.

I never thought I'd end up with the upper hand—certainly not like this, not at this cost.

All I know is, if I return, I vow one thing: I'll never put myself in a desperate position again. No more groveling.

Mma is in the kitchen. If she knew what we were saying, how would she react? A child going hungry when food is plentiful would be too ludicrous to contemplate.

But I don't need her opinion. These past few days, while my brother labored at the quarry, she consoled me with affirmations and hurled insults at the Moabs. But her words were hollow.

Where was she when I needed real support?

I wanted her to draw the line—to say no to the marriage. But that was foolish. She sent me on my way with nothing but an amulet for protection. Where was she two years later when I was banished from the Mouloudji family? When I was fifteen—and alone?

If that had been my daughter, I would have gone looking for her.

CHAPTER 13

A Quiet Mourning

Yasmina

It's eerily quiet on the morning of January 9, 1949. For every degree the mercury rises, cats scatter, dogs retreat to the shadows, and birds stop singing mid-song. I've been back from Fes for two days. At first, everything was fine—Nanette scrunching her fingers into my face, pressing her head against mine with all her might, covering me with kisses. Now, there's a stillness in the air I cannot explain, a rotten-egg smell reminiscent of when I, along with the rest of my family, was in the caves of Tacheddirt. I'm thinking this is earthquake weather when, cutting through the silence, is the ear-piercing, heart-wrenching sound of a woman in pain. The hair on my hands stands up straight. My belly tightens.

Madame Moab has delivered many babies at home, but she's always been stoic. At first, I try to brush it off. A rough delivery, perhaps? But I know better. The baby is in trouble.

When I descend the stairs, I realize the situation is worse than I imagined. I see Monsieur Moab standing over a tiny figure wrapped in a linen blanket. I know.

I've never seen a corpse before, and when he removes the covering, I have to grip the back of a chair to keep from collapsing. There she is—a tiny, perfectly formed angel, with waxy hair and bluish, translucent skin. Monsieur Moab leans down to kiss the child's cupid's bow lips.

"There was nothing we could do," he says.

That I'm able to function in the moments and hours afterward is a miracle. The mind is strange. Like after my divorce, it takes a day for the fog to descend and months to clear.

"Can I help?" I ask.

Monsieur Moab fills a kettle with water and sets it to boil, choking back tears.

"Elise's sister—Helena—is coming," he says. "Could you prepare her some tea? I'll drop Nanette and the boys off at school. We'll take the balcony, of course—to avoid all this. Rolls and fruit are in the car."

Before giving me the rest of the day off, he asks if I can pick up Nanette after school. She's fragile, he says. She needs to be kept busy until six. By then, his wife will be more composed.

"What about the others?" I ask.

"Henri knows," he replies, clearing his throat. He hesitates before continuing. "After school, my boss will put the older boys to work. Helena will give Aristide and Jean a sedative so they can nap. It's all arranged. Oh— and one more thing. Let's not wake the neighbors. Not all of them will think this is a tragedy."

My eyebrows lift in admiration. This isn't the first time Monsieur Moab has managed to give his wife a moment of peace while keeping seven children occupied. I haven't forgotten Fes, but still.

I don't have to, but after he leaves—after Helena puts the boys down and joins Madame Moab in her room—I get to work. I scrub every sink in the house until it shines. I drag every rug outside and beat it with a broom. I scour the bathtub until my hands hurt. I cut out a dozen biscuits and set them on a baking sheet.

By this time, I need to make my way to the Lycée de Jeunes Filles. I can barely put one foot in front of the other. I can't even remember leaving the mellah. I can't get the image of the poor child out of my mind.

By the time I reach the French quarter, I'm more aware. I still can't feel my fingers, my wrists. I trudge past the palace of the Résidence Générale of the Protectorate, past the estates of bankers, bureaucrats, and diplomats, barely lifting my heels.

What pulls me out of my fog is the sound of a helicopter, its blades chopping through the air as it lowers itself on a nearby roof. Somehow being in surroundings where large expanses of lawn lead to grand, gleaming white structures with wraparound porches held up by glowing colonial-style columns heightens my senses and increases my resolve. Nanette's classmates, the ones who call her a giraffe, the ones who tell her she's too skinny and dark, reside in these homes.

None of this removes the feeling I have in the hollow of my stomach. That blessed baby dying. It was all my fault. I hadn't taken my premonition seriously. Had I warned her she could've gotten care?

I once wished the family goat would wander off because I hated milking her. The next day, she was dead—killed by a fox. So don't tell me I don't have power.

I didn't want Madame Moab to have another child. I knew I'd be the one doing the work. But from now on, I vow never to take life for granted. I'll devote the rest of my days to caring for the children she still has.

God gives so many blessings—the shade of a cypress tree, the noisy caw of a slender-billed gull, countless other gifts—but it is He who has control. And as for protection, I'm not even sure God grants us that anymore.

The next thought, I try to push away: *What if everything is random? What if every amulet, every mezuzah, is no more sacred than the metal it's made from?*

I was collateral damage. Amira tried to tell me that in the square. The rumor is the entire Mouloudji family has been arrested. Monsieur Mouloudji is dead. Brahim and his brother are languishing in a Spanish prison. Crimes against the state, they said.

A clock chimes in the city square. I turn and there it is—the Lycée de Jeunes Filles. In fifteen minutes, the gates will spill open with children. For now, I take the time to collect myself.

Mma used to make a salve of eucalyptus to keep mosquitoes away. Now, as I sit under one of the trees, I'm reminded of the unbroken cycle of love and loss passed through generations. Babies are born. Babies die. And so it goes.

In this moment, every clover, every blade of grass, feels infused with meaning. It's as if the dead child is speaking to me.

I close my eyes. I inhale the heady scent of the trees. I let myself sink into the glory of God's creation. I believed back then—and I guess I still do, because of my pagan ancestors—that everything leads back to nature. Even a child who never draws a breath belongs to the earth. It is for her life, and the life of all, that we celebrate.

I imagine placing my sorrow in a box and closing the lid. I'll pay my respects to the stillborn girl when the time is right. But now, I must brace Nanette for what's to come.

When the chime of the clock tower pulls me back to the present, I feel renewed. I touch my earrings—aren't they here to celebrate the gift of hearing? And the vivid hues of pink, red, and green in my tunic—don't they honor our other senses?

Still, the sadness doesn't leave me. With ten minutes left, a tremor of sorrow washes over me. The perfect light-skinned daughter Madame Moab longed for—gone. And the babies I'll never have.

I sit with this feeling for a while until I look up. The giant eucalyptus tree above me—its branches twining into a green canopy—feels like an embrace. I press my feet into the earth. The damp grass wraps around my sandals and tickles the edges of my toes.

I exhale and think of the child.

She will be restored.

Isn't that what Monsieur Moab meant when he said that, under Jewish law, he isn't permitted to grieve a stillbirth? The rabbi will come—once he's finished his other duties.

"Until we have his counsel," he'd said, "a black curtain will hang over us."

CHAPTER 14

Bitter Thorns

Yasmina

The gate is shaded by a low-hanging wisteria tree. Its branches, fern-like and delicate, sway in the breeze, cooling my skin. The gate itself is a work of art, with decorative curlicues of writing and rose patterns in between. But I know why it's been put there, to keep people like Baba and my brother out. They barely tolerate Jews, but it is people like us they want to keep in the shadows.

A swarm of bees land on a nearby branch. I'm so preoccupied by their buzzing I almost don't see her. Not Nanette, but a squat, square-faced girl with dishwater blond hair, dressed in the blue-and-white uniform of the Institut Jeanne d'Arc.

She lunges at Nanette like an uncoiled spring, slamming her against the wall. Nanette's lips quiver, then tighten. I've never seen her so fierce.

From Nanette's past stories, I know who this is: Colette Groban. Standing behind her is Camille LaCount—ringleader, mean girl, and self-styled ballerina. According to Nanette, she lets the slow-witted Colette do the dirty work while she stays pristine. Once Nanette is pinned, Camille steps forward and shoves Colette aside.

"Let me at her," she says.

I feel my heart drum against my chest. Camille may not be physically imposing, but she's a savage, nonetheless. She delivers verbal one-two punches with such rapid-fire speed, you'd think she was Joe Lewis, the number one prizefighter in the world.

"Jew!" Camille says, brushing a finger across Nanette's chin like she was a camel or a horse and not a human. "My papa told me your maman got special approval for you to come here, and I don't have to be nice."

The blood drains from my face. If I could get away with it, I'd rip off her fancy beret, grab her by that Peter Pan collar, and lift her until her shoes dangled like worms. I don't want Nanette to be expelled—but this is different. Then, as if summoned by the gods, a slender-billed gull lands just a few feet away on the grass.

Nanette acts. She grabs Camille by the cape and hurls her to the ground. Pride and fear twist inside me. I can barely process what's happening before the gathered girls start shrieking like a flock of crows. Nanette's face burns red. I know that look—rage, humiliation, and nothing left to lose.

Already taller than the others, she makes herself even larger. When she turns to face the circle, it is in one fluid twirl.

"Wanna know why I don't believe in Papa Noel?" she bellows. "You wouldn't have come to school bragging about stupid Madame Alexander dolls, Hobby Horses, tea sets, and miniature carriage houses. What you should've gotten was a lump of coal. If Papa Noel did exist, he'd be more like your Jesus."

Camille's head snaps back, but not for long. This is the kind of girl who is seldom without composure.

"A Jew talking about Jesus," she laughs. "The nerve."

Nanette doesn't flinch. She jabs a finger in Camille's face. "Jesus was a Jew," she says.

Bravo, Nanette. Don't let them see you're hurt. If Camille smells weakness, she'll move on to someone easier. But who am I kidding? Nanette's the only Jewish girl here. She's a walking target. The Vichy regime ended just six years ago—not sixty. And most of their fathers likely played a part in it. They let the Nazis paint swastikas and scrawl their filth on the walls of the mellah—first with spray paint, later in blood. I might've been new to the city and only 15, but I remember how terrified we all were, especially the Moabs. Yet my mistress sends her daughter to a school staffed by those who would've had no problem annihilating her.

Grabbing my elbows in my palms, I have an awful thought: *Have the years of abuse have made Nanette more susceptible?* When she thinks she can get away with it, like with Henri, she can be very cruel. What if instead of gaining more control over herself, she's going backward?

I clutch my amulet and whisper a small prayer. I squeeze my eyes shut. When I open them, Camille's delivered a left hook to Nanette's face. Nanette collapses, sobbing.

Part of me is relieved. Maybe this will humble her, bring her back to herself—back to how Allah wants her to be. But that thought makes me feel sick. Meekness is what got me into my own mess. My fists clench. The instinct to protect takes over.

Whatever cruelty these girls throw, I can take it.

Maybe it's for the best that I stay back. I don't know what would've happened if the headmaster and principal teacher—a sharp-faced woman in her 30s, hadn't stumbled onto the scene. Just as I'm thanking the lord, what the teacher does next sends my blood to boil. I've seen the look before.

"What's going on here?" the headmaster says with a smirk.

She's not one bit angry at the girls. That her fury is directed at Nanette, emboldens Camille. Even at seven, she already has a punish-me-and-my-papa-will-have-your-job attitude.

"None of us could take it anymore," she says, voice dripping with faux innocence. "Somebody had to hit her."

The headmaster should dismiss the excuse outright. But instead, she nods, gives Camille a warm look, and then turns to Nanette. Nanette stands motionless—only her quivering lip betrays her pain.

"This is your last warning," the woman snaps. "Now. Get up. Quickly."

Nanette rises slowly, eyes fixed on the ground.

My stomach knots.

Don't bury it, child. Let your red-hot tears fall.

"Giant giraffe-girl. No wonder you're slow," the headmaster barks.

A girl who'd been silent until now begins to chant.

"Slug, slug, slug!"

Soon, the others join in.

I gasp and look to the sky.

What kind of school treats a child this way?

Whatever defiance Nanette once had is gone from her face.

I feel my jaw tighten. If I'm this angry, what about Nanette? What if one day she is the one who snaps? I imagine her taking a lit match to the place. Making stray animals bear the brunt of her pain is no less a sin. Already, her tantrums torture her brothers and distress her parents.

"We must rise above this sort of thing," the headmaster says with an icy chuckle. "We don't want to start thinking like her."

And then, with a flip of a switch, her face softens. When her eyes find Camille, her eyes light up with such affection, one would never know.

"Oh, my dear," she says. "Your beret. Are you all right?"

Camile smooths her skirt and reaches for her hat.

"I'm fine. Except my fist hurts. And I'll need to wash my hands—after touching a Jew."

"Camille," the headmaster says with a scolding laugh. "That's too far. If we must have a Jewish girl here, at least let her be a dunce. You know how loud and obnoxious they are."

I clasp my hands around my elbows. Anger rises from my chest, seeping into my arms and fists.

How can Madame Moab support this? Does she really think aligning herself with the French will earn her respectability? She dreams of university education at the Sorbonne for her children, but at what cost? Nanette will drop out before that happens.

If only she saw her daughter as I do. Defeated.

I wait until the iron clangs open to fully leave my hiding place. When I wave in Nanette's direction, her reaction is immediate. As soon as she sees me, she barrels into my waiting arms. It's as if I was supposed to be there. She doesn't even raise the question: *Why not Papa?*

"That pig hit me," she says. "And the head teacher, *my* teacher—You'd have to hear it yourself to believe it."

Grabbing her by the shoulders, I hold her close.

"I did, mignon. I heard."

"You understand. You see."

Her voice trembles. When she looks up, tears are spilling down her cheeks. The skin under one eye is already bruising, turning a deep purplish-blue.

"She got me. But I got her too," she says.

"An onion might help with the swelling. Or if we're lucky, we'll catch the ice cart."

"I gave her a good punch. Shame I didn't land it better."

"I'm glad you didn't. Can you imagine the punishment?"

"They're awful," she says, voice loud and hoarse. "Every last one of them. My eye could swell shut and they wouldn't care!"

I rub my amulet between my fingers.

"They have some devil in them," I say. "Especially Camille. Let's say a prayer—not to let them poison your heart. Your mother doesn't believe in the evil eye, and I only halfway do, but still."

"You think I haven't tried?" she says, sobbing. "If your stupid Hamsa worked, none of this would've happened!"

She collapses against me, breathing in hot, heavy bursts.

If she knew what news was waiting for her, she wouldn't survive it. She's already shrinking, already brittle. I won't let her fall further.

"I have to tell Maman," she says with sudden resolve. "I'm not going back. If she doesn't agree, I'm dropping out."

"Oh, chérie," I sigh. What I don't say is that her mother won't hear her. She'll shut her ears, shut her eyes. She won't recognize Nanette's pain—not even a blackened eye will register.

Don't be so sensitive, Madame Moab will say. *That's why they tease you.*

But I know better. When Nanette finally rebels, it will be in a way no one sees coming. She's already turned her body into a battlefield. What comes next could be worse. But this is 1949. I'm here with this child, doing my best.

"It's useless," Nanette says before launching into a perfect impersonation of her maman.

"Think you have it bad? Try 7,000 years of persecution! I won't allow a child of mine to be coddled by some backwards school!"

Nanette doesn't mention the rest of what her mother will say. The Dahan and Moab families are of superior stock and always have been. It's not unusual to have first cousins marry, but their reasoning! Every one of Madame Moab's children, including Nanette, is destined for a Parisian university.

It strikes me; being ordinary is a fine thing. I want to tell Nanette, "Yes we are unique, but so are all God's creatures. There's honor in humility." But how can my voice be heard over the maman? All I can give Nanette is care.

"I'll talk to your maman," I say, reaching for her hand. "Let's take care of your eye first."

She nods, but there's a sharpness in it—authority. A reminder. I'm Yasmina, the maid. I shouldn't forget it.

"They can't make me go back," she says. "I'll stop eating."

My stomach drops.

"That's not the way," I say gently. "You need strength to reason with your mother."

But my words feel empty. We pass a bank and a row of palm trees. After a long silence, Nanette speaks again.

"If Maman's baby is a girl, maybe she'll fall in love with her. Then she'll stop pushing me to get into the Sore-Bun."

My chest tightens.

"Your maman has a lot on her mind," I say.

"You think they'd get me a tutor? It can't be that expensive. You had one."

Tears sting my eyes. I have to shut them tight to keep them from falling.

"You okay?" Nanette asks.

I don't answer. I take her hand. We need to walk with purpose. Although the old Vichy is dead, the French bureaucrats who either stood by or put it into place still live here. I am not one of those radical nationalists who are calling for independence. Still, these mansions with vast expanses of lawns make me a little sick inside. There are turbaned men, immaculate white figures, whose only job is to walk around with a hose or move sprinklers from place to place. Other men in grass-stained djellabas cut and trim the rows of palm trees to exact specifications.

We pass a row of plumeria, fragrant pinwheels of red and pink. When I remarry, these will be in my bouquet.

"Have you ever seen such beauty?" I say.

"They're all from France," Nanette replies. "Hibiscus, camellias, roses. Papa says the French forget this is a desert. He hates how green everything is—says it's wasteful. But secretly? I like it."

I think of the time the king's father diverted water from our village to a silver mine. But I don't tell her that story. Not today.

A trio of nannies walks by—either pale-skinned Berbers or foreign girls of uncertain origin. Their burqas are stricter than the one I wore when I first met Madame Moab. Even their gloved hands barely grip the handles of the prams they push.

Nanette offers them a shy smile. They don't return it.

A parade of camels and horses marches down the road. A car speeds past. Otherwise, the street is hushed. But as we turn onto Rue Moulay Ali Chérif and then Rue Tinghir, the noise returns. Closer to the mellah, a horse-drawn ice cart pulls into view.

I flag it down.

"A half-franc for some ice?" I say, placing a coin into the iceman's palm.

His eyes burn into me. He thinks I'm the reason for Nanette's blackened eye—though that doesn't stop him from snatching the coin from my hand.

He wraps a piece of ice in a rag and hands it to Nanette.

"Allah be with you," he says to her.

"This will burn," I whisper after we find a bench and sit. "But you'll see—it helps."

Both of her eyes are deep purple now. There's an abrasion at her hairline I hadn't noticed before.

I had planned to give Nanette a lovely afternoon. A small break from it all. But now this day will be burned into her memory for all the wrong reasons.

"How about a café au lait?" I suggest. "And maybe a rose for your hair. I don't think I ever told you how perfect your ringlets are. You don't even have to try."

"I do have the most beautiful hair ever."

It shocks me how hungrily she receives this praise. I would tell her what my mma said about how evil it is to be vain. But then again, let her be.

We locate a table outside a bazaar. Before the waiter arrives, I remove the ice from Nanette's eye and pat it dry. Her face is tense, unsure. I don't know how this makes me feel. How can a child be so tender and dear one moment and so conceited the next?

When Nanette criticizes my own hair, about how frizzy it is when I don't have it in a braid, I think about heading home, but a promise is a promise.

"My aunties think I'm ugly," Nanette says. "Maman too. She wants me to be white."

"I'm sorry, chérie," I say.

"One time, I told Maman that Papa Noel brought Camille a gift," she says. "I knew he wasn't real. Anyway, Maman said if I were better-behaved, he would've brought me a present too. Like I don't already know I'm a Jew!"

I let out a soft sigh. I wish Elisa Moab would bite her tongue. These are the words a daughter will remember.

"Gifts aren't always for holidays," I say. "I saw your maman wrapping a present. I think it was for you."

"A Madame Alexander Doll?" Nanette asks.

"Too small," I say, ignoring the disappointment on her face.

"It would make me feel better."

"It's what's in your heart that brings you joy. No matter how hard things are or what tragedy may befall you, love will help you get through. Just because Camille has turned herself to stone doesn't mean you have to. If you do, you could have a thousand Madame Alexander dolls and it'll never be enough."

"You don't understand what it is to be desperate," she says. "It's not the doll—Maman says I'm getting a sister to hold. I want to show those girls. Every one of them!"

"That'll happen with your accomplishments," I say, trying my best to stay even keel. The yearning in her voice scares me. "You'll have a first-class education. Better than the one I received from Madame Rubin because you'll have an actual diploma."

"I have an idea," she says brightly. "Maman can teach me to have class—to walk like a ballerina. You can tutor me. Papa says you're smart. For a Shilha."

Her face lights up, but inside, I crumble. That word. Madame Moab uses it like a curse. But when did her husband say it? Where was I?

The clock on the red-brick façade of the Banque d'État du Maroc reads 4:10. I'm supposed to be lifting Nanette's spirits. Her father gave me enough money for the cinema and a pack of Junior Mints. But the waiter is taking so long, the film will end late.

"How about we skip the café au lait," I say, "and get you a Coca-Cola instead? Your papa is bringing sandwiches for dinner. Your aunt is with the little ones. He even gave us francs to spend. You're his precious girl."

"With ice!" Nanette says. "And a chocolate éclair. And two roses— one for you and one for me!"

"Pâtisserie Satin it is. Let's linger a little. It's too nice to stay indoors."

"Not too long," she says. "I want a bath and a book. And when you read me a story, can you try with more expression? I know Madame Rubin taught you. You read fast, but the way you say some of the words …"

I pat her shoulder, masking my irritation. She doesn't know that I've built a small library of my own—books rescued from the trash heaps of families who've already left for Israel. The story we'll read tonight wasn't chosen for her, but for the child I hope to have someday.

I straighten the flaps of her collar and tap her gently under the chin.

"You know how you hate when Camille teases you?" I say. "That's how I feel when you call me Shilha like it's a curse. It cuts me."

"But my parents say—"

I stop her there. I want to tell her the rumor about her grandfather—a full-blooded Berber who converted. But I hold it back.

"I keep calling you chérie, mignon," I say, "but you're still unkind. I excuse it because you're not yet eight, and because the French girls are mean to you, I tolerate this. My only hope is when you are old enough, you can make up your own mind. No human being is better than any other."

Nanette covers her mouth.

"I guess," she says.

She guesses? I need to think about how much I'm willing to do for this child. When the Peres family moved to Israel, they left a book behind. *The Little Prince*, the story of a lonely boy struggling to find a meaning in life, but there are lessons he needs to learn first. It's intended for older children like Henri and Laurent, but with Nanette's sassy attitude, the way she thinks she can bend the world to her will, she needs it more than they do. I'm not going to let her get away with it—not if I can help it.

But I won't sacrifice myself to fix her either.

I press my amulet against my chest. It's a reminder: I have a life of my own to live.

CHAPTER 15

Potatoes and Promises

Southfield Michigan Gazette, 30 October 1957

Hugh Jones, son of Conan and Elisabeth, 21 Deer Road, is headed to Nouasseur Air Base located outside Casablanca, Morocco. Since 1953, many of our young men have been stationed there. Although WWII is long over, the Cold War is heating up, which means this North African outpost is becoming a critical staging area against Soviet operations.

Mrs. Jones has asked for a special benediction to be delivered at the end of St. Lucy's 9 o'clock Sunday service. However, we think Hugh's going to do fine. He's smart and hardworking (though he did spend some extra time at boot camp working off a few "minor infractions"), and as long as he doesn't get mixed up in any more hijinks, he'll be fine. Judging from what our Nouasseur returnees have to say, there'll be little opportunity for trouble, though we know Hugh has always been full of … energy.

Hugh – December 1957 – Nouasseur Air Base

1. It's the day after Christmas, and me and two colored fellas—Reginald and Cedric—are slumped over a dozen 25-gallon buckets, working through a truckload of potatoes that came in a few hours ago. The work's as dull and soul-killing as it looks. To make it worse, the Air Force has candy-coated the whole operation by telling us our job is

essential to the 1,500 men in our unit. More important than repairing B-47s. We're not buying it.

"The Air Force can spin it all they want," Reginald says. He's twenty-eight, older, mouthier, and naturally more opinionated. "Only thing worse than potatoes is latrines."

I nod. Potato duty stinks—literally and otherwise. Still, I try to stay hopeful to keep my temper from boiling over. I have a bad habit of jumping in fists first. I've only been in Casablanca a few months, and the military sure hasn't turned out to be the noble adventure I imagined. Cedric and I just got "promoted" from—of course—latrine duty. And honestly, working the mess hall takes more attention than you'd expect. But my heart's still set on bombers. Sooner or later, some officer will see I've got potential. Won't happen if I slice my hand open with a potato peeler or a pocket knife.

Still, I like it here. If I were home in Michigan, I'd be freezing my ass off. It's unusually hot for December in Morocco, but I don't mind. When the sun filters through the slats of the warehouse roof, it warms my face and my spirit.

As for the potatoes—God help me—I'm sick of them. Just when we get a dent made, a new mountain rolls in. Our supervisor, a pimply twenty-one-year-old who can't grow enough stubble to shave, rarely shows up, which means things run … creatively.

Reginald's job, which he hates, is to cut out the eyes and rotten bits before handing them off to one of us to peel. But he can't really do it—he's allergic to pollen or something, and even touching the skin puts welts on his hands. He's always got a complaint, some injustice to rail against, but it's clear under all that, he's a good-time guy with a sharp wit. It's rubbing off on Cedric, who's usually quieter. He tosses a peeled potato into the water bucket and turns to me.

"You're the most ignorant, dumb-as-fuck 18-year-old I've ever met," he says.

He's joking, of course, but it doesn't exactly land.

"You don't know nothin' about Negroes and their trials," he adds, grinning like he's trying to get me all lathered up.

Slavery ended 100 years ago, I wanna say, but before I can, Cedric goes into a rant.

"Damn it all to hell! If the Louisville recruiter didn't promise I'd be behind the wheel of a bomber ..." he says. "He took it back the minute I signed the papers. If I knew I'd be in the kitchen, I never would've given them my John Hancock. All because I'm colored."

Before I can state how ridiculous that is, Reginald chimes in with an Amen.

"I got a 98 percent on the aptitude test," he says. "Said I could pick my job. Not only have I been lied to, I have the hands to prove it."

That I never met a colored fella until Cedric two months ago should've been my first clue I shoulda kept my trap shut.

"Must've been some other reason," I mumble.

Reginald snorts. "Okay, Mr. White-as-a-Piece-of-Paper. What landed you here? Something must've gone foul. Screw an officer's daughter?"

I can be crude too, but I've got a girl back home. And besides, they're wrong. But trying to change two minds at once? Not worth it. Better to play along.

"Last time I went to school was eighth grade," I say. "Recruiter told me it didn't matter—I got an eighty-five on the test. But once I failed the red-green color test, the Air Force stamped *REJECT* across my face."

Reginald laughs. "White boy, poor, no education, color-blind? Surprised they let your ass in."

"I'm not allowed within a hundred feet of a B-47," I say. "I can't even operate a radio tower or do electrical. I'll mix up the wires. At least you two can advance on merit."

"Not in Whitey's world," Reginald says. "Honky, if you think me and Cedric can get anywhere on merit, I've got a bridge for sale."

"Forget it," Cedric says, like we've waded into dangerous waters. "What'd they tell you guys when they put you on potatoes? Some bullshit about turning us into first-class chefs."

"Something like that," I say, still stewing from the 'Whitey's world' jab. "But they're not training anybody. The fanciest thing I've seen made is Shit on a Shingle—mushroom soup and dried beef on toast."

"Screw the US Air Force and the horse they rode in on," Reginald mutters. "Soviet threat, my ass. Aren't you tired of being wrist-deep in potato water? You guys been here two weeks. Me, six months. When the boss man leaves, let's blow this place."

Cedric perks up. "There's a party off-base. Real hush-hush. Booze, women. Out in the middle of the Sahara, but I know a guy who can get us a Jeep. Meet you in front of your barracks at 2 o'clock sharp."

It's surprising how quick the words, "I'm in. Gimme enough time to clean up," come out of my mouth. Or maybe not. Never been to a party I wasn't the guest of honor at. Besides, after two weeks of being up to my ears in my least favorite vegetable, I feel like Mr. Potato Head.

What never crosses my mind are the contingencies, getting lost in the Sahara, running out of gas, and being declared AWOL. My motto is: You only get one go-round in this world. Might as well enjoy it.

CHAPTER 16

Hot Wheels

Hugh

From my barracks, I hear two sharp blasts of a horn, followed by Reginald's voice cutting through the quiet. "Hijinks in the desert!" he calls out, in the loud, brassy voice of a guy who maybe took trumpet lessons once and quit before getting halfway decent.

He's not exactly subtle. Isn't this supposed to be hush-hush? I pull back the blinds and there it is—a brand-new Jeep M38-A1. Cedric's behind the wheel. Reginald's stuffed in the back, leaving the catbird seat open for me and taking brazen to a new level.

"Carpe diem," PRONUNCIATION Reginald says when I climb in. He's been drinking; they both have. I can smell it on their breaths.

"Did you think to at least hide yourselves?" I ask.

"Everything's copacetic. My contact's pretty high up," Cedric says. "He signed the Jeep out to me, but I still have to return it by 8. Otherwise, our asses'll be in a sling."

"A certain lieutenant colonel is all moony-eyed over Cedric," Reginald says, laughing. "Unrequited love, but that doesn't stop him from going to the ends of the earth trying. Anyway, the bean counters take inventory at 8. Then the Jeep turns into a pumpkin and we and Cinderfella here end up in the clink."

It doesn't add up, but what does? I've been in tighter spots. I can get out of trouble easily enough. Flash a smile. Plead ignorance. Worst case, I'm looking at a couple days' punishment. And with the New Year's Eve party at the Triangle Fleet Club only four days away, it's a risk I'm willing to take.

"What about Bossman?" I ask.

"Baby-Face?" Reginald says. "Biggest hypochondriac I ever met. Bet he's curled up with a cold compress on his forehead."

"He's been angling for a medical discharge since September," Cedric says. "Might actually get it."

Like Brando in *Streetcar*, I lean back, take a slow drag off a cigarette, and flick it out the window. The red ash spirals to the ground.

"All right, boys," I say, grinning. "Let's blow this popsicle stand."

CHAPTER 17

Hijinx in the Desert

Hugh

Halfway into our adventure, the siroccos kick up. Not too bad—just enough to wipe out the tire tracks we'd been following. That's when Reginald, who's been acting like our guide, gets turned around. Can't blame Cedric or me—we're new here. I'm not too nervous, though. It's early. We've got time.

So we wait for a caravan to roll by while Reginald stumbles through some French, practicing how to ask for directions. I pull a bottle from the inside pocket of my jacket and take a swig. I'm no alkie like my dad—hate the taste—but it takes the edge off.

Luck's on our side. Just when things look iffy, help shows up like something out of a movie—two guys in a Jeep, heading the same way. From there, it's not exactly smooth sailing, but we make it.

And when we get there—holy hell.

This isn't some dingy little campfire party. We're smack in the middle of the desert. We're in with a bunch of off-duty soldiers in what I imagine is a casbah. Red tents, belly dancers, waiters in red fezzes. And I'll be danged if alcohol doesn't flow like water from a spigot. There are ice chests loaded with Coors, Millers, and Johnny Walker Red. Since observant Muslims don't come near booze, the few exceptions are proof anything can be had for a price. Our boys get it from the commissary and lug it around in ice chests.

After I get a few more drinks in me, I climb on stage. "Did I ever tell you the one about the guy with a duck on his head?"

The crowd roars. I rattle off jokes like machine-gun fire. They say I sound like Henny Youngman. I'm killing it. Even the old lines are landing. And when I step down, I'm swarmed. Painted-up, half-dressed belly dancers slink over one by one, all trying to get in my pants. I don't care. They're A-rabs. Barely covered boobs pressing into my face, a bare midriff, gold-belted hips that jingle when they move, firm buttocks planted in my lap … It's tempting. But the memory of my girl, Bess, waiting for me at home is fresh. Besides, these are working girls, and sex is something I don't gotta pay for. Since I'm tired of it being the other way around at home with Bess, who's always saying no, I allow one of them to kiss me.

I'm not looking at my Timex. Neither is Reginald, who looks like he's three sheets to the wind. Cedric, I can't locate. At 6, after Reginald and I get side-eyed by a couple of GIs looking for a fight, we stumble our way back to the Jeep. After hearing what sounds like Cedric hurling his guts out, we collect him and put him in the driver's seat. He's wasted, slurring his words, but he's driving slow enough. In fact, sometimes I think he's forgotten where the accelerator is.

The sun's sinking fast, bleeding out over the horizon. Luckily, we're behind a caravan of Jeeps and dune buggies. I figure, how bad can the ride home be?

Then the wind shifts, the temperature drops, and I feel it. Uh-oh. When cool air slaps the back of my neck, that's when I know.

The chain around my neck—my USAF dog tag—has been baking against my skin all day. What felt like a mild sting at the party is now a roaring blaze. I've got a sunburn from hell. Full-on, second-degree, nerve-pinging, mother-of-God pain.

Since every chance I get I call these guys candy-ass pansies and worse, whenever I wanna yelp or let out a sob, I hold it. Pretty soon, I'm biting the back of my mouth so hard it also hurts. I try to concentrate on desert sounds; I never knew there were so many. Engines cutting in and out, the hiss of the viper snake, the howl of a sand cat, the sound of the siroccos. All the while, my neck is on fire.

CHAPTER 18

Burned Out

Hugh

The doctor takes one look at the red-brown blisters on the back of my neck, scribbles on his clipboard, and lets out a raspy sigh.

"Well, sir, you've got yourself a second-degree burn," he says. "Go back to the barracks and rest. If you can't, at least stay out of the sun, dammit. While you're at it, lay off the booze, okay?"

I don't know what he's talking about—booze. "Big assumption, Mister. Cause of my Scottish name."

Anyway, it's depressing as hell being inside. I'm in agony. That my skin glistens in places, peels, and oozes pus isn't the half of it. I feel empty inside. The more time I spend in my bunk, the more thoughts of Bess enter my mind. I open my wallet, and along with my about-to-expire Michigan driver's license and USAF ID, there she is. Pale skin, spun-gold hair, apple-pink cheeks, and that pillowy chest. Just looking at her photo makes me tremble.

Outside, Cedric laughs. It's not personal, but my fists clench anyway. Tears sting my eyes. Jesus, I don't even know what I'm feeling. Sadness? Guilt? If I had a bottle of whiskey, I might find out.

For the next couple days, I go soft. Little things set me off—a horn blowing in the distance, soot in the air when I crack open the window.

Three months ago, I said goodbye to Bess. We made quite the couple on the train platform—me in my blues with spit-shined shoes, her in a cream dress and pearls. The air was thick with chimney smoke. My eyes burned. My throat was raw. But still, I remember the moment she unclasped the precious charm from her bracelet and slid it into my pocket. I can still feel her hand on my thigh, the electricity running up my leg and into my groin.

The last letter I got was a week ago. I'd write her back, but I don't have the energy.

The skin underneath my blisters is tender. Doctor said ice, Neosporin, and bandages. Easy to say! The pressure of tape against gauze is murder. Every movement hurts like a bitch. Longing gnaws at me. I don't usually like country music, but Hank Williams' song about the lonely cry of the whippoorwill comes to mind.

Someone needs to tell me, *stop the pity party*. I take Bess's picture out of its plastic sleeve, run my fingers over the deckled edges, kiss it, and place it on my nightstand. I light a smoke, take a couple drags, then stub it out half-smoked. The nicotine calms my nerves but does nothing for the pain—or the wallowing.

Out of five rowdy boys, I'm the fuckup.

Out the window, an inflatable Papa Noel that's seen better days bobs up and down. It brings back memories of Christmases past—the fistfights, the broken bottles, the shotgun blasts. Brothers will be brothers. I still miss Ma. I have this way of calling her. The operator says, "Collect call," and I say "I'm fine, Ma," and she hangs up. No charges that way. Last week, she got a few words in.

"Celebrate Jesus' birthday," she said.

I tuned out before the line went dead. Soon as she started in on the religion. But now, I wish I'd listened.

I dig in my pockets for coins and shuffle down the hallway to the payphone. My fingers tremble as I dial.

"You'd be mad if you saw me, Ma. Second-degree burns. From the sun."

"You'll heal," she says.

"Tell Bess I'm okay."

There's a long silence. If she knew the truth—that I was AWOL, drunk, acting like my no-good father on one of his week-long benders—

she'd take a willow switch to me. He was a boilermaker man. She, on the other hand, rations affection like it's wartime.

"Of all my kids," she says, "you worry me the most, Son," she says. "Always go-go-go. If you ever stop, I'm afraid your head's going to roll off."

What Ma doesn't know is that the minute the brakes go on, desperation sets in. On my belly, face crooked upward so that only my chin's on the pillow, my thoughts start going haywire. One minute I'm crying, the next I'm not.

The window overlooks a promenade of palm trees decked out in tinsel and string lights. Christ, I can't even take a leak when I need to without being reminded this was my first Christmas away from home. I can't close my eyes without thinking of seventeen years of white Christmases; me and my brothers on bobsleds, getting into snowball fights, making snow angels.

I'm on the verge of a full-on bawl when there's a knock. It's Cedric, holding a bowl of cold oatmeal—some remedy from his Creole grandmother. His arms are covered in bug bites.

I wipe my eyes with my sleeve. "Thanks, bud. Looks like the mosquitoes made mincemeat outta you."

Cedric tosses his head and laughs. "I might've scratched myself to smithereens, but I'm upright. Careful, man. Old Memaw's oatmeal remedy only gets you so far. Like Reggie says, you white as a piece of paper."

He spreads the cool mixture on the back of my neck, gentle as anything.

"This is the last time," he says. "How you manage to spend 18 years on the planet and not learn a damn thing?"

Without anything to counter him with, I go to sleep. When I wake up, he's gone.

I'm not completely out of my funk, but the TLC has spun me in a positive direction. I get up, splash cold water on my face, and inspect myself in the mirror. I'm clean for mosquito bites. They don't chew me up like they do Cedric. Poor guy. Soon as I'm halfway better, I'm going to return the favor and bring him some Calamine lotion.

My face is red, and my skin is peeling in places, but I'm still good looking. I might be short, but three-fourths of the natives who run the cafes and storefronts are 5'4" tops. I look at my dimples and the way my head full of hair curls into a pompadour. My pep talk doesn't last long. Two more days go by without much improvement. On day three, I'm finally comfortable enough to sleep.

My bunkmate, a bland, vacant-eyed North Dakotan named Sven— who moonlights as a security guard on account of him being as tall and wide as a damn tree—is always gone. When he *is* here, he's quiet, which doesn't give me a damn clue as to how the hell he feels. Until he drops a tube of Neosporin on my bedside table.

"You were almost out," he says.

Next thing I know, he's gone.

CHAPTER 19

A Bubbly Beginning

Hugh

By the time New Year's Eve rolls around, my face and neck are pretty much healed. So is my mood. The back of my neck is the only thing not restored to its former glory. Cedric, Reginald, and I are headed to the dance at the Officer's Club, which is open to us enlisted men on New Year's Eve and some other occasions. Even workaholic Sven, who I'm coming around to, has the night off. Maybe he doesn't laugh at my jokes, but he got me the ointment, didn't he? And when I complained about the sun corroding my dog tag, he showed me how to use dish soap and ammonia to shine it back up again.

"Can't have your good luck charm get tarnished," he'd said.

I check my look in the bathroom mirror; I'm looking pretty snazzy. My face is still red, and I have the beginnings of a beard, but it's nothing a shave won't fix. I smother my face in Barbasol, wet my razor, and think about how this would've been impossible a day ago. I almost dreaded going, if you can believe it. I thought I'd be red as a lobster, sitting at the table closest to the exit, sulking, nursing the same beer.

Now, it's back to my old motto: Every moment with gusto. Ma warned me to slow down, but I'm pumped. The teary-eyed sap who cried over Bess's photo a few days ago? History. Yes, that picture shows off her assets in all their pillowy glory, but there are girls out there. And tonight, I plan to meet a few. My mind's spinning with one-liners and jokes when I nick my chin mid-shave. I blot it with toilet paper and shrug. It's not much of a handicap—certainly not as bad as showing up with two colored friends. But screw it.

"The girls are here to have a good time, and we're here to give it to them," Reginald says. "Some want a meal ticket outta here so bad, they don't care that me and Cedric are colored. But plenty a man's gotten a girl in a family way."

I think of what the commander said—how Jews want out of this place in the worst way. I'm not trying to get anyone pregnant, unless it's Bess on our wedding night. Not that I want to get married, but there's nothing like a Cracker Jack box ring to keep a girl from running around on you.

I'm here to cut a rug, have a few drinks, and—if luck's on my side—kiss a girl at midnight. We've all got the dances down: the Swing, the Bob, the Lindy.

We're having ourselves a good time when I spot this one girl—a real star. The other GIs have already clocked her. Some recognize her as the Orange Fanta girl, Nanette Moab. Word is, she's just come back from Paris, where she did billboard and cinema ads. She's the picture of a Moroccan beauty: brown-skinned, tall, with curves that stop time—38-24-36, if I had to guess.

I grab a dollar to buy her a drink. When I open my wallet, there's Bess's picture, back in its slot. I shouldn't feel bad. She's at a New Year's Eve dance of her own. The aspirin I took three hours ago is wearing off. The back of my neck hurts, and there's a raised bump on my chin, but if I want to dance with 16-year-old Nanette Moab, I'll have competition. For the first time since I've been in Morocco, I feel short. It's no big deal, but my roommate is six-two and standing next to her. She might be wearing heels, but I'll be damned if they're not eye-to-eye.

She might be a giant, but that doesn't keep her dance card from filling up. I notice with guy after guy, she chooses to sit out the faster tunes, ones in which I could show off my dance moves. Instead, she dances to the instrumental melodies of the day, *Sentimental Journey*, *In the Mood*, and *Moulin Rouge*. I wouldn't call what she's doing dancing. It's like she's on air.

It isn't until after midnight, after many of the guys have taken off, that I seize my opportunity. She's standing with another young woman, who I learn later is her aunt. When the disc jockey announces a slow dance, and she says yes to my request, I take her in my arms. The song is *Moonlight Serenade*.

"How do you float like that?"

She eyes me and says, "I don't talk to red-faced boys who cut themselves shaving." Then she turns away.

In shock, I reach up—yep. Blood spot on my chin, and probably still a touch of sunburn too. Just my luck. The one girl in Casablanca who isn't falling all over me because I'm American.

I look around. Reginald's at some rickety table, necking with a girl. Cedric's gone—God knows where. I give it another try, tell her a joke about Pepé Le Pew, and this time, she laughs.

I've lost my confidence. I'm fumbling, but maybe that's what works. An hour later, she's confiding in me, her accent sweet, her English just shaky enough to be charming.

"My mother—and later the headmistress at my lycée, had me spend hours from when I was 12, walking around with at first one book and then multiple books balanced on my head. To be more Parisian, they said. And I guess it was all worth it because look where I am!"

"Sounds like a lot of trouble," I say, my mind making the comparison to Bess, who might clog, do an Irish jig or polka, but never while floating.

"If I didn't hold my back rod straight and tilt my neck in the right way, my hips would move. Then everything would fall."

Bess begins to fade from my memory. The girl in front of me is beguiling. Maybe it's the days I spent nursing a sunburn, the fact it's New Year's, or me imagining Bess is already with someone else. But seeing this girl with her high, ample bosom, hourglass figure, and her dewy face, all I know is one thing: I must ask her out.

CHAPTER 20

Fawn Drive

Yasmina – October 1966 – San Jose, California, USA

Nanette and Hugh are easy to spot, even from the tarmac. Hugh looks like himself. Red-cheeks, Brylcreemed hair, and a smile as wide as the outdoors. He *has* lost his freckles, and strands of cigarette ash-colored hair dots his temples. Nanette's the same, but thinner. When Hugh steps away, Nanette, who must be anticipating my reaction, tells me having a "kid," the word she uses, doesn't suit her. She's not meant to be a mother.

"They say it's true love from the minute the baby's born, but six years in, my attitude hasn't changed," she says. "Hugh keeps wanting to have another, but how could I? Abi's difficult. You'll see."

She reaches in for a hug. A half-dozen gold bracelets clang at her wrists. One of them—if I'm not mistaken—is thicker than the rest and engraved with the initials *ES*, her maman's. She's wearing Arpège, and a lot of it—an upgrade from the Jean Naté Madame Moab's been reduced to lately.

But when I circle my arms around the folds of her dress, all I feel is bone.

My hand flies to my mouth. I bite back a gasp. How can Hugh not see this? Her weight has always fluctuated, but this is the worst it's ever been.

At their house in San Jose, it's extroverted, charming-as-ever Hugh who gives me a grand tour. Everything is slightly too bright, too clean, too still—as if someone set the stage and forgot to tell the actors to move, talking about having it all—wife, kid, white picket fence. A thought pops into my head: *but why?* Hugh never drank, at least not in front of us. He always said never to be like his dad. Yet there's something about him. I would say his cheeks are rosy, but there's a patchiness there.

My fingers trace the edges of my amulet.

"You don't need to sell me on America," I say unevenly. "I'm more than happy to be here."

But he doesn't get it. "Zero down and the house was ours," he crows. "VA foreclosure. You can get one too, but since you're not military, you'll have to rent for a while."

"We got lucky," Nanette chimes in with a too-bright laugh. "The previous owners had a sick kid. Bankrupted them with therapy. Tragic— but classy enough to clean before they left."

Nanette's always had a streak of callousness, but this … this doesn't sound like her. Still, I'm more concerned with her frail frame than what comes out of her mouth. I start brainstorming how to put meat back on her bones.

The first time she starved herself, I'd just come back from Fes. A few bowls of chickpea soup fixed her. The second time, when puberty hit, it was worse. She barely spoke and was hospitalized for a month while they fed her nothing but bland institutional meals. It was a Russian doctor who finally figured it out.

"When my chest got too big for my costumes," she told me once, "Maman said I couldn't be a prima ballerina. After that, I was done for. So much for Audrey Hepburn—I'd have to settle for Gina Lollobrigida."

They gave her barbiturates to dull the anxiety. It worked. A calm, mellow girl doesn't starve herself. Within two years, she had curves, a full figure, and a look no one could copy—tall, classically Moroccan, with a hint of Berber fire. At sixteen, she was flown to Paris for a photoshoot. Soon, she was in print ads, billboards, and movie theaters all over Morocco.

The house on Fawn Drive isn't expensive, and though it's shoebox-small, it's in Cambrian Park, a neighborhood Nanette says is "up-and-coming," which adds to the stress. Hugh's working at a gas station. Nanette stays home. There's a mortgage, and she says they scrape to pay it. Hugh's out of the military now. Abigail's birth brought medical bills, and her formula was expensive. Nanette's still bitter about it. How long before she starts feeling the same way about me?

I need to get a job—fast.

But any concerns I have about them being broke vanish when Hugh opens the pantry. It's stocked with root vegetables, canned goods, rice, and flour. Then he points to a domed structure in the backyard.

"Came with the house," he says. "We're keeping it because you never know when the Ruskies are going to try to nuke us," he says before launching into a breezy lecture on the Cold War. It feels strange coming from Hugh. He wouldn't know danger if it hit him in the face.

Nanette twists her bracelet. She shifts her weight from one foot to the other.

"Now Hugh, Yasmina doesn't understand," she says.

I fixate on my toes, which are peeking out from the tops of my sandals. It's the middle of the night in Morocco. I'm so exhausted, I can barely stand.

Nanette swallows hard, making her collarbone jut out in the scariest way.

"You must be so tired," she says. "Hugh, Yasmina is tired."

I have to get her to eat. With the pantry door still open, I take inventory: chickpeas, carrots, bouillon, spices. Nanette, who's been following the direction, misunderstands.

"I can cook," she says. "American, French, Italian, Moroccan. You name it. I make it. After you've had enough rest from your travels, me and Abigail will prepare a lavish meal."

It doesn't make sense—this too-thin woman, hoarding food, talking about it like a prize she's never claimed. No woman who cooks should be starving. I remember the second time too clearly: the fever, the confusion, the doctors with their clipped diagnoses and theories. All they did was write about her in journals. No follow-up. No plan.

Hugh hadn't met her yet, but now, standing in this shiny, spotless kitchen, it's him I blame. What husband lets his wife waste away?

As always, it's on me. I've always been the one holding this family together.

She'll make that big meal she promised. Then I'll take over. If spoonfuls of chickpea soup aren't the answer, I'll find another. I always do.

CHAPTER 21

Tea Time

The "lavish meal" Nanette promised arrives a day and a half later. Seeing her and Abigail in the kitchen together—cooking, laughing, tasting—gives me hope.

"Afternoon tea," the little girl says. "I have it with my dolls all the time. But the cups and saucers are much smaller."

"Pardon her," Nanette says before turning to address me. "We've never had a guest over for tea. Ever since her friend's mom took her to the library for Storytime, her imagination's run wild."

Abigail stares into an empty cup.

"It's the thing to do in foggy London," she says. "I wanted high tea, but that's at 5, and Mummy said no."

Nanette points to Abigail and rolls her eyes.

"I told her there was only so much we could do," she says. "But she insisted. She had a list of things she wanted from Fry's, but I told her they don't sell imported groceries, but of course, she knows better than to call me *Mum*, don't you, Abi?"

I smile. The clang of pans and the scent of cardamom and sugar drifting from the kitchen start to quell my unease. Nanette's talked before about making green eggs and ham, about Abigail convincing neighbors to make soup from a stone. She may have made her daughter a target for being "too much," but I can see the love in this room.

Nanette has prepared a feast. Watching her eat will be the real pleasure. And I'm sure once they get used to having me around, the mother-daughter rhythm will steady itself.

My barstool spins when I shift, and I plant my feet to keep from tipping. I laugh—what kind of invention is this, and for what purpose?

Abigail's flattening dough with a pin, and Nanette is helping her. That she has the strength and patience for this—for make-believe, for pastries, for sugar cubes—is a good sign. Her parents never did. In fact, the more this child-woman and her daughter turn a pretend game into something real, the more restored I am. It's more than a mirage, what Nanette's been able to do; here in this steamy rectangular-shaped kitchen with no air conditioning. Abigail's too young to have been more than a small help.

Hot water, mint, and sugar cubes are there to make a tea they serve in porcelain cups with handles and saucers. There are silver trays lined with white paper doilies, bearing sandwiches filled with cucumber and cream cheese. For dessert, along with the Moroccan honey almond cigar-shaped pastries I taught her to make, there is a sticky cake with pineapple rings and cherries suspended beneath the surface, a lemon curd such as I've never had, a delicious yeasty-smelling cinnamon crumb cake clouds that pull apart in my fingers, and a scone that hits my stomach like a stone.

None of this placates me. Nanette's trying to fool me into thinking she's been eating when she's not. She moves food around on her plate. She scrapes the cream cheese from her cucumber sandwich, throwing away the bread and eating only what's left.

It isn't until late afternoon, when we're sitting at the table Nanette calls a breakfast nook, that things really fall apart. That's when she gives me one of her double-dimpled smiles and tells me the last thing I expect to hear.

"We weren't able to get you a green card. I tried everything. I was so lonely."

I don't remember the exact words that followed—just my pulse pounding, jaw clenched, fingers pressing into the underside of the table. Words like *tourist visa, six months, under the table, on the sly*—they fall from her mouth as if they mean nothing.

Time stalls. I sit in silence. Not as a weapon—but because I can't trust myself to speak.

Nanette stares at me. When I don't respond, she looks away.

The disappointment crashes over me like cold water. But I keep quiet. I don't want to say something I'll regret. I reach for my Hand of Fatima and press it to my chest.

Across the room, Abigail stands near the fireplace, looking like she's shrunk two sizes. She's six, but too tender, too subdued. Her eyes are always downcast. The slightest sound startles her. She retreats from conflict like a creature trained to hide.

"My dolly made a mess," she whispers.

It takes everything I have not to sigh. How has this little girl been made to feel responsible for her mother's doing?

"Go to your room," Nanette says. "Grown-ups need to talk."

What don't you want her to know? I think, but do not say. How deceitful you've been! You, with your grand stories of America, where nothing is as you've described. You needn't worry. I have self-control. And what have you done to this little girl?

It's Nanette's voice, urgent and sharp, that returns me to the present.

"Say something!" she says.

A quiet hiss escapes my lips. I reach into my pocket for my prayer beads and put them back. Even this sets her off.

"The beads," she says, exasperated. "Your precious Hand of Fatima. The salt. The incense. It's all too much. Isn't it enough we have mezuzahs?"

I blink. She's angry? She should be on the defensive.

Wasn't your family the same? I want to say. *Your grandmother didn't allow mirrors. Said they were portals for evil.* But I stop myself. That would be deflection.

"You promised me sponsorship," I say quietly. "You said a green card."

"I didn't know how to tell you," she says, lip trembling. "I can't sponsor you and my parents."

My heart sinks. I didn't want to see it, but it was always there. Of course the Moabs wouldn't stay.

"You'll be fine," she adds quickly. "You can make money under the table. Nobody has to tell the government."

My fingers burn. My toes grip my sandals. "And if they find out?"

"You'll be deported. But don't worry, that won't happen," she says, breezy again. "Hugh has more pull than you think. He's cozying up to every Iranian engineer this side of the Bay Bridge; he washes their windows, checks their oil."

"Iranians? I don't understand."

"He's getting you a job," she says brightly. "As a maid."

My hands tremble. I don't mean to be ungrateful. But this—this is my chance.

"I thought coming to America would be different."

"It *will* be," she says. "This is only temporary."

"Don't ask me to take part in your scheming."

She yawns and places tea in front of me. "Everyone's got a little larceny in their heart. Even you."

She thinks she's helping, but all she's done is throw me back into the past—back to when I was fifteen, and powerless.

My voice is steady. "Take me to the airport. I want to go home."

"I need you," she pleads. "You'll be homeless in Morocco."

You're wrong, I want to say. What I haven't told you is that recently, my chances of finding a suitable husband in Morocco have improved a hundredfold. After almost twenty-five years, it was confirmed. The rumor about Brahim and his family was true. I'm not crazy, and I'm not infertile.

The Mouloudjis were German spies. Anything for a franc. But they were so ignorant, so in over their heads. Within a month after discovering amongst my husband's things a copy of *La Vie Ouvrière*, a French Resistance newspaper, a Vichy map, and a document outlining plans for a sweep of several thousand Parisian Jews, I am out of the family. They thought me knowing how to read was a superpower capable of destroying them. When the military records were uncovered, the whole story was told. Less than a year after I joined the Moabs, Allied Forces arrested Brahim and my in-laws. Although Fatima was released, the rest are incarcerated. Brahim died short of his twentieth birthday of typhus. They buried him in a mass grave. My father-in-law and Idir didn't last long after that.

It's the gossiping Madame Mouloudji who gave me my freedom. Just this year, she made a full confession and announced I am not a divorcee but a widow. Absolved, I can now secure a decent husband. I still have some of my looks. There is even the possibility, however slim, with my French, I can secure a government job. So why did I come to America? For the same reason everyone else does.

Nanette's still watching me, twisting her sleeves.

"A tourist visa gives you six months," she says. "Time to learn the ropes."

I don't respond. I just look at her—long and hard. It makes her nervous.

"I need you, Yasmina," she says again, more vulnerable this time, like something inside her is about to break. "Apply for refugee status. Or— another option. We'll save. Pay someone for a fake marriage. Or maybe a real one. There are so many eligible men. Many here are on genius visas. Not Moroccan, but close."

I feel myself softening. This is Nanette. She's always been this way. Her intentions may be a mess, but she means well. She *thinks* she's helping.

"You can forgive me," she whispers.

"In time," I say. "But stop being so deceptive. Trust yourself. Trust me. You don't need to live like this."

"I'll be better," she says. "I promise."

I nod, but my voice is quiet, worn.

"I don't know if your words are true. Tourist visas. Green cards. Under-the-table jobs. It's all ... so exhausting."

CHAPTER 22

The Hand of Fatima

Yasmina

At twenty-four, Nanette still carries the lilting innocence of her childhood. She speaks with that breathy, Jackie Kennedy voice—pausing gently at the end of each sentence, smiling shyly like she's waiting for permission to go on. Beside Hugh, they make a picture-perfect couple. He's a happy-go-lucky ham, sparkling with that too-good-to-be-true energy I once loved in Brahim. The same easy charm. The same platitudes. Only Hugh's comes packaged in American slang.

"You betcha," he says. "You're a good egg."

I've only been here two weeks, but already I can tell the neighbors are wary of the Joneses—especially Hugh. With a cigarette dangling from his mouth, he looks like a man playing at suburbia but never quite fitting in. Still, he trims the hedges, rakes the leaves that constantly drift onto their lawn, and tries his best to play the part.

It saddens me how unwelcome they seem. If a bad boy and his ballerina-beautiful wife can't find their place here, where can anyone?

Abigail, on the other hand, is welcome everywhere. Like a stray cat, she slips in and out of the neighbors' homes, eating their snacks, playing with their children. The women here are not what I imagined Americans to be. They wear scarves, too—but only to cover the plastic curlers they never seem to remove. They're always outside: hanging laundry, pulling weeds, watching. And I understand why Abigail seeks them out. They are steady. Rooted. They would never bring someone over on a tourist visa and call it kindness.

Nanette, for all her charm, is ill-equipped.

She wanted a little girl more than she ever wanted a sister. But from the beginning, it was all complaints.

Abi—that's what we're calling her—is allergic to milk, she wrote in her first letter. *She needs some special formula we can't afford. But if we don't buy it, she never stops crying. I don't know what to do.*

Things didn't get better as Abigail grew. After they moved from Michigan to California, another letter came:

Our apartment is no bigger than a shoebox. It's stifling being trapped with this demanding child. I don't give her the right-sized cookie, and it's like the world ends. And then, when I finally do, she throws it all up.

When I wrote back, I tried to soften her. *She's two, Nanette. What can you expect? You were the same way.* But over time, even I started to doubt myself. Nanette's conviction was so relentless I nearly believed it—maybe Abigail *was* impossible.

And yet, when they visited Morocco, Abigail bloomed at the smallest kindness. When I gave her a Coca-Cola and a rose, she looked at me like I'd given her the moon.

After that trip, Nanette's letters grew darker; less about frustration, and more about despair.

Please come, she wrote. *I am a bottomless pit of emptiness. Underneath it all, I feel so alone.*

When she started making plans for me to immigrate, I found myself going along. After years of taking care of other people's babies, I long for my own family. No wonder I didn't take care in reading the visa application. If I were, I would've realized. The words *tourist* and *visa* are the same in English and in French.

The idea of working "on the sly" might seem humiliating, but I've spent my life on the margins. If Nanette can sort things out, if I can only be patient.

"Give me a few more months," she said

My window faces the backyard, where a narrow creek runs along the fence line. Nanette has scattered river rocks there. Two frogs rest lazily on a lily pad; a turtle, half-hidden beneath a flat stone, eventually crawls onto land. Two weeks in, the room has begun to feel familiar.

There's a Rand McNally map of the world pinned to the wall. Thumbtacks crowd the southern half of California—Abigail's travel dreams. Some are so close together they've torn the paper. I trace my finger across the ocean from Morocco to California and back. Amira's soothsayer, the one who said I would travel far and wide, was right. I have. I've been Yasmina of the Mountains and Yasmina the Barren. Now, like my ancestors, I've become Yasmina the Nomad. Once, right after I married Brahim, I had a dream about ten painted lady butterflies. I thought ten was the number of children we would have.

"Winged creatures shouldn't be pinned in one place," she'd said.

I thought she was being ridiculous. Now I realize I've become the butterfly, and as such, I hold no ill will. Not even toward Nanette. I should have seen the contradictions in her letters. One minute, she was giving me a sales pitch: *You'll find a job tout suite. The valley is flush with money.* The next, she was expressing her disillusionment: *So much for my Hollywood dreams.*

But I'm not going back. This is where the soothsayer's predictions end and my own will begin. I may be a High Atlas butterfly, but I will not drift with the wind. Everything I do now will be deliberate.

There's a knock at my door.

"I have something," Nanette says, peeking in. "I know it's not in great shape—Abi got to it. A little glue will fix it, though."

She holds out the remains of her wedding cake topper: a plastic bride and groom, nearly detached from their satin-covered foam pedestal, the arch of crushed baby's breath. She's trying to make amends.

"Aren't you getting ahead of yourself?" I laugh.

"I remember how much you loved it. You kept saying the bell looked like it was made out of sugar but still made a sound when you shook it."

It wasn't the bell, though. It might be embarrassing to admit, but it was the groom who captured my attention, with his painted-on eyes and thick slant mouth. He may've been amateurish, but in his top hat, tux, and tailcoat, he seemed so debonair.

"Thank you," I say.

Later, alone, I examine him. Once, I thought a man like that was beyond reach, a different species. Now, in America, dare I dream? Back in Morocco, when the matchmakers came calling—even after I'd been approved for my US visa—they said I was "well preserved." Not a single tooth missing.

"Was it the tree bark you used on your gums?" they asked. "Do you use argan oil? Your skin is more youthful than most."

But always, the hourglass loomed. One matchmaker compared me to a salted lemon fermenting in a jar.

"Never as fine as fresh," she'd said.

Even Amira once promised, "Describe your ideal man. I'll stuff him in a suitcase." I joked: *Silk shirt, cufflinks, smells of sandalwood.* I didn't realize I'd described the cake-topper groom exactly.

Nanette's voice calls from the hallway.

"I'll pick up some Elmer's tomorrow," she says through a crack in the door. "I know it's chintzy, but wouldn't it be fun to use it as a decoration at your wedding?"

After telling me to rest up—dinner in half an hour—she walks away.

I set the topper on my nightstand and hum to myself. Silicon Valley isn't what they call it yet, but there's something about this place. A fast marriage to a kind, prosperous American? I could do worse.

First things first: the headscarf must go. I can't transform into the kind of woman a cake-topper man wants while hiding behind it. I spend the next hour experimenting, trying to shape my hair into something acceptable. I twist it into a bun and pin it down—only to see puffs of frizz spring up around my ears like weeds. I'm not sure when my hair became too thick for a single braid. Puberty? The humid air? It was a partial blessing until now that the religion of my home country allowed me to keep it wrapped.

At the dinner table, I wait for someone in the Jones family to gasp or make some other expression of shock. I clasp my hands. I stare silently into my lap. *Am I that invisible?*

Hugh, who smells of motor oil and is still wearing his gas station uniform with his name printed on it in curly-cue letters, *does* give me a surveying look. And Nanette, who's not on speaking terms with Abigail, makes a show out of smoothing her hair and patting her perfectly curled tendrils.

"Don't you love convenience foods?" she says. "Aside from the chicken, the whole thing took fifteen minutes, including setting the table."

On one plate is gluey white bread with slabs of oleomargarine. In a bowl is green mush of some kind. Another plate holds over-salted, under-seasoned boiled chicken. A half-full bottle of Foremost milk sweats on the table.

I'd hoped for something. A glance. A word. Some ceremony to mark the removal of my headscarf. But nothing. Not even acknowledgment. It's just dinner.

"Maybe it's my Moroccan sensibilities," I say. "But you put much more effort into the meal earlier."

Abigail snaps to attention, her neck pivoting so fast it's like she's never heard anyone contradict her mother. She watches silently.

Nanette meets my eyes, then tugs her hair into a loose ponytail, exposing pearl studs.

"No time," she says. "Places to go. People to see."

Hugh, who knows nothing of how mean women are, is oblivious. He frees the top button of his shirt and says, "Jesus Christ and the Holy Ghost, the one who eats the fastest eats the most."

Where have I landed? I wonder. In a place where a man can make uncouth statements before eating, where women talk about food as if it's an inconvenience. In commercials, women talk about Vitamins B, C, D, but get them from a can. As for Nanette, I'd assumed with the tea she and Abigail put together for me, she'd turned a corner. How could what she did have been anything other than an act of care? I still plan on returning that love with a pot of chickpea soup, a healing medicine she will enjoy.

With not one appetizing thing on the table, I go for the bread. But when I take a bite, it sticks to the top of my mouth. I have to use my tongue to loosen it. When I try swallowing, a lump forms in my throat.

Nanette pours a glass of milk, but instead of being sweet and warm with a layer of cream on the top, it's chalky and cold. It takes everything I have not to spit it out.

Hugh, who still doesn't have any idea how mortified I am, scoops a portion of soggy, green nastiness on his plate and takes a bite.

"French cut beans," he says. "You're the best."

I don't know what shocks me more, the praise he's giving or the pride on Nanette's face.

I can't help myself. "You can't be serious!"

"In America, we use a can opener," Nanette replies. "Food's not fresh, but it saves time. Tinsel Town's only seven hours away, you know."

"The food on the plane was better," I say.

Abigail stifles a giggle.

Nanette's smile fades. "Three of the four food groups on one plate. Everyone else likes it. And I used the time I saved to schedule interviews for you. It's a formality. You're an ordinary woman about to begin an ordinary American life. Except for me. I made this happen. I deserve credit."

But it's too much: this "meal," Hugh in his dirty uniform, Abigail's silence, my uncovered hair. One day, maybe I'll understand. That time is a resource. That a woman doesn't have to spend it all in the kitchen. That a man can cook. That a woman can chase her own dreams.

But not today.

Today, I simply absorb it all

CHAPTER 23

The Minx in the Mirror

I can't say Nanette isn't encouraging. When Hugh's at the filling station and Abigail's at school, she tells me my moment has come.

"Hugh and I don't condone San Francisco beatniks," she says, wrapping a curl of my hair around a roller. "Poetry readings, coffee houses. And don't get us started on the Beatles. But you—with your flowy dresses, dangly earrings, and crazy hair—if we can get it under control, you'll fit right in. At the airport, people stared at *you* instead of me. Not that Jackie Kennedy's look isn't still popular."

Men *had* stared at the airport. I'd been offended—they'd looked at my chest, then my face. But they never saw the full swell of espresso-colored curls mushrooming beneath my scarf. If they had, any sway I had over them would have disappeared.

Nanette thinks she has a solution.

"When it comes to cosmetology," she says, pulling and pinning sections, "I never took a class, but I'm a natural."

Whether she has skill doesn't interest me. My mind's elsewhere when Nanette spots a single gray hair amongst my mass of curls.

"Well, I'll be darned!" she says. "Time has to catch up with you sometime."

I take this as a good sign. Instead of feeling neutral or upset, my heart leaps with joy. In Morocco, it was like I was frozen in time. In America, I will age.

Nanette grabs a lock of hair and pulls. "You can wear these curls," she says. "But I need to get enough gel and hairspray to tone it down, so you don't look like some radical Black Panther."

None of it works. Two days later, when I'm introduced to potential employers, Mrs. Afra and Mrs. Behzadi, I'm back to wearing a scarf. For now, until Nanette comes up with a solution. She puts me in a splashy above-the-knee dress and low heels. For makeup, I choose a matching bright orange lipstick and kohl eyeliner. After that, a liberal application of mascara. But instead of fawning over me like the workmen at the airport, the women who interview me have the opposite reaction.

"You didn't tell me she was so pretty. Did you say 40?" Mrs. Afra told Nanette over the phone. "Did you say *forty*? I'd rather let the house go dirty than tempt my husband."

"What about Mrs. Behzadi?" Nanette pressed.

Also no.

"They thought you were a younger, hipper Sophia Loren," Nanette tells me. "They hated the headscarf. Hated the hair. They said your figure would be irresistible to their husbands. Your lashes, your eyes. When I told them you were nothing special, they said, 'Look again.'"

The mood in the house shifts. Hugh said I'd find a job "lickety-split." These were his friends. Now Nanette watches me like I've become a burden.

"I can't believe Mrs. Afra said I shouldn't leave you alone with Hugh," she says. "True, you don't age, but you're ten years older than he is."

All I want is for Nanette to get along with her daughter not to say whatever comes to mind. Like when she told Abigail she was the first pancake because it never turns out right, and the next child she had would be an improvement. Her husband, I have no interest in.

Ironically enough, it's he who comes up with the winning idea. Home from work, leaning back in his recliner chair, Hugh points out, rightly so, that non-Arab "American" housewives in Monte Sereno and Saratoga will hire me with no problem. And they won't try to haggle the price.

"I'll put out some feelers," he says.

"These women are well-traveled, and they love anyone exotic," Nanette adds as if it was her idea all along. "Everything and everyone around them has to look perfect. They're not insecure about their husbands when maybe they should be. I see you in an embroidered apron and a pair of babouche slippers."

"No, Nanette," Hugh says. "She needs English classes."

"That I can do," I say. "But I can't pull off the good-looking part without fixing this."

I point to my hair, which today looks especially wild.

"There are relaxers," Nanette says. "But they burn the scalp. Let's start with Breck. And better rollers."

She believes in beauty as a discipline. *You must suffer to be beautiful,* she always says—and insists I do. The next morning, she sets me under a Jiffy Jet hairdryer in jumbo curlers, then combs everything out and turns my chair toward the mirror.

I'm pleased. She isn't.

"Good thing the natural look is in," she says, spraying a cloud of Aqua Net over me. "This'll hold, but you need a real salon."

"Don't I still owe you—for the flight?"

"We'll figure it out. I've saved a little. Not much. But this matters. Rich Americans care about appearances almost as much as we do."

"Nanette, I can't."

"You must. Even with perfect English, you won't pass the interviews unless you *look* the part."

The comment stings. For some, I'm too beautiful. For others, not enough. But Nanette means well. Within hours, she finds a night class nearby. She books me a hair appointment. She lines up a part-time interview with a Saratoga matron named Mrs. Suzy Shrum.

Everything happens fast.

A week later, I sit at Stephen's Hair-Do of Cambrian Park, draped in a cape. When he spins me toward the mirror, I hardly recognize myself. My hair, now cut just past the shoulders, swings like silk.

"You've pulled off a miracle, Stephen," Nanette says when she sees it. "I knew you were a master, but I never thought … I hope she doesn't look overqualified."

Stephen shrugs her off and tells me to watch the humidity.

"You look fabulous," he adds. "I don't know if you know the word *minx*, but that's what you look like. Do you mind if I snap a photo for my wall?"

I can tell Nanette isn't pleased. On the way to the parking lot, Nanette warns me not to get too stuck up.

"It'll wash out with the first shampoo," she says.

I don't care. I'm on a high. Not only will I look great for Mrs. Shrum, but for the first time in a long time, anything's possible.

Half an hour later, when I'm sitting in the cafeteria waiting for class, I still don't know what a minx is, but I feel as sleek and slinky as a cat. My hair swings when I turn my head. Same rollers, same dryer, same pins as Nanette used—but somehow, Stephen worked magic.

Part of me thinks it's wasted. The men arriving for class look exhausted, most of them Spanish-speaking day laborers. After another takes their seat, a puff of a sigh escapes my lips. No one should ever be that tired.

I want to study at home, but Nanette and Hugh say I have to be here. For the job.

"Your French/English dictionary—it's for travelers," they said. "You need to learn the words of *work*."

The irony is not lost. They brought me here on a tourist visa.

And what about words of *love*? Where will I learn *those*? I need a groom, someone flesh and blood and not plastic; a tall man with a broad smile and hands unblemished by work.

I clutch my amulet and hold it against my chest. The room is too hot. As if in answer, the air conditioning sputters into action. What happens next is even more miraculous than the hair. At 7:00 p.m. sharp, our teacher, a well-dressed dark-haired man who could be an Arab, enters the room. He's younger than me, in his early thirties. I'm close enough to smell the Brylcreem, but not the Chiclets on his breath. That comes later.

Before picking up a piece of chalk, he straightens his cufflinks and adjusts his suit.

Mr. Bijan Tehranpour, he writes, in large, elegant cursive.

"I'm an immigrant too," he says, meeting my eyes like I'm the only one there. "Five years ago, I was in your place. Now I'm an engineer at Stanford by day. Life in Persia—*I refuse to call it Iran*—was difficult. I'm Zartosht, not Muslim. But enough about me. Tonight, I want to know about *you.*"

Just like that, the weight of tourist visas, awkward dinners, and mother-daughter fights slips away.

I'll find the money. I *will.* Even if it kills me, I'm making another appointment with Stephen before my next class.

As I leave, I catch my reflection in the glass door. My cheeks are flushed and my eyes are wide. My hair is still perfect. The Hand of Fatima is cold against my skin.

I think of six-year-old Abigail, how I once gave her a replica of this same amulet to ward off evil. What I don't know is that fifteen years from now, when betrayal rips her world apart, she'll cling to it with everything she has.

CHAPTER 24

Licensed to Lie

Abigail – Los Gatos, California – May 1983

A lot has changed since that fateful Mimouna a decade ago. Nikki, once a precocious little thing, is now fifteen—sharp as a tack, quick with a comeback, and slick enough to run circles around our parents. I'm in grad school now, technically on my own. But if Nikki wants something, she *gets* it. And by the time you figure it out, it's too late.

This last stunt wasn't just inconvenient or embarrassing. It was like a bomb detonated in the middle of the DMV.

In 1983, the California Department of Motor Vehicles is bureaucracy at its worst. Even before the doors open, a line of groggy people snakes around the building. The wait could be unbearable—except this is Los Gatos, not Pacoima. There's nothing dull here. Olivia de Havilland once called this place home. John Steinbeck too, though he moved a lot. The real draw is the landscape: lemon-scented geraniums, mock orange blossoms, and blue sage crawling up the building, their blossoms buzzing with hummingbirds. I'm barely holding myself together—sleep-deprived and fighting to stay alert by tracing the edges of the amulet at my wrist.

Nowadays, with Los Gatos morphing into the West Coast epicenter of Yuppiedom (Ronald Reagan would be proud) this DMV has to be its microcosm. Amongst a turnstile of luxury cars waiting for their permanent plates, there are scores of overindulgent fathers paying slap-on-the-wrist fines so their little brats can keep driving. And then there are the ultra-rich who feel like they can park anywhere they want. Only they don't show up. It's their personal assistants who settle the bill.

That's why, although my people-watching eyes are at half mast, on any given day, there's always some tidbit to feast on. Under the awning are the usual suspects. A hotshot business exec with a tan line on his ring finger flicks his cigarette, allowing the sparking ash to fall on the walk. Behind him is a panic-stricken punk rocker in a Devo T-shirt, safety-pinned jeans, and scuffed sneakers. Her mother stands close, patting her shoulder and offering calm words. Further down, an entrepreneur does his best hand-to-chin Jack Benny imitation, no doubt to show off the chunky gold ring on his pinkie finger and the Rolex on his wrist.

I forgot my sweater in my friend Lee's car, so when a light breeze cuts through the back of my Star Wars tee, I shiver, arms folded tight. Last night, I'd faked a cold over the phone—throat raspy, voice lowered an octave. I'm supposed to be in school, so pulling a Ferris Bueller-style mental health day to go to Disneyland one day early comes at a price. When it comes to college, I'm not a makes-you-want-to-gag good girl always sitting in the front row of the lecture hall, the kind who peppers the professors with want-to-know-more questions. But still, the work has to be done.

Last night, I feigned a cold, coughed into the phone, lowered my voice to a smoky husk, and lied. The only reason I'm at the DMV is because I lost my license. The paper replacement they mailed expired. Once I'm done, it's me, Lee, and Caroline on the road.

I'm half zoned out when a perky, over-highlighted woman in a tennis outfit elbows past me.

"Do you mind?" she says. "So much to do today."

Something about her—maybe the diamond the size of Gibraltar on her hand—makes me nod, like I've got nowhere to be. She makes me feel small. A lot of people around here do. I'm wearing a bracelet with marble beads and two charms: a Celtic cross from my father's mother and a Hand of Fatima gifted years ago by Mrs. Tehranpour.

When the door finally opens, the pace changes. A woman behind a rope starts handing out numbers. Miss Highlights and I end up neck and neck, meaning her little rush was pointless. I'm directed to a line with a view—the Santa Cruz Mountains right outside the window, so close it's like you could touch them. I've lived in San Jose's toughest neighborhood. Gunshots, lowriders in loud backfiring cars—I could never tell which. Now I live here with my two best friends.

On the ride ahead, we'll be traveling along a highway so flat and straight, so devoid of any scenery, drivers need a cup of coffee or a couple No-Doz to stay awake. Fields, pastures, farms, orchards—nothing even remotely picturesque until we hit the Grapevine. But I won't mind.

A clerk pats me on the elbow and summons me to Booth 4, where I find a petite older woman with features so perfect they look like they've been chiseled by scalpel. And then there's the expert way her skin has been stretched across her face like a drum seal. She greets me with a genteel smile, but I'm a snarky 23. Except for my professors, I still roll my eyes at the establishment and "old" people. All I need to look effortless is a T-shirt and jeans. She's way overdone.

Still, she's helpful. As soon as I explain why I'm there, her salmon-pink nails click rapidly across the keyboard. I feel a pang of guilt for judging her—but she doesn't waste time proving me right. As soon as the terminal spits out a printout, her demeanor shifts. She leans in. Her breath is minty but warm against my neck.

"You owe $212," she says.

I'm stunned. She knows I'm broke—my T-shirt, cutoffs, and rainbow flip-flops betray me. Her tone turns smug. I'm not wearing Ralph Lauren for a road trip. Shame on me.

"No checks," she adds. "Too early to verify funds."

Like I'd bounce one.

I sputter. "What? I don't understand." I'm calm, too calm. Mom would've smacked the counter by now. Even Nikki would've turned the place upside down. But not me. I know how to behave. My parents didn't come over on the Mayflower, but I can speak WASP.

She slips me the printout.

"The lesson here," she says, channeling Queen Victoria, "is not to ignore a moving violation. Paid promptly, it would've been $40."

What happens next is surreal. What episode of *The Twilight Zone* have I stepped into? Me, spitting words out; her talking over me, telling me not to fight it.

"The judges in Coalinga are harsh," she says. "That's how they keep the lights on in these places."

"Either the officer got it all wrong or a counterfeiter's out there pretending to be me," I say.

All I get is a now-I've-heard-everything sigh.

"We're going to Disneyland," I say, my voice edging toward desperation. I try to smile, but it slips. "Just me and two friends. Caroline doesn't have her license yet—I don't even know why." I shift my weight from one foot to the other. I glance at the clock. "It's way too much for Lee to drive the whole way alone."

The quiver in my voice convinces her. After typing a few things into a CRT, and pressing enter, the genteel smile returns to her face.

"Ever wonder if it was stolen?" she says. "You reported your license missing June 16. The ticket is dated June 15."

When would that've happened? Where do I go except for school, home, and once in a while to my parent's house? Then I remember—Mom retrieving Nikki from the police station a while back. I hadn't thought much of it at the time. Most teens sneak into clubs with fake IDs. But Nikki? She wouldn't use *mine*—I'd already reported it stolen.

Apparently not soon enough.

The clerk claps to get my attention.

"You're upset," she says, softening. "I would be too. Take it to the authorities."

My head is pounding. The adrenaline's real—but I feel like the floor is made of sand. Even the worst lecture I ever sat through—two full hours of a guest professor droning on about Freud and Jung's complex relationship—I'll take that torture over this, any day of the week.

The only decent thing about this is the adrenaline. It's like someone's given me a shot of it. But the ground beneath me still feels shaky. It takes me forever to get to the door. The girl in the Devo T-shirt is smiling from ear to ear. She must've aced the written test because she has her arm around her mother like after this, they're going for ice cream. For them, it's a beautiful day.

Outside, the sage bush closest to the street is so bright it's like it's been lit by the sun. The hummingbirds, having had their fill a half hour before, have gone on to other things. I don't know why, but this affects me.

CHAPTER 25

Chasing Justice

Abigail

After the DMV, Lee and Caroline pick me up in front of Safeway. We drive for a couple of hours, and I'm half-asleep for most of it. But when we reach the stretch of Highway 33 where Nikki got the ticket, I jolt awake.

The radio skips between country tunes and mariachi music. Out the window, migrant workers squat in the fields—picking, packing, stacking fruit into wooden crates. Decades after the Delano Grape Strike, this still looks like indentured servitude.

I picture Nikki behind the wheel of someone's borrowed Jaguar, flashing the patrol officer a perfect smile, blaming her speed on a bad hair day, and signing *my* name at the bottom of the ticket. She must've been heading to the same place we are. I imagine her laughing. How gullible the small-town cop was! We're both pretty. Who isn't at our age? But Nikki, who has Mom's height and coloring, is hard to confuse with me. I'm three shades lighter than she is and two inches shorter.

Since Caroline's dating a sheriff who knows all the right people, all it takes is a few phone calls for me to get a same-day appointment before a judge. I try to protest. We can do this later. Why *ruin* our vacation? But they'll have none of it. Only problem is, the courthouse is in Coalinga, a blink-and-you'll-miss postage stamp of about 7,000 people. It used to be a mining town. It makes sense Nikki got a ticket there. The clerk at the DMV was right; it's Speed Trap City. It's also the geographical halfway point between my parents' house and Tinseltown.

With Lee's careful driving, we don't have to worry. We arrive at the courthouse a full half hour ahead of our appointment. People don't usually fight their tickets here. It's too remote, which means express service. At 12:30, I appear before Judge Harvey Sloane.

He slams the gavel.

"Dismissed," he says.

When I try to explain—ask about Nikki—he waves me off. No proof. The entire detour takes twenty minutes.

Somehow, it should have taken longer.

All the way to Anaheim, I'm in a haze. Nikki *shouldn't* get away with this. But she always does.

Dinner plans are ruined—Anderson's Split Pea Soup in Buellton is closed for repairs. The Motel 6 is old, dingy, and loud. A letdown. Nikki's last trip south was first class, courtesy of Grandma Moab's credit card—valet, poolside drinks, the works. The bill didn't lie.

We still have fun. The first two days, we barely see the motel. But by the third, we're Disney'ed out and Knott's Berry Farm'ed to death. That night, we stay in.

It's noisy—horns, slamming doors, banging on walls. Motels never land in the good neighborhoods. But we make the best of it. There are six channels on the TV—nine, if you count the Spanish ones. No cable, no VCR.

Caroline tunes the Walkman to a disco station. Soon, we're three women in our twenties, singing along to *Love to Love You Baby*. Then it's *Play That Funky Music* by the Average White Band.

Tomorrow's a beach day. Lee and I take turns painting our toenails. Caroline, who hates the smell of nail polish, tosses her shoes aside and dances on the bed. I want to join her, but my toes are still wet.

Then the music cuts out. Regular programming returns.

A radio talk show host—*Dr. Lauren*—comes on. Her voice, sharp and smug, fills the room. She's not like any psychologist I've ever heard. Her delight in humiliating callers is pure poison.

"You'd have to be a masochist to call in," Lee mutters.

"You're a twit," Dr. Lauren says to a woman asking how to get her husband to listen. "Who are you to deserve attention?"

To another: "You're wasting my airtime. I could be helping people who matter."

We're horrified—but we keep listening. She's a virtuoso of verbal flaying.

And then it happens.

A crackly voice calls in.

"Dr. Lauren," it says, laced with a familiar shrill French-Moroccan accent. "This is Nora from San Jose."

My mother.

Using *Nora.* Smart.

"I'm calling about my daughters," my mother says. "One is twenty-three. Let's call her Donna. The other is fifteen. Let's call her Stacy. I know—big age difference."

"Chop chop, Nora," says Dr. Lauren.

"Stacy's always pushed the rules. But recently, it's gotten worse. She applied for a credit card in my mother's name and charged it up. She also stole Donna's license and got a ticket. I didn't report it. I didn't want her in juvenile hall. Now Donna's furious. She won't speak to me. I think this time, I've lost her."

"So you let your barely-a-teenager daughter commit fraud?" Dr. Lauren says. "You don't need advice. You need a reverse lobotomy."

There's a tremor in my mother's voice. I reach for the dial—but Lee stops me.

"You need to hear this," she says.

"I'm doing my best," my mother pleads. "Stacy wouldn't survive juvie. You're a mother—you must understand."

"I understand," Dr. Lauren says coldly. "And don't play the mom card. If my son pulled that, I'd let him rot in jail."

Lee shakes her fist at the radio. "Right. Like she'd do that."

"Stop," Caroline says softly. "Abi needs to hear this."

Laura continues: "If the last caller was a twit, you're a *double* twit. If you don't want to be a complete waste of human breath, turn her in."

"You don't understand," my mother says. "Donna already has. I want to fix things with her. I want to help Stacy too, but she's dropped out of school. She's not even home half the time. Donna's studious. Stacy doesn't want to be like her."

"Blah, blah, blah," says Dr. Lauren. "No accountability for the teenager."

"I was so busy fighting Donna, I didn't have time for Stacy," my mother says, her voice quiet.

"I'm guessing you were the adult," Dr. Lauren says, her voice dripping with sarcasm.

"Donna was born when I was 18. The hospitals in Morocco were terrible. She was sick. They thought they'd have to airlift her to Spain. So many times, I thought I'd lose her. I was afraid to attach."

"That's the biggest load of psychobabble I've ever heard."

"I loved Donna, and I hated her," my mother says. "From day one, she cried night and day. Colic."

"Infants cry," Dr. Lauren says. "That's why babies shouldn't have babies. As far as being difficult goes, have you thought about Stacy?"

"This isn't the first time Donna's disowned me," my mother says. "A year ago, I got on my hands and knees begging for a reconciliation. Since then, I'd like to think we've patched things up."

"Maybe she should've stayed estranged," Dr. Lauren says. "I don't talk to my mom either. As far as I'm concerned, she's dead. Some mothers really do eat their young."

I wince at the way Dr. Lauren is exploiting my mother, who clearly has a disorder, for entertainment.

"But, but ..." my mother says. "Donna and I had been doing great. I make her special meals. We go out to eat. She's Polly Perfect morals-wise, which I don't like, but—"

"If you raised her, she's no rule-follower," Dr. Lauren says. "The apple doesn't fall far from the tree. I'll tell you what to do, and you have to write this down if you want to redeem yourself. You live in California. Get yourself to a courthouse and file a CHINS petition. CHINS stands for Children in Need of Supervision."

"CHINS," my mother says, like she's hypnotized.

"The court will supply you with an attorney. And your younger daughter, Stacy, or whatever her name is, will get her own attorney too. And don't worry about juvenile hall. They won't keep her long. It's too overpopulated with gang members. Migrant worker spawn, if you ask me."

"Are you sure this is what I must do to earn Donna's trust?"

"I can't tell you what'll work. If you're a twit, you're a twit. Now, off the phone. You've got your work cut out for you."

My hands roll into fists. Mom might not be angry, but I'm loaded for bear. I don't care if Dr. Lauren has a point. This is *my* mom she's messing with.

From there, justice is served swiftly. After a follow-up call from Dr. Lauren, Mom is bullied and shamed into completing the CHINS application with the false assurance Nikki would avoid juvie. Someone called social services; we don't know who. Following that, there's no turning back. Within a week, my parents are deemed unfit to raise their daughter, and she becomes a ward of the court.

A few days later, Nikki's in juvenile hall awaiting her court date. I'm still not talking to Mom, but I heard she's inconsolable.

And my heart breaks—for Nikki, for everything we could've done differently. I wish it had never come to this.

CHAPTER 26

Juvie

Abigail

Nikki remains "imprisoned" longer than anyone expected. *Tough case*, they say. All she has to do to be released is show remorse—but she won't. She shifts blame. Evades accountability. Initially, she's placed with our other grandparents, who've relocated from Michigan, but she abuses the privilege, disappears, and winds up right back where she started. Three months later, she's still not going anywhere.

Weirdly, I have hope for her now. Being stuck in one place might finally teach her something.

But mostly, I feel shame. If I hadn't set the wheels in motion, Mom wouldn't have called Dr. Lauren. It's hard to stay mad at Nikki. I go visit her half a dozen times, each time getting off work early to battle traffic, taking the 237 from Alviso, past the Zanker Landfill, and onto the Guadalupe Parkway where the facility is located. I usually try to avoid this small sliver of town because unincorporated Alviso smells of sewage and rotting fish no matter the season or time of day. As a deterrent, it's as good a place as any for a children's detention center.

The first time I visit Nikki, in the days after her incarceration, she's washed out. But in her faded blue uniform, even devoid of makeup, she still looks older than 15. It's clear from her voice, from the way her hands shake, she's furious. But for some insane reason, none of her anger's directed at me.

A girl walks by, reeking of BO. I point to her and plug my nose.

"Stinks to the high heavens here," I say. "But if that's how you're going to learn …"

But Nikki, who's still stuck on Mom, isn't listening.

She slams a fist on the table.

"How could *she*?" she says.

A guard shoots her a look. She lets out a snort.

"You don't know it's her," I say, convincing no one. "Nikki, have you ever stopped to think maybe you're where you need to be?"

That's when her face goes red.

"According to *who*?"

"All I'm saying is—use your time here. Make it count."

"I'm still pissed. Mom—"

"Don't use that word," I snap. "It's crass. And like I said, it might not even be her."

"You're a terrible liar, Abi. I saw the CHINS petition. It was her handwriting. That's what I get for expecting loyalty."

"She was vulnerable. Someone planted a seed. If she wasn't still talking to that damn radio shrink, she'd be baking a cake with a file in it."

Nikki glares. "Since when is wanting to have *fun* the same as being *out of control*?"

"I didn't go clubbing at fifteen. I still had a good time. My friends and I sang and danced to records. We played Gin Rummy."

"Wow. What a riot. And what did that get you? Perpetual grad school and no boyfriend?"

The jab stings.

"For your information," she continues, "my boyfriend's already back with his ex. So if that's what you wanted—mission accomplished."

"Focus on your future," I say, trying to keep my voice calm. "Put Tiger Beat posters on your wall. Leif Garrett. John Stamos."

"Jus' bored," she says, listlessly.

"If you don't want to study, at least take the free counseling."

She rolls her eyes. "They make us talk to some ex-felon in a therapy hat. What's he gonna do? Give me a roadmap to redemption?"

"Play along. Maybe he'll help you work through your anger toward Mom."

"She's gullible. She always does what the last person tells her to do. That's how *you* got away with everything."

"What do you mean, *I*?"

"I borrowed your license. Skipped out on a pizza without paying a couple of times. But I had *nothing* to do with Grandma Moab and the credit cards or with what happened to the money. That was Uncle Laurent's crazy ex-wife."

In Nikki's face, gears are turning, plots are being hatched and set into motion.

It can't be. No one this age can be this manipulative.

"Okay, Nikki," I say in a level voice. "I know this pales by comparison, but Dad went through your room and found a lot of stuff belonging to me. Bras, underwear, other intimate things. Why?"

"I dunno."

"Dunno's not good enough. I blamed the laundromat; I suspected my roommates."

"If you hadn't used *our* washing machine. Anyway, let's talk about Mom. I *hate* her."

"Don't," I say. "You've no idea what's going on. An across-the-street neighbor said Mom's losing weight again. As for Dad, if he's using and selling again, it'll be your fault."

Nikki gives me a who-gives-a-shit stare.

"If Mom didn't bust me, it was one of your nosy friends."

"Haven't we been through this? The path you were on—it was wrong. This might be your chance to change direction. Get your diploma."

"School here's a joke. Half the girls can't even read."

"Then it'll be easy credits then. You're smart. Go beyond. Challenge some of the coursework. In any other situation, you know I'd want you out. I'd be helping Mom with the cake."

"Don't even joke. I gotta get outta here. My boyfriend's losing patience."

"You've got your whole life ahead of you. Relationships at your age last, what? A year?"

But Nikki, who grabs a lock of hair and starts running her fingers through it, isn't listening.

She lets out a groan.

"If anyone leaves, it's going to be me," she says in a voice too worldly for her age. "But since I don't know how long I'll be here ... I *know* what you're going to say. Study in this hellhole with all these beneath-me losers. Look at me. My hair's as dry as straw. Nothing wrong with the Breck you got me, but can you spring for Paul Mitchell? Also ... blue eyeshadow. Soft curlers. Tanning oil—for the yard. Ryan says he'll pay you back."

Paul Mitchell. Blue eyeshadow. *Ryan'll pay me back.*

Her words echo in my ears.

She gives me a look—half-begging, half-daring. We sit in silence.

Finally, I speak.

"I'll be there for the hearing."

CHAPTER 27

The Vise Grip

Abigail – 1984

"I know you're busy," Mrs. Tehranpour says when I mention the nightmares. "But you need help. You can't go on like this."

At first, I dismiss her. Of everyone I know, it's *Yasmina*—as she now insists I call her—who's been through hell and come out the other side. She never saw a counselor, so why is she pushing me toward one? Still, everything changes a week later, when I physically can't function. Dr. DiSibio has to wake me up.

"Class is over," she says gently.

She refers me to Pansy Parnell, PhD, whose office is a narrow flight of stairs above a mom-and-pop insurance agency. The hallway smells like mildew. Her name is spelled out in plastic diner-board letters, the kind that usually list breakfast specials. She buzzes me in.

I'm not sure what I expect, but when she opens the door, I'm not surprised. She has a youthful face for someone in her 50s, with close-cropped silver hair and thick Frida Kahlo eyebrows. Her dress is an eye-popping green, the color of which you hardly see anymore. She's wearing one of those gigantic Arts-and-Wine-Festival turquoise and gold necklaces old ladies go nuts over.

The interior of the office doesn't look much different from the hallway—battleship gray and sparse, like one day she'll get around to decorating. The contrast between how she looks and her office isn't lost on me, a person who notices. In one corner is a spray-painted over file cabinet and a mini-fridge. In the other corner, a vanilla-looking wing-back chair for her, a hard-as-a-rock futon for me, and a glass and rattan side table with nothing on it except a box of Kleenex and a pencil holder with a couple of knitting needles and a length of yarn sticking out. The part of me that has a place for everything is bothered, but not too much.

There isn't much on the wall other than a framed diploma and a plastic battery-operated clock.

With a generous wave of the hand, she motions me to sit.

"I'll be direct," she says. "When I agreed to take university referrals, I knew there'd be a waitlist. When your name jumped to the top, I was pissed. Big-time. Like, who the hell are you?"

Usually, I'd shrink—shoulders curled, head down. But not this time.

"My research methods professor took pity," I say. "I wasn't sleeping. I couldn't study. I could barely stay awake in class."

"She exaggerated," Dr. Parnell says.

Then she throws her head back and laughs—a low, throaty sound.

"Grad professors notice everything," she adds, with a flicker of respect.

I'm tired of people saying awful things and laughing it off. I decide to push back.

"So what *is* the front-of-line criterion?" I ask. "Hospitalization?"

She leans back and rubs her chin. No apology, but something close.

"Go on," she says.

"You read the intake," I reply. "Surreal childhood. Kafkaesque, even. I knew something was wrong, but when I spoke up—well, you know what they say about killing the messenger. I've been holding it together, mostly. But lately, the past keeps crashing in. That guy on PBS said it best: 'Everywhere you go, there you are.'"

"Jon Kabat-Zinn," she nods.

I bristle at her know-it-all tone, but she's all I've got.

Bit by bit, I tell her about Dad. About Rhonda. Her face softens. Her eyes mirror mine, patient and present. She listens until I pause.

"Wait—Rhonda was your boss and your dad was …?"

"Her dealer. As in, drugs."

She launches into a standard spiel about confidentiality. It's good enough to break the ice. Before long, we're ping-ponging between one what happened and why and another.

I'm still giving her the sanitized Cliff's Notes version. Since I'm studying research psychology, I throw in some stream-of-consciousness psychobabble.

"I'm incapable of being in a relationship," I say. "Every boy I've dated said it. I'm frozen solid from being so strong. Then there's my sister, the budding criminal, safely summering in Japan with a chaperoned group of girls. My parents—"

"Crazy what can happen when there's no guardrails. Unfortunately, I'm hearing a lot of this, with the children of the Haight-Ashbury Summer of Love generation trickling in. Let's stay on track. We have thirty minutes."

I close my eyes, take a breath, and tell myself to focus. I notice the light streaming through the trees outside the window. Cars buzz by from the freeway below.

"I wish you just … knew. Without me having to say it."

"Wouldn't that be nice?" she says softly. Then, with pinpoint precision: "Tell me about the nightmares."

"They got better," I lie. I focus on the yarn, now looped around one of the knitting needles. "I'm making my dad a fisherman's sweater for Father's Day. Granny squares."

Most therapists might allow the deflection. Not Parnell. She leans forward.

"You've barely mentioned your boss."

Just hearing *Rhonda's* name loosens the floodgates. I spill more than I meant to.

"Dad's like a kingpin. His reach is everywhere. My job at FMC, a heavy-equipment company, was supposed to be safe. I can't quit. I need the job to afford school."

She furrows her brow. "We'll circle back. But tell me about the nightmares."

"They stopped when HR fired Rhonda. Until then … they were brutal. I'd wake up on the floor. The dreams were so vivid—she'd grab me by the hair, drag me outside, smash my head into concrete."

Parnell exhales. "Now I see why you got bumped up the list."

"Dad's drug of choice was coke," I say. "I don't know what happened to make him stop. Maybe my mother finally put her foot down. Rhonda was his number one customer."

Before I continue, my eyes go all watery. Dr. Parnell sets a box of tissues on the table.

No tears come, not because I'm not upset, but because I'll be darned if I'm giving Rhonda the satisfaction.

When I speak again, my words are sharper than they've ever been. I'm spitting them out like I'm a no reload needed human nail gun.

"I couldn't understand how she got through HR. She had the hungry, glassy-eyed look of an addict. The other markers were there too: the cheap perm, the bi-level dishwasher blond mullet, the *always* dripping flattened-out nose. The minute I met her, I knew—*a wicked wind blew.*"

Dr. Parnell must've latched on to something because now her eyes are ablaze.

"She couldn't even pretend?" she asks.

"Like druggies are competent? All day, every day, she holed herself up in her office chain-smoking Camels, second-hand smoke wafting into my cubicle, possibly giving me cancer. Doing jack shit. But until I learned about her and Dad, I was able to avoid her."

Dr. Parnell gives me a wise look. "This is when compartmentalization comes in handy. Sometimes being detached is a gift. Until it isn't."

I let out a soft sigh. Boggles the mind the way we humans have to adapt.

"People like Rhonda have short shelf lives," I say. "Usually, I outlast them. But when worlds collide …"

My throat goes dry. I try to keep talking, but my voice cracks. Parnell mutters something under her breath—*bitch*, I think. For a second, I wonder if she means me.

She gets up, grabs a bottle of water from the mini-fridge, and hands it to me.

"Drink," she says.

I take a long sip, then laugh hoarsely.

"Dad thought she was *mentoring* me. She lied about having a USC degree, claimed she'd worked as a buyer. He thought, *why not her?*"

Parnell raises a brow. "Don't you already have a degree?"

"Not from the right place. Rhonda was a liar. But Dad—he vouched for her. That's what stings."

"But the nightmares," she presses. "They were about *her*."

"Work was my sanctuary. Then Rhonda showed up—sitting on my parents' couch, eating Mom's Moroccan cookies, listening to Dad's sad records. Now she's gone, but I still look over my shoulder."

Parnell's voice softens. "You're safe now," she says.

I dig my elbows into the back of the futon.

"I wish I could believe you," I say. "I don't usually fall apart, but mullet-headed Rhonda snorting coke off my parents' coffee table kills me. Good thing the new boss is a garden-variety alcoholic. Puts booze in his coffee every morning to stave off the DTs, but he's totally amiable. He works hard too."

I would go on about how the guy's no cokehead, but when he eats a donut, he's sloppy and the powdered sugar grosses me out, but that's not the point. The sound of construction work outside reminds me we're almost out of time.

A bulldozer beeps. There is a crashing sound.

To be heard, Dr. Parnell needs to raise her voice.

"Can't you find some related employment? Research psychology, right? In a lab somewhere?"

"No one else is this flexible."

Dr. Parnell sets down her pen.

"Next week," she says. "Same Bat Time. Same Bat Channel. And for homework: PTSD and codependency. Both apply."

As I stand, she asks if she can knit next time. It helps her focus.

"No," I say. "I may have been bumped up the list, but I'm still the client."

Outside, I exhale sharply. *Way* too much. Probably said too much.

It takes forever to get to my car; construction vehicles block every route. The clouds have thickened. The air's damp. My wipers are useless. I realize only when I reach the door—my face is wet.

Hunched over the steering wheel, I finally allow myself to cry.

CHAPTER 28

Moving On

Abigail

It takes a couple of months for Dr. Parnell to get to the root, as she calls it. I have one crying jag, and that's it. After that, we spend too much time skimming the surface.

"Academia's my jam," I say. "At least there's structure."

I never broach the subject of PTSD. I figure anything involving trench warfare or jumping out of planes into enemy lines has nothing to do with me. The issue of codependency is thornier.

Dr. Parnell keeps pushing me.

"I don't usually recommend this, but as much as I enjoy you," she says, "I think you need to move. Your father may not have a territory anymore, but seriously."

She's worried about me. She has this crazy idea that Dad has mob connections. That he's laundering money. That my 15-year-old sister is a ringleader. *Move* becomes her mantra. Half the time I think my therapist is nuts, but still, I wonder about San Rafael. Sixty miles and a suspension bridge away from my parents, it would be an easy transfer—Dominican University.

"I'd have to switch from research psychology to counseling psychology, but it's feasible," I tell her one day. "But I'll be taking my problems with me. Like Jon Kabat-Zinn said."

"If you put a goldfish in dirty water and it dies, do you blame the fish?" Dr. Parnell replies. "Sometimes the environment needs to change."

In the last sessions, she helps with logistics. Maybe because I'm a short-timer, maybe because we've become so comfortable, she asks again for permission to knit. I can bring my crochet.

She turns out to be an awful knitter. She always has to take the scarf she's working on apart, but I figure that's not the point. As for me, even though it's July, I make one ski hat after another. We look up when one of us has something big to say. Sometimes we test each other, making sure someone's paying attention.

"It must've been like looking into a funhouse mirror, being a kid in your family," she says. "Everything warped, distorted, ass-backward."

I thank her profusely. "Without you, who knows how long I would've been stuck in a mediocre, not-good-enough existence."

"You would've figured it out."

"Sixty miles might not seem far enough, but I'm still scared. I can't leave my friends behind. Tomorrow, Jonathan—one of the kids I used to dumpster dive with—is coming by with a truck. Who knows when I'm going to see any of them."

I don't expect Dr. Parnell to put down her knitting, but she does.

"The growth you've made is yours alone. And if there's one thing I can promise you—from now on, your life's going to get a whole lot easier."

CHAPTER 29

Cyrus

Abigail

Two months later, I'm standing in an empty studio apartment in San Rafael, surrounded by boxes and wondering if Dr. Parnell was right about life getting easier. The Murphy bed is still folded up against the wall like a question mark. If only there were some natural sunlight coming in.

For the first few weekends, friends visit. We shop. We sightsee in Sausalito's Richardson Bay. Until it gets old. The transfer from Cal to Dominican University isn't as seamless as I thought, which doesn't exactly make me the best hostess.

As far as college goes, even though I haven't changed my major—only my focus—there are endless hoops and unreasonable requirements. I need to take an undergrad prerequisite ASAP, which is nuts because I already have a bachelor's. The only offering is miles away, too close to my parents, making the move feel merely symbolic. Dr. Parnell tries to intervene. Can they make an exception? Even she has no pull.

"Go," she says finally. "One night a week. In and out. You're not there to make friends."

I would have a cow over this, but it's not my style. As for the shrink, I need another appointment, but she's too darn far away. The school I end up at—West Valley Junior College—while not exactly rinky-dink, still feels like a huge step backward. Although grand and lush, situated on 135 acres of prime Saratoga real estate, the first class takes place in a makeshift portable. It's been raining for days. Maybe it's karma—maintenance has to clear a fallen tree limb before anyone can access the main campus. Near the portable, a flood pipe has burst, forcing students to wind their way around puddles of indeterminate depth. San Rafael may be cozy and dry, but ten miles to the south—my old stomping grounds—abandoned cars float through waist-high water.

Inside the portable, it's much cozier. Several space heaters, once sparked up, do an adequate job of keeping us warm and dry, and the 1970s brown veneer paneling provides decent insulation from the noise. The scent of varnish and turpentine is comforting in its familiarity.

I try to keep an open mind. West Valley rivals Dominican in terms of beauty. Still, I'm peeved. The other students are so much younger than me, they might as well be embryos. At least it means I won't be making friends. I sit behind someone who looks closer to my age—a guy in a trucker hat with the initials *R&J Plumbing* embroidered across the front. He's not horrible-looking. Tall and even-featured, with tawny skin and a smattering of freckles across the tops of his cheeks, he might be conventionally handsome if the straw-blond hair peeking from under his hat wasn't so long and stringy—and if everything he wore wasn't wrong: the Budweiser belt buckle, the death metal band T-shirt, the hat.

The girls here might be staring, but I have a feeling their parents— Rinconada Country Club members, all—wouldn't approve. What puzzles me is that even the instructor, Mr. Blair Taylor, a balding man in his early thirties, seems enamored. Why else would he act like he's in the presence of greatness? He's generally speedy taking roll, but when he gets to the trucker hat guy's name, he drags out the pronunciation.

"Greeeeen, Cy-rus W.," he says with a smile.

Mr. Taylor's a decent guy, and when it comes to the housekeeping duties associated with opening a class, he's serviceable. I've had enough experience—not only have I earned a bachelor's degree; I'm halfway through my master's.

He takes a worried scan of the room, like he doesn't have enough students to make a class.

"The syllabus is longer than you're used to—one page, front and back—but you'll find it useful," he says nervously before walking to where Cyrus sits.

"Mind passing these along, young man?" he asks.

Cyrus turns out to be one of those super eager types. Not that I care—I'm people-watching. When he reaches me, he stops for a second before introducing himself.

"Call me Cy," he says.

"I'm Abi," I reply after a pause. "Short for Abigail."

After that, Cy does everything he can to make his presence known. He helps Mr. Taylor with the projector—it wasn't plugged in right. When the vintage Kodak slide carousel jams, he fixes that too. When I'm startled by a sudden flash of rain pelting the roof, it's Cy who reassures me. I'm starting to warm to him when I spot two girls—one in a rabbit-skin jacket with matching earmuffs and the other in a fox-trimmed parka. They stare at him dreamily, like they wish he'd talk to them that way.

I try to focus on the lecture, which is about attachment and the importance of mirroring. Although the slideshow consists of pictures of Mr. Taylor's adorable, chubby-cheeked children, I can't concentrate. I don't know what it is—the pounding rain, the small portable, the rich girls in their furs—but with each click of the carousel, it's like I'm back in high school. My own jacket, purchased years ago with my Lerner's employee discount, is hopelessly passé. And it's in desperate need of a sweater shaver.

Nothing in my closet is new. Nothing looks like it could've been bought at one of those boutiques on University Avenue. Most of these kids went to Saratoga High. I always thought it was frou-frou, but after it came out that Steven Spielberg went there and hated it, it lost its gleam. After Nikki convinced Mom and Dad to use Mrs. Tehranpour's address so she could attend, it lost even more luster.

A few of the kids here still fit the feckless, play-child stereotype so well they might as well have their mascot, Freddie Falcon, stamped on their foreheads. But everyone is pleasant enough. Besides, I'm 24. Time to stop being insecure. Look for silver linings. I am enjoying Mr. Taylor. The pleasure he takes in showing his slides is infectious. A Gerber baby with fat cheeks and a big smile appears on the screen.

"There are so many other ways to love a child," he crows. "My wife makes all their baby food from scratch."

I'm not learning anything new, but it is a break, and I can tell this is going to be an easy A. San Rafael is the dictionary definition of a bedroom community—way too quiet, especially when you don't know anyone. In the last couple of weeks, I've been ticking off the things I don't like. My apartment is too dark. The pull-down bed is heavy and hard to manage. Cooking for one isn't my forte. Takeout is expensive. I think about the way Caroline's dog used to snuggle against my chin. It's possible I miss him most of all.

A rifle of hail hitting the roof jolts me back to the present. A second later, there's a loud boom. Then everything goes dark. My tendency to dress for the weather I want, rather than the one I have, is about to bite me in the butt. I need to get to Parking Lot 3 in a thin jacket and a California-special umbrella that collapses on impact. Once I get to the car, I'll be okay. My windshield wipers need replacing, but at least the heater works.

What I'm not prepared for is what happens next, which is complete overkill. The city of Saratoga is so overfunded, even the campus police are bored of the drills. They need a disaster to keep them occupied. Their sirens are obnoxious. One would think we were in the middle of a WWII air raid. The instructor looks calm. He's been through a hundred of these drills.

"Listen up, kiddos," he says as he unfolds what looks like an emergency preparedness plan and holds it in front of him. "This isn't an earthquake, but the protocol is the same. When I give the go-ahead, you need to follow me to the bookstore, where there are generators for heat and light, and places to rest if needed—if it comes to that. Once the weather clears, we'll get you all home. But for now, it's like it's going to snow."

I expect Cy to chortle and give me a knowing look, but his expression is serious, ready for action. If I didn't know better, I'd think he was a Marine reporting for duty. Nothing about him is average, but he's not a celebrity. Some of the girls groan and reach for their pagers, which I could've told them won't work.

This teacher is ridiculous. Fallen tree limbs? Flooding? Sure. But snow? I'll believe it when I see it.

CHAPTER 30

The Wallet

Abigail

At the bookstore, we bond over granola bars, glow sticks, and scratchy army surplus wool blankets. Again, Cy tries to be the hero. He helps a girl into her oversized parka. He helps me when my umbrella breaks. But by then, the wind and rain have left me sopping wet and chilled to the bone. One of the girls I'd mistakenly labeled as spoiled takes pity and lends me her jacket.

From Campus Police, I learn how big the school really is—it has more than half a dozen parking areas—but I'm only half-listening. It's like these folks have been prepping all their lives for an emergency that never comes. Dear God, get me to my car.

The head of the student center serves hot chocolate in Dixie cups, warning us they'll collapse if we hold them too tight. We're there forever, but really not that long. When there's a break in the weather, security takes us to our cars—four at a time—in golf carts labeled *Rinconada Country Club*.

The wind has died down so much that once I put my Mustang into gear and hit the road—except for a lane closure on Highway 280—it's almost laughable how easy the drive home is. I'm not angry about it, but apparently at least one of the other students is, because a few days later, the school's ombudsman leaves a message on my voicemail asking about "things."

By the time class reconvenes a week later, I'm unsure about the status of the class or its instructor—which is sad. If I have to drop, it'll be six months of my life wasted. Others must feel the same way because as we stand outside the classroom, waiting for our five-minutes-late instructor, we joke uneasily about how he needs to get a grip.

"Does anyone know why the ombudsman called?" a girl says. "I mean, it's not Mr. Taylor's fault. He could be from somewhere it snows all the time—like Poughkeepsie or Pocatello."

"He should've known," someone else interjects. "Last time we had snow, we were in the fourth grade—and we barely had enough for a snowball."

I'm too busy praying we'll get to keep the class to join in. Not only have I put a down jacket on my Macy's card that'll take months to pay off, I've also gotten dressed up for no good reason—wearing the same outfit I wore to Lee's wedding shower and Carolyn's promotion ceremony: a brushed velvet pantsuit and low-heeled Bandolino pumps.

As the minutes tick by, a stream of new students arrives—girly girls in full makeup, wearing the uniform of Gunne Sax blouses, indigo Jordaches, and spotless white tennis shoes. Their sudden presence doesn't register yet. All I notice is that I'm not the only one dressed up.

When someone informs us that the instructor is on his way but running a few minutes late, it feels like I can finally breathe. Not only are we going to make enrollment, but the voicemail didn't mean the teacher was canned.

When I finally get a chance to look around—there's no Cy. At least, not at first.

When he does arrive, at the same time as the instructor; he's somber, head down. I'm surprised at how relieved I am. The new girls giggle and point, but I can tell something's wrong. He's almost unrecognizable. If he were a painting, they'd call it *Study in Brown*—like he's trying to blend in with the paneling. Mr. Taylor looks tired and nervous.

"Gimme a minute to make a phone call," he says.

I can tell from his voice—whatever he's dealing with isn't in his pay grade. What I don't expect is for Cy to turn toward me and mouth the word *CRAZY*.

"What?" I ask. "The teacher?"

"Never mind," he whispers.

When a love-struck girl saunters over to him, I think I have my answer. Dressed for a nightclub instead of class, she's wearing several pounds of gold jewelry and a sheer top-and-pants combo that leaves little to the imagination. The only thing she's covered? Her feet—in fringed white pigskin stiletto boots. And her perfume—it's like she poured Opium all over herself.

What she does next almost makes me feel sorry. Because of Cy, everyone—including me—is a little more put together than we were in the last class. As for not dressing for the weather? I'm wearing Bandolinos. I want to pull her aside: *Don't lose your dignity. Not over a man.* But it doesn't matter. She only has eyes for Cy.

"Are you?" she says with a titter.

"What if I am?" he replies.

This is a side I haven't seen—not angry or defiant, but rude.

I give Cy a *what the hell* look.

He ignores me.

"You guys played Senior Ball," the girl squeals. "And then in the summer? At the Boardwalk? You sounded *exactly* like the Beach Boys!"

If his face wasn't turning red, if his hands weren't shaking, I'd tell him, *Take it easy. She's a kid. Everyone has a crush.* And who are you—a member of a cover band?

It's a good thing I don't, because the next thing I know, Cy looks her dead in the eye and says, "If you put the note in my car the other day, stop."

"Never! Not me," the girl stammers. "You think? You're not even close to my age."

"It was either you or one of your little friends," Cy says, like he doesn't believe her. "*If I can't have you, nobody can.* The ombudsman called the police. Who do you think Mr. Taylor's talking to?"

"It wasn't me. I swear."

After a pause, in which she sighs and looks at her shoes, she says she's sorry. Not like she did it—but like she feels for him.

"Wanna help?" Cy says. "Tell your Saratoga High groupie girlfriends to leave me alone."

Dr. Parnell told me not to make friends. I was going to make an exception for Cy. Now, with how harsh he's being, it's easier not to.

But … a 1960s cover band, really?

"Hasn't Papa Doo Run Run been around forever?" I ask. "Aren't they all in their 40s?"

I can feel Cy letting his guard down—like if there's one thing he's sure of, it's not me.

"Everyone but the lead singer, who's amazing, is interchangeable," Cy says. "I replaced the old drummer. Since then, I've been labeled 'the cute one.' Being in a going-nowhere band isn't as glamorous as you think."

"You're cute in a way, so I guess I understand the attention. But how did the person know? How'd she get to your car before you did?"

"In all the confusion the other day, I forgot where I parked. This place is huge. I felt like an idiot, having security drive me around in circles. When I finally found the car and saw the note—it was nuts. Whoever wrote it is under the delusion we're in a relationship."

"Drop the class," I say. But the moment the words leave my mouth, I regret them. I've taken enough psychology classes. There's no easy solution.

"I'm getting temporary custody of my niece," he says. "The judge said fine, but I think since I'm young and in a band, he's making me take a child development class. I also need the money. Kid needs her own room."

I can tell from his voice he's giving me grace.

"Campus Police is a ways away—near the Viking Bookstore," I say. "After class, if you want, I can walk you there."

The next hour of class goes by in a blur. Things settle. There are more slides, more words of wisdom from Mr. Taylor, who's calmed way down.

By the time we walk out together, Cy and I are able to shift to other things. We learn we have things in common. His parents used to own DK Harryman's. Who knows—he might've been behind the register when Mom said no to Levi's.

"That scene played out dozens of times," he explains. "Immigrant parents don't understand how not wearing the right thing is social suicide.

But it builds character—not always getting what you want. Peaking in junior high never did anyone any good."

I'm so lost in the conversation, it's no surprise Cy sees it first: a wallet sitting on a patch of ice directly behind the bookstore. I'm closer, but since I'm hindered by my Bandolinos, he's the one who picks it up. He's wearing galoshes. I don't expect him to almost slip.

"I'll never get used to this weather," he says as his mittens skid across the icy leather. "Dad's retired military. We moved here when I was 14. Before that, we were in San Diego."

Once he opens the wallet, it's a struggle to get the ID out—frozen to the slot. Strange how he ignores the uneven wad of $100 bills staring him in the face.

"I imagine Chase Clydesdale III will be wanting this," Cy says, snapping the wallet shut. "And since we're on our way to Campus Police— call him lucky!"

It's what this broker-than-a-joke musician *doesn't* suggest—skimming a few bills off the top—that dazzles me.

I've had half a dozen exes. There was the guy who tried to skip out on the restaurant tab as soon as the wait staff changed (I had to go back), and the guy who crashed his car to get out of the payments.

From Campus Center Way to the police station, an ever-so-small spark of trust begins to grow.

When a flash of pink light bounces off the clouds, I take it as a sign. How could I not notice the stunning cornflower blue of his eyes?

But all I care about is the way he's holding on to the wallet—the way he's picking up the pace.

Slow down, I start to say.

But before the words leave my mouth, a single snowflake—and then another—lands on my cheek. It makes me want to laugh out loud.

Our instructor wasn't so over-the-top with his warnings after all.

"Get chains on those tires," he'd said. "And bring a parka next time. We're not in Florida."

Mr. Taylor might've been right about the snow—but wrong about its effects. No mittens, no hat, and I'm still not cold.

Looking into Cy's eyes, all I feel is warmth.

I don't realize it then, but something is shifting. The snowflakes, his smile, the quiet way things seem to settle—for now, it's enough.

CHAPTER 31

The Lie

Yasmina – Pacific Grove, California – 1995

For week one of Bijan's retirement, he makes a point of visiting the beach daily. When he gets home, he throws the door open, bounds into the house, flips off his thongs, and lets go of Cathy's leash. She races inside, tracking sand all over the entryway. This goes unnoticed by Bijan. In his arms is a collection of sand dollars, conch shells, sticks, and pieces of twine. When he reaches the table, he tosses everything but one of the shells into a bowl.

This is a far cry from the man—the ESL teacher/engineer—I fell in love with and married in 1967. In the years since, Bijan built and sold one technology firm after another before finally deciding it was less stressful to stop being a CEO. Why he had to wait until we were both this age to retire is beyond me.

He holds a shell to his ear. "You can hear ocean sounds," he says. "Sixty-five years on this earth, and I'm just now finding this out?"

I try to be humorous, to match my enthusiasm to his.

"Do I need to hire a cleaner to follow you two around?"

Not only does my attempt fall flat, but Bijan senses it.

"You can relax around me, Yasmina," he says. "My days of micro-managing are over. Do what you want. Hire another cleaning lady. Hire three. I won't monitor your spending."

For some reason, this irritates me. If change were so easy, why didn't he do it sooner? It takes a snap of the fingers to trade a suit jacket and silk

Sartorio trousers for an old-school Caribbean-blue Adidas tracksuit with too many zippers, but a personality shift takes excavation. Beneath the polite, debonair, best-kind-of-husband facade is a hard-driving, take-no-prisoners Silicon Valley executive with a limited understanding of human suffering. It's been a long time since he worked with migrants in those ESL classes he once taught.

I can't deny retirement looks good on Bijan. The tension has drained from his jaw, and he looks lighter, happier than he did the day he got his golden handshake. Still, I wonder: is it safe to tell him about Nanette? Ever since what happened, I've been forbidden from speaking to her. He threatened divorce.

Bijan has always been careful with money, but in the 1980s, Nanette and Hugh talked us into joining them in a commercial real estate venture at Los Gatos' Forbes Mill. I encouraged it because, if successful, Nanette could finally have the beach house she always dreamed of. We invested no small amount—much more than Bijan had initially committed to. But the Joneses, who said they'd done their homework, hadn't. We were all scammed.

And then there's how Nikki was turning out. It was bad enough she was wild, but when her influence on teenage Adam began to outweigh ours, the decision was made. It hurt our marriage. Things were never the same after. Although he stayed strong, we never got beyond the superficial arrangement that suited us. We never evolved.

But now, as attachments from the past threaten to converge with those of the present, I decide I have to see Nanette. Hugh was clear. She could die. My plan is to apologize profusely for cutting her out of my life. Then I'll be done with it. Bijan won't have to know a thing.

The first lie is told with seamless ease. I can't believe I'm doing it. This isn't me.

"I'm going to San Jose Monday," I say. "Running errands. One of our properties needs to be ready for sale."

It's alarming—the lies I tell. All in the service of the greater good. I don't usually fear Bijan's temper, but the memory of him all those years ago, after he hung up with the attorney—his voice shook so hard I thought he might have a stroke.

"Talk to them again and I'll leave you!" he'd bellowed.

That's why the lies keep piling up. It's been over a dozen years. Bijan is the right age for heart attacks. My excuse for not using our regular driver is that he has to pick up his grandchildren from daycare at a set time.

"You know Silicon Valley traffic," I say.

I've always been scrupulous about the truth, and now I'm amazed at how much I'm getting away with. Bijan suspects nothing. I might be misleading him, but it's not betrayal. We've more than made up what we lost with other investments, and our son—one of the reasons for our rupture with the Joneses in the first place—is getting his PhD in Cinema and Media Studies from UCLA's prestigious film school.

Still, part of me worries that if Bijan learns of my defiance, he might end things. Someone else bought Forbes Mill, and a grand shopping center annex was built. Every time we pass the Church Street intersection, his bitterness is still palpable.

The morning I leave, I tiptoe downstairs and wander into the kitchen. I haven't even had time to wonder what Nanette's reaction will be when she sees me—or whether Abigail will kick me out. Hugh was friendly when he called. He's never been one to hold a grudge.

"Leukemia," he said. "They caught it late."

It's not supposed to be this light outside, not in April. It's too early for morning sounds, yet I hear the hum of appliances and snippets of birdsong coming in from outside.

I'm not alone with my thoughts for long. The swish of Bijan's tracksuit and the smell of sandalwood and soap alert me to his presence. This is the Bijan I love—the man of gold cufflinks. Only, like his jackets and suit pants, they were part of the great purge. They now sit in a box in the closet, ready to be gifted to Adam on the eve of his graduation.

I'm ready for my own purge, because in less than twelve hours—no matter how I'm received by the Jones family—a burden will be lifted. My forced estrangement from Nanette has imprisoned me. It's as if ever since then, I've been waiting to exhale. Today, no matter what happens, I'll be able to let go. For the part of me that's still superstitious—who knows? Maybe the prophecy of the oracle can once again be fulfilled, and Bijan and I can go somewhere.

It only takes a minute for reality to set in. Instead of placing the fig tree I bought for her in the car where it belongs, it's sitting in our galley kitchen, taking up space. Bijan has to maneuver around it to get to the fridge and back to the coffeemaker. When I see his eyes land on it, my stomach clenches. I wish the florist hadn't affixed a card to a little stake and pushed it into the soil. My heart stutters with a pang.

"Staging the Mountain View house," I say.

But I know better. No one includes a card with a plant unless it's a gift.

Bijan, recharged from yesterday's beach trip, gives me a whimsical look, like he's sorry to see me working. He assumes the card could be for anyone.

After pouring coffee into a thermos and setting it on the table, guilt creeps in.

Why must he be so trusting?

"You'd better get going, dearest," he says. "Or it'll be bumper-to-bumper the whole way back."

"Yes, yes," I reply. "The card is for the realtor."

Bijan is in a jokey mood.

"Totally unnecessary," he says. "And who made you add a florist to your motley crew of opportunists?"

"Let them earn a living," I answer.

Bijan can't blame me for allowing the mystics, tea leaf-reading fortune tellers, and woodland nymphs of my youth to become part of who I am. If I'd added Islam into the mix, it would've been an affront to Bijan. Thousands of years of persecution are not easily forgotten.

"She's a florist," I say, picking up the fig and balancing it on my knee.

"Who, no doubt, interprets dreams," he adds airily before kissing me on the cheek. "You have a hairstylist who reads palms and a masseuse who doubles as a psychic. They all have one thing in common: they see a fine woman with a golden heart and pounce. Now if you don't mind, I'm taking my coffee outside."

It barely registers, his leaving. *A fine woman with a golden heart.*

If what he says about me being naïve is true, isn't he also?

Once he's safely out on the patio, I tap my amulet twice for luck. It's my way of ensuring we'll be returned to each other safely. But when I touch the space above my clavicle, I'm reminded:

My Hamsa is gone.

CHAPTER 32

Bird Ave

Yasmina

The only thing I remember about the trip to San Jose is the end—when Emilio pulls his Mercedes in front of the Bird Avenue address and squeaks the parking brake into place. We're parked in front of a WWII-era house, standard-issue, the kind that used to be a dime a dozen before Silicon Valley happened. Never charming, they featured single-wide driveways on the left or right, a tin carport (because who needed a garage?), and a chain-link fence separating the front yard from the back. One by one, they've either been bulldozed or completely revamped. Yet this one still stands.

I survey the house with a cool eye. Abigail married a good man, but I'd hoped he could support her better. Part-time drummer in a band, part-time fix-it man. It's obvious they're renting—because in terms of curb appeal, the house scores a zero. A homeowner would've planted a flower bed, put down a welcome mat. Oil stains mark the driveway. Tire tracks engrave the mole-hilled lawn. And judging from the broken Venetian blind dangling from a cord in the window, the inside must be just as neglected.

This is the last place I expected the posh Nanette Jones to convalesce. Aside from the fact that she's in the care of her least favorite daughter (she put her faith in the wrong child and, as Adam says, doubled down on it), the Nanette I remember lived large.

At one time, she and Hugh were throwing cash around like Monopoly money, hosting catered backyard parties with 100+ guests and butlers serving champagne in Lalique glasses. Always designer labels. Jewels from

Tiffany. Even her daytime slippers said Dior. This was around the time Bijan began to suspect—without much evidence—that Hugh was involved in some kind of money-laundering scheme. All I knew was Hugh and Nanette were spending their "washed" cash faster than they could bring it in, and in strange ways. Nikki didn't get new clothes. Abi didn't get help with tuition. But every room had mirrored ceilings and a waterbed. All they needed were disco balls.

While Emilio repositions the car to align more closely with the curb, a lanky high school boy cuts in front of us. The near-collision jolts me further into the present. The boy—whose every movement is a synchronization of jutting elbows and knees—walks with his head down, perhaps trying to hide a blotchy, yet-to-be-defined face. What does the presence of this awkward boy mean?

A memory from the spring of 1984 returns. Adam is 15. I'm preparing fried donuts for his school's homecoming celebration, up to my elbows in dough, when the phone rings. I almost don't answer—voicemail is a technology I do not trust. Besides, Adam is late coming home. Maybe this is why.

I wipe my hands with a kitchen towel, pick up the receiver, and clutch it for dear life.

"Mrs. Tehranpour? It's Miss Lathrop. From Saratoga High," the voice says.

A million thoughts swirl. Nanette's daughter Nikki—born the year before we adopted Adam—is using our address for high school. Panic rises in my chest.

"Adam? Is he okay?"

"He's fine. The deal is, we caught him skipping class," Miss Lathrop says. "Worse—he and some other students went on a high-speed joyride. Santa Cruz Avenue. The driver nearly sideswiped several cars. He wasn't the instigator, so we're not pushing for expulsion. But you'll have to deal with the police. The Trans Am they were in was stolen."

She doesn't have to say it. The little she-devil. All I remember is shaking. With Miss Lathrop's voice echoing in my ears, any reply I might've had was a jumble.

"Your son's a nice boy," she said. "But he's veered off the path. I'm not supposed to mention names, but if I were you, I'd steer him away from the circle of kids he's in—especially Nikki Jones. You know she's trying to pin it on him."

I burned the last batch of donuts. I slammed the pan. I cried. I paced.

When Adam came home, I was ready to let him have it—but Bijan had already done so. Adam's eyes were rimmed with red. He was shaking.

"I tried to open the door, to hurl myself out of the car," he said. "But me dying would only hurt you."

"Isn't that a little dramatic?" I said. "No one's caught you—yet."

"I was scared. Nikki was bragging about a suitcase full of money. Said it was from real estate, but it wasn't. Her parents wouldn't miss it. They all had fake IDs. They were heading to LA. They needed me for protection."

I wanted to laugh. Protection? A 15-year-old girl that sophisticated? Because the car belonged to a friend's parent, no one pressed charges. The suitcase never appeared. Nikki was only ticketed for underage driving.

We yanked Adam out of school and enrolled him at St. Andrew's Episcopal. Best thing we ever did. He was devastated.

"Change your mind," he pleaded. "Please."

"It's this or boarding school," I said. "We didn't move from Almaden Valley to Saratoga so you could be someone's lapdog."

"I finally had friends," he whispered.

"Some friends. Miss Lathrop told me Nikki blamed you. A lie, of course. No excuse for being in the wrong place at the wrong time."

He almost whined.

"When school finds out Nikki's using our address," he cried, "they'll kick her out, meaning I can stay. I think Dad'll support me on this."

"Your father is with me one hundred percent. We don't know American schools. It's a wake-up call. He mentioned sending you away. His mother dropped him at a Parisian boarding school and forgot him. Can you imagine?"

By the time we returned to the car, he was inconsolable. I didn't care.

I took his advice. I called the admissions office and reported Nikki. The final step was cutting the Joneses off. Everyone except Abigail. I would've fought Bijan—Hugh and Nanette were Forbes Mill victims too—but Nikki's influence over Adam ignited something fierce in me.

Even with Adam safe at his new school, even though I'd never have to run into Nanette in the parking circle again, I was done. Maybe they would've expelled Nikki. Maybe I'd been too harsh. Had I stayed around, maybe I could've helped Nanette. Maybe I could've steered Nikki in the right direction? A small private school with a dormitory would've done her a world of good. We could've afforded it. Nanette and I could've stayed at arm's length. I don't know how to explain it, but once my mother's instinct kicked in, all that mattered was Adam.

Emilio's cough brings me back. He offers to help me out of the car; I decline. I may be in my late seventies, but I'm not infirm. Still, I clutch the armrest instead of reaching for the door. I thought time would numb the pain. But it hasn't. A jab of sadness. A pang of regret. I hope she forgives me.

Instead of my amulet—Bijan took it to be reset—I grasp the bracelet he gave me for my last birthday. It's set with seven diamonds for each decade of my life, and ten rubies for the High Atlas butterflies I'm always talking about. I treasure it.

One look in the mirror, and Emilio knows.

"You'll have that charm back around your neck soon enough," he says.

"I don't know why I still believe in this nonsense," I murmur, digging for a Kleenex. "Mezuzahs everywhere—even inside the pool house. I kiss it each time I pass. Started when I was a servant in a Jewish household."

"Mr. Tehranpour told me," Emilio chuckles. "Said he banged his thumb nailing it in. 'Not even my wife's religion,' he said."

"I'm not ready to see her. So many years. I can wait."

My eyes rest on the flowering fig tree between my feet. In the kitchen, it took up too much space, but here—with its two V-shaped branches and sparse leaves—it looks delicate, intentional. My florist, Haja, selected it for this moment.

"It will grow into a mighty tree," she said. "Your husband may think you superstitious, but to dream of a fig leaf symbolizes renewal and forgiveness."

Thinking of Haja makes me smile. Like Amira, she's usually right.

What would Bijan think if he saw me handing the plant to Nanette? There are delivery services. A letter. But Haja insisted: "Atonement is never easy."

Sunglasses back on, I tuck a silver-gray strand behind my ear. My plan was to drop the plant and leave. I know it's wrong, but without my amulet, who knows? Maybe cancer will visit me next.

Inside my purse is a magnetic mezuzah. I'd procured it from a store selling Judaica, to give it to Abigail as a peace offering, to protect her house. Only, I'm not sure I can let it go.

Fate must be on my side. I may get to hold on to the mezuzah a little longer because it looks like no one's home. There's a car on the other side of the chain-link fence, but it's been parked there a while. Large white splotches cover its roof and windshield.

"Ready?" Emilio says with only a hint of irritation in his voice.

I step out of the car and bend down to grab the plant, careful not to pull it by its roots as I inch it out of the car. When the pot hits the floorboards, I need to use my foot to stop it from tipping over.

"Can I help?"

"Got it," I say, though my knees will exact a price. My back twinges. I should balance it on my thigh, but that would slow me to a crawl.

Emilio gives me a look, but he knows not to push.

At the porch, I realize someone's home. Through the screen door, I see a neat living room. Abigail must be a good homemaker. It's not yet three, and dinner's already on. The slow-cooked scent of comfort fills the air. I set the plant down with a hurried clunk and rub my shoulder. Then, I make a beeline for the car.

Just as my hand reaches the door, the screen door opens.

"Yasmina?" a familiar voice calls.

My heart drops. I press my fingers to my breastbone.

"Yes," I say, hesitant.

Abigail looks the same. The last time we spoke, I told her to get counseling. There were a few moments after—when she and Cy were dating—but we drifted.

Same Daisy Duke overalls. Same "Boycott Grapes" T-shirt (probably her dozenth). Same open-toed sandals with socks. Only now, her prematurely graying hair is tied up in a Rosie-the-Riveter bandana.

The toddler she's holding; Hugh told me about him.

I didn't think she'd be home. I assumed Abigail would pawn Baby off the moment he dropped out of her womb. Look who her role models were! That she's caring for a critically ill mother is another surprise. Although when she was a child, she took pretty good care of her dolls. I imagine her putting a cold compress on Nanette's head, saying, "There, there."

I can't help but imagine Nanette opening her eyes, wishing it was Nikki who was there instead. Even though I know it's not true. I'm charmed by the way Abigail looks at her boy, how he giggles.

But now's not the time to get sentimental. My plan—drop and dash—is foiled. Who still uses a screen door for ventilation?

"Isn't this a surprise!" Abigail says. "Let me put Uly in his playpen."

One second, she's behind the screen; the next, she's close enough to breathe on my neck. She kisses both cheeks. I was inches from escape, but I underestimated how fast a 36-year-old can move.

"I hope I'm not imposing," I say.

"Of course not. I know why you're here," she says wryly. "Move the car out of the sun. I'll hang out here till you come back."

I lean against the door. "I'm sorry—about your mom. The fig is for her. She used to eat them by the handful."

"She can't take care of it," Abigail says. "But thanks for the kind gesture."

"How's your mother? How's everyone? Your boy—he's adorable."

She narrows her eyes and lets out a humph. A nerve hit. But her face softens.

"Mom's fighting hard," she says. "The rest—I'll catch you up on later."

"I'd stay for a hello," I say. "But the doctor says stay at sea level. Even the slightest elevation sends my blood pressure through the roof."

My voice trembles. I have my share of health issues, but high blood pressure isn't one. I feel my stomach clench. If I keep lying, who will I become? I can tell Abigail doesn't believe me.

"So that's why you moved to Pacific Grove," she says. Then, without explanation, she breaks into a smile. "C'mon in. You've already risked life and limb. I imagine you'll need a rest. Also, you sound parched."

"For a minute," I say, relieved it's Abigail I'm dealing with and not Madame Moab or one of Nanette's brothers.

"Mom will be thrilled to see you," she says. "Stay. She never sleeps for long."

I need to sit down. I need air. When my hand flies to my chest, Abigail notices.

"I thought you never went without your evil eye charm," she says. "Not that you need it. Dad tells me you've made a bundle in real estate."

"It's at the jeweler's," I say, my voice a tremor. "But honestly, the years in America were what brought me luck."

"I can see. Designer labels, fancy car, your own driver."

I twist the knots of my bracelet between my fingers.

"It's not about money," I say. "I don't shop for myself. Bijan does. The car doesn't even belong to me. Can we change the subject?"

"I don't mean to be abrupt," she says. "But things haven't been exactly lucky for us. I thought I'd escaped, with Cy being my one and only. But halfway through my pregnancy, he went ahead and lost his ever-loving mind. What should've been a joyous time was full of tears. In and out of hospitals. It would've been fine, but once there was a child involved, it wasn't safe."

"I'm sorry."

"No need to be. Ever since we separated, if anyone else is happy, it's like I can't handle it."

"Your dad didn't. I don't understand. Cy seemed so salt-of-the-earth. I always admired how authentic you two were."

"We were too real," she laughs. "Insanity crept up on him slowly. He was afraid to tell anyone. Not even me. Last time he was admitted, he thought another patient was his mother. Now, with what's going on with Mom, it's a good thing we saved our pennies. Good thing I got my school psychologist credential."

When she's finished, she looks at me like everything's okay. Whether or not it's true, I don't know. She's like her uncles—too proud to accept help.

"You know what? I get blamed," she adds. "If I'd made a better choice in picking a husband,

if I'd been a better wife. People with cancer get sympathy. You should see all the meals we get now with Mom. No one cares quite the same way with mental illness. You're here to see Mom, not to hear my sob story."

"I'm here for all of it. But about your mom—has it spread? Your dad didn't say much."

"She'd been losing weight, but we thought it was the eating disorder," Abi says. "Three months ago, she joined a UC Berkeley focus group about women in early menopause. A hundred dollars to each participant, plus free food for a month. She was the perfect candidate—thin, young-looking. When they did the bloodwork, they found it. Since Nikki's away again, me and Dad are left to handle things."

One thing that hasn't changed: Abigail still overshares. All this and we're still in the driveway. She also doesn't know how to stay mad. If it were the other way around, I'd be silent.

"What's the prognosis?" I ask.

"Bone marrow transplants don't usually take after 50, so the doctors don't give her good odds. As usual, Mom thinks this doesn't apply to her. She's been weak, but the steroids give her fake energy. She didn't used to be able to pick Uly up."

I would never say it, but this family reminds me of Brahim's. One self-inflicted tragedy after another, and now the devil has visited itself upon them. With the sweetest smile I can muster, even though I know the answer can't be good, I ask about Madame Moab. She must be in her late eighties now. How much must she suffer?

"Grandma's beside herself," Abigail answers, as if reading my mind. "Which I would have empathy for—if she weren't such a pain in the neck."

"Abigail. Don't be disrespectful. She grew up a certain way. Besides, you wouldn't want your grandchildren remembering you at your worst."

"You should've seen her. Going through all my uncles trying to find a bone marrow match, beginning with the Golden Child, moving on to the Lost Boys, before finally getting to Henri. He's flying in from Tel Aviv on Tuesday, staying just long enough for the nurses to harvest his bone marrow and put a Band-Aid on his arm. Believe me, he'll be on the first flight out."

Knowing it was Henri makes the world seem just. The child they treated the worst is the one who comes to the rescue.

"I'd like to see her," I say.

"You know Grandma. She's hurt. She's old. And with what's going on, she'll need someone to blame. I'm afraid it'll be you."

I take a step back. Abigail's cheekier than I remember—not that I don't deserve it.

"I wanted to reconnect. But it seemed too late. Of all people, you should know how difficult it is."

Abigail's eyes soften, and her lips turn upward. "Grandma went home yesterday," she says. "I couldn't take her anymore. She wanted to move Mom to Uncle Jean's house because of the dog. I told her, 'Not as long as I'm here, you won't.' That started WWIII."

I flinch. Years, it took me to get used to having Cathy in the house. It's the Moroccan way. Dogs go outside.

I want to tell Abigail to give her grandmother some space. Who wants two children and ends up with seven? She is a woman to sympathize with. But it's no use. Abigail uses all her education, her fancy words, like a shield. But certain aspects of her remind me of her father. The way she tilts her chin and gives me this look—it's as if she's been possessed by the souls of a thousand Irish matriarchs, none of them happy.

"I should go," I say.

"I'm waking her for her medication anyway," she says slyly. "And seriously, don't you want to meet my son?"

She's letting me off easy. "Of course I do," I say, grateful. "But your mother ... Another time. Let me give you my number."

I fish through my oversized Louis Vuitton for a pen. That my bag is so jam-packed, that I'm so flustered, doesn't help. An envelope spills out onto the porch.

"Looks official," she says.

As I bend to pick it up, my knees lock. It takes all I have to get back up.

"Immigration papers," I say. "I'm bringing someone over—a friend of mine, Amira."

"That's nice," Abigail says. "I'll be sure to tell Mom. She'll see it as some sort of kumbaya reunion."

"Abigail, I want to. I'm trying."

"I know," she says. "After what I went through with Cy ... everything feels like abandonment."

I stifle a groan. By giving Nanette a tree she can't care for and a card I barely thought about, I've reinserted myself into their messy lives. Nanette has her leukemia, Nikki has a worse problem, and Hugh's a slave to his drugs. And Abigail and Cy? I thought she, of all people ...

"Okay. I'll come in," I say. "First, I need to tell Emilio to move the car to a shady spot."

My plan is to take a couple sips of whatever drink she offers, and go ga-ga over the baby—which won't be hard. But if Nanette wakes, I don't want to see her, even if I have to fake a coughing fit.

The next thing I know, I'm sitting on an overstuffed leather couch that squeaks when I move.

Abigail, holding Uly's legs in the crook of her elbow, brings me tea. The intent is there, but the presentation—in a Tupperware cup on a TV tray—couldn't be further from Moroccan if she tried.

"Sorry about the place," she says. "I take care of the inside. I can't afford a man for the outside. So I had to let the yard go."

I'm speechless. When Cy was her boyfriend, he planted gardens and helped them grow. We all admired him. Now, everything looks shabby.

"I remember how overwhelming it was with a little one," I say, trying not to focus on the brown shag carpet.

When she places a bowl of sugar packets on the tray, Uly's foot grazes my elbow. He's at the cherub stage. Alabaster white like Hugh, with Nanette's black hair. The eyes he gets from his father. He hasn't lost the heavenly smell all babies have—like cream.

"It's nice to see you looking so well, Mrs. Tehranpour—I mean, Yasmina. Mom wanted me to call you Auntie. I was just starting to."

My stomach clenches. We've missed so much. I want to reach out and touch her cheek.

"I can't believe it. Seeing you with a baby. So devoted."

Abigail exhales. "I get it," she says. "Mom's hard. I have every reason in the world to go no-contact. But now she's sick … I'm glad I didn't."

I rub the corners of the seat cushion.

"I thought about calling her when Adam left for USC. I heard your parents were in a temporary separation. I heard all the money dried up. No more grand wedding-worthy parties at Park Wilford. I couldn't. The maid isn't supposed to be the success."

"She isn't the same."

"I should've tried harder."

"It wouldn't have worked. You have what she wanted. A stable husband. A beach house."

"I didn't mean to, Abigail," I say, dabbing my forehead. "It was like watching a car crash in slow motion, seeing her life go to pieces. I gave up."

One cough turns to two, then three. My blood pressure rises. Funny how a lie becomes the truth. Fishing through my purse for a lozenge, I spot the mezuzah.

Abigail tilts her head and rubs her elbows. "Are you all right?" she asks.

I unwrap a lozenge and pop it in. "I've been warm all day," I say. "At first, I thought it was the heat, but now I'm coughing. I'm sure it's nothing. But with Nanette's immune system …"

"A rare summer cold," Abigail says. "But I get it. You're missing out. Before the leukemia, Mom got therapy. One time, we drove to San Juan Capistrano. We had lunch. We watched the birds fly in. She even held Uly— at arm's length, like he was a bomb—but at least she did."

I hold my hand to my neck and let out a long breath. "I always knew it wouldn't take much for your mom. A tweak here and there. She had to get over some things. That's why I stuck with her."

We talk more—chit chat, mostly. An alarm goes off. Before I leave, I ask one last question.

"You said your sister was busy. With what?"

I regret it instantly. But Abigail doesn't flinch. Repositioning Uly on her hip, she says what I already know.

"Prison. Five years this time."

"I'm sorry."

"Same old, same old," Abigail says. "Everything's going to be better now that you're reconnecting with Mom. Her remaining friends are all the same type. They've dealt with adultery, betrayal, their kids' sexuality, illnesses. Yet they still think they can throw money at a problem and poof— it disappears. They don't know how to handle this."

I press a fist to my lips. She's pushing me to be my best self.

"When my cough is gone, I'll return," I say. "When she's healthy enough."

Before departing, I give Abigail the mezuzah. "It's a magnet," I say. "So you don't have to worry about putting a hole in the wall."

"It's kinda *woo*," she says, giving me a tired look. "But thanks. Mom's grown to appreciate that kind of stuff."

As soon as the screen door closes, I remember Nanette's last frantic voicemail.

"Call me," she'd said. "Someone—Nikki, I think—took over Maman's identity. All her credit cards are maxed out. People won't stop calling."

My heart went out to Madame Moab, but it didn't stop me from cutting Nanette off. It wasn't just Bijan's philosophy—I'd had enough.

"No one named Moab or Jones has ever taken accountability," Bijan said. "You have to let them go."

Now I see—it was about trust. Bijan couldn't trust. As smart as he was, he couldn't fall for one more scam. And neither of us could trust Adam to do the right thing. As the biological child of Bijan's not-too-bright niece and her impulsive, thrill-seeking boyfriend, his DNA was suspect. But after two miscarriages and no other options, we welcomed him with open arms.

"We have to be careful with him," Bijan said. "It's like his gun came loaded—with the sins of his birth parents. We don't need anything pulling the trigger."

Even now, inside the safety of the Mercedes, the memory brings tears. If only we'd had more faith in our family. If only Bijan hadn't been so judgmental. I plunge my hand into my purse for a Kleenex.

People are so much more than their biology. Bijan and I are Adam's true parents.

As Emilio shifts into drive and turns on easy-listening KARA AM, my eyes fill. As we round the corner at the end of the street, it hits me.

Maybe I don't need to obsess about the evil eye. Sometimes, tragedy happens.

Sometimes you have to grieve.

On the floor lies a branch with a blossom still attached. I pick the flower and hold it to my nose.

"Go back," I say to Emilio. "I want to be there when Nanette wakes."

CHAPTER 33

The Turning

Yasmina

Usually, I admire Emilio's careful driving—the way he holds his hands at 9 o'clock and 3 o'clock on the steering wheel, the way he always allows ample space between him and the next vehicle. But with Highway 280 slick from the first rain of the season, and the latest influx of Silicon Valley transplants unable to keep from cutting us off, I don't know. What happened with Nanette has left me raw. The first time Emilio pumps the brakes too hard and the car skids sideways, I burst into tears.

Emilio tries to help, but there's nothing he can do.

It made me reel to see Nanette this way. Her cheeks, when I kissed them, were soft and moist—she is, after all, only fifty-four. Her timid smile was the same one she had as a child.

"I've finally learned how to live," she'd said. "Now all I want is a chance to prove it."

When the car sputters, I ask Emilio if we need to stop for gas.

"We don't," he says. "Should be a straight shot once we pass Highway 9. The road is dry, and if we leave now, there'll only be a few cars on the road."

I can't stop thinking about Nanette. When she learned I was sponsoring Amira, she was beyond thrilled. It was as if those last twelve years had never happened. She said I was performing a mitzvah. So many years lost—and for what? So I could be a peacekeeper? So I could swallow my feelings?

It came at a price.

With the sun setting over Lexington Reservoir, I reach into my purse, remove the envelope with Amira's immigration papers, and spread them across my lap. My appointment with the US Office of Immigration is already on the calendar. Bijan is helping me prepare.

Thirty-two years after Nanette helped me come to America, it'll be me doing the sponsoring.

Amira Abdallah, age 67, the application says.

Marital status: Widowed – Occupation: Retired

Long after the rain has stopped, when the highway widens at its Scotts Valley plateau, Emilio asks me—belatedly—if I'm okay.

Of course I am.

Soon we'll be at the intersection of 17 and Ocean Avenue, not far from where Bijan took me on our first date. Stephen had just set my hair. I was worried the wind would ruin it. But soon enough, I became lost in the wonder of it all. I'd never seen a carnival, never put a nickel into a 1910-era Nickelodeon, never been on the Tilt-A-Whirl or a roller coaster—this one was made out of wood—never taken a ride into the Tunnel of Love.

I remember how excited Bijan was to show it to me.

I remove my sunglasses and dab my eyes with a tissue. Emilio asks again, "Are you all right?"

"Too many emotions, Emilio," I say. "Sorrow, guilt, worry, gratitude. All in one big ball."

"Life is one big ole ride," he says. "Like the Big Dipper at the end of the boardwalk. But man, aren't we lucky to be alive? Here. Now."

When I close my eyes, it isn't the smooth, shiny man in the suit jacket and gold cufflinks I see—it's raggedy, self-assured Brahim.

What would he have thought of this Santa Cruz? A place where teenagers go to have fun. He'd never had a chance to ride in bumper cars, run into the ocean, or even eat saltwater taffy, cotton candy, and corn dogs.

For years, I haven't been able to think of Brahim without blaming myself or feeling bitter. He was a dumb kid.

As I fold my hands in prayer, my eyes glisten with tears.

God bless Brahim. God bless everyone—his parents, my parents, Idir, Fatima, and all of the Moabs.

"My best friend from childhood, Amira, is joining us in America," I say. "She and her daughter. Can you think of anything more wonderful?"

CHAPTER 34

Amira

Yasmina

Amira is blind now, confined to a world of light and shadow, and her daughter Anusha—who is coming with her and who is a joy to her family—is what we used to call simple, from being born with the umbilical cord wrapped tightly around her neck. Anusha speaks very few words, but she understands more. She can't get around well. But who knows?

"Maybe with physical therapy," Nanette says from her hospital bed.

She's already had her transplant, but even in her weakened state, she urges me on.

"I'm dying," she says. "I've accepted it. Life's about love. Everything else is secondary. You deserve all the credit. Amira would die soon without you."

I do not tell Nanette how untrue this is. It was Amira's ten-year-old granddaughter, Farrah, who placed the collect call informing me of Amira's dire circumstances. Blinded by a parasite of the eye, she had been reduced to a sorrowful state. Amira's daughter-in-law—a good-for-nothing if I've ever seen one—had started a character assassination campaign. Anusha, she could make money on. She planned to put her in the medina. Tourists would donate like crazy. Amira, she could throw away.

Amira's son is blind as well, but after he allowed his wife to make his mother homeless, I have no sympathy. By day, Amira strings beads into necklaces to sell in the medina. At night, she sleeps in an alleyway on a cardboard box.

When the day finally comes for Amira to arrive, our reunion is joyous. She's crying. I'm crying. It doesn't occur to me until after she is here how much I've taken on. She's become a zealot. I figured that, being a Shilha, she could survive anything. She's not the same old Amira, but it isn't a problem for me. However, every time Bijan sees her kneeling in prayer, he's reminded of how fanatics persecuted his religious minority family.

"There's a mosque in Monterey," he says. "There she can pray to her heart's content. For that, and a lot of other things, she'll need a seeing-eye dog."

Even though it's a workable solution, the Quran prohibits it.

But Bijan is insistent. "They both need to become independent," he says. "It's not fair to anyone."

For a while, nothing sways Amira. Even our loyal, smart, well-behaved Cathy—who can't stand getting her paws dirty—isn't clean enough. But after Cathy gives birth to a litter of puppies, the result of an encounter with a Pomeranian (which will never happen again, now that she's spayed), something magical happens. Once Anusha meets feisty, eight-week-old, untrainable Bruno, it's love at first sight.

"Give me him," she says in Arabic.

Amira relenting is the easy part. It takes more effort to get approval from the local Imam. The dog must be specially trained or trainable, which means no Bruno. The dog cannot go any further than where the shoes are kept.

There's no shortage of people willing to lead Amira and Anusha to the inner chamber to worship, but if I'm not around, they'll have to arrange for someone to stay with the animal. After we make a couple of large donations, things speed along.

The first is for a mudroom at the mosque. The second is to Guide Dogs for the Blind, Inc., so Amira—who is far from the ideal candidate—can cut to the front of the line.

When Amira returns from her week of training with her new dog in San Rafael, she's back to her old self. She names the dog *Bashiga*—the Arabic word for *joy*. With Bashiga around, life gets easier.

I have time to get my nails done and my hair styled. I can get a facial. I can shop. As Adam says, a lot of my life has become "outsourced."

Amira is surprised at the change in me.

"It took me years to realize I didn't have to be burdened with work," I tell her. "Fifteen years ago, when we still had all the apartment complexes, I was the one doing all the cleaning. I'd be on my hands and knees until it was too hard to get up, and my hands were raw from all the scrubbing."

"You work and then you die," Amira says. "Life is hard."

"Adam was the one who told me to stop," I say. "I used to take him to the apartment complexes we owned. He grew tired of learning his multiplication tables and doing his homework in empty rooms that smelled like ammonia."

"I don't understand," Amira says.

"Adam explained it to me," I say. "He said a team of eight can do the job eight times faster, freeing us up to rent the apartment out eight times faster as well. In the time it took for me to work, I lost money. It took some getting used to, but I realized my labor was only worth so much."

"Work is always honorable. Even when I was stringing beads together."

"That's what they want us to believe. When we were poor, we were like cogs in a wheel."

"What do you mean?" she asks.

"You see how easy it was for you to be thrown away once no one thought you were useful anymore. Used up and spit out. That's one thing I've made sure of, Amira—neither one of us is ever going to have to live hand to mouth again."

CHAPTER 35

No Thanks

Abigail – November 2010

My decision to spend the holiday with Nikki and her family is ill-advised. I know it, and so does everyone else. Yasmina—who hasn't butted into my life since she insisted I go to counseling—tells me not to put myself through it. She tells me anything can happen. I tell her I want to see the kids. Even Bijan has offered Thanksgiving at their house. I tell her I know Nikki's behavior is beyond the pale, but Dad wants me to take him, and Uly's dying for a vacation.

"I'm a big girl," I say. "I know what I'm getting into."

As a mother, I haven't been neglectful, but I can't say I qualify for mother-of-the-year either. Take the drive down, for example. Who lets an emotionally fragile fifteen-year-old—who's barely had his permit long enough for the ink to dry—drive six and half hours? Who lets their kid navigate freeway driving on Highway 5 in a tin-can of a car with a manual transmission and a clutch on its last leg? So far, no harm, no foul.

All the way through Bakersfield, with his hands at 12 o'clock and 4 o'clock, Uly drives like a champ. I think it comforts him, honestly, given all we've been through lately. That's why I take it easy on him. I don't remind him about which cars to watch for or where the speed traps are. And rather than argue about why Gwen Stefani is better than 50 Cent, I let him have the radio.

When we stop for fuel, Uly spots a Mexican restaurant and asks for a pick-me-up. I don't say no.

I take a twenty from my wallet and place it on the dash.

"Two tacos and no more," I say. "Aunt Nikki'll be insulted if you don't eat."

By the time I click the nozzle into my gas tank, Uly's already crossed the street.

Fifteen years old and already taller than his father, Uly favors bowl haircuts, oversized T-shirts, and pants that hang so loose they end up inches above his knees. Baseball caps, he wears backward.

The old me would've harped on him. The old me wouldn't have let him call me "Dude" or "Bruh," even if it slipped out. I would've told him to pull up his pants. But after a disastrous weekend with his father ended in a 9-1-1 call, I've changed my attitude.

Maybe I went through a lot as a kid, but I never had to sit in an ambulance, listening to my father sputter paranoid word salads about government-implanted microchips.

"Everyone's in cahoots," he'd said.

The heater's been on full blast; soon, I'm roasting. I roll the window down and plug my Razr into the cigarette lighter. That's when a 408 number I don't recognize flashes across the screen, and I know—it's him.

"Collect call from Langley-Porter," a voice says.

A wave of relief. Cy's still in the hospital.

"Yes, yes," I say. Then Cy's voice:

"Can I talk to my son?"

Those six words are a barometer. When he acts like I wasn't the one who gave birth, the conversation won't go well. But I learned long ago—roll with whatever. He'll swing back around.

"Our son's busy," I say. I don't mean to be curt. What I really am is concerned. "We're getting food."

"I can wait," he says.

His voice sounds sad. Desperate, even.

"They taking care of you, Cy?"

"Good enough, I guess," he says. "For the looney bin. Anyhoo, I want Uly to know I'm back to my old self."

"I'm not sure he's ready to talk. After what happened, he needs time. Anyway, I'll tell him."

"I want to talk to him myself."

"That might take a while. Tacos Jimenez must be making their tortillas from scratch—he still hasn't come out yet."

Cy sounds better than he did a week ago, but it doesn't take much for him to go off; just one misplaced word. He's so red-hot I can almost feel the flames through the phone.

"Tacos Jimenez?" he bellows. "What the *hell?* Don't tell me you're in Lebec! I told you I didn't want him visiting Nikki!"

My stomach knots.

"Dad's in Frazier Park, Cy. Sober again, lonely, and wanting family. Some chick's bleeding him dry. What was I supposed to do?"

"I get sick and this friggin' happens!" he shouts. "Why isn't she in prison? Revolving frickin' door. And you, putting your dad first? Not in a million years would I have allowed this. Not my son."

"You know how hard it's been. Ever since that weekend, Uly's been withdrawn. He needs escapism. I figure a little of Aunt Nikki's LaLa Land lunacy might be what the doctor ordered."

"Let's see," Cy says. "Petty theft, grand theft, mail theft, identity theft, wire fraud. Lunacy is right. At least I have integrity. I am not criminally insane. She gets off on screwing people and never pays a dime of rent. Where is she—Beverly Hills? No one's immune, as I recall. Even family."

My shoulders slump in shame. I want to project confidence, but the voice that comes out is fragile and thin.

"I know the other shoe's about to drop, Cy. But she's family."

"Like your grandma? Like your mother?" he bellows. His voice is so intense it's scary. "By eating a morsel of her food, you've made yourself guilty by association. The slime won't wash off. I can't do anything from here, but if I could—man."

"You'd do what?"

"For Chrissake, Abi. Do what normal families do when they want to escape. Go to goddamn Disneyland."

"You're not exactly working, Cy."

"Money's on its way," he says, his voice softening. "A worker here helped me apply for disability. Any day now, you'll be getting a check. Six hundred isn't much, but it's enough to drop your dad at Nikki's and leave. On the way back, take Uly to a show. Six Flags. Even that would be better."

The part of me still angry at Cy for getting sick wants to engage, but he's suffering. And if we're both circling the drain, where does that leave Uly?

I'm about to be kind when I spot Uly. In his hand is a large bag and a can of Pepsi.

"Uly's coming. We barely have two dimes to rub together, and he gets himself a soda."

"Tell him."

"Later. Let Uly have one carefree day, okay? He's looking forward to seeing his cousins. We'll call after dinner."

There's an eerie hiss on the line. My heart aches. I never got to say how sorry I am. I would call back, but he's in the right place. Besides, we have a son to look after—one who's now tapping on the window, waiting for me to unlock the door.

"That was hella good," Uly says as he slides behind the wheel. "Now all I wanna do is dip my toes into Aunt Nikki's swimming pool. Ya think she'll let me drive one of her cars?"

"You know what?" I say. "How about using the Cozy 9 as our home base? It has a pool and a jacuzzi. We could hang out with Aunt Nikki and the kids until dinner. They can visit us there."

"No way," Uly says. "I'm not a Kardashian. No *Lifestyles of the Rich and Famous*. But Mom—those beds are like boards. Their breakfast buffet is cold cereal and powdered eggs. They don't even heat their pool."

I spare him an answer because I created this. Years ago, when Cy was admitted to a Palo Alto hospital for long-term treatment, I took a job nearby. I thought it would be better for Uly to be close to his father. Even then, it was one of the most expensive places to live in the US. But I yearned for a fresh start—a place where no one knew my story. A safe place for Uly.

Now, the decision gnaws at me. He doesn't need to dumpster dive, but is a little grit too much to ask for?

Neither of us minds the silence. For a long stretch, all the way to the Grapevine, that's how it is. I only speak to warn him about the dense fog ahead. But the concentration on his face, the way he leans forward, the way his hands grip the wheel—he knows what he's doing.

"Bruh, I don't know," Uly says. "Like pea soup. Isn't that what they say?"

"Don't drive any faster than you can see."

Ironic, me giving him this advice. Cy's right. I'm a terrible mom. I should've traded in this putt-putt of a car a year ago. As my hands press into the dash, I worry it won't make it up the hill. It's not until we're five minutes from where Dad's staying that we're finally in the clear.

"It might seem like we're having a blast in LA," I say. "But not everything is as it seems. Your aunt's living large for a woman who had her ankle bracelet taken off six months ago. As far as I'm concerned, anything of value gets locked in the car."

"What? Really?"

"Your wallet, those Nikes you saved up for. Anything pawnable."

Uly gives me a look like both his parents have lost their minds.

"A woman living in a mansion isn't gonna care about worn-out Nikes," he says. "That shit's petty, Mom. Small time."

"Small time, big time, any time. Doesn't matter. It's the thrill."

There isn't much else to say, which is fortunate, because not a minute later, we're at the trailer of Dad's grifting on-again, off-again girlfriend.

My heart breaks seeing him—morose, sitting outside on his suitcase, walker and cane spread out beside him on the Astroturf. His face looks less sunken in, and he's dressed pretty sharp. I figured with him sober, he and Misty-Jane would be doing better.

The truth is, he's not exactly sugar daddy material—and when she can do better, she does. I've already called Adult Protective Services. They're not doing anything.

"Got my six-month medallion from AA," Dad says, pointing to the pin on his lapel.

I say something about being proud. Uly echoes me. We've been through this too many times to be enthusiastic. But who knows—this could be it.

"I wish your mom were here," Dad says. "Me sober, both our girls thriving, all our grandchildren under one roof."

"You can't be serious," I laugh. "Between Nikki's rap sheet and my checkbook balance, neither one of us is doing great."

"All the ladies at the park are after me," he says, clicking his seatbelt. "But Misty-Jane's the only one for me."

Dad might need a cane to hoist himself into the back seat, but he's still a silver fox.

By the time he's in, he's exhausted. I wish I could say we banter like we used to, but between his heart condition and riveted-together back, he's slowed way down. Within a minute, he's out cold. When I glance back and see his head wedged between an inflatable pillow and the console, I think of my parents—and their pills.

Whatever cocktail he's on must be potent, because forty-five minutes later, when Uly stops in front of the access road to Nikki's house, he's still asleep. While we wait for one last car to pass, I crank the window and breathe in the ocean air. With each click of the turn signal, my apprehension builds.

According to Google Maps, the driveway to 42105 Pacific Coast Highway is an eighth of a mile long. It passes over a footbridge and winds to a parking circle on the far side of a mountain.

It doesn't hit me until I see it—Cy was right. Everything's one-way and steep. But instead of worrying about sports cars barreling down at 100 miles an hour, I'm worried about law enforcement. In my mind, helicopters are overhead. LAPD SWAT is kicking Nikki's door open.

But the only thing waiting at the top of the driveway is Nikki's 10,000-square-foot Malibu estate.

I give Uly a smile. We made it.

"Done!" he says, like he just pitched a no-hitter.

He should be proud. He's managed to wedge our Aveo into the only sliver of space in the parking circle. We could've gone behind the garage. All around us are Rolls-Royces, Lamborghinis, Bentleys, Bugattis—but Uly's bold that way. I'm the one who feels bad. All those arguments about extras.

"Air conditioning, automatic doors and windows cost money," I'd said.

Now, with Uly's dream car—a convertible Aston Martin—just inches away, maybe I could've spent a few thousand more.

Uly sets the brake and cranks his window open.

"Let's get some air. Grandpa, you up?" he asks.

I hear a faint "Yes" from the backseat, then a humph. Dad might be awake, but it takes a minute for him to orient himself.

"Look at these cars," he says. "I never gave a rat's ass what I drove. Every car I ever had was a beater. Drove them till they wouldn't drive no more. Then I'd get another one. All I cared about was getting from Point A to Point B."

He doesn't mean to, but I wish he'd stop. Uly's bougie enough. All this is making me frustrated.

"Can't you see?" I say. "None of this belongs to her. Her job is to create experiences."

Uly has to know. He's not stupid. The only reason I'm keeping up the charade is for Dad.

"Forget your mom," Dad says to Uly. "As far as I'm concerned, your aunt's smashing it."

I catch Uly shooting me a look. Like, *Really, Grandpa?*

I get being in denial, but if Dad thinks Nikki's a success, then I have a bridge for sale with his name on it. This unexplained wealth—it can only add up to one thing.

I'm about ready to correct him. Then, with watery eyes and a slack-jawed expression, Dad gives me a look like I hung the moon.

"You're the one I'm proud of. I never could've done it. All those years of school," he says.

That's the thing I love about him—his undying faith in his girls, the way his brain goes into overdrive thinking of things to crow about. Impossible-to-please Uly couldn't be more different.

At this very moment, what's uniting us is this house. I'm so busy locking my purse and jacket in the car, stowing the key at the bottom of my shoe, that I don't see it at first. But there it is—a sprawling marble-and-glass structure on a hill, not so much a house as a compound. Manicured grounds. Basketball and tennis courts. An Olympic-sized saltwater pool overlooking the Pacific. Even in daylight, the place gleams.

So we're standing there. To my left is Dad, craning his neck toward the sky with a beatific look on his face. If he's worshiping at the altar of Nikki, who can blame him? In between grifter girlfriends, he's spent the last five years in an ancient, rusted-out trailer in Morgan Hill with nothing but a fox, a coyote, and until recently, a bottle of Johnnie Walker for company.

As for Uly on my right—he's smiling. There's no way I'm selling him on the Cozy 9. Not even if I promise to stop at Anderson's Split Pea on the way home. Even I'm seduced. A small part of me wants to believe in Nikki. That some glorious redemption arc is about to play out. Who gives a shit about the house? The view leaves me breathless. This 360-degree panorama of trees, mountains, and ocean is beyond my wildest dreams.

But it makes it hard to relax. How many signatures did Nikki have to forge for this one? How many false lawsuits will she file to stay? How many people will she bankrupt? A tree isn't just a tree anymore—it's a potential SWAT stakeout. Will a helicopter land on the flat tile roof? Or will they choose the area behind the guest house?

Meanwhile, next to me, Uly and Dad are still oohing and aahing.

"Every house your sister's had since she left Frontera is nicer than the one before," Dad says. "She could host me for a month. In style. What you've done with your place is nice, Abi, but who wouldn't rather stay here?"

Last time you were at my "nice" house, I want to say, *you threw up so much it took a week and a whole lot of vinegar and detergent to get the smell out.* But as much as I want Dad to have a dose of the truth, I'm afraid even clearing my throat might ruin his sobriety. With Dad, it's walking on eggshells. Only now, instead of his temper, it's his fragile self I'm protecting.

For four days, all Dad's going to see is sunshine and lollipops. Problem is, I forgot to tell the fifteen-year-old.

Uly points to an area next to the garage.

"Hate to break it to you, Grandpa, but you see those pods over there? People only have those when they're moving."

I shoot Uly a look. *Stop.* But if I thought Dad would recoil, I was wrong.

"Jesus Christ, kid," he says. "Ye of little faith. Like your mom. If you wanna know, her landlord lent this to her. The last place had problems."

"Lemme guess. Mold," Uly mutters. "What a fraud."

When I see Dad go quiet, I jump in.

"All I want is for us to have a nice time, okay?" I force myself to smile.

"Whatever," Uly says in typical teenage fashion.

Although I'm sympathetic, I signal again—he needs to stop. Gallows humor never helped anyone. Not here.

As we approach the door, I notice Uly's pants are hanging low—for the hundredth time. At least his boxers are nice. I let it go. It's not like I didn't have my own wardrobe disasters. I pulled up saggy socks so many times I thought my legs were the problem, not stretched-out elastic and poverty. Not to mention my eyebrows, the Sun-In. As with Uly, a lot was self-inflicted.

After letting ourselves in through an unlocked door, the first person we see is Nikki's 11-year-old daughter, Blessa.

She asks for my coat and purse. She's disappointed when I say no.

"Mom put me in charge, Aunt Abi," she says, her voice sweet but tinged with fear. "I'm supposed to put your things in the other room. So they're safe."

My jaw clenches, then my stomach. So Nikki's manipulated her daughter into doing her dirty work. Uly, not having any of it, reflexively checks his pocket for his wallet. I told him so. Dad, however, seems amused.

"Here you go," he says, handing his coat and overnight bag to Blessa. "I haven't seen you in forever, darlin'. Aren't you the cutest thing?"

I don't know if I'd describe Blessa as cute. She would be adorable if Nikki dressed her like a kid. What she is is aggressively pretty. Light brown, flat-ironed hair with blonde streaks. Skin plump and hydrated—thanks, I later learn, to regular facials. Waxed eyebrows (dangerous at her age), acrylic nails, and chunky kitten heels she's worn since kindergarten.

Her outfit matches her mother's. Both are channeling the Britney Spears schoolgirl look: long-sleeved, midriff-baring white shirts and too-short plaid skirts. And more: when she leans in for a hug, there's gold powder on her cheeks. Her lips are so plump they look bee-stung.

Nikki's oldest, 14-year-old Josiah, arrives next—almost as polished. Same pillowy skin as his sister. The sun-kissed blond hair (Nikki says it's for commercial work) is perfectly styled. When he gives Uly a high five, the contrast is striking. Josiah, in a pressed linen shirt, pants, and sockless loafers, looks like he stepped out of a magazine. Uly's look is, to be polite, rugged.

Uly's always said it's a Country-Mouse, City-Mouse thing. It's more Urban-Mouse meets Hollywood-Mouse.

After taking Dad's things, Blessa leads him and Uly to the far end of a massive sectional. Uly's full, but I need a snack. I grab a salmon mousse and caviar canapé from a tray and take a look around.

I'm overwhelmed by the number of Hollywood types who've torn themselves away from their own families to be here. Other than Dad, Uly, and the kids, I don't recognize anyone. No riff-raff either. No acquaintances from Nikki's car-thieving days or prison stints.

Nikki, mic in hand, barely acknowledges my existence. For a brief moment, I wonder if Dad was right. Maybe she has reinvented herself. Her schoolgirl outfit is too short for a 42-year-old. Half her paid-for breasts are hanging out. But paired with Blessa, they look like they're in costume.

The only difference? Nikki's wearing the cuff bracelet she got from Japan. Blessa isn't.

The bracelet—cheap cloisonné with red flowers—pierces my heart. I haven't reflected much on Nikki's days as a "teenage model," but watching her turn Blessa into a mini-adult scares me.

She's getting a lot of mileage out of the kid. With her at her side, Nikki's lacquered ponytail and Pretty Woman thigh-high boots look glamorous instead of slutty.

Though the house is full, I'm sure others declined the invite. Nikki would never fit in at the country club.

Addressing her admirers, Nikki is electric—just like when she lit up the dance floor as a precocious four-year-old. She's still as fake as the paper roses on our Mimouna table, but she's mesmerizing.

I've never seen anyone take command of a room like this.

"Gather around," she says, her voice syrupy sweet. "Four years ago today, I looked around and realized I was tired of being someone who lets life happen. That's when I decided to be a changemaker. So I invite you— what do you want to do with your life?"

I've read about charismatic leaders who can convince anyone of anything. Here's one right in front of me.

She breaks down a quote from the Great Buddha into digestible self-help fluff. I'm not entranced. She's like a friggin' cult leader.

Then she introduces a charity I've never heard of. Nikki insists it's an LLC for victims of the Trabuco Canyon fires.

"It's in Blessa's name. Never too early to practice being a girl boss," she says. "We take cash, checks, credit cards. One hundred percent goes to victims. You'll get a full tax deduction. No administrative fees. Who else can say that?"

The applause is thunderous. Somehow, Nikki comes off as a better human than the rest of us. Not only is she devoted to self-improvement and charitable causes—so the fiction goes—her rags-to-riches story is a testament to hard work.

Or so she says.

I feel guilty for thinking it, but ... could Nikki be stealing Blessa's identity?

After Nikki's money grab comes a song: *Hollaback Girl*. I'm sure Uly and I will laugh about it later. Bubblegum pop.

Uly's right. That song is feel-good cotton candy fluff. After it ends, Nikki gives another speech. The room erupts.

I look at Dad—grandchildren surrounding him—more content than I've seen him in years. He's clapping, too.

As for Uly, he was confident behind the wheel. Now, his face is a mask. I don't know what he's thinking. It's a sucker punch to the gut. Cy told me not to bring him. Uly's reaction proves he was right.

This isn't the place for a child. Nikki's one domino away. The whole thing is going to come crashing down.

When I see Dad woozy and unsteady, wine glass teetering in his hand, my face flushes with anger. Blood rushes to my fists. I don't expect much, but he's clearly not thinking.

"Music!" he yells, raising his glass.

Nikki notices but stays in performance mode, gazing at Dad like he's the most perfect man alive.

"My father's here," she says. "Everyone, give him a toast."

Whatever Daddy wants, Daddy gets.

I want to slap the drink from his hand. Six months. And there he is, clinking glasses with Josiah.

"To Nikki Jones," he says. "The hostess with the mostest."

I don't know how to react. So all you need to look good is a borrowed house, some CDs, a few speeches, and a caterer? I can't believe I wanted this for Uly.

"How about everyone makes a conga line?" Nikki says. "How about *Bye Bye Bye*? After that—turkey time!"

Her comment earns a smirk from Uly. Nikki doesn't realize how irrelevant she is. NSYNC? Really? It makes me smile. Uly and I can still share an inside joke. Even from across the room.

But as Nikki leads her version of the song, the room spins. I hear sirens—not music. Not today, but soon.

In the restroom, I splash water on my face and breathe deeply. Just a few more hours. I'm so turned around, I forget which door leads to the hallway.

I open the first door and find coats and jackets piled on a bed. Then I see Nikki—hand in a man's coat pocket.

I slam the door, praying she didn't see me.

The shock won't wear off. Neither does the feeling that I'm the only sane person here.

When Nikki calls us to dinner, Uly—my only source of trust—is relegated to the kids' table. I can't relax. After some discussion, he's finally allowed to sit next to me.

The catered meal, which is meh, goes on forever. Turkey, cranberry sauce, endless toasts and congratulations. Uly and I stick together like Velcro. His eyes are rimmed with red. My legs are shaking.

I wonder if he's thinking the same thing I am.

Cy and I might be divorced, but every Thanksgiving, he leads our family—fractured or not—in prayer. Now he's alone. A plate full of food. He hates: powdered mashed potatoes, canned gravy, Stove Top stuffing.

Before the night's over, maybe I will put Uly on the phone.

But when gregarious Josiah invites him to the game room for pinball, I let him go.

Let a kid be a kid.

CHAPTER 36

The Fix

Abigail

Nikki and Blessa's phony charity is a rousing success. Checks, piles of cash, credit card receipts from Blessa's Square Reader—they all add up. Enough to keep Nikki in this lifestyle for at least another month. When I saw her wrist-deep in that man's coat pocket, it confirmed what I already knew. I could warn everyone, but she'd call me crazy. I've seen her character-assassinate. First ex-husband, second, third. Bada-bing, bada-boom.

You'd think Nikki would hire a maid for the cleanup, but here we are in the kitchen, taking on a mountain of plates, bowls, cups, glassware, and silver. I'm covering the leftovers in foil. Nikki's scraping food into the garbage disposal.

"You saw me with the coat," she says.

I set a dish on the counter. "I guess it was a matter of time."

"This isn't what you think," she says.

The last time she was this cucumber-cool was when she was fifteen and I visited her in juvenile hall. Thank God I'm not naïve anymore.

When I give her my best "too bad, so sad" look, she adjusts. It's subtle—like she's recalibrating.

"Tom had to leave in a rush. He asked me to grab his jacket. He didn't want to leave without donating."

"Don't you have a website?"

"And disappoint Blessa?" she says.

She picks up a plate and wipes it with a cloth.

"I've been meaning to talk to you," she adds. "You see what we've done with this charity. I know how to turn ideas into action. That's what I'm trying to teach the kids. With Blessa soaking up Japanese culture and my connections at Tokyo University, she'll have a full ride."

"She'll be set," I say, deadpan. I wonder if she'll catch it.

Her bracelet is a jarring reminder of her time in Japan. When she readjusts it, it takes everything in me not to react. It's like she's throwing spaghetti at the wall to see what sticks. The more she rambles, the more confident I feel. As long as I keep my wits, she'll never figure me out.

Unable to hide her impatience, she tears off the bracelet and sets it on the sink.

I've seen cuff bracelets like this before. This one's different—silver and black, with a picture of a geisha engraved in it. A child's face carved into silver. Always watching. Just looking at it sends my mind swirling. Who gave it to her? Almost thirty years ago, working at those hostess clubs; she was the same age Uly is now.

I dry the inside of a pot and place it on the drying rack.

"You've come a long way," I say.

That's when she tries to zero in.

"I'm worried about you," she says. "You've worked hard, but have you worked smart? Have you learned from your mistakes?"

Just as I'm about to tell her she sounds like an MLM boss babe, she pivots.

"First thing I did when I got out of prison?" she says. "I asked myself what I could fix about myself. You could do the same. Take Cy, for example."

I slow my breathing. Her mentioning Cy makes me furious. How dare she? But I can't show it. She really is nuts—her problem is that she thinks everyone's as insecure as she is.

"You see this house, the view, this furniture, this artwork, these clothes?" she says, sweeping her hand like a self-help guru. "I got here by taking risks. So I'm asking again—what can *you* change? I mean, it can't be easy for you. I heard the kids talking about Universal Studios. Uly said you couldn't afford it. I'd like to help, Abi, but you know … teaching a person to fish …"

The whole thing is so performative, I want to call Cy. He was right. One thousand percent.

"Listen, Nikki," I say, setting a bowl on the counter. "Save your speeches for another time. As broken as things seem right now—with Cy not working—they'll improve. They always do."

What I want to say is that some things are too devastating to be explained away with fish analogies. Sometimes, we just need to survive. But she'd never understand.

I set the last dish on the drainer and turn to leave.

"I get it," she says.

"No worries. I'm going to my room. Cy's expecting a call. I don't want to disappoint him."

CHAPTER 37

The Gamble

Abigail – Los Altos Hills, California – December 2011

The crabapple trees surrounding the perimeter of Liberty Park High School have given up their fruit. Much of it, overripe, is already on the ground, forming slushy mounds in the mud. With Homecoming approaching, the junior varsity boys—unable to resist anything remotely ball-shaped—will pick off what's left and throw them against the fence with a satisfying thud.

The administrative building, where my office is located, feels like the lobby of the Waldorf Astoria. The cloying smell of gardenia and the stifling air of understated wealth hang heavily. Everyone speaks in whispers. A sign of the times.

Once known for its cow pastures and grape vineyards, the area has been overtaken by Silicon Valley bigwigs. Only a few of the old guard remain—those who remember the children of ranchers and farmers showing up in boots still crusted with mud, smelling faintly of manure. Among them: Judy North, the school counselor; two teachers, Mrs. Gray and Mr. Kemper, who've been here since before Reagan; and me.

I have fifteen years left before I can retire. It bothers me sometimes, but the stability and pension are enough to stay.

Until one day when everything changes.

Judy and I are in my office, sharing a cheese-filled yeast roll, appropriately named a Zombie because it puts everyone into a catatonic state. I don't realize I'm miserable, but there's a ball and chain around my ankle. I have to wear the uniform. My hair is sprayed so stiff it doesn't move. Even my overly fussy blouse and pencil skirt have me feeling like a sausage.

Judy, set to retire in a few months, has already traded power suits and wedge heels for a Hawaiian shirt, denim skirt, and sandals. She has the breezy look of a short-timer.

"What are they going to do—fire me?" she says, referring to her outfit, though I haven't asked. Then she grabs a Coke from her mini-fridge, pops the tab, and pours the amber liquid into two Dixie cups twice the size of a shot glass.

"A hundred extra calories," she says. "But whatever. I'll have time to walk it off."

"I'm only halfway to the finish line," I say. "Caseload's heavier than ever. You never had it easy—but man-o-man. So many kids with autism, ADHD, dyslexia. My reports used to be four pages. This one I'm doing is forty."

Judy puts her fist to her chin and looks at me thoughtfully.

"Times have changed," she says. "I never thought I'd miss the rancher kids. They raised a ruckus, and their senior pranks got out of hand. But they didn't get away with shit."

The boys with cowboy boots left long before my time. For as long as I've been here, big-donor families have run the place. There was never a shortage of WASPy moms with upswept chignons and thin wool cardigans, acting like one-half of a Silicon Valley power couple. What's ruined everything is Google. And parent chatrooms. Now everyone's a diagnostician.

I reach back to scratch an itch at the base of my neck.

"Yeah," I say. "It's demoralizing being a rubber stamp."

"Give me all the tea in China," Judy says, "and it wouldn't be enough for me to stay."

I wish I could go too. I'm about to tell her that when my phone lights up. The ringtone is a rap song. I didn't program it—tech-savvy Uly did.

"Sorry," I say. "Barnyard Hip Hop means it's either my sister or my dad. I forget which."

"Then I'd better go," Judy says, popping the last bite of Zombie in her mouth.

I don't pick up until she's out of earshot. I'm disappointed it's not Dad. After Thanksgiving, he went straight into rehab. Got counseling too. It's a pleasure to hear his voice every day.

"Got a minute?" Nikki says as soon as I answer. Her voice is casual, but also conspiratorial. She doesn't sound quite as supercharged as she did a week ago—but she's still Nikki. I can hear her buttering me up.

"I've been thinking," she says. "I'm sorry for what I said. About teaching you to fish instead of giving you one. The truth is, if my money weren't tied up, I would've sprung for the whole shebang—Disney, Universal, Legoland. After Dad told me about the trouble you're having with disability giving Cy a hard time, I felt terrible."

"It hasn't been easy," I say.

"Later on, I Googled school psychologist salaries and realized—oh my God, Abi. You deserve better. So does Uly."

The only reason I keep her on the line is because I'm amused. Country Mouse and Hollywood Mouse all over again. Does she even have an endgame?

"Did you call to apologize?" I ask. "Because that's not what this sounds like."

"Contrary to what you might think, I care about you. Uly too. I have a proposition."

Her saccharine tone makes me want to gag.

"There's a kid at my door," I say. "Gotta go."

When I hang up, I'm not prepared for what I end up feeling. All night, and into the next day, I simmer. So much of what she said was uncalled for. The pity disguised as sympathy. Disgusting.

What I don't know is Nikki has already sized me up. She tried bad-mouthing my ex and learned quickly that's off-limits. But she did figure out a couple of things. One: there's nothing I won't do for my lanky, next-great-rapper, pinball-playing son. Two: I need money.

With Cy in day treatment and unable to work, no paycheck means no child support. I've already dipped into my 401(k) twice. The more I think about it, the more it burns. The way she gets to live isn't fair. Her money might be "tied up in investments," but at least she has some.

Nikki calls again; I knew she would. I'm in a meeting. Strains of Barnyard Hip Hop fill the room. I'm powerless to stop it—I'm not used to smartphones, unsure how to silence it. My boss gives me a look.

"It's okay. Go take the call."

"I'm in a staff meeting," I whisper, before hanging up.

She calls again an hour later—and she's ready.

"Boring," Nikki says. "Working a 9-to-5? My job at the headhunter's office? First time I've ever had to check in with anyone."

"Listen, Nikki. I don't have time."

"You should," she says. "Have you thought about striking out on your own? You could make a lot more. With your skills, you could get a loan."

"I'm a single mom. Remember? Benefits."

"Nobody said quit. Take a sabbatical."

"Where would I get the money?" I ask. "I've already pulled out as much as I safely can."

"The Small Business Administration," Nikki says. "Your business would be woman-owned. African-American too. You were born in Morocco, and you're American. You might not even have to pay it back."

For someone so smart, her lack of basic knowledge astonishes me. It takes all I have not to gasp. She must sense it, because instantly, she pivots.

"You never could take a joke," she says. "Me, of all people; I know the price of dishonesty. All I want to do is make amends."

"You mean for my adolescent years, when I was falsely accused?"

"I do want to make it up to you. So, I've taken the liberty of starting the application. As much of a spartan as you are, a hundred grand should do it. You don't have to use all of it."

My head spins. I'm so flabbergasted, I duck into an empty cubicle.

"You did what?" I whisper.

"Listen. Hear me out," she says.

But I don't. "Gotta go," I say, flipping my phone shut.

It takes three days for Nikki to try again. I figure even she doesn't have that much chutzpah.

I'm driving home when the call comes. I almost don't answer—but it's been a hard week. Uly's baseball is costing a fortune. Not just the school team, but the travel leagues where college scouts show up. I can barely afford groceries.

"There's a vacant office across from your school," Nikki says. "You can see it tomorrow at noon. I've arranged it. The agent says it has a bird's-eye view of the football field—in case you're feeling nostalgic."

"I'm not saying it's out of the question," I say, wearily. "But please, let me investigate on my own."

Thankfully, she accepts that. Without a reason to stay on the line, she clicks off.

With the ball in my court, I research all night. According to Google, success is possible—if I can find a niche. By morning, I'm more rational. Two hundred an hour sounds nice, but it'll take time to get there. Since she made the appointment, I figure I'll look at the place—just to get her off my back.

"No more interference," I tell her. "From here on out, I'm on my own."

"No, no, no, no, no," she says. "Don't miss out on my expertise. I helped Blessa form her own LLC."

"I'm not a kid running a charity, Nikki."

"Allow me to do the legwork. You can't keep being chief cook and bottle washer. It has to be exhausting. Uly and all those extracurriculars."

"Uh-huh."

"What's your Social Security number? The property manager needs to do a soft pull on your credit. You haven't ruined it, have you?"

That does it. I thought, for once, she cared. But no. All she wants is to scam me.

"Nope. And nope," I say.

With one click, I end the call.

Dammit, Nikki. Who the hell does she think she is?

If the realtor needs my info, I'll give it to him myself.

CHAPTER 38

The Hustle

Abigail

The appointment with the realtor goes well—maybe a little too well. Not only is he scrupulously honest, but the place is also a steal at only $1,300 a month for two treatment rooms and a waiting area. I sleep on it—but not for long.

The next day, when I see the scores of private chauffeurs idling their limousines, the mothers pulling up in their Rolls-Royce SUVs, it gets to me in a way it hasn't before. I decide to go for it. I'm not going to get rich, but according to Google, if I work hard and branch out, if I can get my PsyD and hire people to work under me, my money problems will be solved. Soon, I'll be hanging my own shingle: Abigail Jones, Licensed Educational Psychologist.

The next little while goes by so fast, it's a blur. It's not easy saying adios to fifteen years at the same school. Even so, it's a sabbatical—I'm not all the way gone. From my third-floor office, I still have a view of the football field. Though I'm no longer drawing a paycheck, I still have a connection.

Each weekday from three to four, the Liberty Park High marching band practices. Snare drums, trumpets, and cymbals—expertly played by kids who've had years of lessons—fill the air. Later, if there's a game, the crowd erupts with every home-team score. With preparations underway for Homecoming Week, which we hold in winter, I watch vicariously as teams of students and their parents assemble floats for the parade. My favorite so far is from the ninth graders. In school colors of blue, it portrays a man being dumped into a postal box, the lettering "Return to Sender" spelled out in little curlicues.

Work is so slow sometimes I wish I were Nikki. She wouldn't let the floats pass her by. She'd be out there, guns blazing. She'd be profitable from the get-go—by hook or by crook. But it would be a scam. Thank God she's not involved. I insisted on mailing the paperwork myself. I don't know why I'm relying on her, but these days, Nikki is strangely … reassuring. On the phone, she's quiet. Subdued.

"I hope the money comes soon," I tell her. "I've maxed out my credit cards taking cash advances."

"Don't worry," she says. "So many people are starting businesses, the SBA's processing time is behind. You know how government agencies are. When your bill comes due, I'll cover it. In the meantime—market the hell out of yourself."

With Nikki as cheerleader, I immerse myself in the world of how-to. Of all the materials I buy, the *Marketing Guide for the Health Professional* by Dr. Ted Topper is the most helpful. He gets into the nuts and bolts—emphasizing the importance of developing multiple income streams, maintaining a website and blog, and most importantly, handing out business cards and flyers like candy.

To attract cash-payers, he writes, *image is vital.*

I furnish the office with the finest secondhand furniture my money can buy. I upgrade my look with a new haircut, honey-brown highlights, and acrylic nails from Paris Beauty School. From the thrift store, I buy two linen suits and a wool-cashmere jacket, have them dry cleaned to get the smoke out, and altered for a custom fit. When a cruise ship outside of San Francisco is seized, I win a few pieces of jewelry at a government auction. The only thing I can't hack is shoes. So far, no one's donated suitable Jimmy Choos. I may still be a scrounger, but at least I've leveled up.

These are the smaller expenses. Some of the big-ticket items, I can't get on discount. Test kits, for example. The Wechsler intelligence and achievement tests cost $1,500 apiece. I buy three—one for each age group. Then there are whole batteries that cost even more: the Delis-Kaplan, the Pearson Continuous Performance Test for ADHD, the ADOS kit for autism. It never ends.

You have to spend money to make money, writes Dr. Topper.

So I go further. From eight to ten, Monday through Friday, bearing trays of bagels, cream cheese, and fruit, I make my rounds. Schools and doctors' offices, mostly.

I hit as many places as I can. Stanford-affiliated practices. High-end private schools. Even some nonprofits run by power couples and other schmoozers.

"Can I give you brochures to pass out?" I ask whoever's at the front desk.

The ease with which they accept could never happen with today's cybersecurity. But it's early 2012, and it's not hard for a well-dressed woman of a certain age to infiltrate the upper echelons of Silicon Valley's crème de la crème.

As a scrapper from the plum-orchard era of San Jose—and a seeming reject in my own family—I never thought I'd belong anywhere except among my childhood friends. Lee, Caroline, Jonathan, and Sierra. They moved away a long time ago, ceding the valley to a new crowd of movers and shakers. Except for Sierra—now a ship's captain in Lahaina—who regularly sends Uly and me tickets to visit, I see little of them. Not that I've noticed, but Nikki isn't checking in as much, either.

Client calls come in regularly. But when I quote my price, few people bite. Some ask about insurance (it's not covered), and some try to barter. Manipulation and gaslighting are rare, but when it happens, I wonder: without a PsyD, should I take half? I thought it'd be different. After years of watching Los Altos residents speed through traffic in sports cars, cutting people off and parking with impunity, I assumed they'd be just as reckless when it came to spending on their kids.

As it turns out, I'd been too judgmental. People of means are generally cautious. I'm unproven.

"How long have you been doing this?" they ask several times a day. My twenty years in the public sector don't count. They want to know: *Are you Googleable?*

When I do get someone eager, other problems arise. My plan was to take on an intern and run teen groups. If I fill up, that's $300 per fifty-minute session—not bad. But getting kids in the door at the same time? It's like herding cats. Ballet, bar and bat mitzvahs, bongo lessons, baseball practice—there's only so much time.

And then there's the SBA loan. It's taking forever. Worse—when the credit card bill comes due, Nikki says she's short on funds.

"One of my clients tried to rip me off for $300k," she says. "Had to hire a real piranha to fight him off."

"But my credit record," I say. "You have no idea the hole I'm in."

"Wish I could help. But you know how it is—being busy. People to see, places to go. Oh! Gotta go now. Japan's on the line."

Then the line goes dead.

CHAPTER 39

Business as Usual

Abigail

The sober living house in downtown San Jose isn't far from the old Camera One theater. Dad and I go to the movies sometimes—*The Thin Man, The Maltese Falcon, Key Largo*. It's harrowing how he ended up here after one more relapse, but that's a story for another day. At least he's alive. And one more thing—he has an envelope for me.

"Ya gotta get your mail straightened out," Dad says when I arrive. "Anyway, here it is. From the SBA. You've been looking forward to that money."

"So it wasn't you who filed the change of address?" I ask.

With Dad being such a vagabond, my mail is always getting diverted. The timing doesn't make sense. His trailer on Croy Road has been vacant. Sure, Cy's been there, but he has a permanent address. As for Dad, he's pretty much occupied.

The only question I have as I tear into the envelope is, why does it say *Personal and Confidential?*

"If this is what I think it is," I say, "I've already applied for the next installment. Even though this check's going toward credit card bills—"

Instead of a check, what I see—and there's no mistaking it—is a late notice for the eye-popping amount of $21,586.00. I start shaking. My body boils with rage. The terms are horrendous: eleven percent interest, fifteen-year term, first payment of $245.31 due immediately.

"It's not a check. It's a bill. Oh my God. It's her."

"Whaddya mean?" Dad says, clearly confused.

"You think your youngest daughter's so great—lives in a mansion, drives a fancy car? This is the truth. You want me to be like her? A woman who steals over twenty grand from her own sister."

Dad lowers his head and squeezes his eyes shut. As for me, I need to tamp down my reaction. I don't want to trigger another relapse.

What I want to say but don't is: *Stop wanting me to be as smart as her.* If I were a psychopath, I'd be one step ahead of everyone else, too.

"There has to be a mistake," Dad says, like he doesn't quite believe it. "Lemme call. If she sees it's you, she won't pick up."

Dad doesn't know how to put the phone on speaker, but from the way his hands are shaking—

"Disconnected," he says.

When he can't reach the kids either, he calls Verizon. The news isn't any better.

"With the situation in Japan, they're probably using burners. For their protection. Who knows what those crazies might do?"

I grasp my elbows and let out a sputtering sigh.

"Dad. The only people after Nikki are from law enforcement."

Dad's eyes well with tears. When he finally speaks, his voice is weak.

"Maybe this is the last time," he says.

"I thought I had it dialed in," I say. "You saw me at Thanksgiving, hiding my things. By then, she already had most of what she needed."

Dad lets out a faint sigh of recognition and scratches the back of his head. His fingers grab the edge of his tray table.

"Abi, I'm tired of keeping secrets," he says. "Months ago, your sister offered to help clear out my storage unit. It's trivial, but I should've told you. We were going through Mom's trinkets. I saw her slip a gold-plated Social Security card into her pocket. Damn it all to hell. She said it was hers."

"It wasn't," I say.

I didn't just get my naivete from Dad—Mom, too. Why did I leave it there? Why did Mom even keep it?

"I bought it with my Lerner's money. It was a collectible from Franklin Mint. Too heavy for my wallet," I say.

"She would never. You're family."

"When has that ever gotten in the way? Nothing's personal."

"Betcha it's a loan," Dad says. "Some shady Japanese ripped her off. She has a lawyer. As soon as she gets paid—"

I want to ask Dad if he knows what really happened in Japan. All that "modeling" and not one picture. I could handle the truth, but it would kill him.

When he changes the subject, grumbling that Misty-Jane's garbage disposal is broken and she wants him to go fix it, I let it go.

Inside, it feels like I'm dying. A single tear drags down Dad's cheek. So much regret and sorrow. I don't know what happened to him when he was a kid, but seriously, he's wallowing in it.

I'm about to give up when he brightens. There's still some resilience in the old man.

Casablanca's playing across the street. "Let's go. Afterward, we can talk about it. My take's a little different from Bogie's."

CHAPTER 40

Hardwired

Abigail

Nikki's pretty much disappeared. It worries me. I have a zero percent chance of getting my money back, but after last week, Dad's "one day at a time" has turned into "one minute at a time." In the meantime, after a long day's work, I spend my nights Googling every variation of Nikki's name I can think of. Nikki. Nikky. Nikkii. Nikkiii. Then all the possible misspellings of her last name and the surnames of all her ex-husbands—hyphenated and not.

She must've paid for one of those internet reputation services. Her entire digital footprint is squeaky clean. Aside from her LinkedIn and IMDb pages—which are completely fabricated—everything else has vanished.

Then one day, Polly Muniz, the mother of one of Uly's friends, stops by. I don't know how she found out before I did, but Uly and her daughter Carys are acquainted. Polly and I aren't friends. I already have enough train wrecks in my life. It's early. I'm sharing my standing desk with Luna, who, growing impatient with me and my coffee, is meowing for Fancy Feast. In Polly's hand is yesterday's *New York Times*. She's highlighted an article most people—unless they're eagle-eyed obsessives—would have missed.

"I thought you'd want this," she says. "I know it sounds strange, but I read the 'News from the Southern District of New York' section. I always say you never know. I was right, because—is this her? Is this your sister?"

I want to tell her, *Go back to your life. Leave me alone.* But once I start reading, I realize—I already knew.

"Your son told my Carys about the money," she says. "Terrible. And now this. Now I understand. We could never figure out why you were driving that old junker. I mean, roll-up windows, manual locks. Anyway, I have a feeling once she's locked up, everything's going to change."

I still think Polly's a mess. But for this, she deserves thanks. We exchange pleasantries. She apologizes for being nosy. I'd say no problem, but the bombshell she's dropped has me reeling. When she leaves, I read the article again.

Nicole Ann Jones, age 42, was apprehended yesterday as part of a widespread investigation into passport fraud. According to the charges, Jones attempted to obtain a passport using fraudulent documentation. A separate investigation is underway for her role in a scheme that defrauded ABC Universal Entertainment out of nearly $450,000. If convicted on all federal charges, Jones faces more than 100 years in prison.

What I do next isn't just anger or vengeance. It's drawing a line. Never again will I let Nikki find her way into my orbit. Anyway, it's like they were waiting for my call. How else to explain how quickly I'm directed to the right person?

Detective Roger Fitch of the LAPD's Internet Crimes Division is all ears. To my surprise, he gives as much as he gets.

"It was a SWAT team arrest," he says. "They had to break down the door. The children were there. It was sad. She tried to run."

"No surprise there. That escape artist ran before she could walk."

"What is she—forty-five? Too old to sprint," he laughs. "Her MO now is impersonation. To think she almost slipped past us. If we hadn't confiscated her desktop over the forged passport, we never would've found the headhunter scam."

Those words hit me like a rock. "I should've known better," I say. "Too much unexplained wealth. She asked me for the last four digits of my Social, but that was just to throw me off."

When he asks, I tell him everything—about her childhood, how she was a kleptomaniac from early on. What she did with my license. What she did to Grandma. No remorse. He's building a pattern. Early behavioral issues.

"It's terrible," I say, "One sister being disloyal to another. But it's safer we be adversaries."

"When we spoke to one of her exes, he said the same thing. With Nikki, you're either a victim or an enabler. There's no in-between."

Since Nikki and her lawyer have a right to see the evidence, and I've provided context, I've effectively made myself the enemy. From here on out, Nikki's smear campaign intensifies. It doesn't take long to bear fruit.

When I first spoke to Detective Fitch, he was Johnny-on-the-spot. "Got you on speed dial," he'd said.

Now, his tone is cold. Detached. Almost accusatory.

"Nikki showed us the texts," he says. "You knew the money was coming."

My hands shake. "You don't get it. Nikki set me up. I signed a fake application—completed after the fact. Check my bank accounts. I didn't get a cent."

"She says you were violent. That you beat her up. She was very convincing, I might add."

He can't see me step back. I've been shamed all my life. But not this time.

"As soon as I defend myself, I lose. But it's pure projection. If anything, I was afraid of her. Talk to my friends. Talk to Uncle Henri."

"We ran your profile. Must be hard, living in a rich area with a child and a deadbeat ex. Not that the texts aren't incriminating by themselves. You gave her the go-ahead."

I let out an exasperated sigh. One more lazy bureaucrat taking the easy way out.

"Follow the money," I say.

"Nobody says you weren't double-crossed."

"I can explain."

"Explaining is what the Jones sisters are good at. Too bad nothing you say holds water."

Our conversation goes further south. When he basically tells me I deserved what I got and not to waste his time, my stomach twists into a knot. Then the line goes dead.

For half a day, I wallow. I feel sorry for myself. I'm angry. The idiot couldn't investigate his way out of a paper bag. All morning, my hot water bottle of a dog presses against my belly and licks my chin. She knows something's off.

By 1 p.m., I head to the office. I'd be functional if not for the get-rich-quick schemes racing through my mind. I'm in the parking structure, pulling my briefcase from the trunk when a Ken-doll of a businessman with perfect hair rolls up in a Lamborghini convertible.

I'm not too old to notice handsome. But all I'm fantasizing about is hot-wiring his car and driving off. Impractical. These days, cars are armed to the gills. And I'd definitely get caught. With Uly's dad in day treatment, his grandfather in rehab, and me and Nikki in the slammer—where would Uly go? Misty-Jane's?

I need legitimate employment.

As soon as I return to the office, I call my old boss.

"We hired a contractor," he says when I ask.

The *tsk-tsk* in his voice makes me instantly regret calling. I can almost see him wagging his finger.

"She might not be thorough," he adds, "but she's efficient. And any new contract would have to go through the board. You know how they are."

Asshole.

Now he's given me something to prove. *The Marketing Guide for the Health Professional* becomes my bible. If Dr. Topper wasn't my guru before, he is now. I've had the book for two months, and it's already dogeared. Every other paragraph is highlighted. Every other page, tabbed. Every kernel of advice, I heed.

Write daily, he advises on page 36. *On a timely topic, using bullet points. People like the number seven. Seven steps.*

Not only does this seem doable—given that my bagel and fruit budget is down to fumes—it feels like a way forward. Detective Fitch might be right that I'm desperate, and my old boss might be right about the board, but they've severely underestimated me.

Don't assume people will understand you, Dr. Topper insists on page 138. *Keep communication simple and clear. Bullet points. Too much info is overwhelming.*

Doing the math, if Dr. Topper's right, fifty bullet-pointed articles will replace the amount Nikki stole from me. In no time, I've got six in the hopper. It's easier than I thought.

Then it occurs to me: Topper has his points—but what happens when I don't agree? Some of his philosophy is naïve. He wants me to play the long game. Believe in the "I'm okay, you're okay, we all win" schtick. He never acknowledges that not everyone plays fair. To him, stamina and a strong stomach are all it takes. *Show up,* he says.

But Nikki's out on bond. I'm drowning in debt. And this guy wants me singing *tra-la-la*?

That whole "they go low, we go high" thing? Bullshit. I've lost too many street fights.

If coloring outside the lines is what it takes to survive, so be it.

Knowing the property manager doesn't allow it, I rent the extra treatment room to a subletter. Seven hundred a month for a small space furnished with leftover 1970s rattan covers a lot of rent. Is it dishonest? A little. But I'm not the bad guy.

I don't know it yet, but it's the first step in a direction I never meant to go. Is it in my DNA? It weighs on me like a brick of dynamite strapped to my back—and all it took to light the match was this.

For a while, things go okay. I couldn't ask for a better tenant than Cory McMahon. A new marriage and family therapist, she's perky and sweet. She's endearing. The smallest things thrill her: the ceiling fan, the rattan furniture, the water dispenser. Her wardrobe consists of limp fast-fashion tops, colored nylons, and the same plastic pumps I used to put on my Barbie dolls.

Because Cory accepts insurance, clients are plentiful. When she complains her caseload is full after two weeks, I can't say it doesn't grate on me. She's busy without being cheery. Efficient without being effective.

When someone enters or exits her room, a bell rings. And her sound machine? Does it have to be that loud?

One thing Cory isn't is stupid. She sees me developing my website, writing articles, and hears me telling Uly, "No, you can't use my credit card to buy brie."

Soon, her tone becomes solicitous. Little Miss Do-Gooder.

"You needn't do all this," she says in her chirpy voice. "The carved furniture, the mohair couch, the oil paintings. The testing materials— couldn't you have borrowed them?"

I give her my thousand-yard stare. *You have no idea*, I don't say. Instead, I deflect.

"There's a baseball game across the way," I say. "Somebody must've scored."

"Private schools, I know nothing about," she says. "I grew up off the grid, in the middle of nowhere. The only reason we're here is because my fiancé got a job in tech."

Over the next few weeks, there are changes. City life gets to Cory—in a good way, at first. She goes from chirpy to effervescent. Weekends rejuvenate her. She knew Napa, but the hot-air ballooning, wine tasting, dinner train? That's new.

It doesn't bother me. I have bright memories of Cy and me doing the same.

Then, without warning, Cory walks in wearing a 3-carat sparkler and a designer outfit that costs more than I make in a year. She's insufferable.

"I never imagined—not in a million years—we could afford Versace," she says. "But Tom's company went public. Stock options! I thought it was $1,000. Then I saw the extra zeros. Even my shoes are designer. I forget who they're by."

"Nice," I say with a laugh. "Now that you're high-end, can you stop bugging me about the furniture?"

Really, what I want to say is, *You might have Versace, but I have war stories.*

"I can admit when I'm wrong," she titters. "I want to stay here, of course—the location!—but let's paint. And for sure, we need to ditch the cowbell and get an actual buzzer. You know … to attract cash payers."

CHAPTER 41

The Pretender

Abigail

One thing about Cory—she never gives up. She bakes me cookies. She leaves encouraging notes in my box, with things taped to them: a Hershey's Kiss, a purple ballpoint pen.

Chin up. You'll be turning away business in no time, she writes. Heart emoji, smiley face emoji, thumbs-up emoji.

Then one day, sweet, sunny Cory walks in—gigantic ring still on her hand—carrying trays of homemade cupcakes with multicolored sprinkles and confetti. All out for delivery.

"I hope you don't mind me copying you," she says. "What do they say? Imitation is the sincerest form of flattery."

What she doesn't know is that what happens next—she can't replicate.

I'm about to hit pay dirt. My *Seven Ways* articles have done okay—parents are reading them, especially the one on bullying. Several dozen bullet-point posts are live on my website, but it's when I go off-script and get personal that something clicks. Five hundred views the first day. Ten thousand the second. Two weeks later—one million. Without even realizing it, I've landed on a topic few in the child-rearing space have addressed: how parents can use the principles of restorative justice in practical ways.

I include an example from my own life—changing Uly's name, age, and gender. There's truth in it. As a floundering middle-schooler, Uly did throw a bottle of nail polish at my dresser. It did splatter. He did spend a day helping a furniture refinisher restore it. But the part that went viral?

That's fiction. Reader engagement—what we're all chasing—goes through the roof.

When *People Magazine* runs an article about the birth of Instagram and the re-emergence of the social media star, my ears perk up. Instagram *is* blowing up, gaining a million new subscribers in its first month. Not all early adopters benefit. I will.

Cory, who spends her downtime reading psychology journals, isn't into social media. But when a friend emails her a link to one of my articles, she's dumbfounded.

"What the hell is restorative justice?" she says, pressing a perfectly manicured palm to her forehead. "I would've thought a mom writing about resilience would resonate. Pioneer Woman Survives."

I shield my eyes with my hand. "More than anything, parents want advice," I say, trying to conceal the rise in my voice. "Or they want to be validated for what they're already doing."

"I should at least know what it is," she says.

"All consequences are directly related to the offense. Restitution is always involved. Like—if a kid steals a bike from a store and gets caught, he has to meet with the owner and write an apology. If he damages it, he has to fix it."

I'm subdued with Cory, but part of me wants to shout from a rooftop. I strayed from my usual checklist formula, shared a real-life vignette—and it paid off. I'm proud to have packaged an applied social psychology intervention—used with criminal offenders—into something parents can actually use.

What happens next isn't pretty.

I'm a survivor always have been. But I'm laser-focused on me and mine. Normally that's fine—money's always been tight—but now it's a full-blown panic. Rent is due in five days, and my 401(k)? Completely gutted. Driving for Uber might've been an option, but my car is one piece of plumber's tape away from the junkyard. For the first time in my life, despair has me in a chokehold. I can't even breathe.

What I do next isn't illegal. It's not. It's an act of service—at least, that's what I tell myself when the guilt starts gnawing. I'm not like Nikki. I have an endgame. I still believe that if I follow a careful plan of prescribed rules, Uly and I will have a good life. It's like Topper's *Seven Steps*—but applied to running a family.

I enter the ultra-conservative world of mommy blogging. It's pretend, of course. If I presented myself as divorced with one kid, I'd be a cautionary tale. I want to be aspirational. Instead of one kid, I'm juggling seven. And my made-up husband—who I didn't kiss until the day we married—is the family leader. The internet is all about curated images. Real messiness, unless it's circus-level chaos, gets rejected.

The irony is, if I'd only held out, we could've slept on a friend's couch. Yasmina could've helped. But pride and shame held me back. Business was already picking up—we were going to survive. How did I not see that?

Google Images had just made reverse image search available. I made sure every photo I acquired was for my exclusive use. I went all-in on the farm-life angle: children with blacked-out faces riding horses, milking cows, churning butter, reading by candlelight.

Never show children's faces on social media, I wrote. *Not only will you attract pedophiles, no kid wants their diaper changes and temper tantrums on display for eternity.*

I caught fire at the right time. I made $25,000 in the first two months. While Uly slept, I listened to Matt Coots' podcasts on scaling a business. I learned about SEO links, how to optimize content so it appears at the top when a frustrated parent types something into Google. I was getting enough clicks and subscribers to make serious money.

This was before the internet caught on to how insular this world is—before people learned about Josh Duggar and started "deconstructing."

Even so, in my gut, I knew I was wrong. But I figured I wasn't privileged enough to take the moral high ground. I stayed away from the extremes—avoided the strident *my-way-or-the-highway* tone—but still planted myself firmly center-right.

But when I encouraged a mom to send her marijuana-smoking teen to a wilderness camp, I knew I'd crossed a line. The backlash was immediate. Hundreds of comments. I read the first hundred before disabling them. But I got the message. Going harsh might make me a millionaire, but what good is it if someone gets hurt?

My new gentle-parenting approach caps me at 300,000 followers. But when I take on a sponsor and promote a homeschooling method I actually like, I make $3,000. In the weeks that follow, more crunchy-hippie-mom-type offers come in. I've found a sweet spot at the intersection of motherhood, old-fashioned values, and soft science.

But it's cold comfort.

The shadow side of being a scrapper is the means-to-an-end mindset. If I'm not careful, if I don't stay self-aware, I'll be no better than my sister. One hundred thousand—that's my limit. The $20k Nikki stole, plus my lost salary. I won't take a penny more.

But before I get there, someone else stops me.

One morning, I turn on my computer—and it's all gone.

CHAPTER 42

The Unraveling

Abigail

My hands are shaking. I can't breathe. Not only is my IP address invalid—my Instagram's been wiped clean. My heart's pounding so hard it feels like a jackhammer's stuck in my chest. A half-dozen conspiracy theories swirl through my mind. Was it one of my competitors? A regulatory agency? Nikki?

As soon as Uly walks in—too quietly for me to hear—I know. His anger is palpable. His face is almost menacing, his voice thick and heavy.

When he narrows his eyes and looks at me, all I can think is: *this isn't my boy.*

"I deleted it all. Your creator agreements. Your Square Reader account," he says.

My eyes bore into him with the full force of maternal authority. I might be ashamed, but I'm not going to let my child intimidate me. He may sound like a forty-year-old, but he's still my kid.

"This was my website," I say. "If you have a problem with it—"

Uly deflates. He looks like he's going to cry.

"Are you trying to leave me without a parent?" he asks.

"What? Of course not," I say, trying not to sound incredulous. "I did it for you."

"Have you read your comments? I did. A woman named Alice is suicidal because of you. I had to call the police to check on her."

"You can't believe I'm responsible."

"Alice lives in a converted bus with an unemployed nut-job husband and five unruly kids. She uses a library to go online—so yeah, we all know how evil that is. And what does she glom onto, one step away from a laundromat meltdown? You and your pretend life."

"You have no idea how sorry I am," I say, picking at the chipped nail polish on my fingers. "I've always tried to be authentic."

"If you were sorry, you'd ask about her."

I swallow the lump in my throat. "I stopped reading the comments. Is she okay?"

"Yesterday she logged in from some middle-of-nowhere town in Idaho. So yeah, the police were able to get her and the kids to safety."

"Her kids? I didn't have anything to do—"

"I said her old man was crazy," Uly says, his voice like a razor's edge. "That culty bullshit you were selling had everything to do with her staying as long as she did. If I'm sixteen and can see it, why can't you?"

"It was middle-of-the-road, son. Besides, we were broke. I was scared about being evicted."

"I'm not so much against what you did—but how you did it. Seriously, Mom. A mother of seven? Head scarves, cotton dresses, and dingy-looking aprons. A Jew for Jesus? That's you—covering all the bases."

"I didn't think anyone would be—" I look at my feet.

"Hurt? No, you didn't think. Dad's nuts, Aunt Nikki's in prison, and the only grandparent left throws his money at twenty-year-old hookers," he says. "But you know who I'm most disappointed in? You. You're always down on her, but you're no better."

My heart sinks to my stomach.

"Haven't I always given you a stable home?" I say. "Not like what Nikki's done to her kids. My mistake was keeping this from you—letting you be a bougie kid."

"That's me, Mom. Bougie Uly. I could've quit baseball. Other kids at school have jobs. I could've. It's not like I was gonna go pro. We could've asked Mrs. Tehranpour."

"Not after the way your aunt ripped her off. I'd rather be homeless."

"I read what you wrote, Mom. If Alice died, it would've been two sisters in prison. *Orange is the New Black*."

It makes me sick to my stomach the way he says it—like, *touché*.

After a long pause, with Uly on the verge of tears, he finally speaks.

"Dad might have his issues, but he's a way better person than you."

There's a lot I could say. Uly puts zero expectations on his father. As for me—they're monumental.

"Let me exit gracefully. I just need to make a little more. I promise— no more extreme content."

"You think I'm gonna give you another chance?"

"You leave me no choice," I say, my fists curling into balls. "I'm going to have to sell the Aveo."

"That's unnecessary," Uly snaps. "You have money."

"Tainted, according to you. I'm the one who gets to decide what to do with it—so good luck getting your butt to school."

"You forget Manuel's dad works for Caltrans. He can give me a ride anytime."

When Uly slams the door, it's *good goddamn riddance*. How dare he judge me? But … what if he's right?

I can't even contemplate it.

The next day, when Uly's in his room playing a video game, I dial my IT guy in India to get everything restored. I'm leaving on *my* terms. I'm not letting a sixteen-year-old dictate what I do.

There's no way he can hear me. He's too busy slamming his controller against his desk and yelling, "Damn it, Farmville!" I have no clue what's on Uly's mind. The kids at school are cliquey. They call him "Inside-Out Oreo." His dad's too ill to visit. He's on the verge of being "unhoused."

"Make sure the IT guy knows," Uly yells from the other room. "Whatever he does, I'm shutting it down. While you're at it—make sure you tell him about Alice."

CHAPTER 43

The Reckoning

Abigail

The Board of Behavioral Sciences (BBS) is a California state regulatory agency responsible for licensing, examination, and the enforcement of professional standards for master's-level therapists, such as Marriage and Family Therapists, Licensed Professional Clinical Counselors, and Licensed Clinical Social Workers.

The evidence against me, as cataloged and submitted by Ulysses Grant Green, is incontrovertible. The board has everything. My son collected and forwarded copies of my emails, attached screenshots of the fake Instagram profile I created, and submitted PDFs and other documents exposing financial fraud. But it's the comments from Alice that have the board most concerned.

That I could lose my license takes a while to sink in. When the notifications come, all I want to do is crumple them into a ball and throw them in the circular file. I want to be furious at Uly, but none of this feels like a betrayal. He was torn. He considered this the lesser evil.

Today's letter, though more formal, is no different—smelling faintly of India ink, printed on heavy linen paper embossed with raised letters and a notary's seal. I already know what it says.

But this one is ten times worse than the others.

To: Abigail Jones-Green, LMFT #364123

We are continuing to investigate the alleged ethics violations as specified in our Code of Conduct. Sarah Cohen, PhD, BBS Employee Number 50214 for the State of California, has been assigned to your case.

You have until January 15 to set up an appointment with her for mediation and counseling. Her contact information can be found as follows:

~   ~   ~

Between January 5, when I get the letter, and January 17, when we first meet in her San Mateo office, I learn all I can about Dr. Sarah Cohen. *Keep your enemies close.* When it comes to getting to know this Cohen person, Google is my best friend. It's still a free country, last I checked, and there's no harm in doing research—not when BBS Employee Number 50214 holds my career in her hands. The more I know, the better chance I have of getting on her good side.

Facebook turns up nothing—it's set to private. She doesn't have an Instagram.

On Classmates.com, I learn Sarah Ann Bernstein (her maiden name) was remembered in high school for her tumbling ability and her all-inclusive personality. Scrolling through the yearbook pages, pictures from her junior year show Sarah looking like Madonna from her *Like a Virgin* days. By her senior year, there's been an evolution—she's sporting a bleach-blonde tousled bob with bangs curled into an ocean wave. Her fishing-lure earring and beaded necklace strung on a tangle of acrylic wire would be comical if I hadn't worn the same thing.

With all that pancake makeup and glitter eyeshadow, the only thing teenagery about her is the mouthful of metal. I wonder what in her history led her here. No one chooses psychology without a reason. Was she neglected? What kind of household lets a kid go out looking like a Studio 54 wannabe on Picture Day? Or maybe Sarah's parents had a strong-willed daughter and just gave up trying to rein her in.

None of this tells me anything about present-day Sarah. On LinkedIn, I enter: *Cohen, Sarah Ann, Bay Area, California* and press enter. No photo pops up, but there's a laundry list of accomplishments: She earned her doctorate in Marriage and Family Therapy in 1997. There's a gap between 2003 and 2011, and then she's hired by the board.

From Zillow and Google Maps, I learn Dr. Sarah Cohen lives in a rundown, subsidized apartment complex in Redwood City. She's married to Nathanial Cohen, a work-from-home dad who, according to LinkedIn, dabbles in graphic design and caters on the side.

I hate this side of me. The overconsumption of Sarah Cohen's personal information is not only sickening—it's stupid. None of it prepares me to meet the real-life Sarah. All it does is increase the odds of blurting out something I shouldn't.

When I finally meet her, the difference between Sarah Cohen then and now is startling. Her hair is now a subdued, elegantly styled dark chocolate brown. The only jewelry she wears is a plain gold wedding band. But there's still something familiar—her vivaciousness, her hyperkinetic energy—it reminds me of that heart-of-gold joiner from the yearbook. Her legs, mostly hidden under her skirt, are toned and brown. I can picture her on a balance beam, executing a perfect split.

"Abigail Jones, I presume," she says.

"That's me," I reply, breathy. I tug at the string on my bracelet, hoping she won't notice, but she does.

"Is that a Hamsa?" she asks.

"Kind of, yeah. A Celtic cross too."

After we exchange first-visit pleasantries, she pushes a clipboard with a pen into my chest.

"The usual demographic info and disclosures," she says. "You know the drill."

She's not brusque at all. I'd imagined a Nurse Ratched. Instead, she's endearingly awkward, and a little shy. I forget other people don't have the Joneses' gift of the gab. But with Sarah, I'll soon learn—there's always a method.

Her office is spartan. No-nonsense. I could teach her a thing or two about décor, but the view outside—three mighty oaks—eclipses anything I've seen in a while. The pen she gives me is a cheap Bic—not substantial enough for sensory feedback. If you want to calm clients, use pens that feel good in the hand. I make a note to buy her a Uni-Ball. She'll feel the difference. Her other clients will thank me.

Still, I like the Zen rock garden, the water sounds, and the apple cider-scented diffuser.

Sarah tucks a piece of hair behind her ear and rests her palm on her cheek. It's surreal being on the client side, signing forms, paying fees.

"So your son turned you in?" she says. Her voice is steady and clinical—my own work voice.

"Yes," I say, ashamed. "He's not usually like that."

The look she gives me—curious, with a touch of empathy—almost makes me forget I'm in trouble with the board. My original plan was to say as little as possible, but the kindness in her eyes reels me in.

It's a good thing I have the form to focus on. I'm at the "Mom, Dad, and Siblings" section when my hand starts trembling.

"Can I leave the family part blank?" I ask.

"If it's relevant, include it. If not, no worries."

Her flexibility is the last thing I expected. Truth is, she's missing a lot. Because I'll be damned—it's *all* relevant.

My pain-in-the-ass, half-crazy mom, who died just as she was getting better. My sister, who ripped me off. My dad, now shacking up with some crack addict he met at the Flying J. I bet her colleagues don't have to worry about their 60-something father getting a girl pregnant.

I might be a stoic, but under pressure, I become a motor mouth. That's when I self-shame and give away all my power.

I return the pen to the clipboard. "I won't, then."

My eyes drift to the rocks in the Zen garden—smooth and wet, begging to be picked up.

"Aren't they cool?" she says. "My husband set it up for my birthday. It helps people talk."

I pick up a rock, think better of it, and set it down. She notices. Of course she does; it's her job. If I squirm or breathe too long, she'll log it.

"It's a long story, Dr. Cohen," I say. "I'd rather not share."

"Excellent. Because I don't want to hear it," she says with a wry laugh. "Stories turn into excuses. In this role, I'm not interested. And call me Sarah. I'm not a physician—that's my father-in-law."

She's an odd duck. Doesn't want the story, but she'll get it anyway. She has a way of wrapping even hard truths in warmth.

"What's in store for me?" I ask.

"We're revoking your license, if that's what you want to know," she says. "You can still practice—under supervision. But you'll need to follow my rules. I need to know your character and how fixed it is before I make a final decision. What I recommend goes."

My mouth goes dry. I didn't expect this.

"Without evidence?" I ask.

"You had a chance to respond."

"What about my school work? My Pupil Personnel Credential?"

"Your son's cross-complaint is with the district. That's up to them."

My throat dries up. I cough. She hands me a paper cup of water but does nothing to reassure me.

"So you know," she adds, "the reason I chose your case is because the fraud you committed raises ethical concerns. Most of our cases involve DUIs or sexual misconduct. This one? It's about character."

"Really?" I say, instantly regretting my tone. Not because I'm wrong—but because I should know better.

If Sarah is offended, she doesn't show it. She just jots a note in her notebook.

"I peeked at your demographics. I noticed you're Jewish. Since I am too, we can explore the spiritual side if you want. I used to study to be a rabbi."

"Not too much. I'm secular."

"At your discretion. The BBS allows spiritual counseling if both parties consent. I'm not twisting your arm, but since you didn't want to talk about your family …"

I look out the window. Trees with wet orange and yellow leaves glisten in the late afternoon.

"I'm Moroccan, actually. But that side's gone. All my cultural exposure is basically nonexistent."

"What about the food?" Sarah says. "It's caloric, sure, but delicious."

I shift in my seat. What's her point? Still, if she feels some kinship with me, it might work in my favor.

"It's okay," I say after a pause. "My grandma and mom had a maid who did the cooking. They never learned. Couscous, boiled chicken, too much cumin thrown in at the last minute. That was the extent of it."

I wish I had something better to say. On the Peninsula, Ashkenazi Jews are curious about Sephardi culture. She doesn't need to know my dad was Catholic and my mom worshiped at the temple of the almighty dollar.

"Don't get me started on food," Sarah says, returning to her notebook. "Anyway, let's begin. You collected money under false pretenses. You gave advice you knew could harm people—especially children. One person nearly died. Do I need to go on?"

We sit in silence. She's the first to speak.

"Are there any mitigating factors?" she asks.

"I thought you didn't want excuses."

"Mitigating. Background."

"My sister, who I'll tell you about later, has no safety net. Meanwhile, I walk around convinced I'll end up homeless."

"Let's set a goal for next time. I don't allow excuses, but one thing you can count on is knowing this: God provides for all His creatures. If you share your abundance, you'll be rewarded a hundredfold."

It takes everything not to roll my eyes. Is this where my BBS dues go? With what I'm paying, she'd better deliver. I haven't recovered from Dr. Topper's *Seven Steps*. The last thing I need is a prosperity gospel remix.

"How would you know?" I ask.

"Pardon me?"

You wouldn't, I want to say, but I don't. If my research is right, she never had to attend the school of hard knocks. She probably thinks it's God who's been providing all along.

When she looks at me with kind eyes and asks if I'm okay, my internal rant stops. Her face—so full of optimism, probably a wonderful mother to her kids—is impossible to resent.

"I bet you collected for UNICEF when you were a kid," I say. "Carton in hand, dressed as Florence Nightingale for Halloween. Nurse's cap, toy stethoscope, medicine bag full of sticky bandages that smelled like VapoRub."

"It's that obvious?" she says, voice soft as the Zen fountain behind her. "I trick-or-treated for world hunger. But you got the nurse part wrong."

When I laugh, she grows serious again.

"I might seem nice, but I won't hesitate. What's right is right."

She reaches for my clipboard. "You can finish the rest later. All I need today is your contact info and the one signature."

She leans back in her chair, one hand resting on the armrest. Another one of her *I-encourage-you-to-be-real* poses.

"There's no reason to be afraid," she says. "I'm not the enemy. I might've taken your license, but only temporarily. I'm here to help you get it back."

"It's an explanation, not an excuse," I say. "Uly's dad hasn't been well, which meant I raised him alone. The kid who filed the complaint. I spoiled him. I made promises about school I couldn't keep. Like, work hard and I'll get you there."

A flicker of relief crosses her face.

"This is a good starting point," she says. "Your son made it seem like you were a sociopath."

"He's a good kid. We get along. He just … snapped. I think I know the problem. My old office-mate once said I have a scarcity mentality."

"Who doesn't?" Sarah says. "Unless you're one of the lucky ones. Try raising six kids on one salary—mine. When the youngest starts preschool, my husband can go back to teaching."

I lean back. Maybe I said too much.

"I almost forgot," she says, glancing at her watch. "I know it's unorthodox, but it might be helpful to meet at your home sometimes. I only rent this office on Wednesdays and Thursdays. Seeing how you live would help."

"That'll be fine."

"In the meantime, you can still work—but under my supervision. You must inform all your testing clients about what's happening. Don't tell me it'll be a financial struggle. With the social media thing, you've made enough to last a while."

Not as long as you think, I want to say.

"How much detail?"

"Tell them it has nothing to do with your competence. I'm also assigning you one hundred hours of community service. There's a list of BBS-approved agencies on the table. Starting tomorrow."

"But I'm self-employed. You wouldn't believe the work I've done— the relationships I've cultivated."

"I'm not saying stop," she says, glancing at the oaks. "And I'll ask the board to word their notice in a way that won't harm your business."

I shift my weight from one leg to the other.

What would Uly say if he knew the trouble he's caused? I imagine him at his desk doing Calc homework, stopping to make himself a snack, wondering why I'm taking so long.

Next time, I'll tell Sarah more. Without context, she won't understand. Meanwhile, I'll do what I have to—listen to her talk about God, do the hundred hours.

What I don't know is this: because of Dr. Cohen's unorthodox ways, my penance will take years. Over time, the oak trees outside her window will lose their majesty. The apple-scented diffuser will start to smell artificial. Even the Zen garden will lose its charm.

By the time Sarah's through with me, Uly will be out of college and married.

As for Nikki—she'll be all over the news.

CHAPTER 44

The Visit

Abigail

In the sink is a carrot peel and half a lime. On the bottom rack of the fridge is a chicken covered in foil. I can smell the marinade—jerk sauce. The dishes are done. Uly's making amends; it must've taken him an hour to chop the ingredients, because it takes twenty when we do it together. The aroma of allspice, clove, vinegar, and zested lime fills the air. One rack higher sits a bowl of cantaloupe scooped into perfect half-inch balls. My heart softens. He's taken the time.

Uly isn't aware I've already forgiven him for turning me in to the BBS. I'll never fully trust him again, but I recognize an adolescent, knee-jerk reaction when I see one—even when it escalates into a four-hour rage-a-thon. Lately, Uly's been acting out his disappointments in real time.

I won't let him off easy. Gone are the bento box lunches with chicken cacciatore and breadsticks, the bowls of mac and cheese with smoked gouda, the thermoses of homemade ramen. If he doesn't like cafeteria pizza, Hot Pockets, or fish sticks (an epicurean health nut's nightmare), he can make his own food. I imagine him at his lunch table, eating with a spork—because for him, there are no finger foods—dabbing at his chin with an unbleached napkin.

At first, it was hard not to cook for him. For a while, I'd pour sesame oil into a wok and turn on the burner before catching myself. But it's gotten easier over time. Uly's love language is acts of service. From the beginning, he's wanted food fresh and made from scratch. Otherwise, he might not eat. Not being a chef, I've done my best to oblige. His earliest food memories don't involve the whirr of a can opener, but the grind of pestle against mortar. Me, in a gingham apron, peeling an apple or scooping cheese and melon with the metal tool he still favors. Our afternoon picnics. Days spent in the yard picking bean sprouts, cucumbers, mint, and tomatoes for a tossed salad. As a kid, he'd dig holes with a plastic shovel, searching for an errant lime or kumquat to bury. He'd pop a cherry tomato into his mouth and laugh. I'd pick him up by the straps of his overalls and carry him up the porch steps.

I'm not my mother, who reserved her best efforts for company—Baked Alaska and pineapple upside-down cake. For Uly and me, using monogrammed napkin rings and linen napkins on a Tuesday is nothing special.

None of this is for Sarah's benefit. She's coming over after dinner—she only eats kosher. By the time she arrives, the dishes will be done and put away. For a while, I hoped she'd forget about the home visit. I didn't know how much that could set us back. The way I try to animate our life with small, special touches—how that would lead to an explosion. Not with the way the evening starts, so innocently.

"We need to be done with dinner by the time Sarah gets here," I say to Uly. "Otherwise, with the way we are, she'll think we hired a private chef."

Uly, who still feels like he's in the doghouse, is doing all the cooking. He has his heart set on a marinade—which, honestly, takes forever. The clock on the stove says 6:00. She's coming at 8:00. The chicken needs to be in the oven in thirty minutes.

I'm still angry. I guess a part of me always will be. But in an effort to keep things mausoleum quiet (it's how he studies best), I tiptoe past his door. I crack it open—and immediately regret it. Papers, rough drafts, bottles of flavored mineral water, an empty popcorn bag—everything strewn across the floor. The room smells of mold and BO. My mother would've had a cow.

Sitting on the bed is my hip-hop/rap-loving child, wearing a Warriors shirt and Beatz headphones, singing tunelessly, tapping his feet, drumming on his thighs. He doesn't notice me. The last few lines tear me up:

My goals like a target, I'm tryna hit.

I'm lost, yeah, stuck in the pit.

They say I'm that bruh, but I don't feel blessed

Head full of pressure, can't get no rest.

I always thought rap was poetry for burn victims. I don't know if this is Uly's or if he picked it up somewhere. Either way, it breaks me. If he's sad, I want to know.

"When'd you make the marinade?"

Uly pulls off his headphones. "What? Homework?" he says. "Lemme listen to music."

"Not homework. The marinade."

"You said before the lady's coming. Three hours?"

"Not three—two. I want everything perfect."

"It'll be," he says, lowering his head. "I know you're nervous."

I don't need to mention my license. It's always been there—at least since the board got involved. Everything about him sags. I can hear it in his voice.

"You've been seeing Dr. Sarah for so long, I almost forgot," he says. "Or wanted to. I don't know."

"Forget that, son. When she gets here, introduce yourself, then go to your room. Say you have a project."

I want to believe it'll be fine. But when I return to the living room, all I see is imperfection. I imagine Sarah's home—a chaotic but loving reflection of life. Kids' drawings on the fridge. Fingerprint-smudged walls. What would she think of our cottage? Light birch floors. Matte white walls. Huge, professionally framed paintings that look like Rorschach inkblots. All at once, they seem sterile. I wish I could twitch my nose and replace our modular sofa with something overstuffed and cozy. I wish we had a clutter of family photos on the walls. Luckily, I've done the next best thing—gone to Target.

Once the chicken's in the oven and Uly is chopping vegetables, I start opening bags.

"What do you think?" I say, holding a pillow to my face. "The place isn't homey enough, so I bought two. One says *Live Laugh Love,* and the other says *Family.*"

"How do I know what looks good?" he asks, then changes his tone. "I hope you don't think this'll get your license back."

"Of course not," I say, placing a pillow on the sectional and giving it a karate chop. "Toss me the Febreze. These smell like jute."

I take a step back to survey the room.

"What do you think?"

"They look uncomfortable," Uly says. "I bet they itch."

"It's the trend," I say. "Anyway, when you're done, help me move some furniture. The sectional's so scattered it looks like an unfinished puzzle. She'll think we never sit together."

"It's fine, Mom. What kind of therapist/mentor?"

I reach into a bag and pull out a candle—one smells like coffee, the other like peaches.

"Dr. Sarah's got this big, noisy family. I want her to know that even though it's just us, we live in a home, not a museum."

Uly, pushing sectional pieces around carelessly on the hardwood, tells me to stop.

I let out a sigh. A wicker basket goes in front of the cherry-scented Glade Plug-in I placed earlier to mask the Lysol smell.

"Since it's too late for a shower, I bought you this," I say, tossing him a bottle of Axe. "And can you spray your room with Febreze? In case she wants a tour—scratch that. Don't let her see your room. And if you use the downstairs bathroom, don't touch the hand towels or the guest soap. They're for company."

"Okay, Mom," Uly says. "But first, lemme finish cooking."

I watch as he measures rice, puts it in the steamer, and sets the timer.

Once he's gone, I set the table. Bone china on charger plates. Irish linen napkins with matching table runner. Silver napkin rings. A rose in a vase.

We're okay. Dinner's at 7:15. But we don't count on Sarah knocking fifteen minutes early.

We're in the middle of our palate cleanser—chilled melon balls with lemon and an edible flower.

I greet her with a smile and a hug. She reciprocates.

"Sorry I'm early," she says, bright and cheerful. "But I couldn't—"

As soon as she sees Uly at the table, her expression darkens.

"I hope I'm not interrupting," she says. "You must be Uly."

Uly casts his eyes downward, his shoulders slumping like a turtle retreating into its shell. "That's me. The little narc," he says.

I feel bad for him. "We're almost done," I say. "Uly, if you want, you can finish in your room."

At first, it's okay, Uly's leaving. But as the minutes tick by, there's an awkward silence. I catch Sarah glaring at me—searing, accusatory. I don't know why. I'm used to people shifting their emotions, Mom in one of her crazier moods, Cy, but I don't expect this.

When Sarah's eyes narrow to slits. I don't understand. I've been giving it my all—working, learning, trying. I have no idea what I've done wrong.

I want it all to go away.

"Sit," I say, placing a teapot on the side table and pointing to two gold-rimmed glasses. "They belonged to my grandmother. For Moroccan mint tea."

My attempts to appease her do nothing.

She wags a finger. "Your dinner. All this. You lied."

I take a step back. I don't understand. I feel betrayed. The last person I expected to shame me—especially over nothing—is a therapist.

"You mean dinner? We try to make each night special. Making memories."

"When you said you were broke, when you said you were too busy to volunteer—I believed you. I cut you break after break. Man, was I naïve."

"You don't understand."

"Oh, I understand. Linen napkins. Pansy garnish. And this house—spotless. Don't tell me you don't have help. This takes time and money. Things you claim not to have."

"Uly helps," I say, and I'm not lying.

"I'd believe you, except for the napkins," she says. "I didn't think I'd be walking into the lobby of the Empress Hotel. Who irons these?"

"Thrifted napkins are cheaper than paper. And I have a steamer—takes two seconds. The flower? From the garden."

In one breath, the wind goes out of her.

She realizes she's overreacted.

I'd feel empathy for her, but I'm too angry about what she's put me through. Her house must be a disaster. A passel of under eleven-year-olds, a preoccupied husband. This woman, with whom I've formed an uneasy bond—turns out she's clueless. She says she knows history but knows nothing about how Moroccan Jews keep a home. If she thinks this is fancy, I'm giving her the diluted, half-Irish version.

Her eyes brim with tears. "I'm sorry," she says. "It's against Jewish law to jump to conclusions, but I'm so exhausted. It's me going through the motions. It's hard to find the energy. Working with the BBS, it's lies and deception all day long. Most are nowhere near as contrite as you, so when I saw your house …"

"The secret is to keep things minimalistic," I say. "Otherwise, there are too many tchotchkes to dust. Some stuff I bought because you were coming. As for the big dinner, Uly was trying to say sorry …"

"You have to admit, you complain to no end, too much about the trials of being a single mother," she says. "I felt sorry and was ready to arrange for volunteers from the synagogue. And there's one more thing I'm ashamed of; because of your sister, I distrust you. All it took was a linen napkin and a garnish."

I give Sarah a long look and exhale. I never thought I'd be sizing her up, but as high and mighty as she is, she is no different from everyone else. Once anyone learns about my family, it's like I'm on trial. *Hide your wallets! Guilty until proven innocent!* At least she admits it.

"I used to worry I was like her," I say. "Until I read that we inherit traits from all four grandparents. Siblings aren't necessarily similar. But I get it. Both of my parents were cheats. Even Uly said it. Apples and trees."

"Maybe the apple doesn't fall far," Sarah says. "But it can roll away. You, my dear, are a work in progress."

"I've treated Uly like a baby bird—bringing worms back to the nest instead of letting him forage on his own. It's a Moroccan thing. It's an only-child thing. I felt like I owed him. He's been such a good kid. Until recently, he never gave me a reason to think otherwise."

"No explanation needed."

"Okay," I say, laughing. "But since you blew up, does this mean I get my license back?"

"Very funny," she says. "Your mentorship isn't over."

"Speaking of which—I found a project. Uly's team is holding a benefit for East Paly kids who can't afford to play baseball. I'd like to help."

Sarah gives me a disapproving look.

"Not grand enough?"

She sips her tea. "I'm glad you're receptive," she says. "And it's a blessing you and Uly are getting along, and that he helps."

I'm not sure what she's getting at. All I know is this is enough for one night. I had hoped for breezy conversation, but it never came.

As I close the door behind her, she offers one last apology.

"This has been very productive for us both," she says.

As soon as the door clicks shut, Uly appears.

"I heard shouting," he says.

"I thought I knew what to expect. But wow, did that go south. We fixed it though."

"I hope you don't lose your license," he says. "No one will be sorrier than me."

"Sarah still thinks I need straightening out. She's probably right."

"Like me and the nail polish."

"She wants me to grow—but it's like no matter what I say, it's never good enough. Anyway, time for bed. School tomorrow."

CHAPTER 45

The Auction

Abigail

I've always liked those cheesy 90s movies. The heroine gets hit by a car or knocked out by an asteroid, and she's thirteen again—or aging backward. My favorite is when there's some sort of switcheroo. Maybe it's because I can't help but imagine my own trading-places scenario. Nikki's life in a minimum-security prison actually doesn't sound bad. Three hots and a cot. No responsibilities. No worries about whether I'm good enough or how things will look.

My movie is about hanging out at the Frontera Women's Prison. I'm reading and doing crossword puzzles while Nikki takes my place at the Fourth Annual Pasta Feed and Charity Auction. That's how uncomfortable I am with these people. If I can't switch places, let me hang out with the chefs in the kitchen—or the custodians.

If Nikki were here, she'd arrive looking like a rock star and smelling like a million bucks, a vision in silk taffeta. Her stretch limo would pull up to the front circle, valets attending to her every need.

She'd be fashionably late for maximum impact. She'd exit the limo legs first, the tops of her thighs exposed as if by accident. Once standing, she'd shake back her exquisitely coiffed black hair—fresh from a trendy NYC salon. She'd tip the valets so generously they'd scramble to open every door, leading her in like part of an entourage.

Her jumbo-sized double D's, always threatening to pop out of her dress, would enter the room before she did. The low-cut gown, wildly inappropriate for this crowd, would turn off the women. But the second she spoke—magic. They'd be scrambling to lend her their minks.

"To keep out the chill," they'd say.

"Let me tell you about my latest project," she'd say to the Who's Who of Silicon Valley. And once they were buttered and basted, she'd tell them about the ground-floor opportunity.

But we're not stuck in a movie. Nikki's in prison, doing a reasonable job writing her memoir of 99% lies. I'm the one here, having arrived in time to drop off foil-covered trays of fettuccine Alfredo and spaghetti marinara. No valet. No limo. No taffeta. No glamor.

Having parked the Aveo in the dirt lot across the street, it takes two trips to schlep the food into the country club's kitchen.

I'm wearing my best thrifted dress—a vintage Betsey Johnson—and too-tight shoes that make me limp. I dabbed on some perfume my ex gave me, but my fingers still smell like garlic.

Volunteer work done, I'm left to "enjoy" the dinner and auction. I use that term loosely. I feel like a fish out of water, never having been to one of these events. I'm wedged between two dressed-to-the-nines couples who clearly know each other, judging by how they talk over me. Unfortunately, it's assigned seating.

My watch says 5:45.

Sarah—my plus-one, and never late—should be here any moment.

It's been four months since our work began. I hope this auction represents the culmination of that work. I've given her hell—been judgmental, defiant, dishonest. But she stuck by me. She knows the real me, not the paper-roses version. At our last meeting, I laid it all bare. My worries about Uly. Insecurities from childhood. It has to end.

"You're a work in progress," she said at our last session, her voice brimming with authority.

"What do you mean? Aren't I almost done? I'm a good person. I'm a therapist. I understand people."

"To a degree," she said. "Empathy is a skill. Your parents couldn't teach you because no one taught them. You had generations modeling how to be self-absorbed. That's how it began. Let's see how it ends."

"I took their example. I learned what not to do."

"But you didn't learn how to *be*."

"Are you this hard on everyone?" I asked. "I'm repentant. I truly am. So grateful no one got hurt. I even put out a message."

"You sold people on a dream," she said. "An unattainable version of perfect country life. You think they didn't feel bad when they couldn't come close to what you showed them? And when they failed, you told them to lean in. To try harder."

"Because I was starting to believe it myself."

"The first volunteer work you chose was related to Uly. Even this one benefits your community. I want you to look *outside*."

My chest tightened. My skin flushed. Sarah was 100% right. I can be single-minded—especially when it comes to securing Uly's future. But was she calling me mediocre?

"Doesn't everyone do that?" I asked.

"It's the mission of the soul to look beyond the self."

A crackle from the loudspeaker brings me back. I scan the room. No Sarah. Could there have been an accident? Or did she blow me off?

I remind myself: it was *my* elbow grease that made this event. I should be proud. All imaginary Nikki did was get out of a limo in a tight dress and schmooze.

In my purse is a wad of what gamblers call "house money"—fourteen fifty-dollar bills earned after I flipped a limited-print hardcover art book on eBay.

Sarah probably wouldn't want me to bid. But how else can I prove I've changed?

I glance around. Hours over the stove like an Italian grandmother— tomatoes, basil, onion from my garden. Pasta from scratch.

Other tables are bidding on wine and dessert. I don't want to make a wrong move. It's been a while since Sarah lost it on me, but it lingers in the back of my mind.

At 6:00, still no Sarah. I start thinking the worst. Is she angry? With her, I *feel* like I belong.

One of my dress straps slips off my shoulder. I pull it up. My feet are throbbing. I slip off my too-small shoes and stretch my toes.

A heavily perfumed, champagne-blonde woman at my table gives me a look of displeasure. She turns to her friend.

"Are you bidding on the 2004 Silver Oak Cabernet?" she asks. "Or should I?"

Her friend says something inaudible. I don't care. Wait until they see me bid $1,000. I might look average, but I've come a long way from dumpster-diving for playthings.

I fiddle with my bracelet. When I look up, Sarah's there, looking marvelous.

Her hair has grown—I hadn't noticed. Now it's long enough for a chignon, secured with a rhinestone pin. Others might find her brown pantsuit and practical heels too utilitarian, but compared to her usual, she's made an effort. My anxiety evaporates. I want to protect her. Sarah might be unorthodox, but she's gifted. A mensch in her community. That her entrance barely registers is disheartening. Maybe two or three people recognize her. If we were in NYC or Long Island, it'd be different.

"We had a mini-emergency at home," she says. "No one to watch the kids. I would've called, but I was in the thick of it. Anyway, I'm excited. Aren't you? The raffle—I bought us each a ticket."

Before I can respond, the booming emcee begins.

"Hot air balloon ride over Napa," he announces. "Winner: Alexandria Pearce. Mrs. Pearce, please come to the front for your prize. Next up— lunch at La Foret with Laurene Jobs."

"My sister would know what to do with that prize," I joke.

I can't even imagine myself across from Laurene Jobs. We'd sip martinis and pick at salads in silence, counting the minutes.

"The rich rely on connections," Sarah says. "Not a bad idea, really. Too many people pretend merit is king. It's not. Both matter. Cultivate relationships."

Dinner hasn't even been served, and the champagne blonde and her bespectacled husband have already bid $3,000 for a $200 bottle of wine—

and won. A waiter uncorks it and pours. Sarah covers her glass with her hand.

Three thousand for a bottle of wine? What will my $1,000 get—*a cork*?

These people are out of my league. I might volunteer again, but I'm never doing another dinner. The other couple at our table spend an equal amount on another bottle. When the waiter returns, Sarah and I both pass.

Despite the early hour, the women are getting sloppy drunk, gossiping about someone named Patty, who's had so many collagen injections one eyebrow sticks up. Another woman is allegedly having an affair with the pool boy—and who could blame her?

The blonde spills wine on her friend's dress.

"Good thing we ordered white," she laughs, dipping her napkin into her water glass.

Everyone but Sarah picks at their meals. Carbs from spaghetti and fettuccine? No thanks. Sarah, who ordered the vegan option, clearly has a perfect metabolism—she's going to town.

Then comes the dessert bidding. This is the kind of thing Sarah *would* want me to do. Nothing in it for me. The only thing better than giving is doing it anonymously.

"German chocolate's my favorite," I say. "I'm going to try."

I don't know why I want her approval, but when she says, "Atta girl," I feel warm.

Bidding is fierce. Thirty seconds in, I'm outbid by a techie in a green shirt and horn-rimmed glasses. I try a few more desserts. No luck. Me and Green Shirt get into a bidding war with a man in a checkered blazer. A naked bundt cake goes for $2,000.

"Going once, going—"

Just when I think it's sold, Sarah raises her paddle.

I'm stunned.

Sarah, who just six months ago said she returned to work out of necessity, is fully in the game. You'd think every child in Project Open Hand depended on her.

"$2,500. $2,700. $2,900. $3,000. $3,050."

"Sold for $3,050," the auctioneer says. "To the pretty lady with the diamonds in her hair."

All eyes are on Sarah. The other couples at the table look at us like maybe they've misjudged us. We're now worth knowing.

$3050 for a naked Nothing But Bundt cake. Value: $50.

"Remember what I said about us all being part of a community," Sarah says. "My family will be fine. There are children in the Bay Area who go to bed hungry. They need the money more than we do."

Part of me thinks she's a fool. Didn't she chastise me for choosing the wrong charity? And don't bid what you don't have. Allow the drunken rich people.

"But what about your kids' tuition? Your retirement?"

"With God's blessing, we'll have enough."

The idea of *enough* is so unfamiliar that a breath catches in my throat.

And here she is—Sarah. A template for all humanity.

As the waiter slices the cake, I realize none of this is about money or scarcity. It's not just apples and trees. I may have been trained to be selfish, but living in Silicon Valley reinforced it.

When would I have stopped with the website? *Look at me. Look at my perfect life. Look at my farm, my home, my husband.*

Sarah forks a bite of cake into her mouth and smiles.

"There's nothing like a Nothing But Bundt Cake," she says. "Better than homemade."

I take a bite and return her smile.

"Thank you, Sarah," I say, setting my paddle on my lap. When the next item comes up—two box seats to an A's game—I'm ready.

CHAPTER 46

The Witness

Hugh – Morgan Hill, California – 2012

A sliver of red floats across the sky. A hummingbird drones, pecking at the rectangle of window not covered by blinds. A fat blur of white appears at eye level. I look away. When my eyes return, it's gone.

I know I'm home, but how'd I get here?

I don't have time to think about it—someone brushes past me.

"Today's your lucky day because Miriam's here," a sing-songy voice says.

Before she tugs on the string that lifts the blinds, before light floods the room, I see the small of her back. She has a roll of fat around her midsection.

I've never seen this woman before in my life.

My trailer is just how I left it a week ago. But instead of sitting in my Barcalounger with the remote, I'm prostrate in an at-home hospital bed. The windowsill is stained yellow and covered in dust. On the mantle is a picture of 18-year-old me in my Air Force uniform—crew cut, wool jacket, brass buttons. Mom put it there seven years ago. I scan the room for my Marlboro Lights, but the only thing there is my clean-as-a-whistle ashtray. The cigarette smell still lingers, permeating the carpet, the sofa, my blankets. But there's not a bottle in sight. I quit drinking and drugging for good a year ago.

I try to speak, but what comes out is a gurgle, like I'm underwater. I know I'm dying. Too much pain. I can't feel my hands or arms. It's like all the blood has drained from my face. My heart's frozen—an engine in need of a jumpstart.

"Why are you here?" I manage to say. The words are a struggle.

"I'm your nurse. You don't remember?" Miriam says, applying a wet cloth to my forehead. "I've been praying."

I try to speak again, but choke on the words—*Assigned by who?* This time, a rattle escapes from my diaphragm. I flinch and try to catch my breath.

Miriam brings me a mug of water. I open my eyes and see the outline of an angelic face, bathed in sunlight.

"Take small sips," she says, pressing the cup to my lips.

Dread seizes me. My bones ache. The last thing I recall isn't a memory, it's a feeling: I'm on my way out.

Nanette—or her ghost—grabs my arm. I yank it away.

"You okay?" Miriam says.

"Am I dying?" I ask.

A flash of fear crosses Miriam's face, then composure.

"You are," she says, with a gentle lilt. "Are you afraid?"

"It depends," I say. "How long, Doc?"

The joke lands—Miriam laughs and gives me a look that says even on my way out, I'm still a charmer.

"Silly," she says. "I'm barely above an orderly. I could look at your chart, but I haven't since I started keeping vigil. Last night, you were thrashing. Red splotches on your extremities. We were about to bring in the priest."

The lightbulb realization—*I'm on home hospice*—makes me shiver. I don't fear death, but I haven't lined up my ducks. I don't want to leave without seeing my girls one last time. Dammit all to hell.

One minute, I was truckin' down Highway 101 to see Nikki at Frontera. The next, here I am.

My chest tightens. First one tear, then another. My cheeks are wet.

I notice a space on the wall where the paper is peeling. My mother put it up herself—blue geese and pink ribbons—after I moved here when Nanette died. An eighty-year-old woman on a stepladder, brush loaded with wallpaper paste, strips taller than her 4'11" frame. I'd been too devastated to help. Within a year, she'd need a cane; three years later, a walker; a year after that—gone.

Another rush of pain. I can't breathe.

Miriam dabs my cheek with a Kleenex.

"There, there," she says.

Without moving my neck, I examine my arms. They're unrecognizable—waxy and dead, like a figure in Madame Tussaud's. The only thing I can move is my face. My throat doesn't feel like mine.

"I'm cold," I whisper, each syllable a strain.

"You can expect that," Miriam says. "Your body can't regulate its temperature."

She drapes a thin blanket over me. My bones crush under its weight.

"My daughters?" I say, spitting out the words with great effort.

"Your sister Emmy in Montana got in touch with your oldest," Miriam says. "She's trying to pull strings to get your other daughter on the phone. Permissions and so on."

I groan and try to turn onto my side—then remember I can't. This nurse won't give me a smoke, but I want one anyway. Miriam's trying the impossible, and I thank her for it. My girls—that's what I'm thinking of. Nikki, in prison for the second time, is losing privileges by the day.

I don't know when I blacked out. I remember being racked with guilt. I planned to camp out in the parking lot—be the first visitor in.

"Is Abi coming?" I ask. My throat feels like it's full of marbles.

I already know the answer. She's in Mexico with Uly. She'll be fine without me. But I have an apology to make.

"It wasn't easy," Miriam says. "Emmy finally located her. She was in a town with no reception. If your grandson hadn't gone to an Internet café three towns over to check his Instagram, who knows when."

"It's her penance," I gurgle.

Abigail being in Mexico—that was the nutty counselor's doing. Abi said she wanted to make a difference, to look beyond herself and Uly.

"There are street kids with no parents," she said.

"Maybe not so nutty," Miriam replies. "Abi and your grandson are trying to get here but I don't think they'll make it in time. Took them a day to reach Guadalajara. Last I heard, they were at the airport arranging a private plane."

Tears pool in my eyes.

Miriam touches my arm. "I'm sorry," she says.

Silent tears stream down my cheeks. How did I end up alone? As a young man, I partied too much, had too many friends, fought too much with my wife. I should've paid more attention to my girls.

"If and when Abigail gets here, and for as long as you need me, I'll be here," Miriam says, gently lifting my head to place a pillow beneath it.

It feels light. Soft. It occurs to me that this pillow, this blanket, and this caring soul are enough. I'll settle things with my girls. I'll watch over them from heaven.

Miriam holds a bottle in her hand.

"Open your mouth," she says. "This will make you comfortable. And water—but sip it. After some rest, you might be able to talk more."

When I wake, I have no idea how much time has passed. It's daylight. Miriam must've retrieved Dad's old table clock from the closet and wound it—it's chiming.

I focus. The smell of cigarettes has been replaced by antiseptic. An adhesive bandage covers a scratch on my hand.

I'm connected to a drip. I feel better.

Miriam reappears. This time, she's a shape—an all-white curve floating across the room. A hummingbird perches at the window. I imagine it nesting, waiting for its partner.

"Nanette," I whisper.

The medicine must really be helping—no gurgling.

"It's me, Mr. Jones," Miriam says.

"I could've sworn you were her. You're tall. You sound like her. That French accent …"

"Mr. Jones," she laughs. "I'm five feet tall. And a classy French accent? I wish. My first language is Russian."

What? It's like I'm in a fog. I need something to ground me.

Then I remember—I don't want Abigail to see me like this.

I'm *dying* for a cigarette.

Now that I can move my arms, I pantomime the act of smoking, hoping for the impossible.

Miriam tells me they were worried about withdrawal—because of all the burn marks. Then she retrieves a cigarette from a hidden drawer, lights it, and sets it in an ashtray.

"I can't let you smoke," she says. "But the smell might help calm you."

The sight of the cigarette, its orange-red tip, stirs the craving.

I inhale the scent of nicotine and let out a breath.

Hell, I'm glad I'm still here. I try speaking. My harebrained idea: the more I talk, the longer I stay alive.

The clock chimes 3:45. Abigail and Uly are on a plane.

Nikki—I love her as only a father can. She gets out. She goes back in. I'm glad Nanette didn't live to see it.

Tears fall.

"Do you have time to listen to an old man?" I ask. My voice is raspy, but thanks to the drip, it's not painful.

"Only for you," Miriam says.

"You're an angel on earth."

"Don't be silly."

"You keep saying I'm crazy. But I'm not. Anyway—I don't remember how I got to this popsicle stand. How long have I been waylaid?"

"They found you five days ago. You had short periods of lucidity, but for the first few days, you were out."

"Last I remember, I was in my truck."

"You had a heart attack. Luckily, it happened at a truck stop. An officer found you slumped over. You were in the emergency for a couple of days. Stabilized, then sent home. Your sister Emmy helped with that."

A shiver runs down my body.

The fact that I can move is both a blessing and a curse—everything hurts.

"Should I be scared?"

"Depends. People who believe in an afterlife tend to have an easier transition."

"Jesus has saved me."

What scares me isn't dying—it's the pain. And I'm not ready. Is Nanette in purgatory? Or has she made it to heaven? She *wanted* to be good—but she wasn't right in the head.

Abigail, who I made sure was baptized—she'll be fine. Purgatory's where helpful Jews go.

"One of my daughters, Nicole Ann—she's sinned and sinned. If she doesn't change, she'll face the wrath of God. When I imagine her burning for all eternity, I can't bear it. Do you think Jesus would?"

"I'll keep her in my prayers," Miriam says.

For some reason, that brings me comfort. I close my eyes. The bird is back at the window; the eerie hum of its wings is unmistakable.

I'm going to die. I can hear it in the rattle of my breath. It scares the bejesus out of me. Still, part of me is resigned. What a waste of a life.

"Talk more if you want, Mr. Jones," Miriam says. "My job is to bear witness."

Miriam has all the qualities I like. She is soft. Kind. Strong. I don't care that she's fat. She could've been my girl. Like a rolled-up tube of toothpaste with only one good squeeze left, I need to talk. It comes out in one big glob.

"I remember scarfing down one of those hot dogs spinning on a roller at a convenience store. Picked up some smokes, matches, and a Pepsi. Figured I was six hours from Nikki. Thought about keeping company with a truck stop doll. I've been so lost … but a voice from above—God's—told me no."

I pause. That's not how I want to be remembered. If I've only got a few words left, they shouldn't be about hot dogs and hookers.

"I don't want to die alone," I say, my voice barely a whisper.

"You won't," Miriam says. "I'm here."

I exhale. The tension leaves my body.

When the clock chimes four, I clench my jaw. Abigail must be over Los Angeles. I pray she lands in San Martin. San Jose to Morgan Hill during rush hour would be impossible.

Miriam lights another cigarette and places it near my tray. I inhale.

"You believe in the Bible," she says. "Any scriptures you want to hear?"

"Is there a verse for a man who's squandered his life? For someone broken like me?"

"There is no one so lost they can't find their way home," she says. "Or so lonely they can't find comfort in the Lord."

"I took others with me. I didn't mean to. My wife, bless her soul, was mental. As moldable as clay, no more than a child in most ways. And a petulant, injured, lashing-out one she was. If I told her the moon was green, she'd believe me—even if it was two inches from her face, glowing orange. So I got to do whatever. She left me once but came back. I had sway over her."

"We all have regrets," Miriam says.

My stomach twists inside.

"Nikki's a hot mess, but then again, so is Abi. Nikki might be in prison, but Abi's traipsing all over Mexico trying to atone. For what, I don't know. Pray for her too."

"I get it. Some people are in real prisons, and others are in prisons of their own making. The latter might find it easier to escape, but they all need our prayers."

"You don't know my Abi," I say. "When she was a kid, there wasn't a hill she didn't want to die on. So into justice, I thought she'd grow up to be one of those people who march."

"Some kids are like that," Miriam says. "But she grew out of it, no?"

I summon the energy for a speech.

"Always had problems with her. My wife used to say the oldest kid is like the first pancake."

I pause.

"I didn't mind Nanette being jealous. I was at the center of their world."

With no judgment, Miriam nods for me to continue.

"Nanette had zero self-control. She could be vindictive for weeks. Get into it with her and she'd enlist half of San Jose for support. My priest says Abi was the scapegoat—that I need to apologize. Says we failed Nikki too. Gave her too much of what she didn't need, not enough of what she did."

"Kids are hard," Miriam says. "Don't know how my husband survived our son's puberty. Too much testosterone for one house."

"Abi was two or three when it started. 'I hate you,' she'd say to Nanette. Didn't even know what those words meant. When she was five, whenever Nanette sent her to her room, Abigail would kick and scream and pound at the door. 'Let me out of here. I don't deserve this!' she'd yell. Maybe she was right. But cross my wife and she'd go into a white-hot rage. Man, could she carry a grudge."

What I say next chokes me up.

"To keep the peace, I had to give Abi the belt."

"Ah, the belt," Miriam says, like she knows it too well.

I struggle to swallow. I cough. But I've got to get this out. Miriam presses a cup of water to my lips. I drink.

"You'd think it'd faze her, but she was stubborn," I say, my voice sandpaper-dry. "At school, she was a mouse. Selectively mute, they said. But at home, she didn't know when to stop. When we had our second baby, the dam burst. Abi says Nikki became Nanette's flying monkey—and vice versa. Both my girls are good with words, but flying monkeys?"

Miriam looks hazy, like she's bathed in white. She rushes to my side. Now when she gives me water, it's by the dropperful.

"Are you sure you don't want a priest?"

"You're better than a priest. An angel on earth."

This time, Miriam doesn't call me silly. She just looks at me with those amber eyes.

"I can't give last rites. I'm not Catholic."

"You—and Abi, if God allows. She's been better since I quit using. But she's still bitter. Says trying to get affection from her mother was like touching a stove and not knowing if it was hot or cold. I was the only one. So how dare I disappear into addiction?"

"The real you is warm, committed, good. Drives all night for one daughter, hangs on for the other. I'm not the only one who sees it. We know these things."

"Why doesn't Abi see it? My good soul. When a boy she dated went too far, I had a couple of Italians from the car lot rough him up. Even that was wrong. She says I'm the reason her picker's off."

The clock chimes 4:15. Whatever grip I have on this life, I'm losing. If Abi can't make it, I'll visit her in a dream.

"I once was the apple of a young girl's eye."

I let out a long breath and feel my spirit start to leave. I'm at the ceiling, with a bird's-eye view. I thought I'd have clarity, but the opposite is true.

Where am I in time? 1959?

"I can't die," I say to Nanette's ghost. "Not with Baby Abi on the way."

Miriam's disintegrating before my eyes. A disembodied voice shakes me awake.

"It's okay, Mr. Jones," it warbles. "It's 2013. You're in Morgan Hill. Your daughter landed in San Jose."

Oh no. It's not possible.

I take a breath and settle back into my body. I close my eyes. Miriam presses another cup to my lips.

Please, God. Let me last just a little longer.

But I can't. The sticky honeysuckle nectar on Miriam's fingers sends me spinning. It's 1958. I'm a 19-year-old enlistee stationed at Sidi Slimane Air Base. Strong. Sharp. I reach for a gun—but my arms are immobile.

Miriam swoops in, dabbing my face with a cool cloth.

"Mr. Jones!"

My eyes snap open. I'd be frightened, but Miriam's voice is soft as wind. The chill of the cloth against my forehead grounds me.

She rolls a sliver of ice across my cheek.

"We've gotta get your fever down," she says. "You're delirious. I'll put more Ibuprofen in your drip, but for now, talk to me. It's the only way to stay sane."

"I tried to take care of Nanette. I was still drinking."

"She forgives you," Miriam says.

Water runs from the tap.

"I never should've taken that first drink. That first toke. I wanted life's perks. But there were consequences."

Miriam's footsteps come closer. At my bedside, she lays a towel across my face and neck.

When she speaks, it's with clarity.

"Self-medicating," she says. "People do it to numb pain. Then they tell themselves stories."

"I didn't know," I say, blinking back tears. "By the time I realized …"

"Ask and repent. God will forgive you."

"When Nanette died, we were legally separated. Her ma said I was the cause. They buried her as Nanette Moab. Forget Jones! Got a scripture for that? Crippling guilt."

"Isaiah 1:18–19 might help. May I read it?"

"If you think it's a good one. I've only just returned to God. I wanted to go when I was married, but my wife said no."

Miriam tilts her head, listening. Then begins to read, her voice floating over me:

Come now, let us argue it out, says the Lord.
Though your sins are like scarlet,
they shall be like snow;
though they are red like crimson,
they shall become like wool.
If you are willing and obedient,
you shall eat the good of the land.

My hands clutch the cold bedrails. My legs scratch against the blanket. But her words anchor me.

I summon the last of my strength.

"For fifty years, I've been on a death spiral—singing the blues on repeat."

"God knows. Depression."

"Have you ever heard of Jimmie Rodgers?" I ask. "My favorite bluesman. His voice, especially on 'TB Blues,' sums it all up. He knew he was gonna die."

"How could I not?" Miriam says. "My dad didn't even speak English, and 'Waiting for a Train' was his favorite song. Be as sincere as Jimmie Rodgers and God will forgive you. That's what I believe."

"On my turntable is a record. It's yours now. When you get home, play 'TB Blues' and think of me."

Before she can answer, the clock chimes again. My body thrashes under the blanket.

It's 4:30.

Please, God. Let me live long enough.

Next to me, Miriam thumbs through her Bible. A pendant slips from beneath her blouse—a dull silver replica of the Ten Commandments. I feel myself breaking open. With a whoosh, my spirit leaves my body.

This time, for good.

I'm at the ceiling again. All I see is my form—still, peaceful.

Miriam stands over me, bathed in white, except for the glowing orange orb at her neckline where her pendant rests. She never said if she was Christian or Jewish. It doesn't matter. She was exactly who I needed—an angel helping me cross into the arms of Jesus.

By the time she pulls the blanket over my head, I've already floated away.

"Go on home," she whispers, her voice a fading melody. "God is waiting."

The glow from Miriam's pendant dims into silence. Her voice, a soft memory.

"God is waiting."

Her words linger just a moment more.

And then—nothing.

No more air in my lungs.

No more weight to carry.

The world will continue without me.

CHAPTER 47

The Envelope

16 February 2015 Carmel Pinecone

For one hundred years, your best source for the Carmel and Monterey Valley's local news.

Pacific Grove Police have issued a scam-watch after scores of elderly residents fell victim to a crime ring operating within the walls of an Elmwood, New York Women's prison. A person of interest has been identified. However, according to the warden, the case is on hold due to the unreliability of the main witness, also an inmate. All of this finds the community in an uproar. Adam Tehranpour, whose 89-year-old mother Yasmina was one of the victims, is outraged. "How much proof do they need?" he said. "Not only does Nicole Ann Jones know my mom, she's been victimizing her for years."

Yasmina

The envelope, from Riker's Women's Facility Elmwood, pushes its way through the mail slot. I can tell it's from Nikki without even looking because Bruno, our toothless white fluff of a dog, never barks like this when we get advertising circulars or political ads. He has a nose for trouble. He whines, claws at the door, chases his tail—which isn't doing any good—because there it is: the letter, sitting on the plush carpet like an unshucked pearl. How many times have I been conned by her promises, only to find that behind her syrupy-sweet persona is a hardened shell? Just thinking about how she might start—*Esteemed Auntie*—I can already feel the knot forming in my stomach.

My attendant, Lucia, who will never understand what a good boy Bruno is, tosses a thick black braid over her shoulder and tells him to stop. *He's our early warning system,* I want to say, but she's too busy propping a pillow behind my back, gripping the handles of my chair, and wheeling me to the table.

"Nobody wants me to read them," I say, pointing toward the carpet. "But as I told you once before, I owe it to her mother. I could've intervened. Maybe none of this would've happened—but I didn't."

"Your loyalty belongs with the mother, not a daughter who's caused so much harm," she says.

As she drops a rose into a vase and wraps a set of utensils in a napkin, I heave a sigh.

Lucia has been closer than a daughter to me, but lately, she's been more on my son Adam's side than mine. It's like they're ticking off items on a bucket list that doesn't belong to me. Even the way she's set the table makes me wonder what they're up to. The crystal, the china, the linen napkins—it reminds me of the Carmel Valley restaurants Bijan and I used to frequent, the kind of places where it was hard not to bump elbows with movie-star locals like former mayor Clint Eastwood. Is that what they intended?

It must've taken all morning to make this plate—turkey sausage and a cold couscous and prune salad, surrounded by a circle of oranges.

Without commenting, I mush a sausage with my fork and pass it under the table to Bruno.

"Don't ever stop!" I whisper.

When Lucia spoons a sad-looking dollop of cottage cheese onto my plate, I grimace. After over fifty years in this country, I'll never get used to the texture or taste. If they really wanted to get things right, she'd have made me *raib*, a yogurt I used to make when I was a maid in Morocco—sweetened with a savory orange blossom syrup.

"Good for bones," she says, without looking at me. Good old Lucia. She'd rather pretend-struggle with the blinds than acknowledge my question.

"By the way, Adam called," she adds. "He's coming over."

You'd think I'd be looking forward to a visit from my sweet son, but all I want is for it to go away. He thinks I'm naïve. Thinks I can't fend for myself. It was Bijan who perpetuated that. He said having a carefree wife was a sign of a man's success. I'd grown up with rural ways, but he wanted me to go *la-di-da*. He wanted a nouveau-riche Carmel Valley matron, one of those chatterboxes with nothing substantial to say except, "Life is beautiful."

When it was important to, I fought back.

"This is not who you married," I said once.

I'm tough—always have been—but it's a side I've hidden from my son. Now that I've gotten myself caught up in the latest Nikki scandal, he thinks I can't take care of myself. It doesn't help that instead of humming along as usual, my body now requires round-the-clock monitoring. The doctor said the body keeps a tally, and I guess he's right.

It started when I wrote a large check to a man from a roofing company. Before that, everything was fine. But the man cashed the check and never came back. How was I to know Nikki was behind it? Now, if Adam isn't gathering evidence against her, he's trying to figure out ways to take my freedom.

"I thought you'd be safe," he said when he confronted me. "Even behind bars, she has a hold on you."

"She doesn't," I sputtered. "I don't know why everyone thinks that. I didn't know it was her. The man said he was a contractor. He knew so much I thought he was one of your friends. I'm not the only one—Mrs. Conrad, too."

"It's you I'm worried about, Mom. I don't know what's gotten into you lately. You fall for dangerous shit, and the people you *can* depend on— like me and Lucia—you treat like enemies."

All you do is take things away, I did not say. It's like the two of them are buttering me up for something.

But not Nikki. Her letters are always encouraging—and that's the problem. Miss Suzie Sunshine has a way of making me feel like I still have a lot of life left in me.

I remember my hands shaking. "In one of the letters, I told Nikki the roof needed fixing."

It wasn't like Adam to have steam coming from his ears. When he slammed the cabinet so hard it nearly broke a hinge, I was shocked. Other men are like that. Not Adam.

"Good God, Mom!" he said. "I told you not to respond. Maybe she can't commit wire fraud in prison, but she can still find a hundred ways to take advantage."

"She wrote about how things were. I wanted her to know it wasn't perfect here. I'll stop. But her mother, rest her soul—I don't want to abandon her."

"Yeah, yeah. Lucia told me you had that hang-up. Let me go over everything. Give Nikki enough for shampoo or cigarettes to trade—but don't reveal anything. You've heard of the dark web? All she needs is a partial Social Security number, and there's enough online to fill in the blanks."

I felt my skin prickle. "But, but—" I sputtered.

"Let me handle it!" he said. "My fear is she's trying to worm her way onto this estate. And if you do like last time and write the parole board on her behalf, I'll ask for conservatorship."

My face falls whenever I disappoint him. Now that he's spoken to me in such a manner, it's like I stop breathing for a moment. I'm not stupid enough to write another "Nikki's reformed" letter—but maybe he's right to be afraid. If only everyone would stop making me feel so diminished.

Ever since that day, when Adam gave me his speech, my mind has traveled to strange places. What did his investigation reveal? My heart sticks in my throat. Maybe Nikki already hired someone to go to the "darker" web. Nikki might be 3,000 miles away, but *I'm* the one imprisoned.

That's the part no one understands. This fear—of being used, cast aside, controlled—it's not new. It didn't start with Nikki or Adam's threats of conservatorship.

My hand reaches for the necklace I've worn on and off for over seventy years. For solace, I say a prayer to the woman who gifted it to me. I never believed in evil—only in good. But Mma must've known differently.

"Mma. I still remember how your fingers lingered around my neck the morning you presented it to me on my wedding day."

I was only thirteen.

CHAPTER 48

The Andisheh

Yasmina

The faint sound of a car outside pulls me from my thoughts. Confused, I squeeze my eyes shut. When I open them again, all I see is the ocean. But the sound is enough. How could I ever think I had agency? Yet I did. At twelve and thirteen, fleet-footed in goatskin sandals, everything in my mountain domain was within reach. As a member of a High Atlas nomad tribe, I'd herded my sisters into the forest. There, we'd spend hours bent over baskets, picking mint. I'd teach them to lay each sprig in as delicately as if it were a prize.

You'd think the memories would be fuzzy. But they're sharp, as if they happened yesterday. For so long, I've wanted to reclaim the confidence I had as a child. That's why it takes so much to return me to the present: the smell of mint, the sound of Lucia pouring tea and stirring it with a cinnamon stick, the steam on my face.

And sitting by itself, to the right of my plate—familiar enough to be overlooked—is the *Andisheh*, San Jose's out-of-print Farsi-language newspaper. The *Andisheh* comes from Bijan's culture, not mine, but I relish it all the same. A smile erupts across my face, though I return to neutral before Lucia can see. I unroll my napkin and let the silverware clink onto the tray. The message I want to send: I won't be placated so easily.

In most matters, I'm yielding—living for the happiness of others because it brings me joy. But now, in honor of the fierce girl I once was, I want to do things differently.

I marvel at the newspaper. It must have taken Lucia a month to track it down. She's activated something in me. She doesn't realize she's brushed against a sacred memory. After Nanette passed and Bijan and I patched things up, the *Andisheh* became part of our Sunday morning ritual. Though Farsi was different enough from my mother tongue—and from Arabic, my second language—to be challenging, Bijan's poetic voice made even the dullest stories come to life.

I didn't mind hearing about the latest comings and goings in Silicon Valley. Stories about mergers, acquisitions, venture capital, and the different kinds of silicon chips going into products that could do anything.

"What do you think?" Lucia asks, unable to contain her excitement any longer.

I don't tell her it's the epitome of boring to slog through without Bijan. Instead, I offer a polite thank you.

Her sorrowful, long-lashed eyes give me a pitying look, as if I don't already know how few grains remain in my hourglass.

"Once we're done here," I say, "take me to the sea."

"You'll need a ramp," she says. "Adam checked. It's against city ordinances."

Her comment stretches me to breaking point. I imagine her and Adam wagging their fingers at me. Bijan and I should have installed a retractable ramp forty years ago, back when regulations were lax—when they still let barges sit abandoned in Monterey Bay. We never thought we'd need a ramp. He surfed. I skied on the water.

Even the new mayor—who campaigned against overregulation—couldn't stop it. Apparently, the city must look perfect from all angles, even the air.

"The new guy, then," I say. "Good with his hands. Not a big macho. At low tide, maybe he can smooth out the sand and wheel me down. Or he can carry me."

Lucia pretends not to hear, but the way she fusses with the drapes tells me the answer is no. It's fine for her to carry fragile old Bruno down—but not me?

Assuming Adam's behind this too, a plan starts to form. My son is 300 miles away, working in the film industry. Lucia has her days off. Her substitute probably won't be as alert.

I hate how angry this is making me. On Monday, I'm calling my attorney.

"Change the will," I'll say, even though I would never do it.

To think—I was going to give Lucia the deed to the four-plex on Ravenswood. It would've been like winning the lottery. And Adam, his wife and kids? An animal refuge would appreciate the money more.

If Lucia could do this one thing for me, doesn't she know it would bring her back into my good graces? I'd open my pocketbook wide. I'm not stingy. I've given thousands to the survivors of the original Moab family. The children who were once in my charge in Morocco are now in their sixties and seventies—a proud bunch who chose to move north to Oregon and Washington rather than stay in pricey Silicon Valley and beg. I helped them resettle.

The only local Moab still nearby is Nanette's grandson, Uly, a sophomore at CSU Monterey. His dorm isn't far—an old Fort Ord barracks. He visits often. When I help with expenses, he blushes, but he still cashes the checks.

After Lucia wins her "battle" with the drapes, light floods the room. I turn away from the glare and fix my eyes on a photograph of an old Berber woman. The proper term for our tribe is Amazigh, not Berber, but I'm an old woman now and old habits are hard to break. Bijan and I bought the photo when we were newlyweds, back when the MOMA gift shop was right there. It was during the height of Western fascination with Morocco.

Though *Daguerreotype #1: La Vieille Femme Berbère du Maroc, circa 1912* was always just a souvenir, my feelings about it have changed. It's as if someone spun me around and, in some feat of reverse magic, I became old. Now I could pass for the twin of that ancient, long-dead High Atlas woman. And it bothers me more than a little. My once-brown skin is now a faded sepia, and my face—creased with deep lines—looks like an apple left out to dry.

The picture makes me feel like it won't be long.

What I really am is tired. Clutching my amulet, I let sleep overtake me.

CHAPTER 49

The Ramp

Yasmina

"Rain is here, Miss Yasmina," Lucia says. Her radiant, sing-song voice makes me feel guilty about the plans I'd made before Tylenol and a long nap restored me. Adam is right about me trusting the wrong people. Maybe they really are looking after me.

"We must make the best of our day," Lucia adds. "You want the balcony? Low tide is the best time. No get sprayed."

I'm thinking I can trust her—but when she moves closer, an envelope slips from her pocket. She scrambles to retrieve it, but it's too late.

"The letter from Nikki!" I say. "Read it."

"Your son said—"

"Is he here? Besides, Nikki's not taking advantage of me again. It'll be difficult watching her go homeless, but I'm starting to come around."

My words, while not altogether true, convince Lucia. She reluctantly removes the letter and lifts it out of its envelope.

"My brother's in jail. Drugs. Now he does twelve steps."

"Good for him."

What I don't say is that I wish there were a recovery program for what Nikki has—wire fraud, larceny. Over decades.

"Sorry I kept this from you," Lucia says. "I read it now."

And then, in her already hoarse voice, she begins.

"Esteemed Auntie. How precious you are. Thanks from the bottom of my heart. I don't know what I'd do without your gifts. With the money, I bought cigarettes—the only currency that matters. I'm studying Buddha, learning about karma. Mine is very strong, so no more mistakes. When I get out, I'm turning around."

When Lucia stumbles over the word *mistakes*, I stifle a laugh. Odd phrasing, considering a years-long crime spree.

"No muestra remordimiento," Lucia murmurs.

"Bijan never wanted me to tell anyone I was a maid in Morocco. Nanette was the daughter of my employer, so Nikki's not really my niece. But in memory of her mother, I've been putting fifty dollars on her account every month. After this, instead of money, I'll send Bijan's books on spirituality. That way, she can read about karma. What do you think about two care packages? One for Nikki, one for your brother?"

"Sure, Señora," Lucia says, impassively.

She grips the handles of my wheelchair and bumps the tires over the sliding glass track separating my bedroom from the veranda—hard, as if her thoughts are elsewhere. The sudden, unbraced movement rattles me from my neck to my tailbone. I've been in a lot of pain. My doctor, who happens to be from Yemen, is concerned.

"My mother used to pound turmeric root and cumin seeds into a fine powder," he told me. "Her fingers would turn yellow and orange. She'd say, 'Be careful. Time is a mortar. All of us, if we live long enough, will crumble to ash.'"

He said that to the wrong person. I don't have osteoporosis—a second opinion and a bone density scan proved that—but arthritis has stiffened my hands so much it's hard to put on my amulet in the morning. My fears about Nikki and the dark web have lessened, but I still slump in my chair like a wilted flower.

I'm thinking of Nanette—grateful she never saw me like this—when Lucia's touch brings me back. She places one hand under my shoulder and the other near my neck. In one deft motion, she lifts me to a sitting position.

"I take care of you," she says.

I wince in pain, but once I'm outside, the panoramic view of Point Lobos and the burst of chill air on my face make me feel ten years younger—more effective than sleep, better than Tylenol. What would a walk on the sand, a chance to dip my toes in the water, do?

"Better," Lucia says, sensing my improvement.

"To be sure," I reply. It surprises me how my voice no longer sounds weak.

"Being out—good for soul. But the Esselen tribe says the wind can be a fiend."

"Let me dip my feet?" I ask. "In honor of them."

"How about I wheel you to your old iron bistro set? You can be closer to the ocean. You can't go to the water, but you can pretend."

Her comment makes my cheeks burn. The bistro set is supposed to be on the beach, not the veranda. In our retirement, Bijan and I had breakfast there every morning. If the wind kicked up, our old gardener, Arturo, would set up a tent, Esselen gods or not. Remembering those dinky chairs—how they crimped the sides of Bijan's thighs, making his legs look like sausages in silk casing—brings a smile to my lips. We tried plastic, even wood.

Bijan never once complained about aging. He loved our routine. From his chair, he'd release the *Andisheh* from its cardboard tube, remove the rubber band, and smooth it out like an ancient scroll. For years, we sat across the table, taking turns reading that paper. Later, when macular degeneration took hold, we adjusted.

"Darling, do you mind reading this time? My eyes are tired," he'd say, and it always made me a little sad.

Toward the end, we sat so close our bistro chairs clanged like bumper cars. By the light dappling through our lone cypress, he'd read a few words, then pass it to me so I could read the rest in poorly accented Farsi. Bijan would laugh and correct me gently, always making some joke about never having to stain his fingers with newsprint again.

As our hearing failed too, I made sure we read when the ocean was at low tide, so I wouldn't have to raise my voice over the crashing waves. More often than not, we'd walk along the shore. Bijan would roll up his pant legs, and we'd let the water rush over our feet. Occasionally, a stronger wave would hit, and we'd shuffle back, laughing. If there was one thing about him—he never gave up. I know he'd be disappointed in me if I did.

A tidal wave of spray crashes onto the veranda. Lucia's soaked. So am I. A flash of an idea enters my mind.

Next Monday, when Lucia's off, I'll ask the new guy—Gustavo—to build a ramp. I figure a little cash in an envelope will improve his life immensely. I might not be able to solve the problem of Nikki—not without her breaking me like she did her mother—but ordinances I can handle. And whatever the fine is, I'll pay.

By the time I'm forced to remove it, I'll already be dead.

CHAPTER 50

The Amulet

Yasmina

Assembling a ramp from the second-floor veranda to the beach takes Gustavo exactly one day. After that, wheeling me down is no problem. Once there, he helps me with my sandals and lets me dip my feet into the freezing water. Then, something unexpected happens. My amulet slips into my bra. Feeling around the back of my neck, I realize the chain has caught on a button.

Damn loose clasp. Damn struggling fingers.

Without being asked, Gustavo unwinds the chain from the button and fastens the necklace around my throat. A wave of icy water rolls over my feet, plunging me into a world of memory.

We're at the beach. It's windy and cold, like we're not in Pacific Grove but in Big Sur, where the sea is always choppy. Pages of the *Andisheh* are flying around, and we try in vain to save them. We're both shivering in our tracksuits. Only, Bijan's angry. Pieces of sea glass have washed up on the shore, and he can't stand walking over them. Me, I don't mind.

"John Steinbeck could've drunk from that glass," I say.

But Bijan isn't having it.

"One man's trash is another's garbage," he replies.

He's lively, spirited. Neither of us knows he's almost at the end.

Things escalate—I don't remember how. Bijan calls me a Shilha. It's a minor betrayal, him using that word. That's what the elite in Rabat used to call us—peasants.

I realize now it was just another slur for being poor, akin to calling someone an Appalachian or a hillbilly. I'd tell him now he should be ashamed. That woman in the MOMA picture—I bet she was a proud Shilha until the day she died.

Recalling Bijan like this makes me shiver. Why not remember one of the many peaceful days when we walked along the shore, the sand so fluffy and dry it didn't even register our footprints?

Another wave washes over my feet. At the center of the sky, a sliver of sun peeks out from behind a cloud. Tilting my head upward, I feel a single drop of rain strike my forehead. I pull my hood over my head and shiver.

"You decide, Señora Yasmina," Gustavo says, his voice feather-light.

Soon, it's really raining. Large drops land on my head, the edges of my sleeves, and the arms of my wheelchair. Gustavo opens an umbrella and brings it near. We sit in silent meditation, watching the waves retreat from the water's edge, leaving behind tangles of seaweed. I curl my toes into the wet sand. I press one foot onto a piece of kelp and feel it pop.

Gustavo speaks first.

"Still want to stay?"

"For a minute. If you don't mind."

"As you wish," he says.

His voice is tired but pleasant, like the coo of a dove.

I tighten my jacket around my shoulders. How worn out he must be after building the ramp! And here I am, about to ask him to snap my jacket.

"Remind me to call Adam," I say. "Whatever he's paying you, it's not enough."

"Gracias," he replies.

With his umbrella protecting me from the rain, we stay awhile longer, watching the waves inch toward us. Quiet waves lap over the shore, gentle as a lullaby. At low tide, the Pacific really lives up to its name. The water kisses my feet and lingers before retreating.

This sensation—and the caw of a gull overhead—evokes another memory. It rises in my mind like a bird in flight, solid and sure, as if God retrieved it for me and gave it back as a gift. In it, a swirl of amber sea glass appears before my eyes, each piece shaped into a heart by its hundred-year tumble through the sea.

Then it occurs to me: I am not too old to fight. I may have started in circumstances identical to the woman in the photo, but my life has taken turns no one—not even I—could have predicted. If Lucia had any idea what it took for me to get here, she'd know it would take more than ocean water to knock me down.

"My cousin says you're perfect," Gustavo says. "Like you came from the sky. Like a rich lady on *Shahs of Sunset.*"

An awkward, uninvited laugh escapes me. "Glad to have your interest," I say. "My husband used to tell everyone I was from Casablanca or Rabat. He wasn't a liar—but there was a lot he left out. It stung at the time, and we argued about it, but now I understand. Anyway, remember the picture in my bedroom? Of the old woman? She is me. I am her. We're from the same tribe."

Gustavo gives me a skeptical look. He thinks I've gone crazy.

"Have you heard of the Shilha people?" I ask. "We're mountain nomads. Half the time, we starved. My village, Tacheddirt, was extremely primitive. Except for a few people who hid with us during the war, we never had visitors. We were as isolated as they come."

I clutch my jacket to my chest. Gustavo can't imagine I was ever poor—I can see it in his face. A woman who throws money away on a ramp?

"I'm sorry," he says.

"Oftentimes we *did* eat. It wasn't bad. And we were almost always happy."

"That was a long time ago," Gustavo says, then corrects himself. "You look young."

"Don't try to fool me. I'm old. The month and day of my birth are unknown. But the year—1926—is certain. That's because Baba planted a tree for each child born. All we had to do to know our age was cut off a branch and count the rings."

Gustavo is puzzled.

"I'm sure it was the same for your grandparents," I add. "Morocco only started keeping statistics when France established the protectorate in 1912. And no bureaucrat was hiking 6,000 feet up a mountain to write *my* name in a ledger."

"Colonialism," I say. "Villagers starved and blamed the gods. But the Europeans—oh, they used more than bullets. They diverted water. They stole food."

I'm about to say more when Gustavo suddenly begins picking up pieces of sea glass and hurling them into the sea. His outburst surprises me. What he says next isn't a speech—it's an explosion.

"If I could go back, I'd tell our ancestors—don't be stupid!" he shouts. "Kill them all, I say. *Kill them all.*"

Seeing him like this shatters the image I had of him. From what little I know, he collects sea glass, flowers, and bits of shell to take home to his children. But now I wonder: what is the brick and mortar that builds someone's soul?

Behind every militant, there's a story. I can't imagine the horrors he's lived through.

Maybe because of my naivety, my views on colonialism are more nuanced. My parents were children when the French protectorate was formed. It didn't affect us—at first. By the 1930s, the roads were in. Schools were being built. We were connected to a world of possibility.

Still, Gustavo has me thinking. We'd lived atop that mountain for thousands of years. But within fifty, hunger forced us out.

When he centers himself and takes a breath, my worry turns into admiration. A man with passion and fight who can regulate his emotions. With Nikki getting out of prison in the next year or two, I could use someone like him—someone to protect me.

After pointing out a bald eagle overhead, Gustavo begins telling a nostalgic story about how he met his wife. But his words are drowned out by the thrum of a helicopter. By the time I can hear him again, he's changed the subject.

"Tell me about your childhood," he says.

It's hard. After so many years with Bijan—loving, but a bit ashamed of my past—I've absorbed some of that shame. Marrying a 39-year-old Berber woman with no formal education was Bijan's one act of defiance, a thumbed nose at the affluent, neglectful parents who parked him at a French boarding school and forgot he existed. It wasn't until my documentary-filmmaker son—who thrives on interviewing "people like me"—that I started talking. And only when the camera was off.

"As a child, I was told Tacheddirt was the highest place on earth. And who were we to question it? We were within arm's reach of Anzar, our god of the sky. Getting there was like climbing a spiral staircase."

From Gustavo's expression, I can tell he wants more.

"When it was warm enough," I say, "Baba and Mma—our word for mother—and we children would tend to the animals and gather food."

"You were nomads, but you stayed in the same place?" he asks.

"For generations, yes. We always returned. Baba used to say, 'When the food runs out, we leave.' But we stayed. From 1928 to 1932, Baba helped build the road that would eventually cut through the Tizi n'Test Pass. Even after meeting so many strangers, we still slept in tents. Only in winter would we excavate a nearby cave."

Gustavo encourages me to continue, but there's not much more.

"My recollections are sensory," I say. "The warmth of Mma's embrace. The henna tattoos on her face and arms. The citrusy scent of the argan trees. But those are the sweet memories of youth."

"Childhood is like a dream," he says. "But every trance must end. Something always comes to wake us."

I rub my amulet between my fingers, feeling its familiar weight.

"I was thirteen. A mere child," I say, my voice thick with memory.

Blue lights flash in the distance. Sirens slice through the silence—police cars growing closer. But instead of fear, I marvel at how quickly things change. In the time it took to catch my breath, the dreams of my childhood were gone.

Now, as I grow older and my body fails me, I know: I wouldn't go back.

I'm where I belong.

I close my eyes and see Bruno curled up safely in his bed. As I take in one last breath of salty air, the hum of the ocean faint in my ears, I'm not thinking about Adam or Lucia, or even about being on borrowed time.

Bruno will be looking for me.

CHAPTER 51

Alerts

Abigail – 2022

The soft hum of a sound machine fills the room, the ocean waves rising and falling in a rhythm I've come to rely on. Dad died a decade ago, but I still feel the echo of that loss. Maybe it's because we got there an hour too late. I'll always regret that. The nurse said he had my name on his lips. That was a shocker. I'd been angry. I'd let him down. I still have his last voicemail—the one I never answered—saved on my phone.

On the anniversary, I'm snuggled under a comforter, fuzzy socks still on my feet. One animal is lying across my knees, and another is nestling her graying muzzle against my chin. A series of Alexa alerts is about to go off. The first is a reminder: at 7:00 a.m., it'll be time to give Shawnee her heart medicine. Many more will follow—notifications for wake-ups, birthdays, appointments, medications that need refills, subscriptions about to expire, and news I want to stay on top of.

I wonder what Dad would've thought of all this technology.

"Baby girl," he would've said, "take care of the dog but mute the rest. Life's too short for that nonsense."

Although I'm more like Dad than I care to admit, in this regard, I'm nothing like him. I appreciate having an electronic secretary. I've even programmed Alexa to alert me anytime an article comes out about Nikki. Ever since she was released from prison three years ago, I figured it was a good idea to monitor her comings and goings.

Before today, there hasn't been much Nikki news. There are the dozens of social media posts, the PR blurbs touting her chain of concept restaurants and plugging potential franchise opportunities, the self-aggrandizing blog posts. Since Nikki's release from Frontera—her third incarceration, the serious one—she's been the picture of rehabilitation. Only, I don't believe a word of it.

Some alerts make me angry. Like the one that led me to a glossy feature in *Lo Angelina* Magazine's "Most Dynamic Women of 2018." She must've conned someone into greenlighting that one. Those shiny black-and-white pages, complete with an insert that smelled like Chanel No. 5, might have impressed others, but what I couldn't gloss over was her face. There's this aging malevolence, like her portrait—much like Dorian Gray's—has finally caught up with her.

Decked out in furs and fine jewelry, she has a cobra draped over her shoulders. She's stamping out a cigarette with a stiletto. She's dangerous. She's bad. She's irresistible.

Other alerts cause second-hand embarrassment so painful I can barely read them. They confirm my suspicion that she has zero self-awareness. Like the link to her YouTube channel *Crazyass Bazillionaires*. I watched the first episode, then blocked the rest. Who wants to see a couple of Keystone Cops—Nikki and Husband #4—pretend they're self-made power players who hustled their way to a billionaire's table? One episode has her jet-setting to New York, Milan, Tokyo—all part of a busy week for Nikki Jones and her entourage.

But this morning's alert, delivered in the same robotic voice Alexa uses to tell me my Amazon order is on its way, doesn't just humiliate—it rocks my world. She's been arrested again, hasn't she? My sister's been dragged away before. *Dammit all to hell*, Dad used to say. *That little shit made the national news.*

She's been mentioned in the *New York Times* before—the Southern District of New York. But now, arrested after scamming the wrong rich woman, Nikki's not just facing serious charges—she's gone full-blown notorious. I always knew our family would be famous.

It's like a bullet whizzed by and I ducked my head just in time. She's my doppelgänger. It's only by accident—birth order and the arrangement of DNA—and by God's grace, I'm not the one sitting in an 8x8 cell, wearing an orange jumpsuit, eating slop. And now that I've created space in my life for Zen, I'm no longer fantasizing about three hots and a cot.

I spend my free time researching. Always, I circle back to: *Why?* It becomes a quest.

In the week that follows, Ellin Watkins (aka Victim #1) looks me up. She's a woman on a mission, searching for her role in all of this. I end up with nothing but mad respect for her. It takes courage to step out of the bubble, take a hard look, and come out better than before.

I've always taken pride in seeing reality clearly—but man, was I wrong. I joke about my family and their criminal enterprises, but there are things about them I may never be able to acknowledge. And who's to say what the truth even is? By the time Nikki hit her teenage years, I'd already moved out.

Nikki's summers in Tokyo are a blank. I'd ask her—or ask someone to ask her—but you can't trust what she says. She'll tell you she was on Japanese TV. She slept with John Stamos on the Shinkansen. She sat with Lady Di and held hands with an AIDS patient at Narita Red Cross Hospital. She studied business at the University of Tokyo.

For answers, I reach out to her ex-boyfriend. He might've been shady in high school, but he's not a liar. We meet for lunch at a hotel café in Vegas, where he works maintenance.

"Those two summers!" he exclaims. "It was don't ask, don't tell—but I knew. Her old bestie was doing it too. She hooked her up. 'Hostessing.' Nikki was scared of losing me, so she sent money. Lots of it. By the end, she wasn't the same. She was always full of shit, but after that—she was next level."

After our conversation, I stumble across a 1984 article from a tabloid. In it, "journalist" Arthur Hopkins writes about an 18-year-old from California named *Nikkii* (yes, with a double i) and a 19-year-old Czechoslovakian named Katherina. He first met them in Ginza, handing out fliers and chatting up passersby.

I know right away—*Nikkii* is 16-year-old Nikki.

Reading the article breaks my heart.

Nikkii Stevens, age 18, wears a short, flowy dress and heels. She says both were "five-finger discounts" from her sweetheart back home. Nikkii—likely a pseudonym—says she's "super excited" to be in Japan. But in two months, she hasn't landed a single modeling job. "That's okay," she says. "I have lots of leads." In the meantime, her landlord—also her recruiter—has her working the hostess clubs.

"Everything's working out for the good for me anyways," she says. She's already friends with a famous American actor who frequents Ginza. She won't name him, but he's promised to open doors for her in Hollywood.

It doesn't take long to find the journalist. Arthur Hopkins is 75 now, semi-retired and living in Florida. Within five minutes, he's on the phone.

"About that piece ... I feel terrible," he says. "I was there for a gossip rag, trying to get Keanu Reeves. I didn't know anything back then. Forgive me. I knew they weren't of age, but if a girl could get her parents to sign the form—it was legal trafficking. Those girls were exploited. Working at those clubs didn't even pay rent. They had to do more to survive. And their parents—those poor parents—were conned into delivering their daughters to the devil."

"I can't stop thinking about it," I say. "Child trafficking. I called because ... it's about Nikkii."

"Of course," he says. "What a character. Her Japanese wasn't even as good as mine, but she could read the flier pretty well. 'One free drink and you getta talk to me.'"

I stare at the phone. "Japan is where she went wrong," I say. "I won't go into it, but we didn't come from a great family. You know that feeling—watching *Goodfellas* and realizing Ray Liotta's character reminds you of your dad? Or when the plots of *Ozark* and *Breaking Bad* seem weirdly plausible?"

He exhales. "I had an icky feeling even then. Your sister—she was a name-dropper. Grandiose. Glib. Her brain hadn't fully formed. I was more interested in Katherina, but she said she was all talked out."

"Did you have any idea?"

"It was a scam. Thousands of cute but not spectacular Americans— hundreds of girls a month—pouring into Tokyo? Yes, I was complicit. But if it makes you feel better, I've spent the last decade doing penance. I serve on a UN panel. The actress Ashlynn Ford's on it too. She went to Japan the same year your sister did."

"I already tried calling her."

"Ashlynn's shared what she needs to. She's been public about her assault. Said she wouldn't have made it home if her mother hadn't signed a record deal. Since then, she's turned her life around. Look at her website— she's like Gloria Steinem."

There's not much left to say. When we hang up, I go back to Ashlynn's website.

Broke and alone, forced to work in a hostess club, she describes what she endured as exploitation on a grand scale—emotional, sexual, economic. And the worst part? Her abusers were enabled by governments.

Never married, with no children, Ashlynn has spent the last forty years healing the world.

I wish I could say the same for Nikki.

CHAPTER 52

Nikki

21 February 2022 The Boston Crier

FROM THE SOUTHERN DISTRICT OF NEW YORK FEDERAL COURT

Retired detective Roger Fitch has reason to celebrate. After a week-long manhunt in which 54-year-old career criminal Nikki Jones managed to evade authorities, she was finally apprehended in an alley behind her Los Angeles concept restaurant, *Bitchez Eat Breakfast 2*.

A serial fraudster with a rap sheet spanning 30 years, Jones has been charged with aggravated identity theft and wire fraud. Ellin Watkins, ex-wife of NFL star Roger Watkins, is listed in court records as Victim #1. According to documents obtained by *The Crier*, Ms. Watkins was being treated for Stage 4 cancer when she hired Jones as an assistant. Watkins claims Jones swindled her out of more than a million dollars.

Jones was also incarcerated in 1996 and 1997 for grand theft, and in 2011 for passport fraud and aggravated identity theft, after defrauding an entertainment company of more than $500,000. Detective Fitch, who led the 2011 investigation, deserves much of the credit. Hand-picked by Ms. Watkins as her private investigator, Fitch has been her strongest advocate.

The government lauds Fitch's persistence, citing his dogged determination and exemplary forensic work. In an exclusive interview with *The Crier*, Detective Fitch told us, "It was the least I could do. I regret not going after Jones harder in '11. If I had, she would've gotten a longer sentence, and she and Ms. Watkins—a vulnerable single mother—never would've crossed paths."

Initially, Fitch was hopeful about Jones's plea deal. "I'd prayed that in federal prison, she could be reformed," he says. However, after a former cellmate implicated Jones in a crime racket involving ex-cons targeting elderly residents of a Pacific Grove beachfront community, his hopes were dashed. Although her participation in that scheme could not be verified, Jones was released in 2016 for good behavior. "By then, we had reason to believe she would re-offend," Fitch said.

Court records obtained through the Freedom of Information Act indicate Jones's victims are numerous. Although none agreed to a full interview, a 2011 police report includes a statement from Jones's sister, Abigail Jones-Green, a successful educational psychologist with offices in Palo Alto and Menlo Park. She claimed her sister defrauded her out of $20,000 and provided Fitch with a wealth of background information, confirming that Jones's history of antisocial behavior goes back decades.

A source close to the Jones family disclosed that Nikki spent two years—from age 15 to 17—as an entertainer and hostess in Tokyo's Kabukicho red-light district. "It was a fake modeling scheme," the source said. "After that, her self-esteem must have taken a nosedive. All Nikki's crimes afterward had to do with wanting to inhabit the lives of people she admired—to get close to them." The idea that these early experiences were formative has merit, as her criminal behavior escalated dramatically after her return to the US.

When *The Crier* reached out to Jones-Green for comment, she declined. The last time she saw her sister was in 2011. "Nikki can talk almost anyone into anything," she once said. "She has a way of getting them to return to the same poisoned trough. Being a relative, I want to believe."

When it comes to Jones being a smooth talker, we concur. She is a master of self-promotion and manipulation, with a persona built on lies. Almost all the information on her LinkedIn page is false, and we could not verify any details listed on her IMDb profile. She claims multiple college degrees and reports an impressive work history, though records show she dropped out of Saratoga High School in 1984. She didn't receive her high school equivalency until 1998.

In 2017, her charm landed her a three-page spread in a local lifestyle magazine. Photographed in high-contrast black and white, she's shown in one image stamping out a cigarette with a stiletto. "People see me as edgy and dangerous," she's quoted as saying. "But I'm a girl-next-door from San Jose. All I had were the values instilled in me by my late parents. It took grit and hustle to get to the top." It's no small irony that, at the time of publication, she was using Watkins's money to fund her extravagant lifestyle.

In 2019, Jones used some of that money to launch *Bitchez Eat Breakfast 2*, a restaurant chain whose concept and menu were stolen word-for-word from the Kansas City-based LLC that owns *Bakin' Bitchez*. Records show that she and Husband #4 obtained COVID relief funds to keep their venture afloat. That same month, a professional videographer helped her launch *Crazyass Bazillionaires* on YouTube. In the channel's early episodes, Nikki and her husband present as bumbling power-couple wannabes. In later episodes, she's flanked by a fawning entourage—friends of her much younger husband—and a stylist. She's shown jet-setting to New York, Milan, and Tokyo. All part of a "typical" week for Nicole Ann Jones.

It was that YouTube channel that ultimately helped close the case. "*Crazyass Bazillionaires* was a gift," Detective Fitch says. "We were able to track her movements and match them to credit card receipts. We're grateful. That's one more grifter off the street." Nikki Jones, who was released last week on a $150,000 bond, declined to be interviewed for this article.

30 April 2022 Advocate Podcasting Group - Los Angeles Bureau

This is Brad Haackle here for the *Advocate Podcasting Group*. This episode, our 31st, is called **"Parasite."** I didn't think I'd be going down this rabbit hole, but last week, I ran into old friends Ellin Watkins and Kristi Adams at the 2022 Youth Center Gala at the Shrine Auditorium & Expo Hall. They're not gay, but I'm adopting them.

The first thing I have to say is—the evening was electric. It was such a treat to see them together. Over the years, they've worked tirelessly to fundraise millions to benefit LGBTQ homeless youth. Ellin, a sizzling raven-haired beauty with tawny skin as flawless as the day is long, looks twenty years younger than her age.

Kudos to her daughter, Elouise Watkins, who might be in the running for best stylist in LA. She dressed her mother in a stunning butter-yellow Givenchy gown paired with strappy silver-toned Louboutins—a perfect complement to Ellin's luminous, effervescent personality. I'm sure her deadbeat football coach ex-husband rues the day he let them go.

Kristi Adams' return to the LA scene is also much heralded. We haven't seen much of her since she settled into obscure domesticity in the late 1990s. A vibrant confection of a woman now in her mid-60s, she's a vision in cream, with expertly colored dark blonde hair and expressive, doe-like brown eyes that still carry a hint of melancholy.

It's easy to remember how mesmerizing Kristi was all those years ago when she was Hollywood-adjacent OJ and Nicole, Robert and Kris. It's no surprise she tore it up on the dance floor. Proving she hasn't lost any of her mojo, she took home first prize in our 1970s disco dance contest.

When I asked what brought them together, I expected the usual: *We met at Pilates / LA Spiritual Center / Charity Event*. And this is where the tea comes in. What a shocker—it turns out both were swindled by the same con artist.

Without going into specifics—because I don't want to give this chick, Nikki Jones, any more publicity than she deserves—she ingratiated herself into Ellin's life, drained her kids' college accounts, and opened and maxed out credit cards to the tune of over a million bucks. She did a number on one-time friend Kristi, too.

With Kristi, Jones overstayed her welcome, squatting for months in Kristi's beachside guesthouse, entertaining men at all hours, refusing to leave until she was formally evicted. Before that, she gaslit Kristi into nearly leaving her husband.

Ellin and Kristi, having bonded over Nikki, are now on their way to Vegas, where Ellin's hosting a charity golf event at the Bellagio. I thought about going when they invited me, but once I found out this con artist's older sister was going to be there, I took a hard pass. Some people never learn.

That's it for now. Smash the subscribe button and hit "like" if you want to support the channel.

CHAPTER 53

Detox

Abigail

ALEXA: "VIP Scheming featuring serial fraudster Nikki Jones and husband Fredrik Laudermilk" will air tomorrow at 8 p.m. central on CNBC. Do you want me to record it for you?"

A month ago, I spent an afternoon with a production team giving them the scintillating scoop. It wasn't the smartest thing I've ever done, because since then, it's been all over the news. Her shame is now mine. Half the time, I want to pull the covers over my head. The only good thing was meeting Ellin and Kristi, two of Nikki's celebrity victims. Before the taping, we attended a golf tournament nearby. I'd thought Ellin would want to burn me in effigy—but what a lovely woman she was. After she returned home, Kristi and I spent two days hanging out poolside at the Bellagio, laughing at the irony. Vegas is Nikki's playground, not ours.

I knew it would be detrimental to interview with *Entertainment Tonight*, but I did it anyway. Slathered in sunscreen and sipping sangria, I decided I had to stand up for what was right. I've dealt with fallout before. Bring it on.

When Nikki's given a rebuttal, she pulls the old DARVO routine (Deny, Attack, Reverse Victim Offender). It's right out of the perpetrator's guidebook. Make a fuss, act believable. Have a mountain of evidence? Who cares. *Alternative facts.*

When Nikki does call me—I knew she would—the Barnyard Hip-Hop ringtone plays. The first thing I think is, *The nerve of her, keeping the same number.* She sounds older than I remember. Sharper, too. Her voice could cut through a phone line.

"How dare you take over my life!" she rages. "Ellin, Kristi—I saw the pictures."

I unlock my door and step into my office. "Of all the things you could've taken offense over."

"They're using you," she snarls. "Laughing behind your back. You, showing up to a big-dollar event in an upcycled prom dress! I bet you dyed the shoes to match. Hope you know one of their earrings costs more than your whole 1990s thrift-store wardrobe."

I want to laugh in her face. "Are you done?"

"They aren't your real friends. Never will be."

"Contrary to what you believe, life isn't about how many people envy you."

For a moment, she simmers in silence. It's meant to be a power move—but with me, it falls flat. When she finally speaks, her voice is full of venom.

"Pull the plug on the show," she says. "Or you'll spend your whole life looking over your shoulder."

"Cut the hyperbole, Nikki. The feds are putting you away. I have empathy. You were really wronged—but the public needs protecting."

"If you really cared, you'd be loyal," she fumes. "What's coming out is fake news. Ellin was in it, you know. I was framed. It'll ruin me trying to prove it, though, so my attorney's doing a plea bargain. By the time she's done, my sentence will be whittled to nothing."

"Why are you telling me this?"

"So you know I'll be back."

I steady my voice. "Think I'm scared?" I ask. "You're delusional. I pity you."

"I can talk anyone into anything, remember? Isn't that what you told the producers?"

"This is the last time. I'm blocking your number."

After I click the phone off, I feel grimy. All those old feelings resurface. The sins of the father *and* the mother. The shiny veneer Mom worked so hard to cultivate. She'd go on about ballet, tried to project genteel sophistication—but for her, class was spelled with a capital K. As a kid, I thought it was all legit, but we were imposters, stand-ins for actual human beings. The realization leaves me breathless.

As for my interview—I stand by it. It's not like I wrote a burn-it-all-down memoir. All the main players except for me and Nikki are gone. I tell myself I don't care about what's to come.

Seeking a kind ear, I call Uly.

"I wouldn't have done it," he tells me. "But as far as her doing damage? Don't worry. Her ride-or-dies drank the Kool-Aid a long time ago. They hate you."

"I wanted to change minds."

"Denial ain't a river in Egypt, Mom," he says with a sigh. "You should know that. Make no mistake, I'm Team Mom all the way. My wife too. Mariah wants to organize a watch party with your true family."

A month later, the Vegas taping feels like a lifetime ago. When the episode airs on March 1, I'm sitting in Uly's sparsely decorated Oakland apartment. Mariah, his wife, her mother, and her sister are there too. A few wedding pictures hang on the wall—blending cultures. They're jumping the broom. Uly's breaking a wine glass with his foot.

Mariah, who's as kind as the day is long, places a charcuterie board on the table. It has a million things on it: crackers, cheese, olives, fruit.

"This is your vindication," she says.

This is progress. Until recently, she'd believed there were two sides to everything—that the truth always lies somewhere in the middle. When she says it's time to break out the pretzels and popcorn, Uly, sad for his cousins, tells her to stop. Only ten minutes of my interview makes the cut. They used the most salacious parts. I'm equal parts sad and guilty.

When it finishes, Mariah's side is stunned. They're not judging. Family is everything. Nikki's the one who did the betraying, not me.

"Maybe it's time for a Nikki detox," Uly says after a silence.

"Maybe it's time for me to stop asking why," I say with a smile.

Mariah, who's stayed close, rests her forehead on mine.

"It can't be easy stepping away when your whole family's imploding," she says.

"We have our meltdowns in public," Uly says.

Uly's right. Dad dealt drugs to half of San Jose. Cy had a mental health break during a city council meeting. I say I want privacy, but I don't. I am the only witness. Who else remembers peering into her bassinet—Nikki, the perfect pink cherub, sucking on a toe? I was there when the two-year-old wind-up doll with no audience morphed into a wily seven-year-old who always got her way. Strange now, I have no emotion left. What sympathy I have is for the child, not the adult.

CHAPTER 54

Chatty Baby

Abigail – Casablanca – March 2023

At baggage claim, Uly wraps an arm around my shoulder and leads me through a wall of travelers—business types, recognizable by the distracted looks on their faces and the way they meticulously scroll their devices for notifications and emails after hours of Airplane Mode. The others fit into one of two categories: locals in modest-modern or regional garb, or noisy tourists from Israel, Europe, and America.

This is my first visit to Morocco in almost sixty years, and with almost no memories left, I'd imagined this airport as a dusty outpost where I'd step from the tarmac into a swirl of diesel fumes and camel dung. Turns out, Mohammed V International—which serves a metro population of three million—is as large and polished as any mid-size airport in the US. Spic and span. Modern, too, given the new-car smell emanating from each tray, seat, ramp, and counter I come into contact with. At baggage claim, another scent fills my nostrils—WD-40. If I took the *Go To Morocco* podcasters at their word, I would've expected bait-and-switch scam artists and overeager merchants or taxi drivers. Maybe it's because Dad and I saw *Casablanca* together. The only thing close to a swindle is the money exchange, where they try to sell us a use-it-or-lose-it debit card. There's too much security. Outside of customs, it borders on overkill.

Morocco isn't a quasi-military state. It's not like behind every newspaper is a turbaned spy in a silk suit. But try convincing me. The last time I was here, Mom constantly warned me of the dangers. One misstep, and a boogeyman with a knife would carry me off to God knows where.

"Kidnappers love little girls," she'd said. "Especially American ones with freckles and straight red hair."

But I *do* need to escape. So when Adam asks me to be in an offbeat documentary about Jewish tourism in Morocco—expenses paid, and I can bring Uly—I don't say no.

That Uly has mixed feelings about being here is no surprise. Until now, I've been bitter about this place. And now I'm expecting him to pivot. He's heard how, in 1967, my grandparents and uncles were forced to leave behind everything they owned. I don't know all the geopolitical reasons why it happened. You'd have to ask Uly. He took Jewish studies in college. He attended Aida Heckman's lectures on the displacement of Jews in the Middle East and North Africa and peppered her with questions. Not that he liked her answers.

One thing about Uly: he's never going to turn down a free trip—especially now, bitten by the travel bug, with a chance to rack up Hilton hotel points and get reimbursed for expenses. In preparation, he listens to dozens of podcasts and scours solo-travel Reddit pages. The podcasters—who usually own tour companies—discuss the beauty and wonder of Morocco with a dystopian twist, always ending with a "we alone can save you" message. The Reddit pages are what you'd expect: *never again* horror stories one acquires from traveling anywhere.

This might be why Uly's chewing on a toothpick and cracking his knuckles. Vigilant and never far from my elbow, he doesn't allow himself to look down. His face wears a look of grim concentration. When his phone pings with texts from Mariah and his mother-in-law—who've stayed behind in Barcelona—he doesn't answer.

"I know what they're worried about. The Gibraltar to Tangier Ferry," he says. "Is it dangerous?"

I'm about to say—*Pick up. Talk it out*—when the baggage carousel grinds to a start. Right away, we spot our bags. Mine has a blue pom-pom on it, and Uly's is pink—because he's color blind and it was on sale. After gathering our luggage, Uly signals me to follow. When we pass a tall man with a camera around his neck, Uly shoots me a look I can't quite explain. It's not until we're through the automatic glass doors leading to the passenger pickup area that he says anything.

"Mom. I know you're friendly, but this time, *pleeease*. Don't engage. At least not until Adam gets here."

I fish around in my backpack for my sunglasses. Uly, never without his Ray-Bans, tips his hat and readjusts his backpack. I roll our suitcases closer to the pavement. As a puffy cloud drifts lazily by, I squeeze my eyes shut and am transported to 1964. I can't wrap my head around Mom ever being twenty-three. But there she is—ill-tempered and worn out from a week of travel. We'd been arguing all day, as I recall. Not that we ever got along. Even her womb was hostile, judging from how little she always ate.

The luggage is old-school, which means no wheels—only adding to her overwhelm. It also explains why she was so abrupt. The situation blew up in Lisbon. Burdened with two large, stuffed-to-the-gills bags and a tired four-year-old, Mom had one of her nuclear tantrums. I remember people looking at us, pointing, whispering in a foreign language. But she didn't stop. Not until a policeman walked over. The last straw had to do with my Chatty Baby doll. I'd been treating her like she was real—fussing with her layette, changing her diaper, feeding her with the fake plastic bottle Dad got me. Too many times, I'd pulled her string.

"Doggie bow-wow and cookie all gone," it said.

"You see me struggling. But no. Instead of being a normal child and making yourself useful. Day and night, night and day, you cart that stupid doll around!" Mom screamed.

"I can't hold both," I said, eyes filling with tears.

A few minutes later, I'm on an airport bench, kissing Chatty Baby goodbye, leaving her there.

After that, I wasn't just angry—I was impossible. The milk they served at the hotel was sweet and warm. An abomination. The sheets were scratchy. The bath water too hot. At least Mom was thankful I'd grown out of my milk allergy.

My attitude didn't improve until Morocco. But only because Mom scared me into compliance.

"Warfare in the streets," she warned.

A ping, the smell of diesel fuel, returns me to the present.

"Adam texted," I say. "He's on his way."

CHAPTER 55

Crossroads

Abigail

If anyone can make Uly feel better, it's Adam. He's chill without trying to be, with a sense of ease that can't be faked. He's on time. I can't help but marvel. From behind the window of Adam's late-model Mercedes SUV, the sun catches the metal of his aviators, illuminating the smattering of freckles across his nose and the tops of his cheeks. His eyes are warm—brown with specks of green. The halo of auburn hair framing his face gives him a look of otherworldliness.

Uly, who's been pacing the passenger pick-up area ever since we stepped outside, is too stressed to notice any of this. After shot-putting our suitcases into the backseat and jumping on board, he lets out an exasperated sigh.

I rush to embrace Adam. And then, the cursory kiss-on-each-cheek greeting.

"It's been too long," I say.

As for Uly, he's in the backseat trying to decompress. Best to leave him alone. Still, I feel the need to apologize.

"The *Go To Morocco* podcasts you sent over told us to be careful," I say.

"It's the Jewish studies class I took," Uly adds. "No offense. I want to be here—I do—but still. Things were bad in the 1960s."

"None taken," Adam says, looking at Uly, not me. "There was instability in those days. But did you know they're talking about restoring citizenship? For both you and your mom. As far as the podcasters go, there's danger everywhere. Name any developing country."

I try not to react. Adam's candy-coating things. Uly showed me Dr. Hickman's lectures about how Jews in North Africa were treated.

Still, I have to applaud Adam's effort. Everything he says is laced with positivity and conviction. He's Yasmina's crowning achievement, the absolute cream of the crop. Like his father—only without the judgment or hyperkinetic energy. Same magnanimous smile, same slim physique. You'd never know he was adopted.

"How'd the time go by so fast?" I say. "I don't know if I told you, Uly, but I used to babysit Adam. A dollar an hour—a generous wage for such an easy-peasy kid."

My praise must embarrass Adam. After he flashes that smile—the result of years of orthodontics—he tells me to stop.

Meanwhile, there's Uly, drumming his fingers on the console. On edge since the moment our Air Maroc flight hit the runway, he has no interest in reminiscing.

"How are the police here?" he asks.

Adam cranes his neck. He has an expression on his face like he's trying to puzzle something out.

"Fine," he says, before deftly changing the subject.

"How about the Cabestan for dinner? Great food, better atmosphere."

I watch as Adam steers the car past the Royal Terminal and onto the N11.

"Anything you wanna hear?" he asks. "The radio stations play American music—rock, punk, disco. No country."

Then he turns the dial to a techno-pop station, plunges his foot on the accelerator, and shifts the SUV into high gear.

"There *are* speed limits here," Adam adds. "But I know where the cameras are."

Adam's reassurances seem to satisfy Uly. He lets out a long exhale. Later, when a Drake song—his favorite rapper—comes on, I see him bopping along.

"I didn't think Mariah would enjoy this," he says. "Maybe I was wrong."

Meanwhile, I'm disappointed. I expected Casablanca to be modern, but it didn't *sink in* until I saw it. Long expanses of fast-moving freeway shine platinum in the sun, plowing their way through tunnels and snaking over long stretches of land. No camels. No mirages. No citadels. Very few ocean views. Advertising billboards are everywhere. Dominating the lanes are trucks carrying cargo from one city to the next.

An occasional overpass breaks the monotony. Only then do I see fleeting images, vestiges of Old Morocco: a man driving crookedly on a bicycle next to a lane of traffic, a modestly dressed woman pushing a cart of fruits and vegetables. Otherwise—except for the landscape and the Byzantine architecture with geometric motifs—I might as well be in any rapidly expanding city in the US. Construction is everywhere. So is opportunity.

As three low-hanging clouds move across the horizon, I allow my mind to skip forward to tomorrow. This isn't the Old Casablanca of my imagination—exotic, full of danger and 1940s-style intrigue. Nothing here helps Uly and me get closer to our heritage. It only amplifies my doubts.

One thing I don't question is the expertise with which Adam will approach his documentary. He never scripts anything. His idea to focus on Jewish tourism might sound dubious, but that's how I felt about his other films.

His narrow-interest, slice-of-life pieces have covered Zoroastrianism in Iran (because of his dad), the Delano Grape Strike 50 years later (at my suggestion), the story of Armenian immigration in Fresno (because of his wife), and the use of Guide Dogs for the Blind among Muslims. That last one—filmed shortly before Amira died—included footage of Yasmina and Amira trying to get a mosque in progressive Santa Cruz to allow dogs. It was comedy gold—how the Imam and his followers used pretzel logic and reinterpretations of the Quran before finally giving the green light for Amira's dog to sit beside her while she prayed.

A cluster of clouds moves away from the sun. The warmth—the burst of light—returns me to the present. Adam points to a turbaned man in a djellaba riding a scooter.

"You see?" he exclaims. "Even in this, the most European of cities, you'll find Moroccan culture. You have to get over the juxtaposition. There's graffiti on that overpass, but the drawings are done in the Shilha tradition. Nothing can equal them."

When Adam steers the Mercedes onto Autoroute Casablanca-Agadir, the sun disappears and the landscape changes again. Rays of light beam onto the concrete. The sickle-shaped streetlamps that line the avenue are illuminated, too. They remind me of the swaying fronds of a palm.

The closer we get to the hotel, the more it resembles a construction zone. Stately palm trees still line the streets, only now they're dwarfed by scaffolds and skyscrapers.

None of this matters—Adam's relentless enthusiasm, Uly's trepidation, the modernity of this place.

Returning to the land of my birth, I had no idea how freeing it would be.

CHAPTER 56

The Rose

Abigail

U nlike Bijan with his cigars, cognac, and gold jewelry, Adam exudes rumpled chic—a hand-dyed cotton shirt and jeans amid Cabestan's opulence. I smooth my sarong as a waiter refills our crystal glasses. Outside, the Casablanca sunset burns gold across the harbor while businesspeople from around the globe seal deals over vintage champagne.

Adam opens the menu and tells us to order what we want. In his smile is the gentleness Bijan and Yasmina used to fret over. Needlessly, because look at him. He's unapologetically himself.

"Don't mistake kindness for weakness," he once said in one of his documentaries. "It's a strength."

I spear a piece of asparagus and allow it to melt in my mouth.

"The last time I was in Morocco, I was four," I say. "Mom was a walking advertisement for how not to travel with a child. No bag of toys, no crayons or coloring books, no water."

"She was never any good at organization," Adam says.

"In Morocco, I was with a family I'd never met, speaking a language I didn't know," I say. "I had four cousins, all boys. Testosterone overload."

"So you don't have much to tell us," Adam says with a laugh.

I would feel slighted, but his voice has a certain don't-worry-be-happy buoyancy to it.

"My memories here are clearer than you think." I trace the rim of my glass. "But they're tinged with trauma. Better to make new ones."

Uly sips his wine, eyes darkening. "I would've died if that happened to me. Never could handle change."

"Dad was far from perfect," I say, "but he was the only one who gave affection. Every day I'd stand on the curb waiting for him to round the corner."

"Mom told me your mother wanted a divorce," Adam says. "If she'd stayed in Morocco, everything would've been different. She would've remarried, eventually made her way to France, Canada, Israel—but she chose to return."

"I can't imagine, Mom. You must've been a wreck," Uly says.

"I was miserable," I say. "Missing Dad, the whole Moab family telling me to stop whining."

"My mom told me stories," Adam says. "It wasn't all bad."

"Yeah. There were cool parts. Men in red fez hats, women in hijabs, terra-cotta terraces, ancient archways, persimmon trees. You'll see, Son."

"And my mom?" Adam asks.

"All I remember is her giving me a rose."

"I wish Mom was well enough," Adam says.

"To see this homecoming," I say.

"The first time I came here, everything coalesced. Stories about Mom as a young girl. When the Berbers and the Jews coexisted. The documentary is just an excuse."

"Is this another one of your projects where you want us to trust the process?"

"I haven't mapped it out," he says, pulling a scrap of paper from his pocket. "I know what I'm going to say about Marrakech. Tell me if this sounds too trite. 'Marrakech is a seductive, sometimes emotionally exhausting city. It must be interpreted with every one of the senses.' Other than that," he adds, "I'm letting things unfold organically."

CHAPTER 57

Ballet Shoes

The Bronx News

12 March 2022

Morocco has long relied on tourism. Twenty-five percent of its workforce is connected to it in some way. It also represents 8% of Morocco's GDP. One population no one's ignoring are Jews of Moroccan descent. Between 1948 and 1970, 300,000 of them left. Only 2,500 Jews, mostly wealthy and well-connected, remain. The reasons for the exodus were many. And although some resent the Moroccans' tendency to rewrite history in rosy terms, one thing is clear: the government is welcoming them back with open arms. With their support, the Council of Jewish Communities of Morocco has worked tirelessly to restore and safeguard Jewish heritage sites.

Additionally, after a long period of neglect, the city of Fez has restored the 17th-century Slat Alfassiyine synagogue, and cemeteries and Jewish quarters (mellahs) are being reinvigorated. And now, Morocco is the only Arab country in the world with not one, but three museums dedicated to Jewish history. And now that Morocco has established diplomatic ties with Israel, Jewish history and culture is being included in the school curriculum. However, when we spoke to travel agent Don Banks to talk about trends, we got another side. While he's enthusiastic Jewish tourism is exploding, he warns that not everything's as advertised.

"Things have improved, but that might be because there aren't many of us to pick on," he says. "And not everyone's rolling out the welcome mat. Some travelers have been subjected to anti-Semitic slurs. I tell them, 'Don't go into the mellah without a guide. Someone else might be living in your childhood home, using your mother's bellows to sweep the hearth. Someone may be wearing one of your father's old hats. But accept it, you left it behind. It isn't yours anymore.'"

Continued on Page 25

Abigail

The taxi weaves through evening traffic as I mention visiting the Israelite school in Rabat.

"It doesn't exist anymore," Adam says flatly. "I told you before. We can see the old cemetery instead."

I lean against the cool window.

"Too bad. Algeria and Tunisia had better Jewish schools. Probably why Morocco hasn't produced as many great storytellers."

"Let's not get into the weeds," Adam says, rubbing his temple. "You know my style is lighthearted." He outlines his plan—pretending not to speak Arabic while guides gossip, vendors claim Jewish ancestry, all captured with his trademark humor.

I raise an eyebrow. Pure Sacha Baron Cohen. Not my right to disapprove, but if I had the funding, my documentary would expose the sons and daughters of the Vichy. Some stories can't be told through laughter.

Streetlights flash across my face as I gaze out the window. Morocco's harshness isn't to blame. My grandmother manipulated and strived as if she had no choice—a self-absorbed delusion passed through generations like an heirloom. Our birthright. But the real villains were Europeans, placing Jews in the middle of their three-tiered system, their pokers stoking hatred that still smolders.

"Not everything is funny," I tell Adam.

"I can't help it. My whimsy—I get that from my mom," he says. "It's her Moroccan upbringing. It's why I belong here. I get to be in my lane, although I wouldn't know how to deviate from it. Can you imagine me doing this in Iran? There was nothing light in Dad's background. 'Jet-setting parents dump their son at a Paris boarding school and forget about him.' There might be a story there, but it's not one I want to tell."

This must resonate with Uly because, all of a sudden, his face becomes animated.

"I've always admired your approach," he says. "Oddly specific. Your mom was so hilarious in that dog movie, I thought I'd pee my pants laughing."

"She never meant to be funny," Adam says. "Her quasi-Jewish rituals. Me, growing up not knowing the difference between one tradition and the next. I always thought she was unique in her flexibility, but when I learned the way of the Shilha, I knew I had to put my own spin on things."

"Your mom tries on religions like other people try on jackets," I say.

Adam doesn't mention how superstitious his mother is, how she went haywire after my mom died, buying up magnetic mezuzahs, putting them on file cabinets, inside my car. She even sent one in a care package for Nikki.

"That's where the humor is," Adam says. "As far as being culturally diverse, Mom was at the top of the heap."

"Is," I say with a tilt of the head.

"Of course. It took her a while to recover after Dad died, but she's still kicking at 96. You know what's crazy? Around the time you guys came back into our lives, she and Dad started really communicating. After that, it was like they were on a second honeymoon. You wouldn't believe how much fun they had."

I'm not worried about Yasmina. Her golden years with Bijan were perfect. Her body might be failing, but her mind is sharp, and she has plenty of fond memories to think back on. The person I'm concerned about—at least for the time being—is Adam. Will American Jews be as open-minded when it comes to Yasmina's son? I imagine him being shooed away because it isn't his story to tell. It pains me to imagine him so maligned.

One of the other reasons I agreed to this was to give Adam a level of access and credibility he wouldn't otherwise have.

For the rest of the ride, we're quiet. It's dark, and jet lag is starting to set in. Then, as if bothered by our silence, Adam pipes in.

"I heard about your sister," he says, his voice cutting through the darkness. "Saw the true crime show. You were brave to participate."

Uly's hand tightens on my shoulder, his exhale sharp and deliberate.

"We're not talking about that," he says, each word clipped like pieces of broken glass.

Adam's apology comes quickly, but the damage is done. The taxi slows for a red light, bathing us in crimson.

"Uly and I want this to be over," I whisper.

CHAPTER 58

The Memory Keeper

Abigail

The Moroccan Jewish Museum sits like an unassuming box on a residential Casablanca street. As Adam films us examining artifacts and photographs, I can tell from his expression that none of this footage is going to make the final cut. Only the simulated jeweler's studio catches his eye.

Afterward, we stop at a roadside restaurant for a pick-me-up of shish kabob and couscous. Beneath my feet is a sickly kitten with an infected eye. When I mention a vet, Adam touches my arm.

"Don't," he says. "They'll just see you as another naïve American."

The whole way to Rabat, all I can think about is the cat. It doesn't help that I spot another two or three on our way to my grandparents' old house. We'd been told not to go, but Adam's gentle persuasion is enough to gain us entry.

Even though we are greeted with nothing but kindness, I freeze. Too many memories surface—the picture window I opened as a child, the terrace I climbed onto. The terracotta maid's quarters stand closer than I remember, barely seventy-five feet from the main house.

Each room unlocks fragments—the familiar curve of a sink, the tiled edge of the bathtub. Adam, literally vibrating with secondhand excitement, pulls Uly through doorways.

"Your grandmother slept here," he announces, his borrowed memories seeming as real as my own. He traces nail marks on a doorframe. "Your great-grandfather's mezuzah." His fingers linger reverently against the wood.

As for the woman—I'm ready to hate her. The last thing I expect to feel is empathy.

"How did we live?" she asks. "What did your grandfather do? What made them leave?"

I've prepared myself to hate this woman, this occupier of my family's space, but her questions disarm me. She speaks of the house like a custodian, not an owner.

"Be grateful it's me here," she says through Adam's translation. "My mother would have chased you with a broom."

As her story unfolds, unexpected sorrow washes over me—her life has been marked by hardships I never imagined.

"There's a sense of gratitude in the way she speaks," Adam adds quietly, translating. "Like the home belongs not to her but to the ages."

"I was seven when we came," the woman says, her voice distant. "A burned-out shell, but better than the streets."

"In a metal box, my mother found pink ballet shoes." Her eyes brighten. "Too big—made for a giant. But mine, I wore them to threads."

"You don't remember them leaving?" Uly asks, his face visibly softening.

"It was ransacked when we arrived," she answers.

Uly coughs, doubt evident. I share his suspicion, but she said she was seven. Memories at that age are unreliable.

"In the mountains, we were safer—but we starved," she continues. "Here, gangs ruled. Police never came." She straightens with unexpected pride. "But school, that changed everything. I learned to read, to count." Her weathered hand sweeps toward the window. "Now the neighborhood heals."

I look at Uly, then at Adam. Their eyes are misty. It takes me longer to soften. This should be ours.

Still I feel a shift. When Adam picks up his camera and begins filming, a space opens in my heart.

CHAPTER 59

Familiar Ground

Abigail

Without Mustafa, navigating the walled labyrinth of Fes el-Jdid's old mellah would be impossible. Even Adam—who never forgets a direction—would be lost in these ancient passages.

"Better than Go To Morocco," Mustafa boasts about his podcast, cigarette dangling as he removes his Vespa helmet to reveal a crown of brown curls. He carries himself with the princely elegance of well-to-do Moroccans—half self-promoting entertainer, half hero, with the edgy handsomeness of a 1950s film noir actor. Adam admires him enough to make him assistant cameraman in training.

Although Mustafa insists his first job is taking care of us, he takes his new position with great authority. After leading us to the heart of the medina, he insists we need refreshment.

"My uncle has store," he says. "I take you there."

Part of me wants to protest. I've made it clear I might be warming to Moroccans, but I don't want to give them any more tourist money than absolutely necessary. Mustafa knows this.

"No need to buy," he says. "Be aware, one lady I took here—from Idaho, USA—went into shock. 'Too amped up, too much bling-bling,' she said. Too much hard-sell no good. My uncle nice. He not care."

After his speech, Mustafa flashes a smile, and two dimples form on his carob-colored cheeks. What he doesn't know is that it takes a lot to shock me. I grew up in a party house. I have a criminal sister. The only thing I need to worry about is me—having a visceral, negative reaction to a country that still feels inhospitable. They didn't formally kick us out, but they made life so impossible that 99% of us had to leave. It's hard to be polite.

It wasn't long ago—1967—when my grandparents stuffed a lifetime of possessions into two suitcases. Uly learned from his class that the Six-Day War was probably the last straw. Dr. Heckman said the King of Morocco had been pro-Israel—he was the one who'd tipped off Israel in the first place—but the people in the streets rioted, looted, and set things on fire.

My grandparents—64 and 56 when they were forced out—brought two teenage sons with them. For the next decade, until his death, my grandfather bussed tables at Meyer's Delicatessen, riding city buses six days a week for minimum wage plus tips. Mr. Meyer adored him.

The square drowns us in sound—singers, drums, flutes, cymbals creating a beautiful chaos. When Adam reaches for dirhams to tip the musicians, Mustafa grabs his wrist.

"Keep your wits," he warns. "Last week, someone draped a snake around a tourist's neck. Twenty American dollars to remove it."

Uly nods knowingly, mentally confirming everything from Go To Morocco. Despite his caution, I notice him leaning into this place. As for me—maybe because I was born here—long-dormant nerve endings spring to life with each step deeper into the medina.

A haggard woman pulling a cart loaded with melons walks by, followed by a turbaned man on a bicycle. The smell of straw permeates the air. I shut my eyes. My ancestors walked these same streets. My green-eyed great-grandmother, who lost her sight to a parasite—I never met her, but she was tall. She wrapped her long brown hair in her only prized possession, a silken headscarf. Everything else was rags. She had no shoes. The baby came first.

Mustafa said there'd be too much to take in—and there is. The medina is ancient, and its roads are too narrow for cars, but bicycles and scooters are plentiful. I need to keep my wits about me. Above me, a solitary bird missing half its feathers pecks at itself.

The rudeness of this place, the lack of regard—has it always been this way? To some, there are only two choices: destroy or be destroyed. Before

I can contemplate it more, a young girl dressed in Shilha garb approaches. An older woman grabs her sleeve and gives her a look like, *Stop your dreaming*. What's strange is, with the late afternoon sun bouncing off a window, everything about the child shines—her buckles, her jewelry, her headdress. If I didn't know better, I'd say she was glowing.

Mustafa leads us across the street, where the aromas of cumin, cinnamon, ginger, pepper, and lamb waft through the air. Among a carpet of palm fronds in an open stall, a man squats over a cookstove, stirring a tall pot. It's not lunchtime, and he's already attracted a crowd. Uly stops. Mustafa pulls him away.

"Wait," he says.

Adam wants to stop too. "My mother told me about these places," he says. "Cheap eats. No utensils. She'd use bread to scoop the food."

"On your left. Souk El Oulad Dahou," Mustafa says.

And there it is, wedged between a bakery and a buzzing-with-fruit-flies produce market. The shop glows—bling-bling indeed—flickering light washing everything metal in orange. A floor-to-ceiling study in excess: part curio shop, part tourist trap. Inside, television voices in Arabic nearly drown out the street singers.

With each step, a new scent—patchouli oil by the door, cinnamon near the wooden puzzle boxes, mint beside the pottery. Swords hang alongside T-shirts and camel leather canisters. Above it all, a macabre row of preserved chickens stare with formaldehyde-fixed shock, feathers meticulously glued to their skins.

I have to look away. Treat animals fairly, please.

At the back of the store is Mustafa's uncle, El Oulad Dahou. When we're introduced, he's standing in front of a display of antique jewelry.

"I repaired this myself," he says. "Pick what you want. I give discount. Anyone who helps my nephew is a friend."

He offers us tea. Samples of almond butter with ground ginger and dates are served on paper liners.

I've become enamored with a display case, although I still don't want to buy. Inside is a silver necklace held together by decomposing leather and glue. On it are ten tiny filigree Stars of David.

"For your Hanukkah," El Oulad Dahou says. "It's 100 years old. I'm restoring it."

"Uh-huh," I say, attempting disinterest.

If, as Adam says, every shopkeeper swears he's part Jewish, I must remember not to be so harsh. But here he is, a random guy peddling trinkets my family and others were forced to leave behind—for a small fortune, no less. I step up to the case. It contains more jewelry than the entire three-room Jewish museum in Casablanca.

"You sure?" the shopkeeper says. "I could show you."

My fingers recoil as if from a viper. A tide of emotion rises in my chest.

"I don't know," I manage, seeking Uly, who's across the room, head buried in antique postcards.

"Mom!" he says, voice breaking with excitement. "The address—Impasse Moab. That's us!"

My hands fling to my chest.

"What are the odds?" Adam whispers. "You have to buy it."

"Damn straight," Uly says, his eyes shining.

"A small miracle," I say, steadying myself against the counter. "That street in Rabat was named after your great-grandfather. With one gunshot, he scattered invaders scaling the mellah walls. Became a local hero overnight."

El Oulad Dahou, who understands more English than I thought, looks at us with pride, as if he unearthed it for us. There are smile lines around his mouth. His eyes are soft and soulful, but that doesn't mean he's always this way.

So far, everyone in Morocco—from Mustafa, to the hotel doorman who carried our bags, to the woman occupying my family's old home, to him—has rolled out the red carpet. But why? Are these people truly good? Or do they just want our money?

I have to remember El Oulad Dahou hasn't done anything wrong. He wasn't even alive when my family left. But it's like resentment from a time before my birth is encased in my muscle memory. If only I could allow some of it to melt away, I could believe in the essential goodness of people.

I'm afraid Nikki's ruined that for me. If this were really a rude place, how do I explain Yasmina's warmth? It came from somewhere.

Because no matter how much money she accumulates or how old she gets, her goodness is an everlasting ember. Her hugs, the way her nylons felt when little-girl me crawled into her lap. That she is Moroccan matters little. Nothing can cancel my loving feelings. She once told me, "It doesn't matter who you are. A person can choose to be generous and kind, to live up to a moral standard. Or not."

Across the souk, Adam grabs a sword, momentarily cutting it through the air like Ali Baba. Such imagination. His father insisted he become a doctor or engineer. He fought back hard. I'm grateful he did.

"Your grandfather with his gun wouldn't have scared me," he says. "But I wouldn't have been out there in the first place."

Uly is at the front, looking at the display case. He's talking to the shopkeeper, negotiating. I grit my teeth. But he's an adult. He can buy what he wants. When it turns out all he purchases is a postcard, I'm relieved.

It's been days since we've listened to the news. But nestled in the only wall space not stacked to the gills with merchandise are two small slimline TV sets bracketed to a wall. In front of them, with his back to us, is a slight young man. On one screen is a replay of the Moroccan soccer team's surprising win, probably the only reason the man is letting the boy ignore us. On the other, a Twitter feed plays. From America, I'm guessing, because Twitter isn't as big elsewhere, and the subtitles flashing across the screen are in English. El Oulad Dahou stops what he's doing, walks over, and taps the boy on the shoulder.

"My son's obsessed with all things America," he says. "I have a brother in Orlando. When he's 14, I send him to school there."

When he finishes speaking, he gives the youth, still glued to the screen, a hearty squeeze.

"I need to work on my English so I can meet the beautiful Taylor Swift," the boy says.

"Let's not be rude," his father says before turning to us.

"If you buy necklace today," he adds, "mention name of my store in movie—Souk El Oulad Dahou Fes—and I give even better price."

It's not my intention to displace old resentments onto this poor man, but I can't help it.

"No thanks," I say. "If it was worth anything in the first place, we would've taken it with us."

Mustafa shoots me a pained look. Dimples, easy manner, gone. El Oulad Dahou looks crestfallen. I feel like a heel. Whenever I'm rude without meaning to be, Uly comes to the rescue.

"I might make another purchase," he says. "Movie-maker discount, right?"

It stops me short.

"El Oulad Dahou, you are a fantastic craftsman," I say apologetically. "If it weren't for you, these artifacts would've been lost forever."

El Oulad Dahou gives me a timid smile.

"It costs a lot to get good education in America," he says, waving a hand. "I don't like Internet teacher."

Either Adam is tired of swordplay or remembers why we're here, because he and Mustafa begin setting up equipment. After giving Mustafa a few instructions, he addresses the youth.

"Twitter is not the place to go for news," he says. "It doesn't take much to trend. Young people in America who go to bed with their electronics have the attention span of a gnat."

El Oulad Dahou smiles in recognition.

"Only on Twitter can local news from some hole-in-the-wall town dominate the web sphere for a nanosecond before burning out," I say.

Uly, now focused on the display case, looks at the youth and then at the TV.

"We walked into the right store," he says. "Closed captioning in English. Did you see the soccer player dancing with his mother? I'd do the same if I had a chance."

"I'd dance with you, but my knee would need a shot of cortisone first."

While Adam films musicians outside, I drift to a display of brass and silver teapots—long-spouted, squat-bodied vessels warm to the touch. I consider buying mint, its scent already clinging to my fingertips.

Then I see her.

Nikki's face fills the television screen. *Life-Long Swindler Missing*, scrolls beneath her image.

My heart stops.

Adam, returned and sorting through shirts, glances up with studied indifference. Uly catches my eye, frantically motioning: *change the channel.* Before anyone acts, the feed switches to Hakim Ziyech driving downfield, stadium roars drowning everything—even my racing thoughts.

Uly, who until yesterday was conflicted about visiting Morocco, is right there with him. Surprisingly, Adam, not being a sports guy, doesn't care.

"Here's the plan," he says. "We leave now. Film more. Then we grab some grub."

"Sure," Uly says. "But I'll catch up with you later. I want to get one more thing."

CHAPTER 60

Tiny Stars of David

Abigail

A t first, there's not much to capture on video. We wander through the souks, past leather workshops and stalls stacked with goods. I don't spend a dirham. She will be found. She entered through the back to avoid the cameras.

We enter the main square just as it begins to come alive. The sun's gone, but there's still light. Lanterns—paper, glass, metal—float or hang still, their intricate carvings casting lacy shadows across the medina.

Clusters of entertainers populate the square: acrobats, snake charmers, storytellers. A man strums a three-stringed lotar. Drummers pound out a steady rhythm while women in brightly colored skirts clap hand cymbals with wild precision. A singer belts heartfelt folk songs. There's applause. And then there's my son, who's more of a Rockin' Moroccan than I'll ever be, unable to stop his body from moving.

I tilt my head back and allow my mind to drift. Grandma once told me about the Algerian musician she almost married. I wonder—was it a song like this that won her heart?

A beggar woman approaches, offering to tell my future. I'm curious. But Mustafa warns, "Give her five dirhams and you'll be swarmed with more."

Still, we're in the locals' part of the square. They're here for the show, not to prey on tourists. I doubt she's a scammer. Not that I believe, but Yasmina once had a soothsayer tell her the wildest things—and every last one came true.

"For twenty dirhams," the woman says, "your family is rich in love. A baby is coming."

I laugh. Loving, yes, but blending my family with Mariah's Afro-Latina's has been tougher than I expected. And Uly and Mariah have no plans for a child.

My mind flashes to my sister. I push the thought away. She will be found. She entered through the back to avoid the cameras.

"Dinner," Mustafa announces.

We eat at a cluster of picnic tables under the stars—couscous, chicken tagine with walnuts and pomegranate. No dessert.

As we head back to the riad, Uly stops me.

"We said just food and knickknacks," he grins. "But I changed my mind."

"What'd you do?" I ask.

"I wanted you to go home with something," he says, slipping a tiny necklace into my hand—Stars of David on a fine chain.

My throat tightens.

"I was going to give it to Mariah," he says, "but I want you to have it. Don't worry. He tried to jack up the price, but I guilted him. I told him it already belonged to us. All I owed him was for the keeping of it—and his craftsmanship."

Each star has a small diamond. I rub one between my fingers.

"So delicate," I whisper. "Thank you, Son. Dr. Heckman would be proud."

I tuck the necklace into my pocket. Another memory surfaces. My mind reels back to my twelfth birthday when Yasmina gave me a silver Hamsa charm—something I still treasure, though I never wear it anymore.

"Be someone who adds to the world," she said. "Luck comes and goes. You might be broke someday—who knows? But the love you make, that's what makes you rich."

CHAPTER 61

The Heirs

Abigail

"How about we take the Marrakech Express?" Adam says. "The train didn't exist when Mom was here in 1941, but I imagine she was on something very much like it. But how brave was she? Fifteen years old? You know, she never told me until I was grown that she'd been married before. Her first husband's family rode her through the desert and threw her on a train. Discarded her. Just like that."

"Are you sure she'd want us to?" Uly asks. "If it were me, I'm not sure I'd want to retrace that."

"Mom says her life changed for the better. She met Amira on that train. And at the other end was your great-grandmother. She had her issues, but Mom ended up being quite fond of her."

I'd read about this kind of thing in novels, but it's still hard to imagine—Yasmina, treated like chattel. All the steam and smoke, the stench of dung, the buzz of men in djellabas doing business, hash pipes dangling from their lips, women for sale, ducks, geese, chickens, snakes. It must have been suffocating.

I touch the tiny Stars of David necklace at my collarbone.

"Her faith must've been what got her through," I say.

"She did travel second class, but for most of it, she was the only Amazigh. She didn't know how to dress, what to say. Nazi guards. Barbed wire transports. There were camps. I have to hand it to her—the trauma could've hardened her, but it didn't. She became a mother. Not just to me. To everyone."

A warmth spreads through me. Yasmina, Mother Earth—nurturing, life-affirming. Her kindness lingers in every space she filled.

The warmth is still there the next day when Uly helps Mariah and Nilsa overcome their hesitation about Morocco. By noon, after picking them up from the ferry in Tangiers, we join an organized tour. Forget the documentary—it's lovely watching Mariah, giddy with excitement, feed an orange to a camel. Nilsa, wrapped in traditional garb rooted in her Dominican Afro-Latina heritage, gives belly dancing a shot. But the real highlight is riding in a sidecar through the mountains with Benjamin, a former lawyer turned tour operator.

Two at a time, he takes us up to the tomb of Rabbi Shlomo Bel Hensh, maintained by Fatima, his adopted daughter. There, while we pray, Fatima—Muslim—prepares a kosher lunch for us.

Later, I see Uly kneeling before the tomb. He stays still for a long time. I don't know who he's praying to or what it's about. But when he rises, there's reverence on his face. Mariah sees it too. She clutches his hand and kisses it.

I wish I'd noticed Uly's need for ritual and tradition sooner. He wants to know where he comes from. For too long, I'd wrapped myself in the outsider role, not realizing how isolating that had become. I was too busy surviving, always focused on the next step. But faith, when practiced sincerely—feeds the spirit.

"Our kids, if we have them, are going to know," Uly says. "You modeled by example. But I need to build on your foundation. Don't feel bad. I'll make mistakes too. Maybe I don't know my roots yet, but if there's one thing I've never doubted—it's your love."

After that, there's nothing left to say.

By coming here, we've gotten a glimpse of the past.

But Uly, Mariah, Nilsa, and I—we are the future.

EPILOGUE

Abigail

I n February 2024, just short of her 98th birthday, Yasmina dies. Adam is there, as are his wife and daughters. In the end, she was more curious about others' well-being than her own. Her final words, spoken first in Tachelhit and then in English, were, "I'm ready." As requested, she is buried next to Bijan among a grove of pine and cypress trees not far from the Point Pinos Lighthouse—fitting for a life that illuminated so many others. For a while, Adam is too devastated to work. His documentary, intended to be lighthearted but ultimately too sentimental, never comes together—especially after October 7, when antisemitism, already on the rise worldwide, explodes.

As for Nikki: She was at the courthouse all along, putting on makeup in the bathroom to make sure she was ready for the paparazzi and their cameras. Before reporting to prison to begin a five-year sentence, she gives an interview to a TV news station. Her exact words at the end of the interview are, "I'll be back." I believed her. In prison, she behaves. She takes restaurant management classes and volunteers in the prison library. Nikki always claimed karma affected her double. Until recently, I thought the opposite was true, but in the end was so banal and commonplace it proved that even she could not defy the laws of physics. She was leaving a restaurant in Gustine, California—not Tacos Jimenez, but a place like it. Anyway, she has a bag of tacos and a Diet Sprite in hand. She barely steps off the curb when a truck barrels out of nowhere—and she's gone. If you thought she was all over the news before … I hope she rests in peace.

Sarah Cohen and I remain kind of friendly. She's a nut-job as my dad said and she's crossed a crazy amount of boundaries for any therapist let alone someone on an ethics board. But not only has she helped me with my Nikki detox—which became a lot more complicated after her death—but she also has several philanthropic projects in the works. I'm happy to help fund them now that my business is doing so well. Several months ago, out of the blue, the board expunged my record. No explanation given, but I suspect it's because everyone wants this chapter closed. After all, there's no shortage of psychologist influencers posting controversial content online.

For privacy's sake, I'll keep my update on Cy brief. Medication has dulled his edges. He's not as funny as he used to be, but he's no longer out of control. Still a fine man, still salt of the earth. For those who hope we'll reunite: no way. His girlfriend is more tolerant than I am.

I've had to make brave choices in this hard life. Yasmina said I'd reap the rewards, that I'd move beyond surviving to thriving—and she was right. For the first time in a long time, there is joy. My circle of life is complete.

In a month, Uly and his wife will make me a grandmother. Their little girl, Jasmina Altagracia, will be a beautiful blend of everything—Moroccan Jewish, North and Sub-Saharan African, Dominican, and Scots-Irish. Nilsa and I are over the moon. She's already making and freezing mofongo, dumplings, and plantains. I'm giving our granddaughter my old Hamsa—though I doubt she'll need luck. A vintage store in town has a Chatty Baby doll I've had my eye on. I'm crocheting up a storm—layettes, blankets, booties—and working on a quilt. Across the border, at the bottom, I will stitch these words: *Do not forget.*

About the Author

Debby Show is a licensed Marriage and Family Therapist and School Psychologist based in California. With years of experience working with individuals and families, she brings a deep understanding of human behavior, relationships, and generational dynamics to her fiction. Though this is her debut novel, Debby has honed her craft through coaching, writing workshops, and a lifelong passion for storytelling. Inspired by real history and intimate truths, her work explores how the past shapes who we become.

She also happens to be the sister of a rather infamous public figure—and while this is a work of fiction, it draws inspiration from real-life experiences. That said, the spotlight in this story belongs to the generations of women whose legacies are woven across time.